THE HASHTAG KILLER: AWAKENING

BY JESSE BLAIR

For information, permissions, or bulk orders, contact:
Blair Media Press
Los Angeles, California
Thehashtagkillerseries@gmail.com

All rights reserved under International and Pan-American Copyright Conventions.
U.S. Copyright registration pending.

First Edition, 2025
ISBN 979-8-9934850-2-7 (Paperback)
ISBN 979-8-9934850-3-4 (Hardback)
ISBN 979-8-9934850-0-3 (eBook)
ISBN 979-8-9934850-1-0 (Audiobook)

TABLE OF CONTENTS

CHAPTER 1

A BURNING APPETITE

Jeff, the charismatic and obnoxiously upbeat food blogger behind *Eating With Jeff*, was mid-livestream, parked on a dimly lit road in the Hollywood Hills. He dug into his latest review, a greasy cheeseburger dripping with sauce and all the fixings. The livestream buzzed. The live chat filled with a mix of praise for his enthusiasm and playful trolling.

"Alright everyone, you see it. Now I gotta taste it. Time to give this burger the Jeff test," he said.

Suddenly, the backseat folded down.

A masked figure crawled out from the trunk into the second row of Jeff's minivan. The mask was grotesque, with two hashtags painted over the eyelids and a wide, painted-on smile frozen in place.

Before Jeff could react, his head slammed into the steering wheel.

Once.
Twice.
Three times.

Dazed and bloodied, Jeff slumped forward, barely conscious. He didn't even fight back.

The live chat erupted.

"WTF?"
"Is this real?"
"Is this part of the show?"
"Jeff what's going on?"

Jeff lifted his head just enough, blood dribbling from his mouth. One eye was already swelling shut, his nose crushed.

He choked out a single word.

"Why?"

The killer leaned in, voice barely above a whisper.

"Because it's you."

Without hesitation, the killer pulled out a coil of razor wire and looped it around Jeff's neck, yanking it tight.

The killer drew closer, his lips brushing Jeff's ear.

"That's what my followers expect… true honesty. However brutal it may be, that's what I give."

The words were so quiet only Jeff heard them. His eyes went wide with instant recognition.

Jeff thrashed, panicked, desperate, but he was no match and was overpowered.

The live chat lit up with frantic comments.

"Oh my god!"
"This is insane! How is this happening?"
"What kind of sick joke is this?"
"This can't be real!"
"Did anyone else catch that? What did he say to him?!"

The killer didn't say a word.

He tightened the wire. Jeff screamed.

Blood poured from his neck as the blades cut deeper, sawing into flesh and tissue. His struggles weakened. His screams fading.

The wire bit through muscle, deeper and deeper, until, with a sickening lurch.

Jeff's head tore free. Blood spewed from his neck like a geyser.

Jeff's lifeless face was frozen in an expression of agony. His body slumped into the seat, leaving the killer holding the severed head like a trophy.

In a final, sadistic display, the killer moved Jeff's jaw like a ventriloquist's dummy. He stuffed the half-eaten burger between the bloodied lips, smearing grease and gore.

"I'm *Eating With Jeff*," the killer sneered, his voice dripping with venom.
"And on today's episode… I'll show you just how much of a piece of shit I really am."

The chat went wild.

"We're calling the police!"
"You're being tracked!"
"You're dead, you sick freak!"
"Show us who you are coward!"

Unfazed, the killer turned to the camera, still clutching Jeff's head like a grotesque puppet.

"Let's ask the audience and take a vote. How's that sound, Jeff?"

He tilted the head in a macabre nod.

"Do we leave you here to be found… or light up the car?" His eyes lingered on the screen, scanning the flood of frantic comments.

The chat exploded.

"Call 911!"
"You sick fuck!"
"This has to be fake!"
"I hope you die!"

The killer smirked, scanning the flood of comments, searching for the ones unhinged enough to play along.

Then, with manic delight, he read one aloud:

"I don't care. Burn, baby, burn!"

A wild, cackling laugh escaped the killers lips. He was completely unhinged.

Stepping out of the van, he grabbed Jeff's tripod and planted it firmly in the dirt, angling the phone just right to keep the flames, and the fear, front and center.

The livestream continued.
The audience was still watching.
The horror was far from over.

Methodically, the killer began dousing the van with gasoline whistling a tune as he did it. He took his time covering the inside and outside. Every move was calm, precise and premeditated.

He stepped in and out of frame, taunting the viewers and waving erratically to the camera.

The chat spiraled into hysteria.

"This isn't real!"
"Someone do something!"
"The cops have been called! They're on their way!"
"You monster!"

But this is L.A.
And they're deep in the Hollywood Hills.
Help is miles away.
And LAPD won't be coming fast.

The killer finished soaking the vehicle in gasoline. Jeff's lifeless body was soaked with gasoline and blood.

He stepped back and exhaled, savoring the silence.

Slowly, he reached up and removed his mask.

He let it fall to his side, and the camera caught a final glimpse—jet black, with neon-pink hashtags glowing over the eyes and a stitched-on smile that pulsed with the same eerie hue.

Then he vanished. Where did he go?

The livestream kept rolling. A flick of the lighter. The sharp snap of a cigarette igniting.

Then, from the chat, the last desperate demands flooded the screen.

"Show us your face, you twisted fuck!"
"I hope you suffer!"
"You coward! Face us!"
"Trace the IP! Someone stop him!"

The killer slowly exhaled. Smoke curled past the lens.

"Caption this," he murmured, striking a match against the book in his hand. He flicked it through the open window.

The flame caught instantly.

He flicked the cigarette in after it.

Within seconds, the car became a roaring inferno, fire devouring metal, glass, and flesh alike.

The killer watched, his eyes locked on the blaze as it climbed higher.

"Ladies and gentlemen, the BBQ Jeff platter will be served shortly. Fresh. Hot. Made to order… just for you."

His let out a maniacal laugh.
The chat went into over drive.

"You fucking monster!"
"Freak! You sick freak!"
"Go to hell, you bastard!"
"How can you live with yourself?"

He didn't flinch.

Instead, he lifted the phone and angled it toward his masked, grinning face.

"Thanks for tuning in to another episode of *Eating With Jeff*," he said, his voice calm, almost playful. "I was your special guest tonight. Hate to dine and dash… but you'll have to catch me next time."

A sharp, deranged laugh escaped him.

"Man, you can smell it from here!"

He propped the phone near the flames, framing the chaos perfectly.

"Ta-ta, L.A.!"

His footsteps retreated. Moments later, tires could be heard screeching as a car peeled off into the night.

The fire raged on.
The livestream kept rolling.
And the comments… they didn't stop.

CHAPTER 2

THE FALLOUT

The Hollywood Hills were uncharacteristically chaotic. News vans jammed the winding roads near the scorched remains of Jeff's car. Yellow police tape fluttered along the perimeter as officers and K-9 units swept the terrain, searching for any trace of evidence.

Behind the barricades, reporters elbowed for space, microphones raised, voices urgent as they broadcasted the grisly details to millions watching live. Patrol cars idled nearby, their lights casting a steady pulse of red and blue across the crowd. Uniformed officers maintained the perimeter. In the distance, the Hollywood sign loomed above the hills, a surreal backdrop to the chaos below.

At the center of it all, a press conference was underway. Mayor Victor Lang stood at the podium, flanked by LAPD Chief Christopher Parks and Captain Eugene Cunningham, their faces grim beneath the flashing lights.

Then, with a practiced stillness, Detective Lieutenant Byron Maxwell stepped up to the mic. Maxwell, a 20-year homicide veteran, exuded a controlled intensity as he addressed the crowd.

"What we have here is a gruesome act of murder," Maxwell began, his voice low and firm.

"We're urging anyone with information to come forward immediately. Over the next several days, our team will be canvassing the area for potential witnesses and reviewing any available surveillance footage, though given the remoteness of the scene, we know that may be limited."

Maxwell stepped closer to the mic.

"This was a deliberate, calculated, and horrific crime," he continued.

"I followed *Eating With Jeff* myself. He came off like a decent, fun-loving guy. We owe it to him, and to this city, to bring the person responsible to justice."

The reporters clamored, cameras flashing in rapid bursts. A lone woman reporter's voice sliced through the crowd. She wasn't seen, she was only heard.

"Detective Maxwell, do you believe this is the work of a serial killer?"

Maxwell sighed and raised a hand to calm the growing frenzy.

"Let's not jump to conclusions. This is still the early stage of our investigation, and speculation won't help us catch whoever's responsible. What I can promise you is this…we will find whoever did this."

The questions erupt again. Louder, more chaotic.

Before it escalated, Chief Parks stepped forward shutting down the press conference.

"Thank you, everyone. No further comments at this time."

Reporters persisted to ask more questions, to which they were ignored by officials. But the damage was done.

The story spread like wildfire, with local networks breaking into live coverage.
The Hollywood Hills had become ground zero for a full-blown media circus.

Damage Control

As the press conference wrapped up, Detective Maxwell was ushered into a sleek black SUV with Mayor Lang, Chief Parks, and Captain Cunningham. The tension was palpable as they drove away from the chaotic scene. Suddenly, the mayor slammed his fist on the divider.

"Privacy, Now!" he barked.

The partition slid up. He turned to the others and exploded

"What the fuck is going on? Some influencer gets his head severed and his body burned on a goddamn livestream and now every news outlet on Earth is camped out in my city! I want every beat cop on high alert. This city cannot afford another goddamn crisis!"

Chief Parks's phone buzzed, cutting through the mayor's rant. He glanced at the screen, his expression darkened.

"It's the District Attorney," he muttered.

The mayor groaned, rubbing his temples.
"Oh God. This didn't even take twenty-four hours."

Maxwell reclined in his seat, a faint smirk tugging at his lips. "Well, you decapitate a guy and burn his body on a livestream, and yeah, the DA might be interested."

Chief Parks shook his head, the dreaded look on his face said it all.

The car slid to a stop outside City Hall. Maxwell stepped out as the chief's parting words echoed, low and deliberate.

"Lieutenant Maxwell, this is your case. Whatever you need, resources or personnel, it's yours," the Chief said, pausing. "This is why you're the best. Your reputation precedes you."

He lowered his voice slightly. "You've got an entire city watching So get to work."

"Yes sir."

"We'll talk later Byron," Captain Cunningham said.

The SUV peeled off toward City Hall. Maxwell, meanwhile, headed into police headquarters with determination. As the lead senior investigator on a high-profile case, all eyes were on him.

Inside, officers greeted him with nods and handshakes, a sign of the respect he carried. Several beat cops assured him they'd be extra vigilant on their patrols. Maxwell had earned his place. Known for his sharp instincts and an uncanny ability to crack complex cases, he was the department's best investigator. So if anyone could solve this, it was him.

At The Killer's Hideout

While the police and press spiraled into chaos, a different scene unfolded in a dimly lit hideout.

The killer sat hunched over a bowl of cereal, the cold glow of multiple monitors casting eerie reflections across his masked face. Each screen replayed the press conference in real time. Every frantic word. Every desperate promise.

He smirked, chewing with slow exaggeration. The crunch echoed louder than it should in the silence.

Setting the bowl aside, he stood and walked to a whiteboard covered in names.

Jeff's name was slashed through in red.

Below it, a new name gleamed ominously: Samantha Sinclair.

Her social media feed flickered across the monitors. A carefully curated life of fashion, luxury, and beauty, filled with sunsets, trips, and designer products. The killer circled her name slowly, almost reverently.

"You're next," he sneered.

He stood facing the whiteboard as his shadow stretched ominously across the room.

CHAPTER 3

SAMANTHA SINCLAIR: BEAUTY, BRAINS, AND TROUBLE AHEAD

Samantha Josephine Sinclair, a twenty-seven-year-old L.A. native, seems to have it all. Her inherited family home, a beautifully remodeled, three-story seven-bedroom, nine-bath estate in Marina Del Rey that overlooks the beach, a symbol of luxury and generational wealth. But beneath its glamorous exterior, the nearly 100-year-old mansion holds secrets.

She lives alone. She is the queen of her castle. And she's extremely careful about who she allows into her home, or her life.

Her house is her sanctuary. Built during Prohibition and passed down through generations, it's rigged with secret tunnels and escape routes most people will never see. It's also protected by a state-of-the-art surveillance system installed by her father, a retired expert in digital forensics. Every inch of it is her domain.

On the surface, Samantha appears to be the epitome of success: a luxury car in the driveway, designer clothes lining her closet, and multiple income streams to keep it all flowing. She has her own money. Yet, her father still deposits $15,000 into her account every month. Money she doesn't need, but accepts because he insists. Maybe it's his way of easing the guilt for being absent most of her life. Samantha calls it what it is: guilt money. A monthly apology for a childhood spent overlooked, distracted, absent, and paid off.

But make no mistake, Samantha works. She makes it a point to prove, to herself more than anyone, that she can stand on her own.

By day, she's a top-tier makeup artist at *Glam Haven*, an exclusive cosmetics boutique for celebrities and high-profile clients. She works by appointment only. Her books stay full.

By night, she's *Simply Samantha*—a lifestyle and beauty influencer with more than a million followers per platform. Her brand is a blend of luxury, glam, sass, and carefully curated realness. Brands crawl to be featured on her feed. Her audience? Fiercely loyal. They don't just follow her; they believe her. Support her. Defend her.

She knows the best lighting, the right filters, and those magic angles that make everything pop. But behind every shot is a dozen takes. Behind every take, a little voice asking if this one is finally enough.

While she thrived on Instagram and TikTok, it's her YouTube community that held her heart. They've watched her grow, cheered her on, and bought into her world. With everything monetized, content creation has become a full-time, high-revenue career.

One of her most beloved ventures is *Samantha's Attic*, an online store named after the oversized attic in her home. She sells out-of-season designer pieces to her followers at deeply discounted prices. Sometimes for next to nothing.

"I'd rather sell it to my community than hand it over to a thrift store," she once said. "They can thrift with me. This is for them. They love me. I try for them."

She lives for the aesthetic. Samantha is the definition of a modern fashionista, always dressed in something daring, stylish, and designer. Her weeks are filled with spa appointments, photoshoots, collabs, media invites, and romantic dinner dates. She jets off on weekend escapes, hits the hottest concerts, and never misses a chance to show her followers the highs of her life. Champagne in one hand, phone and ring light glowing in the other.

Her beauty is striking. She's mixed with Puerto Rican, French, and what looks like a hint of something Middle Eastern. The ambiguity only adds to her mystique. Her skin is luminous. Her curves are sculpted, thanks to a fat-transfer breast augmentation and a subtle BBL, all with toned thighs to keep it looking natural. She trains at *Elite24Fit,* one of L.A.'s most exclusive gyms, where hot bodies, bold personalities, and viral reputations collide daily. A place to be seen, and to get seen.

But her hair? That's her pet peeve.

It's long, voluminous, and beautiful. But only because she works tirelessly to keep it that way. She spends hours taming every strand, fighting the frizz that hints at her natural texture, something she's never fully embraced and still feels self-conscious about. Her portable straightener and backup kit never leave her side. It's her go-to 2-in-1 rotating iron and brush she swears by. Between the L.A. heat and the Santa Ana winds, she's learned to be ready for battle.

For years, she wore hazel-green colored contacts. Then one day, she took the plunge. Eye color surgery. Now, when people ask if her eyes are real, she doesn't hesitate to say: Yes! Because now, it's the truth.

Samantha knew how to play the game. Whether it was scoring a comped meal or a luxury gift from one of her many smitten fanboys, she got what she wanted without ever giving too much. She kept everyone at arm's length. Enticing, yet never fully available. That was the key to her appeal.

She's hot. She knows it. But it's her control that defines her. The mystery. The execution. The power to shape her own image, to pull the strings, to always stay a step ahead.

At least… until everything would begin to unravel.

The Call

The sound of running water filled Samantha's sleek, modern bathroom as she belted out an off-key rendition of a pop song, her voice echoed against the tiled walls. She's no singer. But in her mind, she's a Grammy winner.

Steam swirled around her as she stepped out of the shower.

Catching her reflection in the mirror, her eyes landed on her surgically enhanced D-cup breasts.
She smirked, giving them a playful shake.

Her hourglass figure glistened in the humidity, curves highlighted by the glow of the vanity lights.
She grabbed a plush towel and wrapped it snugly around her body, pausing for one last look. She stepped into her bedroom.

Her phone vibrated non-stop on the dresser, texts, notifications, and unread messages flooded the screen.

Samantha didn't care.

Let them wait.

She plopped down in front of her vanity and let her hair down, preparing for her grueling hair and makeup routine. It was date night.

"Molly, where are you girl?" Samantha called out to her frou-frou dog.

Her French bulldog came scrambling into the room, her little paws skittering on the hardwood floor. Samantha scooped her up, planting a kiss on the dog's head.

"There's my baby. Mommy's going out tonight, so no boys for you to growl at," she cooed. "Maybe."

Suddenly, her phone rang..
The screen lit up.
Free Meal Mike, her date.

Setting Molly down on the bed, the dog let out a grunt and flopped onto her side.

Samantha smirked and picked up.
"Hey you, there you are," she said, her voice sweet but impatient.

"Samantha?" Mike replied eagerly, his tone dripping with nervous excitement.

"Who else would it be, silly?" she said, rolling her eyes. "What time are we meeting? I'm almost done getting ready."

Her voice laced with a deliberate vocal fry, the kind that drives some men crazy. Samantha knew how to push buttons, and she enjoyed it.

"We can meet at 7:30," Mike said.

"Might as well just say 8," Samantha teased, laughing.

"Okay, 8 it is," he retorted.

"Great. I'm thinking steak, maybe sushi… or even Mediterranean," she mused, her voice carried an undertone of mischief.

"God, you sound so hot."

Samantha rolled her eyes feeding off the compliment. "You love my voice, huh?"

"What's there not to love?" Mike confessed.

Meanwhile, her fingers flew across the screen as she texted *Free Meal Jason* simultaneously:

"Can't wait for tomorrow night, babe. Let's do Italian. I'll text you where."

Back to Mike, she giggled. "There's this French restaurant I want to try, *Le Cher*. Ever been?"

Mike hesitated for a second, likely calculating how much the evening will cost. "Uh… no, but sure, we can go there."

"Come on, Mikey," she pandered. "I have a brand-new outfit I've been saving just for tonight. You'll be the very first to see."

Mike folded. "I love your outfits. I'm looking forward to it."

"Perfect. See you at *Le Cher* at 8. Byyyee!"

She tossed her phone onto the couch, a plush, velvet masterpiece that looked custom-made and expensive as hell.

Turning to Molly, she smirked. "Molly, should I finally fuck him tonight… or make him wait two more dates?"

She laughed, amused at herself.

Her Frenchie snorted and buried her head into the pillow, her expression practically screaming: *This bitch.*

As Samantha returned to fixing herself up, more text messages rolled in, another three from Free Meal Jason, trying to lock down tomorrow night's plans.

She smirked. "Boys, boys, boys…"

After some thought, she went with a shimmery white mesh V-neck lace-up bodysuit, sheer and daring, its delicate embroidery catching the light with every subtle movement. The see-through fabric clung to her like a whisper, barely there yet impossible to ignore. She paired it with denim shorts so short they barely kissed the curve of her full, rounded backside.

She completed her outfit with silver, sparkly high heels for a touch of glam. She knew she was a little clumsy in them, but that had never stopped her. Besides, they were brand new, and tonight she was ready to break them in.

"These are the go-to shorts, Molly," she said, turning to her and popping her hip.

Samantha carefully perfected her makeup, blending eyeshadow, applying false lashes, and contouring her face to sharpen her already killer cheekbones. Her hair fell in loose waves as she gave herself one final once-over in the mirror.

She snapped a quick selfie, angled just right, and uploaded it to her story with the caption:

Ready to slay the night away! #DateNightVibes

It was chilly out, so she grabbed a cropped leather jacket that barely grazed her butt. Teetering slightly in her heels, she laughed at herself, but didn't care. It was all part of the look, or maybe the persona.

"I'm out, Molls!" she called out, opening the garage door and sliding into her pink Tesla.

She shot Mike a text:

"On my way"

The Perfect Life, Or So It Seems

Samantha's world is curated to perfection, down to her pink Tesla with diamond-studded license plates. Everywhere she goes, she makes an entrance.

Samantha always performed, even when no one was watching. It wasn't fake. It was armor. A shield against the silence, against the ache she still refused to name. Sometimes, the armor felt too heavy. The pressure of always being "on brand."

After a media gala last fall, she came home in full glam, sat on her closet floor, and just let herself break. The pressure of being *Simply Samantha* had finally cracked through the surface.

Phone still in hand.
The post's caption from that night?

What a night to remember! I'm celebrating it with all of you! #ForeverGrateful #LivingMyBestLife

To her followers, coworkers, and admirers, she is the glowing embodiment of beauty and success. But behind the carefully crafted image, Samantha's life is as transactional as her relationships.

Her DMs are a revolving door of admirers, eager brands, and influencers looking to collaborate. Deep down, she longs for something real.

She's a hopeless romantic, though she'd never admit it. That longing? She suppresses it and buries it behind flawless selfies, curated captions, and a life designed to captivate.

She knows the game. Flirt, tease, keep her options open. But sometimes, on still nights or long drives, she wondered what it would feel like to stop playing. To want just one person. To actually mean it.

Samantha plays the part flawlessly, slipping into her persona like an actress in a film.

But tonight, everything was about to change.

A chain of events were about to unfold, leaving her dependent, vulnerable, and in need of a real connection. One she can no longer ignore.

And she has no idea that she's already been marked as the next player in the killer's game of revenge.

This time, the stakes are life and death.

Outside Samantha's House

As the sleek Tesla glided out of the driveway, the gate closed behind her, sealing off the mansion.

She disappeared down the street, lost in her own world, music blasting through the speakers.

A dark sedan sat parked nearby.

Inside, the dim glow of the dashboard lights illuminated the killer's mask, resting on the dashboard.

His fingers drummed lightly on the steering wheel before he stepped out, clutching a small pink package wrapped with a neat bow.

He approached Samantha's gate, crouching to place the package down.

He didn't notice the small security camera discreetly perched above the doorway.

Dressed as a delivery driver, he retreated to his car, unaware that his face had just been caught on tape.

Minutes passed. He vanished into the shadows.

CHAPTER 4

DINNER PLANS AT *LE CHER*

Samantha pulled up to *Le Cher*, her pink Tesla turning heads as it glided to a stop. Light, breezy music pulsed from the car, "Summer Feelings" by Lennon Stella and Charlie Puth spilling wistfully into the night air. The valet approached with a polite smile, catching the infectious energy of her arrival.

"Evening, ma'am," the valet said, holding the door open.

Samantha stepped with poise, almost. Her glittery heels betrayed her as she misstepped, and the valet hurried to steady her.

"Oops," she said with mock embarrassment, brushing her hair back with a playful smile.

"Be careful Miss," he said. "Wouldn't want to ruin those shoes, or your night."

She batted her lashes. "You're sweet. Here's my car."

She handed him the key with a coy smile, grabbed her purse, and sauntered toward the entrance. No tip. Just a quick tap of her phone to drop him her aaInstagram so he could follow her. She had no intention of following him back either.

Le Cher and La Pierre are arguably the most sought-after, stylish destinations in Downtown L.A. The kind of places where reservations are mandatory and Friday nights buzzed like a beehive.

She sashayed into *Le Cher*, her glittery heels tapping against the floor. Inside, the soft glow of chandeliers reflected off polished marble floors. The downstairs portion of *Le Cher* was chic and intimate, with low lighting and plush velvet chairs. A two level bar complimented the restaurant. Upstairs, a secondary restaurant and rooftop bar awaited—*La Pierre*.

Mike's face lit up the instant he saw her. He waved her over.

"Hey you," Samantha said, her voice lilting as they exchanged a hug.

Mike bent toward her for a kiss, but she tilted her head just enough for his lips to land on her cheek. She smiled, shrugging it off with her usual charm as she gave him a playful nudge.

"You look stunning tonight," Mike said, his gaze trailing over her form-fitting bodysuit and barely-there denim shorts. Her outfit did more than turn heads, it commanded attention.

Over it all, she wore a designer leather jacket with just the right amount of attitude, likely Versace or Prada. Every move she made, from the way she adjusted her outfit to the way she carried herself, felt rehearsed and designed to captivate.

"Aw, thanks," Samantha replied, giving him a playful nudge. "You don't look so bad yourself mister."

Mike kept it sharp yet casual with tight black jeans and fresh Jordans, a nod to his sneakerhead obsession. His shirt was partially unbuttoned, revealing just a glimpse of his defined chest beneath a tailored sports coat. A sleek Rolex and a set of understated wrist beads completed the look, while diamond studs in both ears added just enough flash to hint at success without overdoing it.

A sharply dressed host in a fitted black suit greeted them at the stand. "Good evening. Welcome. May I have your name for the reservation?"

"Yes, for Michael Alexander Theodorou," he replied confidently.

"It'll be just a few minutes," the host said after confining Mike's name and reservation time.

"No problem, thank you." Mike shook the host's hand, smoothly palming him a $20 tip.

They sat down on a small bench nearby. Samantha crossed her legs with care, her shorts riding just high enough to keep things interesting. Mike's gaze lingered a little longer than he intended.

She caught him staring and smirked.
"Like what you see?" she teased, raising an eyebrow.

"Always," Mike admitted with a chuckle.

Samantha settled back, naturally slipping into conversation about her latest collaborations while Mike listened supportively, nodding at all the key buzzwords and asking the right questions.

Watch Your Step, Gorgeous

After a short wait, the host returned. "Your table is ready please follow me."

Samantha rose, her movements graceful, until her heel wobbled. She stumbled forward letting out a gasp.

"Whoa, careful!" Mike said, catching her arm.

Samantha giggled, brushing her hair from her face. "Ugh, these shoes. I'm still breaking them in."

Her hair, perfectly styled earlier, now carried a hint of frizz. But instead of ruining the look, it added to her charm. Her striking outfit still traced the shape of her body with daring confidence. As she stood tall, her denim shorts inched higher, skimming just past her comfort zone.

A couple nearby snickered rolling their eyes as they watched Samantha struggle.

Samantha caught it in her peripheral vision but lifted her chin, refusing to acknowledge them.

Mike noticed too.

"They're just jealous," he whispered with a smile.

Samantha laughed, resting her hand on his. "You're sweet, Mikey."

There was something about the way she teetered between poise and unpredictability. She was every bit the fashionista. Confident and stylish. But there was a charm in how she never quite masked her slips and stumbles.

Feeling the couple's trailing gaze, Samantha didn't bother adjusting her outfit. Her pride kicked in. Fixing anything now would've only validated their amusement. So she let it ride. Her shorts hugged tighter with each step. The draft brushing higher than she'd prefer beneath her jacket until they were out of sight.

As they approached the staircase, Samantha hooked her arm through Mike's. The elegant steps spiraled downward, dimly lit by a golden glow, just wide enough for the two of them to walk side by side.

Samantha glanced down at her glittering six-inch heels and exhaled.

"Careful now," Mike teased with a grin. "Don't want you taking a tumble."

"Don't jinx me," she warned, squeezing his arm as they began to walk down.

Each step was deliberate, her heels echoing faintly against the polished surface. Her hand clung tightly to Mike's bicep, her body leaning into him slightly. A strand of hair fell forward, partially covering her face. She turned to look at Mike, letting out a small smile.

He caught it and returned one of his own.

She rested her head on his shoulder. A momentary exchange of comfort and closeness.

But just as fast, she pulled herself up.

Don't get too attached, she reminded herself.

She brushed the loose strands of hair away from her face in an attempt to stay in control. Mike was wildly attractive. He had a way of making her feel grounded, something she wasn't used to.

But Samantha didn't allow herself to catch feelings.

Not for anyone.

Still, she had been ignoring numerous texts and DMs all night. Out of all the guys in her rotation, Mike is the only one holding her attention. At least for now.

As they reached the bottom of the stairs, the ambiance transformed. The restaurant was simply breathtaking.

A massive aquarium lined the walls, its hazy blue glow casting light over exotic fish drifting through vibrant coral. Overhead, the ceiling opened to reveal the upstairs dining area with it's sleek bar. French artwork adorned the walls, heightening the romantic, opulent atmosphere.

The entire place felt like stepping into another world that was luxurious, inviting, and intoxicating.

"Wow," Samantha breathed.

"Yeah, it's something, huh?" Mike said, watching her reaction.

She allowed herself a small, genuine smile. "It's… romantic."

"Right this way," he said with a polite smile, leading them to a cozy table tucked beside the glowing aquarium.

Big News At The Dinner Table

Samantha debated whether to take off her jacket. It didn't do much to hide her outfit, but tonight was meant to turn heads.

After a beat, she slipped it off and draped it neatly over the back of her chair. The jacket came off, unveiling the outfit she'd clearly curated to turn heads.

The bodysuit clung tightly, scandalously pushing up her perky breasts, the thong-like cut dipped low at her hips. Her snug, frayed denim shorts sat low on her hips, hinting at the curve and separation of her toned frame.

Her accessories complimented the look: a pink smart watch, sparkling earrings, a delicate gold chain, and a slim gold bracelet with tiny rhinestones

Mike's eyes drifted before he cleared his throat. "You really look amazing."

"Awww thank you," Samantha replied with a slight tilt of her head, feigning modesty.

The waiter handed them menus and stepped back, leaving them in their own world.

She crossed her legs, almost gracefully, until her knee accidentally bumped the table, rattling the glasses and sending a splash of water over the rim. Samantha laughed, brushing it off. Her other hand instinctively rubbed her knee to soothe the subtle sting.

She propped her elbow on the table and rested her chin in her hand, holding her composure. Her eyes locked on Mike, a playful glint sparking behind them.

"So, you want the real version of my day or the Instagram-friendly one?"

Mike smiled, his eyes locking with hers. "I'll take the real, unfiltered version. Please."

Samantha batted her eyes and launched into her story. The lighting was dim. The glow from the aquarium cast a dreamlike hue across the space. Candles flickered faintly at every table.

For Samantha, the mood felt perfect. A balance of indulgence and control. She knew she was the center of attention without giving too much away. As they settled into their night, the lighting reflected off Mike's sharp features.

At 6'2" with broad shoulders, a chiseled jaw, and an athletic build, Mike carried himself with quiet confidence. His strong bone structure and calm assurance were holdovers from his college basketball days, where he played point guard for UCLA. He was consistent, reliable, and known for leading his team through high-pressure games.

But life after college shifted his focus. Mike graduated with a degree in civil engineering and landed a solid job at a respected firm in Los Angeles. Still, he never let go of his love for basketball.

Every other weekend, he volunteers to teach kids the fundamentals of the game. When he wasn't coaching, he refereed local games. The kids adored him. Their parents respected him for both his patience and his passion.

Mike could have his pick of women if he tried. He's no stranger to wandering stares from women or flirtatious smiles from coworkers.

Yes, Mike could pull women if he really wanted to. But lately, and especially tonight, his focus is entirely on Samantha.

There was something about her, a mix of beauty, brains, and just enough sass to keep him on his toes. He wasn't blind to her flaws or the way she flirted without meaning to. But still, he couldn't help himself. Whatever it was about her, Mike was trying, even if he wasn't entirely sure why.

As Samantha stretched across the table to glance at the menu, a strand of hair tumbled across her face. She brushed it back casually, her eyes met his.

"What?" she playfully asked.

"Nothing," Mike replied, shaking his head. "Just thinking about how lucky I am tonight."

Samantha smirked, tilting her head slightly. "You're such a sap," she teased.

As Samantha chatted away, gesturing animatedly about her day, Mike watched her with a faint smile. Beneath her vapid chatter, the endless talk of followers, collabs, influencer events, press parties, and her work as a makeup artist, he caught glimpses of something deeper. It was in the way she paused when talking about things that mattered, or the way she smiled when something he said actually landed.

Maybe tonight's the night, Mike thought.

He lost count of their dates by now, though he knew this must be at least their eighth or ninth, but that's not the point. What mattered was that she's here, sitting across from him, sharing this night with him.

Tonight wasn't just about her.
Tonight was also about him.
And he had some exciting news to share.

Not many people knew, but today he received official word that he'd been promoted to lead a major project at his firm. A government contract, no less. It was the kind of opportunity that could define his entire career. At twenty-nine, he was the youngest ever to head a campaign of this scale.

And he was proud of himself,
Proud of how far he has come.

Yet there she was, Samantha Josephine Sinclair, decked out in her unapologetic outfit sharing this achievement with him.

She might be a little self-absorbed, sure.
But he saw something deeper.
At least… he hoped it was there.

The waiter arrived to take their orders. Samantha debated between the scallops and the lamb before finally settling on the scallops. Mike went with the filet mignon.

"So, what's the big news you were hinting at earlier?" she asked, leaning in slightly.

As she spoke, one strap of her blouse slipped from her shoulder, sliding down in a way Mike found undeniably seductive. Her top was already low-cut, revealing the soft curves of her décolletage, and now it looked like a nip slip was dangerously close to happening.

Samantha, however, seemed completely unbothered. She casually adjusted the strap, as if this sort of thing happened all the time.

Mike couldn't help but admire her brazen confidence. She'd worn a jacket earlier for modesty, but the restaurant had gotten too hot. Her outfit now on full display. Her hair, once perfectly styled, had begun to frizz slightly with each animated turn of her head. The subtle dishevelment only enhanced her allure. Despite himself, Mike found he was even more drawn to her.

"I got promoted," Mike said, finally answering her question. "They're putting me in charge of a major project."

Samantha's eyes widened, her usual sass vanished and a mix of genuine surprise and joy spread across her face.

"Oh my god, Mike! That's amazing, Congratulations!"

She leaned forward in excitement, her strap slipping off her shoulder as she clasped her hands together. Hair fell over her face, but she swept it back with practiced ease, fixing the strap without a second thought.

"We must toast to this. Waiter!" she called out, cutting through the gentle hum of conversation.

She scanned the room for him, unbothered by the glances her enthusiasm attracted, and continued waving.

Mike laughed, shaking his head with a grin.
"I'm not arguing. Get him over here."

Samantha turned to him, smiled, then kept waving until she caught the waiter's eye.

"Yes, waiter, over here please!"

A Toast To Temptation

Samantha and Mike continued vibing, their energy easy and electric. When the drinks arrived, Samantha grinned and lifted her glass. As she raised her arm, her strap slipped again, sliding lower over her shoulder, teasing just a little more skin.

"To Mike and his well-earned promotion," she said with a wink in her voice, a trace of vocal fry adding flirt.

Mike raised his glass, his eyes drawn to her exposed shoulder and the way her top clung to her body. He pushed the heat aside and focused on the toast.

"Here here," he replied, voice composed, though his thoughts were anything but.

Their glasses clinked, the sound cutting through the ambient buzz of the restaurant. Samantha took a sip of her drink, then adjusted her strap again with a quick flick of the wrist, unbothered by how her outfit seemed to have a mind of its own.

Mike chuckled under his breath. She was a mix of chaos and confidence, and somehow it was magnetic.

He knew she liked to play hard to get, but tonight she was here with him and that was all that mattered.

Dinner had delivered: amazing food, great conversation, and a spark between them that couldn't be ignored.

As they finished their plates, Samantha reached for her glass and raised an eyebrow. "One more round?"

"How many is that now for me?" she laughed, her eyes carrying a sparkle.

"Who's keeping count? Tonight's about celebrating," Mike retorted.

"You're right, it is" she agreed, letting a smile creep across her face. A strand of hair fell in front of her eye. She looked relaxed, unguarded.

Warmth pooled under her skin. She wasn't sure if it was the cocktails or something else. Her phone buzzed again. Mike noticed.

She glanced down. "Let me silence this thing, it's getting ridiculous."

Mike shrugged. "Hey, I know you're a busy influencer. That's a 24-hour kind of job."

"Yeah…but sometimes it's just about being in the moment," she replied, surprising even herself with the sincerity in her voice.

Mike's heart lifted. This felt different, like a rare glimpse of something deeper in Samantha. Maybe she wasn't as self-absorbed as she let on.

"I feel like doing a shot. Let's do it!" she declared suddenly, brushing her hair back from her face.

Mike indulged her. "I'm ready when you are."

Samantha finally caught the waiter. "Two double Patrón shots, with two limes please."

When the waiter left, Mike gave Samantha a look. "Let's head up to the rooftop after this."

"Oh yeah, the stairs again," she laughed, recalling her earlier stumbles.

"Don't worry, I got you," Mike smirked.

They both laughed. Samantha felt herself getting more comfortable.

The waiter returned placing the shots on the table, and Samantha smiled. "What should we toast to?"

"To this night. To being here together," Mike said, holding her gaze.

She nodded, meeting his eyes. Then he reached over taking her hands. She didn't pull away. Instead, she let her fingers intertwine with his.

Both straps of her blouse slipped down her shoulders, revealing just enough to leave Mike entranced.

She released his hands, leaving the straps where they were. Unbothered. Raising her shot glass, she smirked.

"Cheers."

They knocked back the Patrón shots in unison. Samantha winced, laughing it off.

Mike signaled for the check, peeling bills from the folded stack he always carried. Samantha watched impressed. This was what she loved most: confidence that didn't need to be loud, generosity that didn't ask for attention.

Trouble At The Girls Bathroom

Samantha excused herself and headed to the restroom to check her makeup. Buzzed but balanced, she felt surprisingly at ease after their toast.

The line was long with chatty women. Samantha sighed, pulling out her phone to check her notifications.

As she scrolled, her heel caught the edge of the tiled floor. She stumbled, and fell right into a short, portly girl holding a bright, fruity cocktail. The drink sloshed out of the glass, splattering all over the girl's outfit and onto the floor.

"Ugh, watch where you're going!" the girl snapped.

Samantha immediately tried to apologize, brushing her hair from her face and regaining her balance. "I'm so sorry, it was an accident. Let me...."

The girl wasn't having it. One look at Samantha's expensive outfit, flawless makeup, and confident posture, and she made a snap judgment.

"Bitch, you spilled my drink!"

Samantha took a calming breath. "Look, I said I'm sorry. It was an accident. I'm willing to…"

The girl's friend chimed in, egging her on. "She thinks she's too good for us. Look at her."

Samantha rolled her eyes, her patience thinning. "Get over it, okay? It's not that serious."

That set the girl off.

Before Samantha could fully turn to walk away, the girl grabbed a fistful of her hair near the collar, yanking her backward. Samantha let out a sharp scream as she stumbled, only to be shoved hard into a nearby table. The wooden corner slammed into her ribcage, knocking over a couple of glasses as she crashed to the floor.

The entire room froze, the air thick with tension. Samantha gasped for air, struggling to collect herself as the girl kept yelling.

"You're not gonna ruin my night, you fake-ass Barbie bitch! You ain't better than me!"

The girl began kicking wildly. One kick missed. Another kick scraped her thigh, but the next one struck her hard in the same side that slammed against the table. A sharp stinging sensation shot through Samantha's ribs, pulling a cry from her lips. She curled in on herself, trying to shield her side.

A security guard rushed over, quickly assessing the scene. Samantha was on the ground while the girl loomed over her, still cursing.

"You're out," the guard said firmly, pointing to the aggressor.

The girl tried to argue, but another female guard joined in, grabbing her arm.

"Let's go," the second guard said, strong-arming her toward the exit despite her protests.

Samantha, still dazed, propped herself up. The first guard extended a hand, helping her to her feet.

"You okay?" the guard asked, her tone softening.

Samantha brushed her hair back, trying to regain her composure. "Yeah, I'm fine. Just… wow." She exhaled deeply.

Mike had heard the commotion and peered to get a better look, watching as the girls were escorted out. Heads were turning, eyes following the chaos as sharp voices echoed the room. The aggressor was still hurling obscenities, her crude defiance drawing murmurs from nearby tables. Samantha, visibly shaken but composed, headed toward the bathroom to gather herself.

Inside, she braced herself against the sink, clutching her purse like a lifeline. Her fingers trembled as she dabbed at her face, trying to fix her lipstick, smooth her eyeliner, and hide the shine with more foundation.

That bitch almost killed my buzz, she thought bitterly, replaying the incident in her mind as she reapplied some foundation.

Just another hating-ass bitch.

She refused to believe that she had provoked anything. What mattered now was getting back to Mike and the good time they were having.

She reached for her cordless curling brush, then froze. She'd left it at home. *Of all the times,* she thought.

With a disgruntled groan, she ran her fingers through her hair, trying to tame the frizz. Some strands still refused to cooperate. Her stomach dipped at the thought of Mike noticing. The heat had already worked against her earlier, and now, after everything, it felt impossible to fix completely.

"Damn that bitch," she muttered..

Her reflection stared back, messy, yet still stunning. Her denim shorts clung low on her hips, slightly rumpled from the scuffle. The fabric had ridden up, baring more skin than she intended. She tugged them down, checking herself again. Thankfully her clothes weren't stained.

One strap of her bodysuit had slipped loose during the fall, threatening another reveal. She eased it back into place, but it still sagged slightly.

Her leather jacket dangled off the same shoulder the girl had grabbed. She could still feel the imprint of her hand. A shiver ran through her. She eased the jacket back up, but the collar still felt off, like it might slip again if she wasn't careful.

She closed her eyes, trying to shut it all out. The ache in her side pulsing beneath the surface.

"I'll be okay. I've been through worse." She took a few deep breaths, drawing strength. She wasn't all the way back, but her glow hadn't left her.

By the time she returned to the table, purse in hand and jacket draped snugly over her shoulders, her composure seemed fully restored. Her strides were steady, head held high. But as she smoothed the hem of her shorts and sat down, Mike caught the faint tremble in her fingers.

She forced a relaxed smile, masking any self-consciousness, but a small voice in her head wondered if he had noticed how shaken she really was.

As she settled in, Mike's gaze flicked over her, catching the tension in her shoulders and the way her fingers toyed absently with the edge of her jacket.

"Everything okay? I heard some commotion near the bathroom," he asked, his tone light but edged with concern.

Samantha shrugged, brushing her hair back and forcing a dismissive smile.
"Bitches being bitches, I guess," she said, rolling her eyes. Her voice carried a faint, hoarse edge.

Mike could tell something was off, but he didn't press.

Samantha, meanwhile, was determined not to let the bathroom incident hijack her night. She cleared her throat, willing herself to pull it together.

"Come on, Mikey," she said with a playful smile, her voice back to its usual rhythm.
"Let's go upstairs to *La Pierre*. I want another drink and soak in the views. This really is a nice place."

Mike hesitated, debating whether to ask more.

But before he could, Samantha abruptly blurted out, "I'm happy to be here with you."

Was that genuine? She wondered as the words left her lips.

I think it is… and I think I'm finally going to let him spend the night, if he plays his cards right.

Mike stood up, but Samantha hesitated, the lingering pain catching her off guard.
Careful not to show any discomfort, she smiled at him and said, "Help me up, Mikey."

He closed the space between them, offering his arm with a smile. She stood slowly, her fingers grazing his as she slipped her arm through. A wince tugged at her lips as she shifted her stance, but she hid it behind her smile, resting her hand over his.

They moved toward the stairs, his presence grounding her with each step. She allowed herself a flicker of vulnerability, holding herself together beside him.

I'll shake this off, she told herself.
The thought firm and final.

The Elevator Ride Up To *La Pierre*

As they made their way toward the elevators, a couple ahead of them spoke in hushed tones, wrapped in their own bubble. The space was intimate, filled with the low murmur of nearby conversations. Only a small group could ride at a time, and Samantha and Mike stood close behind. The couple's voices drifted back toward them.

"Did you hear what happened in the Hollywood Hills?" the man asked, his voice low but clear enough for Mike and Samantha to catch snippets.

"Oh my God, yes. How horrible," the woman said, the concern evident through her words.
"I heard he was a popular food influencer."

"Geez… what the hell did he do to deserve that?" Her tone landed somewhere between surprise and unease.

Mike and Samantha weren't paying much attention. Samantha pressed closer to him, her head resting once again on his shoulder. Mike, ever the gentleman, let her. They were too wrapped up in each other to care much about the world around them.

"Do you remember his handle?" the woman asked.

"No, not really," the man murmured. "But damn, what a way to go… car set on fire?"

A pause, then: "You think it was a mob hit? Because that sounds like some mob-like shit."

Just as the conversation reached its peak, the couple stepped into the elevator. The doors slid shut, taking their voices with them.

Samantha rose onto her tiptoes and kissed Mike lightly on the cheek. She wasn't sure why, maybe after the run-in at the bathroom, she just needed to feel safe. To be close to someone who made her feel protected.

She didn't know what had come over her, but something about the night made her want to stop performing. To be real. To be present.

It was their turn next to step into the first set of elevators. Pressed against the back wall, Samantha let herself rest against him, her breath slowing as the elevator ascended toward the rooftop.

When the doors opened, they joined a short line for the second elevator. Nearby, the couple from earlier kept talking, their voices carrying over the chatter of the waiting area. Mike and Samantha caught fragments as they stood close together.

"It had to be a mob hit," the man said wide eyed.

"You think it was cartel-related?" she asked.

"The cartel? Who knows?"

"Yeah, those things don't happen unless you piss off the wrong person." the woman affirmed.

"Over a livestream? That's just next-level wild shit," the man said in disbelief.

"And they pulled all the videos down," he added.

"They had to! Ugh, I don't even want to see it. Even if it does come up…nope," she groaned.

"Yeah, there's something more to this. Some sort of connection to someone," he muttered.

"Boy, LAPD has their job cut out for them," the woman said shaking her head.

Samantha and Mike exchanged a glance, smiling faintly. To them, it was just another night in Los Angeles, chaotic, loud, and full of gossip. They shrugged it off and turned back to each other as the elevator doors slid open.

Finally, it was their turn.

The doors slid shut behind them, leaving them alone for the brief ride. The chemistry between them was palpable, unspoken and undeniable. Samantha held onto Mike's arm for balance, her steps composed, heels brushing lightly over the floor. The feel of him beside her eased the haze in her head.

Mike noticed her jacket had slipped slightly off one shoulder, revealing more of her figure. His eyes fixated, not even pretending to hide the way he was drawn to her.

Samantha's curves were impossible to ignore. Full, smooth, and balanced in a way that seemed effortless. Her thighs were shapely and strong, the kind of definition that looked sculpted, not exaggerated.

And yet, there was a gentle allure to her. Feminine. Athletic, yet still soft to the touch in all the right places.

Most people assumed her curves were all natural.
She didn't correct them.
She liked it that way, drawing eyes without ever seeming to try and keeping them second-guessing just enough to stay curious.

As they stood in the center of the elevator, she turned toward Mike, her hair cascading partially across her face. Without hesitation, he reached out and delicately brushed it back.

She sank into his touch, their eyes locking in silent understanding. They came together at the same time, the pull between them magnetic, and shared a kiss that felt impossibly right.

His hands rested lightly at her sides, offering a steadying presence, while her arms slipped around his neck. The kiss was sensual and unhurried, an intimate exchange neither of them wanted to end too soon.

A faint chime signaled their arrival at the rooftop, breaking the spell. They pulled back, still smiling as if they had just been caught sharing a secret.

Samantha took his arm again, steadying herself as they stepped into the open air. The DTLA skyline glittered against the night sky, and for the first time all evening, Samantha felt completely at ease, grateful she had chosen to spend the evening with him.

CHAPTER 5

HE'S MINE TONIGHT

In the heart of Downtown Los Angeles, *Le Cher* and *La Pierre* stand as one of the city's premier hotspots. Located on Hill Street between 4th and 5th, this place dazzles with breathtaking panoramic views of the skyline. *La Pierre* is the rooftop and it is split into two levels. The lower restaurant with live music and the upper lounge, complete with it's own bar and seating. Here, couples savor romantic nights, friends clink glasses, and influencers strike poses for their followers. It's a place where people go to be seen.

Tonight, the energy was electric, chatter and laughter filling every corner of the rooftop.

Mike led Samantha toward the bar, navigating through the bustling crowd with ease. She clung to his arm, her steps measured, syncing with his pace while masking the ache in her side after what happened earlier. Her feet threatened to drag, but she wasn't about to let on. Not tonight. Just smiles. Good vibes.

"What can I get you two?" the bartender asked as they approached.

Samantha immediately noticed her. The bartender's short haircut was meticulously styled, with a subtle flare that highlighted her sharp features. It was eye-catching and enough to make Samantha pause and admire her look.

"I'll have a mojito," Samantha said, adjusting her jacket as she looked at the bartender.

"Same," Mike added.

"And a shot of Patrón too," Samantha tacked on, nudging him with a smile. "Come on, Mikey, we're celebrating."

"Oh? What's the occasion?" the bartender asked, her grin aimed squarely at Mike.

"I just got promoted," he replied casually.

"Well, congrats," the bartender said, eyes flicking over him. "I like hearing about people moving up in the world. You know what? I'll buy your shot and take one with you."

Samantha tensed. The bartender's focus lingered too long, her smile just a touch too familiar. Mike, either indifferent or oblivious, didn't seem to notice.

"Sure, we can toast *our* good news with you," Samantha said, looking up at him. Her voice was light but pointed, drawing his attention back to her. A strand of hair slipped over her eye; she quickly shook it loose to avoid any miscues.

The bartender chuckled. "Of course, dear. Whatever you say," she replied, casting one last glance at Mike as she delivered the line.

More like his good news, the bartender thought.

Samantha caught the prolonged gaze out of the corner of her eye and the undertone behind the chuckle. Her heart began to race.

I swear this bitch is asking for it.

She turned to face her fully, fixing the bartender with an icy stare. Samantha's hazel-green eyes caught the light, flashing a silent warning. The bartender met her gaze, her expression calm and unbothered, her icy blue eyes detached and piercing. Samantha felt herself being sized up. She couldn't blink, couldn't show weakness, as their eyes remained locked.

I know your type, the bartender thought. *Enhanced everything. Trying too hard to keep the attention on you.*

Don't look past me like I'm not worthy of him. I am. I'm worthy of anyone, The words flared in her mind, silent but certain.

"BRB, guys," the bartender smiled, stepping away to make the drinks.

Yeah, bitch. Go do your job, Samantha tracked her with her gaze.

Samantha forced herself to relax, smoothing her hair back into place and letting out a slow breath.

Don't let this bitch get to you.

She suddenly felt Mike's arms wrap around her from behind. She reached for his hands, letting herself lean back into him. Looking up, she caught the glow of his hazel eyes and smiled.

When the bartender returned, she placed the drinks on the counter and raised her shot glass.

"Ready?" she said, glancing quickly at Samantha. Before she could respond, her gaze turned back to Mike, locking eyes with him. "To people moving up in the world."

Samantha snatched her glass from the counter. She looked up and tucked a loose strand of hair behind her ear, bracing for the toast.

"To people moving up in the world," she echoed, louder this time, making sure to glance between Mike and the bartender.

Lifting her arm sent a sharp jolt through her side, a pointed reminder of the nasty spill earlier. Still, she smiled and refused to flinch. She ran her fingers through her hair again, more out of reflex than need. Anything to center herself and push through the pain. Her smile came easily, but it served as armor all the same.

They clinked glasses. As they knocked back the shot, Mike turned to her with a reassuring smile that grounded her. A flicker of relief passed through her. Samantha looped her arm around his.

"Come on, Mikey," she said brightly. "I see a couch we can sit at."

Mike reached for his wallet, but the bartender waved him off.

"Don't worry, hun. I trust you. I'll keep it open without a card. Enjoy your night together."

Her tone sounded pleasant, but Samantha picked up on the fake-friendly undertone, something sly beneath the surface.

Their eyes meet briefly.
Samantha's gaze was sharp.
The bartender's?
Indifferent, with just a hint of knowing.

As Samantha turned to lead Mike away, she adjusted her jacket and smoothed her hair again. The bartender glanced at her slightly disheveled appearance and gave her a subtle look as if to say:

Get it together, girl.

Then, with a practiced smile, she turned to the next customer, dismissing Samantha entirely.

Samantha clenched Mike's arm a little tighter as they headed toward the couch, her thoughts racing.

I don't like that bitch, she thought, forcing herself to reset.

She wasn't in the mood to compete. Not tonight. Not like this.

She didn't have the energy to decode whatever that look meant. She just needed Mike.

Right now, he was her safe place.

They settled into an inviting couch tucked away from the crowd, the vibrant energy of *La Pierre* pulsing around them. With drinks in hand, they clinked their glasses and took a sip.

Samantha rested her head against the sofa, a strand slipping across her cheek. Mike noticed and carefully brushed it behind her ear. Their eyes met, and in hers, he read the faint unease she couldn't quite hide.

"You know," he said, moving closer, his voice gentle, meant just for her. "I'm happy to be here with you. Only you." His voice gentle, meant just for her.

Samantha smirked. "Of course you are mister."

Turning toward him, she crossed her legs and cozied up beside him, her toned thighs brushing his. She nestled in close, and he wrapped an arm around her. As she got comfortable, her jean shorts dipped slightly, revealing the faint outline of her bodysuit's thong line against her skin. But Samantha stayed completely at ease, focused only on Mike and the growing intimacy between them.

Mike smiled and inched closer for a kiss. She met him halfway, their lips connecting in a tender exchange.

As their lips parted, Samantha found herself thinking:

He's mine tonight.

She tucked herself into him, her arm sliding around his as she rested her head on his chest. She closed her eyes and exhaled, savoring the calm beneath the illuminated DTLA skyline.

Whatever tension lingered from earlier had faded, replaced by a connection beginning to take shape. They sat together, no words, just the rhythm of the city.

CHAPTER 6

THE COLLAB COUPLE

Samantha and Mike remained on the couch, drinks in hand, absorbing the rooftop's electric atmosphere. The city lights shimmered around them, blending with the chatter, laughter, and soft beats of the music.

"It really is nice up here," Samantha said, her thoughts drifting on her growing affection for Mike.

"I wouldn't have it any other way tonight," Mike replied, his eyes on her. His hand slid to her leg, his palm tracing slow, deliberate lines along her thigh. Their lips met again for a kiss, one that felt as natural as it was electric.

The moment was disrupted by another couple settling onto the couch in the corner to their right. The man carried a light kit, a camera, and other accessories, while the woman carefully balanced two drinks. She set them on the table and sat down, waiting as he returned with two more vibrant cocktails.

As he adjusted his setup, the woman teased, "Good thing we're tucked in the corner, especially with you and that bright light."

"Bright light? You mean my *showstopper light*," he quipped with a smirk.

"Yeah, exactly," she replied, rolling her eyes. "That's why we're way over here, away from everyone."

The man laughed, shaking his head. "Hey, we're having a good night, right? It's a collab, but come on, we're at *Le Cher*. I mean, this is *Le Cher!*"

"Bonswa, Cher!" the woman said enthusiastically.

The guy glanced up from his setup and grins. "On my way. Call me if you need me," he said, winking at her.

They both laughed at their inside joke, referencing one of their favorite games: *Mafia III*.

The buzzwords caught Samantha's attention. Her world revolves around glam and social media, so the word collab instantly perked her ears. Their voices also sounded familiar, reminding her of the couple she had overheard earlier, the ones talking about the murders.

"I'm just glad drinks are included in this collab," the woman said, swirling her cocktail. "Still not feeling a buzz, though, and I've had four already. Plus, the mini shots before we even got here."

"Your tolerance is ridiculous," the man replied with a chuckle, tightening the last adjustment on his equipment.

Curious, Samantha sat up, brushing her hair out of her face. Her eyes locked onto the woman's striking white hair, styled to perfection.

She carried herself with a modest yet alluring aura, the kind of presence that doesn't need to try too hard. Her deep, intense eyes contrast against her perfectly styled white hair, which has just enough flare to be striking. She moved with grace, blending elegance with an exotic charm, a presence that seemed to command the space around her.

Samantha adjusted her outfit, still self-conscious about her hair but determined to stay composed. For some reason, she felt compelled to speak.

"Your hair is gorgeous," she said, a little awkward but completely sincere.

The woman turned, her smile inviting. "Oh, thank you, hun." She was used to compliments, Samantha could tell by the way she carried herself that this kind of attention didn't faze her.

Emboldened by the drinks, Samantha arched forward. "Who do you see? Like, what stylist gets it looking like that?"

She gave a small, bashful laugh. "I actually do it myself."

"Shut up!" Samantha exclaimed, genuinely impressed.

"And you get it to look this good? Wow. You could give me some tips, I usually manage, but my hair's got a complete mind of its own tonight," she added, pointing to her frizz.

"You look good, girl," the woman replied encouragingly.

Samantha grinned, "You should start a channel or a blog!"

"I keep trying to tell her that," the man beside her interjected with a grin.

The woman waved him off modestly. "I couldn't do that. I'm more of a behind-the-scenes kind of girl."

"I'd subscribe in a heartbeat," Samantha insisted. "Do you do hair for other people? Like, are you a stylist?"

"I get asked that a lot," the woman said with a modest laugh.

The man jumped in again. "I've been telling her that too, people would pay good money for her skills."

"Exactly!" Samantha agreed. "I know I would."

"Girl, sometimes I hate doing my own! No way I could do other people's hair," the woman said, shaking her head. They both laughed.

"Hashtag hair problems," Samantha joked.

Their easy banter drew Mike into the conversation. He stepped closer, introducing himself and Samantha. The couple reciprocated, introducing themselves as Aya and Bobby.

Both Black, they appeared to be millennials. Samantha caught the grey patch in Bobby's hair, a distinct feature that added to his look. His rich curls had a texture that often made people assume he was Afro-Caribbean or had lineage somewhere in South America.

"Is that a birthmark?" Samantha asked with curiosity.

"From my years selling timeshares," he joked. "That's why I had to get out of that business."

They explained they were collaborating with the restaurant on a special promotion they'd both been looking forward to. Bobby mentioned he was a food blogger who is a contributor for *Feeder L.A.* and also runs social media accounts for a few L.A. restaurants. Aya works independently in IT and computer repair. The two also do marketing, sometimes teaming up on freelance gigs for other restaurants and businesses.

"I mean, its L.A. Everyone's out here for something. Everyone has a story," he said.

"This is true," Aya added in full support.

Mike remained, patiently letting Samantha steer the conversation. He chimed in occasionally, but it was clear he enjoyed seeing her so engaged.

Samantha turned to Mike, who had been listening intently, watching the exchange. He smiled, patient as always, allowing her to connect with the couple.

"What are your pages?" she asked, eager to make new connections.

They swapped social media handles, diving into talk about Instagram, TikTok, and YouTube. The usual chatter, changing algorithms, trying to stay relevant, and keeping up with trends. Samantha was in her element, talking about how to build a brand and create engaging content.

As their drinks dwindled, Samantha stood, trying to maintain her composure. She no longer clung to Mike's arm, determined to keep it together. She adjusted her outfit. Aya noticed the slight wobble in her step and the practiced laugh Samantha gave, clearly trying to stay cute for her date. Aya smiled, remembering those days.

"I love your heels, girl. You're pulling them off!" she said, eyeing them. "You look great."

"Thanks. Still breaking them in," Samantha replied with a small laugh. The compliment lifted her spirits.

The compliment and the timing gave her just enough breath to feel like herself again, even if only for a little bit.

She felt a little tipsy but didn't want to show it. The dull, throbbing pain in her side still lingered from earlier, the result of the hard fall. Her right side had slammed against the corner of the table before she hit the floor.

She masked it well, but the impact had left her sore. Still, she refused to lean on Mike for support. She didn't want to seem dependent. She wanted to walk away on her own, composed and in control.

Steady yourself, girl.

They said their goodbyes, and Samantha led Mike back toward the bar, feeling like she had successfully navigated the night's social dynamics.

"Let's go see the band," she said, still buzzing from the evening and eager to keep the energy going.

As they left, the night manager sat at the monitors, reviewing footage. Something he'd seen earlier nagged at him. He hoped to catch Samantha before she slipped away.

CHAPTER 7

DANCING THE NIGHT AWAY

"I need to close out with the bartender before we go," Mike said, gesturing toward the bar. Samantha walked beside him, measured and poised despite the slow ache in her side. She wouldn't let discomfort ruin her night, or give the bartender any sense of an advantage.

As they approached, the bartender finished serving another customer and turned to Mike with a smile that bordered on flirtatious.

"We're heading downstairs to the other bar," Mike said, sliding his card across the counter. "Not sure how tabs work here, but let me square up first."

The bartender, rinsing out a few glasses, nodded. Her gaze flicked briefly to Samantha, who had subtly claimed Mike's arm. The message was clear:

He's mine tonight.

Catching on, the bartender played along with a sly grin. She bypassed Mike entirely and turned to Samantha.

"You know, I've been working on a new drink recipe. Want to give me your opinion?"

Samantha, keeping her cool, brushed back her hair and shrugged. "Sure, why not?"

Minutes later, the bartender returned with three brightly colored drinks, setting them down with precise, deliberate movements. Though her demeanor remained friendly, Samantha sensed the underlying tension, the unspoken power play between two women quietly vying for dominance.

Sizing her up, Samantha noted the bartender's lean, athletic build, clearly all-natural. Confidence radiated from her, but Samantha refused to feel threatened.

"How often do you work out?" she asked, her voice light, conversational. But her grip on Mike's arm remained firm.

The bartender's lips curled in amusement. "I used to run track in college. It stuck with me, but these days? Three, maybe four times a week."

Mike, seizing the chance to join in, added, "I played basketball at UCLA."

"Nice," the bartender said, her smile widening. "I went to Cal State L.A."

For a split second, Samantha felt her plan backfire. The bartender and Mike exchanged a glance, bonding over their collegiate athletic pasts.

Before that connection could deepen, Samantha cut in.

"Let's toast again," Samantha said brightly, her voice cutting through the air. "To your promotion tonight, Mike." She raised her glass, her eyes locked on his. "And to *our* great night together."

Mike caught the underlying message. Samantha's words were for him, but the subtext was clearly aimed at the bartender:

Back off.

The bartender gave a knowing smile, careful not to overstep and raised her own glass. "Cheers."

As they clinked glasses, a strand of Samantha's hair fell over her right eye. She didn't bother to fix it, too focused on holding her composure.

When she raised her arm again for the toast, a flash of pain crossed her face. She masked it with a smile, recovering in a heartbeat.

Did he notice? She wasn't sure.
If he did, he didn't say a word. Mike's eyes stayed glued to hers.

Keep it together. Look good. Don't let it show.
"Cheers!" Samantha repeated, beaming at him.

The three of them downed their drinks together. Samantha set her glass down with a confident smile.

"Nice kick to it," she said, acknowledging the bartender's concoction. "I like it."

"Same here," Mike added.

The faint sound of music floated up from the lower level, and Samantha seized the chance. "I hear the band playing, Mikey. Let's go see who they are."

Mike reached for his money clip, pulling out $150. "Is this enough?"

The bartender nodded. "More than enough. Thank you. I really hope you two enjoy your night."

Her words carried a hint of genuine goodwill, but her lingering gaze on Samantha suggested she understood the night wasn't hers to claim.

"Last call's in an hour," the bartender added as Samantha tugged Mike's arm. "Feel free to stop back if you want a nightcap."

"Thanks," they both said in unison, but Samantha was already pulling Mike away before he could offer the bartender another glance.

As they descended to the lower bar, where the band played, Mike glanced back, sensing the bartender's path might cross theirs someday.

Her grip on his arm held a quiet determination, something that caught him off guard in the best way. Mike found it deeply endearing. This side of her felt new, and he wanted her to feel safe enough to let it stay.

The sound of live music buzzed through the air as they stepped into the room, its rhythm threading into the atmosphere. Samantha's energy seemed lighter now, her earlier edge softening as they moved into the crowd.

The Elevator Ride Down

Samantha and Mike stood waiting for the elevator, the dim hallway lighting casting soft shadows around them. Samantha rocked on her heels trying to ease the ache in her feet.

No more stairs. She glanced down at them.

They were killing her, but she wasn't about to be one of those girls, the ones walking barefoot through the grimy streets of Downtown L.A.

The mere idea made her shudder. *Broken glass, or worse... God, no thanks.*

Finally, the elevator doors slid open. Samantha hurried inside, ignoring the throbbing pain in her feet. She grabbed Mike's hand and looked back at him, her hair falling haphazardly over her face.

"Hurry, before someone else comes in," she said, playful.

Mike followed her, a smile playing on his lips. As she moved, her shorts lifted, causing another slight wardrobe malfunction, but Samantha refused to let it distract her.

Mike stepped, and Samantha hit the close button with a snicker, watching the doors seal shut before anyone could join them. She leaned back against the elevator wall, letting out a soft sigh. In her state, her guard was beginning to slip.

She glanced up at Mike, her hair falling in messy strands over her face. "I give up. I'm definitely having a bad hair day, Mikey," she said, laughing at herself.

Mike took a step closer, his gaze softening as he reached out to brush a strand from her cheek.

"Shhh," he murmured, placing a finger over her lips. "You look hot either way, Sam."

The nickname caught her off guard for a second. Sam. It felt intimate, like a term of endearment just for her.

Her heart skipped a beat as Mike tilted her chin up, his hand gentle and sure against her skin. Their eyes locked before he inched closer, his lips capturing hers in a kiss as intentional as it was tender.

Samantha got lost herself, wrapping her arms around his neck as she kissed him back, the world outside the elevator forgotten. The kiss deepened, the intensity between them building. Her hands traveled down his shoulders before one reached lower, grazing against him with a playful yet deliberate touch.

This is what I'm working with tonight. A sly smile tugging at her lips as her touch lingered just long enough to tease.

The elevator dinged, and just like that, the world came rushing back.

Samantha stepped back, brushing her hair from her face as she straightened. The doors slid open and she reached for Mike's hand. Together, they walked out at a slow, confident pace, their connection evident as they moved toward the music.

The First Song

As Samantha stepped out of the elevator, the vibrant beat of a catchy song filled the air, making her pause. She turned to Mike with a playful smile.

"You can dance, right, Mike?"

"Absolutely," he declared.

Samantha grabbed his hand and pulled him onto the dance floor. The rhythm surrounded them. As soon as she started to move, the ache in her feet and side faded. It was just her and Mike now, their bodies moving in sync, lost in the music and the night.

She brushed his lips , electricity flowing through her. A deeper pull stirred inside her, but she held back, maintaining her composure as they moved together on the dance floor.

Mike surprised her, taking the lead and mildly spinning her before drawing her back into his arms.

Nice moves, she thought, a smile tugging at her lips.

The world fell away. Samantha laughed, her tension finally breaking.

Neither of them noticed the night manager watching from the edge of the room. He let out a sigh of relief, though his concern over the earlier incident still lingered. He considered stepping in but thought better of it. The last thing he wanted was to ruin their fun. Instead, he gave a subtle nod to the security guards nearby.

"Keep an eye on her," he told them before heading back toward the kitchen to oversee some pending orders.

Meanwhile, Samantha and Mike remained immersed, dancing together as the music played on. The world could wait, this was their night together.

A Moment To Catch Their Breath

The music faded. Heat pooled under her jacket, sweat blooming just beneath her hairline. Her styled look she walked in with? Gone.

At least my makeup's holding up, she thought, clinging to that one small win.

"Shall we sit down?" Mike asked, noticing how she had started fanning herself.

She nodded, letting him lead her to an empty table tucked into a quiet corner away from the lively crowd. As they sat, a waiter approached swiftly.

"Last call for the kitchen. It's closing in 30 minutes," he informed them.

Realizing the dancing had sparked their appetites, they both decided to order. Each selected an appetizer and added two more drinks to the tab. Samantha shrugged off her jacket as they settled in, the motion revealing a light sheen of sweat on her chest. She grabbed the menu and began fanning herself, hoping to cool down.

In doing so, one of her straps slipped off her shoulder, the fabric sliding just enough to reveal more than intended. She glanced up at Mike, her lips curving into a faint, knowing smile that held a hint of amusement.

Mike swallowed hard. Heat rose in his chest. Samantha looked good. The kind of good that messed with your focus. He shifted slightly, doing his best to stay composed. The last thing he needed was to stand up with a situation he couldn't exactly hide.

Instead, he grinned. "You dance pretty good," he said, leaning back in his chair, trying to focus on anything but how much he wanted her right now.

"And you managed to keep up with me in those heels," he added. They both laughed.

"Hey, we're celebrating, right?" Samantha replied, her eyes locking with his.

Wow. This is new, he thought, catching the softness in her voice. *I've never seen this side of her before.*

Mike reached across the table taking her hand. Their gazes lingered, and she felt her pulse quicken, but she kept her composure.

Just then, the waiter arrived with their drinks. Samantha offered a polite smile, subtly adjusting her strap and top as he walked away. She let out a soft giggle, an unspoken whoops aimed at Mike.

I want to keep this night going, she thought, glancing back at him. Her hand was still wrapped around his.

Meanwhile, the night manager, still concerned about the earlier incident, spotted them from a distance. He didn't want to ruin their evening, but he was determined to talk to Samantha.

"Stay near the exit and radio me when they're about to leave" he whispered to a security guard.

Their appetizers arrived just before the kitchen closed, offering a welcome reprieve from the alcohol. Their table felt like a safe haven, tucked away from the chaos of the night. Samantha and Mike ate slowly.

"You're pretty good at this whole night-out thing," Samantha teased, still fanning herself with the menu.

"You're not too bad yourself, Miss Social Butterfly," Mike shot back with a smirk, raising his glass for a toast.

As they clinked glasses, the energy between them simmered. The band played low, the night neared its end. Tucked into their corner, they spoke in near-whispers, trading laughter and looks only they understood. The night felt far from over. Neither of them wanted it to end.

82

CHAPTER 8

LET'S GO HOME

It was time to leave. *Le Cher and La Pierre* were closing, and Samantha had already decided that she didn't want the night to end alone. She wanted it to end with Mike.

"You ready?" She glanced up at Mike. "Do you want to stay downtown, or follow me back to my place? I'd rather not end the night just yet."

Mike recognized the invitation for what it was. No further explanation was needed.

He hesitated, considering the long drive and how many drinks he had. "What about getting a room downtown? *The Transcontinental Hotel*, maybe?"

The tallest building in DTLA, 73 floors into the sky, with an elegant restaurant on the top floor. Another must-see, must-eat spot in the city.

Samantha's eyes lit up. "I love that hotel," she said with a smile, her readiness to end the night with him fully apparent. She reached for her glass and downed the rest of her drink.

"Let's go, Mikey," she said, reaching her hand out toward him.

He stood, guiding her to her feet. "Lead the way."

As Mike helped her into her jacket, a security guard radioed the night manager. "They're getting up now."

The night manager sprang into action. He didn't want to make a scene, but he couldn't let her leave without speaking to her. He headed toward the elevators, hoping to catch her before she disappeared into the night.

Samantha and Mike made their way out toward the elevators when the night manager spotted her.

"Miss! Miss!" he called out, his voice rising above the chatter of the exiting crowd.

Samantha ignored him, brushing her hair back and pretending she hadn't heard.

"Is he trying to get your attention?" Mike asked, glancing back.

Samantha sighed, pressing her lips into a thin line. "Wait for me right here, please," she said, releasing his arm.

Mike nodded, stepping aside as she turned and walked toward the night manager. She wasn't about to let anything, or anyone, ruin the rest of her evening.

"Miss," the manager said again as she approached. His face was serious but polite.

Samantha stopped a few steps away, arms crossed. "What is it?" Her tone curt.

"I need to talk to you about the earlier incident," he began.

"Look, it's been handled. I'm fine. Let's not make this a big deal."

"Miss, I just—"

"Listen," she interrupted, her voice calm but firm. "I'm about to leave. If there's paperwork or something, send it to me later. I appreciate your concern, but I've got it under control."

The night had been perfect until now. Samantha could feel the stress creeping in as the manager refused to drop it. She knew he meant well, or maybe he was just covering the restaurant's liability, but she wasn't in the mood. She just wanted to leave with Mike. No distractions. No issues.

Still, the manager pressed on with more questions. Samantha could feel the strain, emotionally, physically.

The throbbing returned. Subtle at first, it sent a slow pulse beneath her ribs. Not unbearable, but enough to make her wince, her hand reflexively clutching the spot.

Mike noticed immediately. His face clouded with concern.

"Are you hurt?" the manager asked, his voice turning serious.

Samantha immediately dropped her hand, unwilling to show any sign of fatigue. "I'm fine."

Mike instinctively moved closer, but she raised a hand, signaling him to stay back. She didn't want a scene. She didn't want fussing, especially not from him.

But the night manager wasn't done. "Did you want to file a police report? We don't tolerate this kind of activity at *Le Cher*. We saw what happened, and we'd really like your help in addressing it."

Samantha rolled her eyes. "A police report? Over this? LAPD wouldn't even waste their time." She gave a half laugh.

The manager hesitated. She wasn't reacting the way he expected, she clearly just wanted to move on. But still, he persisted. "I don't want to disturb your night, but we'd really like to make this right for you."

She turned her head, refusing to look at him. "You can start by leaving me alone."

The throbbing intensified, made worse by the stress of the conversation. She pressed a hand to her ribs, inhaling sharply.

"Please." She paused, took a breath. "I have to go. My date is waiting for me."

The manager made one last attempt, pulling out a card. "Please."

Samantha shook her head. No.

He hesitated. "My wife follows you," he admitted. "I know who you are.

Mike caught that last part. His posture stiffened as he started toward her, something protective in his eyes. The manager changed his tone, suddenly all smiles.

"Follow our page and reach out. We'd love to invite you back and host you properly next time."

The mention of a future invitation softened Samantha. She thought of her new friendships with Aya and Bobby. *They'd love that.*

Still cautious, she gave the manager a final look.

"Okay," she said, reluctantly exchanging handles with him and taking his card.

"Are you parked in valet?" he asked.

"Yes, but we're going to be in downtown," Samantha replied.

She wobbled slightly. The manager caught it.

"How about we call you an Uber? On us. There and back," the manager offered. "Both of you can leave your cars here, they'll be safe."

"Sure. Then please call us an Uber home. We stay on the west side."

The manager obliged. Mike's hand found the small of her back Samantha, and looked up at him, her hair falling over her face once again.

"Let's go home, Mike."

"Yes, let's." He brushed her hair back from her face, his hand resting lightly on her back. Samantha cracked a small smile.

As they waited for the Uber, the manager directed them to a quieter area. Samantha wanted to take the edge off and asked, "Do you mind if we have one more drink while we wait?"

The manager agreed, eager to keep things calm.

Samantha and Mike sat together, sharing the same side of the booth. Her head rested against his shoulder as they sipped their drinks in silence. Samantha appreciated the brief reprieve.

The Uber arrived soon after. As they walked out of *Le Cher* hand in hand, Samantha felt a sense of closure. The night hadn't gone perfectly, but it was ending the way she wanted, with Mike by her side.

The night manager stood off to the side as they waited, a subtle reminder of the stress Samantha was eager to leave behind. Mike ordered a coffee to go.

"Good idea," Samantha said, her vocal fry slipping through with exhaustion. "Let's share."

As they waited for the elevator, Samantha subtly adjusted her outfit again, making sure everything was where it should be. *No more distractions. No more wardrobe malfunctions.*

She never thought of herself as insecure in her own skin, but maybe after what happened tonight, a sensitivity had crept in, one she wasn't ready to admit.

The elevator doors opened, and they stepped in with another couple. Samantha's mind briefly wandered to Aya and Bobby's night, but she quickly pulled herself back to the present and back to Mike.

Mike didn't ask, but she could tell he was piecing things together, sensing there was more to tonight than what she was letting on. He didn't press her for answers. He knew she didn't want to dive into the drama.

They exited the elevator, and Samantha slipped her arm through Mike's, planting a gentle kiss on his cheek as she pressed herself closer.

Mike smiled, offering her a sip of the coffee, which she happily accepted.

The Uber slid to the curb. Samantha sank into the seat, her head resting on Mike's shoulder as the city lights streaked past on their way downtown.

Finally, she let herself relax, letting the tension fade. They were finally going home together, and that was all that mattered.

The Uber Ride Home

The hum of the city faded as the Uber wound through downtown, but the silence between them felt heavy. Mike tried to focus on the calm of the ride, but his mind wandered. He glanced at Samantha, noting how her body language had shifted since the night manager approached them.

Something was off. The tension in her was subtle but unmistakable, and ever since she returned from the bathroom.

He couldn't put his finger on it. The curiosity simmering in him all night finally bubbled to the surface. The bartender's forwardness hadn't helped, but Samantha had stayed social and composed through it all. Now, it was clear the night had taken a toll.

Loose strands framed her face, her hairstyle telling the story of the night. She brushed them back in a fleeting attempt to keep it together, then looked up at Mike with a faint smile. She took a sip of coffee, hoping it might soothe her throat.

"What happened with him?" Mike asked, hesitation still clinging to his voice.

Samantha moved carefully, a sharp jolt of pain flaring in her side. Her hand still clasped his. She sat up slightly, turning toward the window to collect her thoughts, trying to shake the memory loose. She didn't want to rehash it. Not now. Not after everything.

Mike watched her reflection in the glass, noticing her jacket slipping from her shoulder again. It looked stretched, tugged slightly out of place as though the evening itself had left its mark.

"Sam?" His voice gentle, breaking her daze. She turned back, strands of hair falling across her face.

"Let's just not," she murmured, her voice barely above a whisper. Everything she had been holding in from the night hung between them.

Mike's brow furrowed. He wanted to comfort her, but her eyes said it all. Now wasn't the time.

"Just kiss me," she said, the words frayed with fatigue and want.

He moved closer, lips brushing hers, gentle at first, testing. When she didn't pull away, the kiss deepened, her head tipping back slightly toward the window as his hand found her cheek.

The chaos of the night fell away. It was just them.

Her heart pounded. The alcohol, the long night, the swirling emotions, it all caught up with her at once. She pulled back, breath unsteady, lips tingling.

"Stay with me tonight," she whispered, unsure if he heard.

Mike tightened his hand around hers, a subtle affirmation. The song changed on the radio.

"Summer Madness" by Kool & The Gang played from the speakers as the car merged onto the freeway.

"I love this song," she said.

She rested her head on his chest, fingers tracing lazy circles. Her jacket slipped fully from her shoulder, bare skin brushing his arm. Mike pulled it back up carefully, earning a faint smile from her.

They shared another kiss before she settled against him, her eyes fluttering closed.

The coffee sat between them now, its warmth fading. Samantha's hand remained in his, her body relaxing as she let herself drift.

Mike brushed his fingers through her hair as the Uber carried them toward West L.A. The song's melody floated over the speakers. Samantha closed her eyes, surrendering to the calm as Mike's hand remained clasped in hers.

CHAPTER 9

THE NIGHT AIN'T OVER YET

Samantha felt the salty ocean air kiss her face as the Uber approached her Marina del Rey home. She had always loved this feeling. It was a sign she was home, a calm she cherished deeply. This house wasn't just a symbol of luxury at her age; it was a gift of love from her late grandmother, a connection she held close to her heart.

Her grandmother had been her world, especially during a childhood shaped by her father's demanding surveillance job and her parents' eventual divorce. Memories flooded in of her grandmother's joyous laughter, their walks along the beach, the countless hours they spent in the kitchen together. Even now, Samantha often felt her presence in the house, like a quiet guardian.

She missed her fiercely. But this home was a gift of love, a sanctuary she deeply cherished. Her father, ever the protector, had installed a state-of-the-art security system so intricate and discreet that even the most seasoned intruder couldn't crack it. At least, not yet.

Samantha never took her safety for granted, not now, with a threat lurking in the shadows she didn't yet fully grasp. As the car slowed to a stop, she stirred.

"We're here," she murmured, her voice heavy with fatigue.

She pushed the door open and slid out slowly. Her shorts rode higher, revealing a little more than she realized. Too tired to care, she left them as they were. Mike couldn't stop himself from stealing a glance, a small smile tugging at his lips.

Taking his hand, Samantha led him to the door. A small pile of packages sat waiting, including a pink box she didn't recognize, left by someone far more sinister than the usual delivery drivers.

"Mike, can you be a dear and bring these inside?" she asked, fumbling with her keys.

"Sure," Mike said, gathering the packages. "Is this a regular thing for you?"

Samantha chuckled. "More than I care to admit," she said as the door swung open.

She slipped away briefly to disarm the alarm. The system's beeps counted down before a chime signaled it was deactivated. she was back, fingers dancing over the panel as she swiftly rearmed it.

"Don't worry, Mikey," she teased. "I won't keep you prisoner. You can wake me up if you need to leave."

"I've got no place to be but here with you," Mike said without hesitation.

She smiled, her walls lowering a bit more. "Living alone, this is non-negotiable," she explained, pointing to the alarm system.

"I feel you," Mike affirmed.. "I've got my CCW. Had to leave my piece in the car before going into *Le Cher*, though."

Her eyebrows lifted. "My dad would definitely approve."

Their conversation faded as they stepped inside, Samantha moving through the house, flicking on it's lights. *At last, the night's over,* she thought, a small smile tugging at her lips.

But her body felt it. The alcohol, exhaustion, and unspoken emotions creeping in like a slow tide.

Mike set the packages on a side table. She didn't notice the pink box tucked among them.

"Hey, where's your bathroom at?" Mike asked.

"Straight down the hall. "When you hit the painting, veer right into the guest wing. It's the second door on the left, across from the linen closet."

As he disappeared, she went to the kitchen and pulled out a bottle of prescription-strength ibuprofen from a drawer. Other pill bottles rattled forward, a container of muscle relaxers rolling into view.

Nope. I have company, she laughed, her fingers squeezing the bottle before pushing it back. *Muscle relaxers would feel amazing after that spill.* She shook her head dismissing the thought.

"It's okay," she whispered to herself. *Endure. He's here. No turning back now.*

She popped the ibuprofen tablet and chased it with water. Closing her eyes, she waited for the familiar relief to seep in.

Something's better than nothing, she told herself, wishing it was the stronger medication.

Catching her reflection in the mirror, she smiled faintly and inhaled deeply. *You wanted this night with him.*

The sound of a toilet flushing echoed down the hall.

"Sam?" Mike's voice carried through the quiet house.

His first time here, she thought, a genuine smile tugging at her lips.

She turned toward the hall. "Here I come, Mike. Just follow my voice."

Her heels danced across the tile floor, her energy lifting in a wistful almost theatrical beam. She let the mood overtake her.

Meanwhile, outside, the air had turned colder. In the shadowed distance, the killer's car idled. His mask, black with white and pink hashtags scattered across it, sat on the dashboard like a haunting symbol of his twisted obsession. The house's inconspicuous cameras captured everything: the car, the slow drive-by, and the danger creeping closer. Yet the killer remained unaware he was under surveillance.

Back inside, Samantha and Mike were oblivious. For now, it was just them, the night, and the pull of an undeniable connection waiting to unfold.

Home Sweet Home

"Molly! Dodger!" Her voice softened as she repeated their names, the strain giving her words a raspy allure. Mike found it sensual, a glimpse of how she pushed through the night, clearly shaken by something but unwilling to let it overshadow the evening.

She made her way to the refrigerator, retrieving a chilled bottle of champagne and two glasses. With a bartender's touch, she popped the cork, the festive pop echoing through her meticulously decorated home.

"Let's keep the celebration going," she said with a smile as she poured.

Mike took in the surroundings as he moved about, appreciating the elegant yet cozy vibe. Her house was stunning, a reflection of her: bold, charming, with a hint of subtle extravagance. Décor filled the space, but everything was meticulously curated. Each piece felt intentional, nothing out of place, not even a speck of dust. It was clear she cared for this home as much as it cared for her.

"Your place is amazing," he said, his voice full of genuine admiration.

"It's my sanctuary," she replied, handing him a glass. "It was my grandmother's house. She left it to me when she passed."

Her voice softened at the mention of her grandmother. "She was everything to me. I practically grew up with her since my dad's job kept him traveling so much."

Mike nodded, sensing the depth of her connection.
"Cheers to Grandma," he said.
"Cheers to Grandma," she echoed with a faint smile.

Their glasses met with a quiet clink before they each took a sip. As Mike's eyes roamed the pristine space, Samantha could almost feel his next question forming.

"I have help keeping it like this," she admitted lightly. "A housekeeper. She's been with my family since my grandmother was alive. A longtime friend. But I try not to give her too much to do when she comes by."

Samantha gestured toward the living room wall, where a row of framed photos hung neatly.

"See that one?" she asked, pointing to a photo of her as a young girl in a Dodgers cap, standing beside her dad at Dodger Stadium.

"My dad and I have been Dodgers fans forever. Growing up, he got us season tickets every year, no matter how busy he was. It was our way of staying connected," she said,

Mike smiled, still looking at the photo. "Looks like you've been a fan from day one."

"I still am," she replied proudly. "He still gifts me those season tickets every year, without fail. It's a tradition I look forward to. We even went to the World Series together. I even kept the stubs."

As she moved to adjust the digital thermostat, Samantha hummed under her breath, the memories warm in her chest. The system responded with a low whir, filling the quiet as the house grew more comfortable around them.

Mike chuckled. "That's pretty special. You must have some amazing memories."

"The best," she said, her eyes sparkling. "Dodger games were one of the few constants in my life. Even when things got tough, those nights with my dad meant everything."

She took another sip of champagne before calling out again, "Molly! Dodger!"

Still no sign of her pets. Samantha shook her head with a smirk. "They must know I have company. Giving me space, as usual."

"Maybe you'll meet them," she added with a playful wink.

Mike smiled back. "I'm sure they'll love me when they do."

She moved past him, her heels barely brushing the tile, jacket still clinging to her shoulders. She drew in a breath, braced a hand against the counter, and lifted her glass toward him.

"Cheers, Mikey. To your new promotion. I'm really happy for you."

She remembered the countless times he'd mentioned it, the long hours he'd been putting in. And while she supported him, she couldn't deny she had kept him at arm's length, until now.

A nagging thought crept in.
Could he turn into what my father was?

She remembered how it was really her grandmother who raised her. Her mother had divorced her father years ago. He had always been too busy, too emotionally unavailable.

Her mother had moved out of state, remarried, and started over with a new family. It had strained their relationship for years. Only recently had things begun to improve, and now Samantha finally understood why her mother had left.

But she brushed the thought aside. Tonight wasn't about that. Tonight was about being here with him. And she wanted him.

"And to you being here to celebrate with me tonight," Mike said, clinking his glass against hers. "Cheers, Sam."

With their glasses in hand, Samantha led him to the living room. "Come sit with me," she said already heading toward the couch.

It was lavish, sleek, and straight out of a high-end designer catalog.
Another thought flickered in Mike's mind.
Could her taste and lavish lifestyle be something I wouldn't fit into?

He had grown up with a modest background. But he pushed the thought aside. Tonight wasn't about that. Tonight was about being with her.

Still moving toward the couch, her steps wobbled slightly, whether from exhaustion or the champagne, he wasn't sure. But she managed to sit gracefully. As she eased into the cushions, her shorts dipped lower, revealing the delicate line of fabric that teasingly curved along her hip.

She didn't notice.

But Mike did.

And damn, he found her sexy.

He followed, settling beside her on the plush, pillowy couch. She grabbed the remote and turned on the TV, the screen casting dim over the room. As the ibuprofen kicked in, the dull ache in her side finally eased, offering a brief, welcome reprieve.

"I want to put some music on," she said searching for the remote.

Turning to one side, she bent forward and rifled through the couch cushions, her shorts sliding lower as she searched. The curve of her thong-cut bodysuit was nearly all exposed now. She looked like she was melting out of her clothes. Mike's gaze lingered, heat curling low in his chest.

Samantha knew exactly what she was doing. One last tease for Mike. She slipped the remote from its hiding place and dangled it between her fingers, a playful gleam in her eye. As she popped up, the bounce made her jacket fall off one shoulder, a subtle invitation that didn't go unnoticed. Their eyes locked. Seeing the jacket hanging off her shoulder,

Mike's hand found the edge of her jacket, his fingers grazed her skin as he eased it down her arm. She didn't stop him, her eyes saying it all:

Undress me.

The jacket fell away, baring her shoulders. Her perky breasts strained up against the thin straps, which now looked seconds away from slipping completely.

She turned on her playlist, music spilling through the house, setting the mood even more.

Curling her legs up over his, she reached for her glass.

"Mike, please," she requested.

He passed it to her, fingertips brushing hers. Her strap slipped down her shoulder as she raised the glass, tousled strands of hair falling across her face. The night clung to her in the best way, leaving her undone yet unbothered.

She lifted the glass in a silent toast. He followed, their eyes locking as they drank together, emptying their glasses in perfect unison. A quiet toast to the night, and to whatever came next.

Samantha readjusted, pulling her legs back and tossing them over his lap, turning to face him fully. Her low-cut top left little to the imagination, her curves front and center. Mike couldn't pretend not to notice.

Make your move, Mike. Here I am.

Mike edged closer, the magnetism between them now impossible to ignore. She lifted slightly as he reached for her, her other strap slipping from her shoulder like an invitation. Their eyes locked. That look sealed it.

They met halfway, lips crashing in a heated kiss, arms wrapping around each other beneath the dim light.

An Unexpected Phone Call

Mike's hands slid down her back, pulling her closer. His touch was tender and deliberate, yet insistent. She felt the warmth of his hands through the thin fabric of her outfit, his fingertips tracing the curve of her waist before slipping lower, inching toward her hips. The sensation made her pulse quicken.

Her hands were just as eager. She slid them underneath his shirt, feeling the firm muscles of his chest. The air between them grew charged, their connection hot and heavy, their hands exploring each other with rising urgency.

The kiss settled. Samantha pulled back to meet his eyes, her chest rising and falling with anticipation. Her body ached for what was coming next.

"I could kiss you all night," Mike murmured, rock-hard beneath her as she sat in his lap.

Samantha was about to respond when the phone on the table started vibrating.

She ignored it, pressing kisses along Mike's neck, but it didn't stop.

With a sigh, she finally reached for it, wincing at the pain in her side.

She squinted, blocking out the ache, hoping Mike wouldn't notice. Tossing her hair back, she glanced at the screen.

"It's my girl Alison. Give me one minute, Mikey."

Mike gave a small motion, *No worries.*

She flashed him a quick "one-minute" signal and picked up the call.

"Ali, baby! What's up?"

"Girl, how did it go tonight? Did you go out with Mike or Sebastian? Oh, and I saw Terrance at Starbucks, he was asking about…"

Alison's voice was loud as hell, but before she could finish, Samantha cut her off.

"Bitch, I'm tied up right now! Mike told me about his promotion today, and we went out to celebrate at *Le Cher*!" She puckered her lips at Mike in a playful air-kiss.

Mike smirked.

"Ohhh shit! Popping bottles over there!" Alison teased, her voice laced with curiosity.

"It's been a good night so far, but honey, he's *here,* so I gotta go."

"No way!" Alison gasped. "You let him come over?!"

She knew Samantha never brought just anyone to her place.

"Yeah, it just kind of happened. It was a long night at *Le Cher,* but I'll tell you everything later, okay, girl?"

"Bitch, I *want* the details!"

"You'll get them! *Bye*, Ali. See you tomorrow."

With a relieved sigh, Samantha hung up and turned to Mike.

"Not me about to put this phone on Do Not Disturb" she said, shaking her head.

Before she did, she scrolled to his contact name. With a flick of her finger, she deleted *Free Meal Mike* and simply left it as Mike. A small smile tugged at her lips as she silenced her notifications and placed her glammed-out phone back on the table.

"No more distractions," she sighed, satisfied.

Turning up the volume, music filled the house. A Drake song played in the background.

"Big Drake fan, huh?" Mike asked.

"I love The Drake," she said with an unexpected nerdiness.

Mike gave her a puzzled look. "The Drake?"

Her laughter was immediate. She waved it off, shifting the focus back to the them..

"You know, Mike... I don't really bring a lot of people here," she admitted.

He looked at her, sincerity in his eyes. "I'm happy you did. And it means a lot that you feel comfortable with me."

She smiled. A brief hesitation. Then, she gave him a knowing look, and he moved in to kiss her again, this time with even more passion. Her hands found the hem of his shirt, pulling it over his head in one swift motion.

Their bodies came together again, their kisses full of hunger and growing need. The heat between them was boiling over. She could feel herself growing wetter with every kiss, every touch. He kept kissing her, trailing down her collarbone and into her chest. She let him lead, eyes fluttering shut as she gave in to the feeling of him against her.

Her bodysuit inched lower, the straps now hanging loose, exposing more of her skin. Her breasts were nearly spilling out, but she didn't stop him, and she didn't want to. She guided him forward with the rhythm of her body, his lips trailing across her chest.

Her breast slipped free as Mike's hands moved down to the waistband of her shorts. They were already riding low on her hips. His hands moved over her exposed skin, sending a shiver through her, guiding her with his touch. He knew how to hold her.

Samantha didn't resist. She kissed him back with aching desire. Mike climbed on top of her, and she let him, her shorts slipping further off. The tension between them deepened. It was magnetic now, impossible to ignore, and it made her want him even more.

She inched back just enough to meet his gaze.
The flush in her face unmistakable.

"Come upstairs with me," she whispered. No more waiting.

Mike helped Samantha to her feet. She glanced up at him, her lashes fluttering. Without a word, she took his hand and led him toward the stairs. They moved slowly, the air thick with anticipation, each step drawing them closer to what neither of them wanted to delay any longer.

CHAPTER 10

NO TURNING BACK

Samantha led Mike toward the stairs, the tension building with every step. Music filled the house, its rhythm syncing with their movements.

As they climbed, the air felt electric. Samantha gripped Mike's hand tighter, pulling him closer. The recessed lighting cast a low amber glow across the stairwell. A charge ran through her body and not from the alcohol. No, this was something real. Something natural.

The sound of her heels echoed with each step. Mike's shirt hung loose around his shoulders, his chest exposed. Samantha's straps slipped down her arms, her breasts barely held by her top. Her shorts clung low on her hips, waiting to be tugged away. She led him on. No turning back.

With a push, the double doors swung open, revealing her space. Her sanctuary. Her domain.

Her bedroom was decadent, lined with mirrored accents and sleek decor. At the center of it all sat a round king-sized bed with dark grey plush outlines. Its bedding was immaculate, made of 100% pure viscose from bamboo. The scent of her lingered in the air, intoxicating.

A cream-colored rug surrounded the bed, its texture thick and inviting against the polished floors.

Mounted on the opposite wall, a massive curved widescreen TV dominated the space, sleek and ultra-modern like something out of a high-end design catalog.

The blankets were a deep purple, the sheets a sleek stone silver. Pillows were perfectly arranged. A chrome vanity with a large mirror reflected the dim light, and in the corner sat one of those grand gothic-style chairs, something out of *The Addams Family.*

Another door led to the balcony, offering a breathtaking view of the ocean. Cosmopolitan. Chic. Ultra-modern. Every detail curated with designer precision.

Her closet was practically a boutique. A separate room lined with sleek shelving, mirrored walls, and rows of designer shoes displayed like art.

Her bathroom? Impeccable. A full glass walk-in shower took center stage, complete with rainfall fixtures and a marble bench for lounging. The vanity gleamed under the lighting, every surface pristine, every product perfectly arranged like a magazine spread.

She stepped inside, and her shorts slid to the floor, revealing the full curve of her plush, rounded butt. The thong framed her perfectly, cutting sharply around every contour.

She walked to the window, her hips swaying with quiet confidence, each step sending a ripple through her curves. Mike watched, drawn in by the rhythm of her movements and the hush that seemed to follow her.

She turned to face him.

"Mike…" she whispered.

The room was dark, lit only by moonlight spilling through the open drapes. A quiet silver glow washed over them both.

"Yes, Sam?"

In the hush of the room, their eyes met. She was beautiful.

She turned around slowly, the moonlight tracing every curve of her back.

"Unlace me," she murmured, her gaze fixed on the balcony doors.

The laces hugged her ribs, running down the curves of her waist. He stepped closer, fingers grazing the fabric as he slowly loosened them. With each pull, more of her skin emerged. An almost inaudible breath slipped from her lips as the bodysuit began to give way.

The next song in her playlist started, "A Night Off" by Drake and Lloyd from the *So Far Gone* mixtape. The music played in the background as she turned, walked up to him, and kissed him hard. Pulling him onto the bed, her bodysuit slipped away, and her breasts spilled free with elegance.

Mike unbuckled his belt, letting his pants fall to the floor. His lips trailed along her neck and collarbone before moving lower, kissing each breast. She felt herself unravel beneath him, every kiss undoing her a little more. She took his hand, guiding it to the snap crotch of her bodysuit, silently inviting him to release it. Letting him take control, she lay back and surrendered completely.

Mike pulled free, stripping fully before easing himself inside her. Samantha, already wet, drew in a breath, a moan slipping free as he entered her. He slowly pushed back, then pressed in again, coaxing another breathy sound from her lips.

"Yes, Mike," she whispered, sinking deeper into the pleasure.

His strokes were slow, deliberate, filled with passion. Another moan escaped her lips.

"Yes, Mike," she said again, her voice trembling as if to reassure him.

"I want you," he murmured, gripping her hand tightly.

"You have me," she breathed.

He extended deeper, drawing a higher-pitched moan from her, one she couldn't hold back with how good he felt.

The song still played in the background as Mike found his rhythm, moving in sync with the beat. This wasn't just sex, it was feeling. She felt so damn good around him, every inch of her responding to every inch of him. Samantha knew exactly how to move, how to control herself, gripping him with every motion. She edged closer to the headboard, anchoring herself as his rhythm deepened.

Just like in the song, her heels stayed on. She slipped out of the last of her clothes, now fully naked with him. Mike hovered over her as her hands pressed against the headboard, a quiet act of surrender. The energy between them was electric, intoxicating. The music wrapped around them, pulling their bodies into perfect sync.

"You feel so good inside me," she whispered. The words sent a shiver through him, urging him on.

They kept going, just the two of them, lost in the rhythm of each other. With a sudden surge of energy, Samantha pushed him onto his back and climbed on top, her movements fierce and hungry. Her breasts bounced as her hair tumbled in messy waves around her face. Mike's hands roamed her curves, fingers finding her nipples and teasing them until another moan spilled from her lips.

He sat up, capturing her breasts in his mouth. Every touch, every lick, was deliberate. Her lips traced his chest, his neck, before finally meeting his in a kiss both sensual and fervent. His hands never left her, exploring every inch he could reach.

"Give me all of you," he whispered, his forehead resting against hers. "I've been waiting for this moment."

Samantha stretched back, still riding him, her eyes locked on his with unflinching intensity.

The song built in the background.
"Yes, Mike. Fuck me!" she screamed.

Something primal lit a fire in him. He flipped her over, putting her on all fours, and drove back into her just as "Don't Love Away" by Adrian Marcel pulsed through the speakers.

She dug her hands into the headboard, bracing herself as he found his rhythm. His deep, steady strokes matched the music perfectly.

"Oh my God," she gasped, her voice rising higher. "Don't stop, Mike… keep going!"

He moved in perfect sync with her, the slick warmth of her body gripping him and pulling him deeper. Sweat beaded on his brow, dripping onto her back as his pace quickened.

Her hair clung to her skin in damp strands, her body shining under the moonlight. She took everything he gave, each thrust more intense than the last. Her moans broke into gasps, then into sharp cries that pierced the stillness.

Mike gripped her hair, watching for her reaction. A playful scream burst from her lips, she loved it. He tugged again, firmer this time, and she cried out once more. Laughter spilled from her, pure delight as she gave in completely, letting him take control.

They kept going, shifting positions as "Come Together" by Chris Brown featuring H.E.R. poured through the speakers. Her playlist became their soundtrack, setting the perfect mood. Now they sat entwined, arms wrapped around each other as he eased into her from the front, their bodies moving in unison.

"I'm so close," she gasped, gripping him tighter and kissing him faster.

He felt it building in her, every sound and motion pushing them both closer. Her moans turned into cries of pleasure, her voice climbed higher.

"Oh my God… oh yes, oh my God!"

A scream tore from her as her body trembled against him. Pleasure crashed through her in waves, her nails digging into his back. She surrendered to it entirely. He felt everything. Her spasms around him. The slick heat. The pulsing surge of her climax.

Their hair was damp, bodies tangled, and sweat slick on their skin. They didn't stop. Mike was close now too.

As he pulled back ready to finish, she whispered, "It's okay, Mike."

Samantha was on birth control. She never missed a dose.

"Are you sure?"

"I'm fine. Trust me."

He couldn't hold back any longer, releasing fully inside her.

"Oh yes," she moaned, her body arching and eyes rolling back as they came together. Still connected, breathless, sweating, trembling, she felt him soften inside her, the subtle shift that told her everything.

Samantha looked at him. He looked back at her.

Then, she smiled and pulled him into an embrace, sinking into his arms.

The sex had been incredible. It was everything they had built up to. The tension and the anticipation were worth every second.

As the music played on, they lay together in silence, both wondering what came next. Something told them this was only the beginning.

CHAPTER 11

THE MORNING AFTER *LE CHER*

Daybreak arrived, and Mike was the first to stir. The comfort of the bed surrounded him, the sun hitting his eyes, nudging him out of sleep. He glanced over at Samantha, still peacefully resting beside him under the covers. Her clothes and shoes lay scattered across the floor, remnants of the night before.

Usually an early riser, Mike was up before her. The alarm system was still armed, making it clear that sneaking out wouldn't be happening. He lay back watching her sleep. Her body still tucked under the covers with only her face exposed. She rolled over and the blanket slipped down.

That's when he saw it, something he hadn't expected.

The covers had fallen just enough for his eyes to drift to her side. A large bruise marred her ribs, deep purple in the center, its edges blooming in shades of red and blue. It looked like one of those inkblot paintings a psychiatrist might ask you to interpret. Much larger than he would have imagined, almost the size of both his hands.

His heart sank. It all clicked into place.

He hadn't meant to see it, but there it was. The bruises explained everything. Her shaken state after the bathroom, her quiet need for him all night. The way she clung to him as they walked together. The subtle grimaces she tried to mask with quick smiles or playful kisses, it all made sense now.

Samantha had been assaulted last night, and it all traced back to the incident in the bathroom, with the girls being escorted out and the manager's frantic search for her. Mike had assumed it was about something else, maybe a collab. He figured the manager had recognized her from social media. But now, all the dots connected.

His mind replayed the night. He remembered how disheveled she looked when she returned to their table. How her movements slowed, each step careful, like she was trying not to jar anything. Usually so poised, Samantha had been visibly shaken.

She always cared about appearances, especially around him. Confident, radiant, that's who she wanted to be. But the bruises and pain had been impossible to hide. And still, she had pushed through.

Mike stared at her now, thinking of how much she'd endured in silence doing everything she could to forget.

A twinge of guilt settled in his chest. *Did I make it worse by not noticing?*

Samantha never wanted to feel like less than herself with him. She had tried to enjoy the night, but he hadn't missed the tells.

When the bartender flirted with him, she tried to brush it off, but a faint grimace crossed her face as she lifted her glass. He caught it, even if she masked it. Now he understood. It hadn't just been discomfort. It had hurt. She had been performing strength.

When they mingled with the collab couple, she kept the energy up, but the pain must've been gnawing at her. He admired her resilience. But he also felt conflicted.

Was I too slow to shut the bartender down? Did I make her feel exposed? Was I somehow enabling it?

He remembered when the manager approached. Samantha clutched her side, her smile forced, stress rising in her voice. No one else would've noticed, but he saw it now.

She hadn't wanted him to see her pain. She had worked so hard to seem fine. She even danced the night away.

He wished she'd told him. But he understood why she didn't.

Now, as she lay beside him, fresh bruises on her ribs, his heart swelled with tenderness. She had been so strong and determined not to let the night unravel.

The least he could do now was help her heal. Physically and emotionally.

But first, he'd surprise her with breakfast in bed.

Breakfast In Bed

Samantha woke to the scent of something delicious elevating through the house. She inhaled deeply, her senses coming alive with the smell of breakfast being cooked downstairs. She was slow to move, reluctant to leave the comfort of her bed. Instinctively, she reached over, her hand brushing the spot where Mike had been.

It hadn't been a dream. Mike was actually here, in her house. Their night together felt like a blur of emotion. The intimacy. Their connection. Glancing at her phone, she was surprised at how late it was. She stretched with a groan, her body protesting as she tried to pull herself from the bed.

"Felicia, play my morning playlist one," she muttered to her home assistant.

House music filled the room. Bright, rhythmic, and full of energy.

Looks like Samantha's awake, he said to himself. *Better hurry.*

He had taken the opportunity to raid her fridge, determined to pull off a surprise. Mike could cook, and really well. Self-taught, he had perfected a handful of recipes, and this felt like the perfect time to put his skills to use. As he worked, he smiled to himself, knowing Samantha would appreciate the effort.

The spread he laid out was impressive: a vegetable omelet, crispy home fries, and toasted sourdough. He even tossed together a quick fruit medley with a splash of citrus and honey. It was nothing fancy, but it worked. The omelet looked light and balanced, but filling enough to count. Despite her fridge being mostly stocked with meal-prepped dishes, he had managed to pull together the perfect breakfast. Unexpected, but thoughtful.

Upstairs, Samantha was still struggling to get out of bed. As she pushed herself upright, she winced. A sharp pain flaring in her side, a cruel reminder of the night before. She glanced down at her ribs, her expression darkening at the sight of the large, purpling bruise that had bloomed overnight.

"Fuck, those torta bitches," she muttered, her anger reigniting at the memory of the altercation.

The pain was intense, but she had to push through. She dragged herself to the bathroom, brushed her teeth, and splashed cold water on her face. When she finally looked up, the full extent of the bruises came into view, and a wave of unease settled in her stomach.

This is bad, she thought to herself. *I probably need to treat this somehow.*

Grabbing her silk robe from the hook, she wrapped it around herself. The deep purple fabric, embroidered with an elegant white "S" on the chest, felt cool and smooth against her skin. She tightened the belt, hoping it would be enough to shield the bruises from Mike's eyes.

Taking a deep breath, she gathered her strength and made her way downstairs, gripping the banister for support. She forced a smile, determined to greet him with her usual energy.

When she stepped into the kitchen, the sight of the breakfast spread touched her heart.

"Good morning, Mister. This smells so good," she said, her voice light but sincere.

She walked over and placed a gentle kiss on his cheek. Mike smiled, took her hand, and kissed it. The way he did it made her feel cared for.

She lifted her arms to hug him, eyes closing as a sharp twinge flared in her side. She winced, bracing herself against his back, unaware how much the shift gave her away. She drew a quiet breath, masking the pain as if nothing had happened.

"I'm glad you like it," Mike said as he turned around. "I thought I'd surprise you."

She admired the spread, but Mike wasn't finished yet. There was fruit to chop, and the biscuits in the oven were almost ready, he had decided to swap them in for the toast he originally planned.

"Thank you so much for this," Samantha said.

Mike shot her a sly smile. "You can thank me by going back upstairs. I wanted to bring you breakfast in bed."

She hesitated. The pain in her ribs worsened, throbbing like someone had kicked her with a steel-toed boot.

When Mike turned his back she instinctively pressed a hand to her side. A sharp jolt ripped through her torso, forcing her to stifle a wince.

Just keep it together until Mike leaves, she thought. She didn't want him to see her struggling.

Forcing a smile, she said, "Okay, I'll go back upstairs."

She popped up from the chair, adding a little bounce to her step to keep up the charade of being her usual self. But when she reached the stairs, her hand gripped the banister a little too tightly, steadying herself as her body began to betray her.

Mike's eyes followed her with concern.

Each step was harder than the last. By the time she reached her bedroom, she had to brace herself against the wall, her free arm hanging at her side.

Just hold on a little longer, she thought.

Her playlist played low in the background, nudging her forward. At last, she sank onto the bed, her body melting into the mattress. Staring at the ceiling, she focused on her breathing, waiting for the pain to pass. The music offering her some comfort as she waited for Mike to come upstairs with breakfast.

Breakfast Is Served

Mike finished preparing breakfast, adding the final touches to the plates. As he tidied up, his thoughts drifted to Samantha. She was trying to act like everything was fine, but the signs were there clear as day.

I'm just going to tell her I know, he resolved. *She needs to rest and recover, and not keep this up for my sake.*

He set the plates aside and wrapped an ice pack in a towel, hoping it would help with the swelling.

As he searched for a tray, Samantha's voice floated over the speakers, her words guiding him.

"If you're looking for a tray, they're in the long cabinet," she called from her bed.

He smiled, pausing mid-search.

"No, Mike, I'm not watching you on camera," she teased. "I just know every inch of my house."

They both laughed, the exchange cutting through his concern. He finally found the tray, an elegant mirrored piece with what looked like genuine silver detailing. A custom design, no doubt. Another reflection of Samantha's impeccable taste.

He carefully arranged the food, then made his way upstairs. As he stepped into the bedroom, Samantha's face lit up. Still tucked beneath the covers, she slowly began to sit up, her movements deliberate and cautious.

"Oh, this is nice," she said, eyeing the spread.

She remained still, balancing herself carefully.

If I can just not move too much, then I'll be okay, she thought.

Mike placed the tray beside her but didn't sit down just yet.

"I have to grab one more thing," he said, turning back toward the stairs.

"What is it?" she called after him.

When he returned, he held the ice pack in his hand. Samantha's eyes widened.

"We need to get the swelling down, Sam," he said as he sat beside her.

"Oh, Mike… you saw," she murmured, a mix of embarrassment and surprise in her voice. She hadn't wanted him to notice.

"Please, Sam, just let me help. You can tell me about it later."

She hesitated, then nodded.

Mike helped her sit up and placed the ice pack against her ribs, holding it there. The sudden chill made her shiver, but the relief was immediate. She closed her eyes and let out a slow, measured exhale.

Her breathing calmed. Without a word, she reached over and took his free hand to hold.

They sat like that for nearly twenty minutes. The ice soothing her injury while Mike stayed by her side treating her. Breakfast could wait. Right now, this was what mattered.

Samantha moved slightly, guiding his hand to the affected area. She loosened her robe to reveal the injury.

His face etched with concern. And yet, even in her vulnerability, she radiated strength.

"Keep doing that," she whispered, her voice laced with relief.

She laid on her side holding his hand over the ice pack. He kept patting her ribs gently, the cold slowly melting away some of the strain. She squeezed his free hand, as if drawing strength from him.

The ice pack melted away, Mike got up to prepare another one.

"I'll be right back," he murmured.

Samantha exhaled. "And I'll be here."
The pain dulling slightly.

"Do you need any medicine to ease the pain?" he asked.

"It's too early for muscle relaxers," she replied with a weak laugh.

"No, Sam, I meant something simple. Over-the-counter."

"I'm fine for now, thank you, Mikey. Just another ice pack, please." She glanced up at him with a, grateful smile.

"Alright," he said.

"There's a solid ice pack in the freezer, one of those reusable ones from a package. Just bring it up with you."

Mike headed to the kitchen while she lay back down, keeping the remains of ice pack on her ribs. She closed her eyes, focusing on the slow, controlled rhythm of her breathing, knowing she'd need to gather her strength again soon.

When he returned, she was lying still, her chest rising and falling in steady breaths.

"Here you go," he said, placing the fresh pack against her ribs.

"Thank you," she said and smiled.

Time To Get the Day Started

"You can eat if you want," Samantha said, her hand resting on Mike's. "Don't let me keep you from that wonderful meal you made."

Mike shook his head and kissed her. "We eat together," he said. "Just let me take care of you first."

Over the next half hour, he continued tending to her injury. Between treatments, they shared small bites from the tray. The food had gone lukewarm, but neither of them seemed to mind. Samantha glanced at him between bites, feeling a quiet comfort settle between them. .

Then a sudden thought jolted her. "Fuck," she muttered.

"What is it?" Mike wondered.

"Our cars. They're still at *Le Cher*," she said, her voice tinged with dread. "And it's Saturday."

"You don't want to go back there, do you?"

Samantha sighed heavily, remembering the notification she'd seen earlier. The manager had reached out through a DM, once again leaving his number and offering to arrange another Uber so she could retrieve her car. Just thinking about it made her stomach turn. She didn't want to talk to him, but she knew avoiding it wasn't an option.

"I just… I don't feel like dealing with him," she admitted.

Mike nodded. "Whatever you need, I'll help. If you don't want to face him alone, you won't have to."

She gave him a grateful look, her shoulders relaxing. "Thank you."

Mike glanced at the clock. It was already past 1:00 p.m. "We'll figure it out," he reassured. "But first, we finish eating.”

Clearing the Air

“Yes, you’re right,” Samantha said, her tone lighter now. Her morning playlist continued to hum in the background, upbeat house music filling the space. One of her favorite tracks, “Come Back Around” by Moon Boots and Cherry Glazerr, began to play. She perked up energized by the sound.

“Okay, let’s eat!” she said playfully, adjusting the ice pack against her ribs and fastening her robe.

Mike smiled, relieved to see her more at ease. He brought the tray closer, as they began eating together. The meal was incredible. Warm, buttery biscuits that melted in her mouth, a perfectly cooked vegetable omelet, and crispy yet tender homemade home fries. Samantha savored every bite, feeling her body respond to the nourishment.

“This is amazing, Mike,” she said between bites.

“I’m glad you like it,” he replied, watching her carefully.

The recovery juice Mike made was the final touch. Packed with fresh fruit and greens, it gave her an extra boost. As she sipped it, Samantha could feel herself improving. 50% better, at least.

They exchanged glances, and finally, Samantha sighed and began to open up about what had happened the night before in the bathroom. She described the confrontation, explaining the women's aggression, how it escalated, and how she ended up getting hurt. Mike listened in disbelief, shaking his head as he absorbed every detail.

"Sam, you should've told me. "I could've done something."

"I know," she admitted. "But I didn't want to ruin the night for us. It was important to me."

Mike frowned but didn't press. "You're more important to me than any night. If anything ever feels wrong like that ever again, you tell me. Please."

She nodded, the talk shifting from one subject to the next until it lingered on the past couple of months they'd been seeing each other. Samantha hesitated, then confessed:

"Look, I know we're both single," she said cautiously, "and normally, I'm not the jealous type. But I guess I felt… I guess I just felt…" She paused, sighed, then continued. "Vulnerable last night. I was hurting. I may have overreacted."

Mike eased forward, recognizing how hard it was for her to admit that. His gaze stayed on hers.

"Samantha, anytime we're together, my entire focus is on you. I'm not seeing anyone else. I haven't been since my last relationship ended over a year ago. I want you to know that."

She smiled, reassured by his words. "Thank you. And I'm sorry if I came off a little... possessive. I don't know, that wasn't like me."

"Don't apologize," Mike replied. "You were dealing with a lot last night. I'm just sorry if I did anything that made you feel insecure."

"No," she shook her head. "That wasn't on you, Mike. It was just... everything. I didn't expect it to hit me like that. Being hurt, feeling exposed... it just got to me."

A quiet understanding passed between them, their connection deepening with every honest word.

"So, how about I make us dinner tonight?" Mike offered trying to lighten the mood.

"I've got this go-to dish. My Salmon Alfredo Recipe Number Three." He grinned, leaning closer. "I'll even make enough for you to meal prep."

"You have jokes, mister," she shot back, crossing her arms. "All my playlists have deep, intentional references that reflect my taste at the time," she said, defending herself like she was being cross-examined.

Mike chuckled. "So, how about it?" He drew a little closer.

As the song swelled in the background, Samantha pointed to the speaker and sang, off-key as always.
"Come back around, come back around, won't you please come around because I want you this time."

She smiled at Mike, the lyrics carrying a playful, unspoken message. He caught it instantly and moved in for a kiss. One Samantha gladly returned.

Mike laughed. "You sure know how to lighten the mood, you know that?"
Then, catching the lyrics, he added, "And don't worry, I won't skip town either."

"I try my best," she smiled.

He could see another side of her emerging. It was quirky, lighthearted, and endearing. Samantha was slowly becoming more comfortable around him, and Mike wanted to show her that his intentions were genuine. Not just through words, but through action.

As they finished the last bites of breakfast, she gave him a big hug, holding on a little longer than usual. She truly appreciated his kindness.

"Thank you, Mike," she said, her voice full of gratitude.

"For what? You don't have to—" he began, but she gently placed a hand over his lips.

"For being here. For everything so far."

She picked up her fork. "And for this amazing breakfast." She took a bite, then gave him a playful look, beckoning him to come closer. As he did, she stole a kiss.

"Good. To. The. Very. Last…"
Another kiss.
"Bite."

Mike hugged her back tightly. "I'm glad I could do this for you."

CHAPTER 12

AN UNEXPECTED GIFT FOR ALISON

Samantha glanced up from her phone, the conversation with the night manager from *Le Cher* still stuck in her thoughts. Their DM exchange had wrapped smoothly, finalizing the plan to pick up their cars. She sighed, dreading the idea of interacting with him again.

She looked over at Mike, who was sitting on the edge of the bed, tidying up the remnants of breakfast.

"Shall we take a shower together?" she teased, a playful smile curling on her lips.

"Music to my ears," Mike replied, grinning. "I'll just finish cleaning this up first."

Before she could respond, the house's speaker system chimed:

"Motion detected. Front gate."

Samantha's smile faded as she gestured for Mike to hand her the remote. She turned on the TV, and the security camera feeds sprang to life across the large screen. Mike froze, surprised by the sophistication of the setup with multiple angles and split screens, all showing her property in crystal-clear detail.

She zoomed in on the front gate to find Alison waving dramatically, her manicured fingers fluttering in the air.

"Sami baby, come buzz me in!" Alison's voice echoed through the intercom.

Samantha groaned inwardly. "Alison, I didn't know you were coming," she said into the intercom.

"Hurry, bitch! I gotta pee!" Alison called back. "I just finished my nail appointment at *Felipe's*, and Sergio was asking about you!"

Samantha rolled her eyes and buzzed her in. She loved Alison, they'd been friends since the 5th grade. But today was not the day for her energy. Alison was a hot mess and while Samantha often indulged her antics, she wasn't in the mood to deal with her friend's drama, especially in front of Mike.

Samantha turned to him. "She's… a lot. Just a heads-up."

"I gathered that," Mike said, chuckling.

"She knows about you, by the way," Samantha warned. "If she says something superficial or tries to stir the pot, don't take it too seriously, okay?"

"I won't," he replied.

"She's been trying to get me to go to New Orleans with some guys she recently met. The last time I went on a double date with her, the guy she wasn't interested in tried to hit on me instead. If she brings up Jake and Darren, just… ignore it, okay? Oh my God, why am I even telling you this?" she said, laughing nervously.

"Don't worry. I have sisters. I've seen and heard a lot over the years." His voice was calm, his smile reassuring. "You're fine. I got it."

Samantha sighed, swinging her legs over the edge of the bed. A sharp pain shot through her ribs, making her wince. She instinctively pressed her hand to the ice pack still resting against her side.

"I'm gonna need a minute to get downstairs," she said, exhaling slowly.

"Do you want me to help?"

"No, I'll be fine. Just… please let her in and sit her down on the couch. I need her visit to be short, that's all."

She tapped into her smart home controller unlocking the front door with a quiet click. "The alarm is deactivated

Seeing her flustered, Mike tried to lighten the mood.

"Relax, Samantha. It's all good, take your time. I got this."

Mike walked downstairs. Alison was already fiddling with her phone when Mike opened the door. She barely glanced up before striding in, her towering heels clicking against the floor.

"Wow, you're tall," she said, giving him a once-over. "And hot. Sami, you didn't tell me your boy toy was a whole snack."

Mike smirked, keeping his cool. "She's upstairs. She'll be down in a minute. Make yourself comfortable."

Alison dropped onto the couch like she owned the place, crossing her legs and scrolling through her phone.

"You trying to make yourself at home here, or are you just visiting?"

"Just visiting," Mike said, keeping his tone neutral.

"Good," Alison replied with a sly grin. "Samantha doesn't do roommates."

Mike ignored the comment and headed back to the kitchen, giving Samantha time to get herself together. Upstairs, she steadied herself against the bed, taking deep breaths to push through the pain.

"Just keep it together," she whispered to herself.
She adjusted her robe, brushed her hair back, and made her way carefully to the stairs.

As she descended, leaning slightly on the banister, Alison's voice floated up to her.

"Sami, I'm dying to tell you about this new guy I met last night. He's an investment banker, drives a Porsche, and—"

"Alison," Samantha interrupted, her tone firm but polite. "Give me a second to sit down before you launch into your stories, okay?"

Alison gasped, jumping up from the couch. "Oh my God, are you okay? You're walking like a grandma."

Samantha bit back a sharp retort, lowering herself carefully into an armchair. "I'm fine hun, just a little sore. Long night."

As soon as the words left her mouth, she regretted them.

"Uh-huh, I bet it was," Alison said, giving Samantha a teasing look. "So, are you going to introduce me to Mr. Tall, Dark, and Handsome over there?"

Mike stood in the kitchen doorway, arms crossed, amused by the nickname but staying quiet for now.

Samantha shot Mike an apologetic look. "So… this is Mike. Mike, meet my best friend, Alison."

Alison's eyes lit up with mischief. "So this is Mike. Sami's been holding out on me. Where'd you find him? Tinder? The Whole Foods? Or did you snatch him from one of your media events?"

Samantha groaned, pressing a hand to her forehead. "Alison, please."

Mike, ever the gentleman, stepped forward. "Nice to meet you, Alison," he said, extending a hand.

Alison took it, her manicured nails glinting in the light. "The pleasure's all mine," she purred.

Samantha sighed, irritated that Alison wasn't picking up on her tone. The frustration was starting to build.

Alison strutted back into the living room after using the bathroom, freshly adjusted and picture-perfect. She wore a skintight dress that showed off her curves, paired with a matching sun hat and very high heels that she commanded with ease. Her blonde-dyed hair, styled strikingly similar to Samantha's, glinted under the sunlight. Alison tried hard to mask her Latina roots, even softening her accent, but certain words always gave her away.

As she made herself comfortable, she begged Samantha for details about the previous night, her sharp eyes flicking between Samantha, still in her robe, and

Mike, still in yesterday's clothes. It didn't take long to connect the dots.

"So, you two had a good night together," Alison teased. "Good for you, Sami. Looks like Mike made it onto your nice list."

That was the last straw. Samantha's patience snapped. She retorted sharply in Spanish, her voice rising with frustration:

"¡Eres una tonta! ¡Te estás haciendo ver como una idiota! ¡Deja de hablar de mi noche con él o sal de mi casa ahora!"
("You silly girl! You're making yourself look dumb! Stop talking about my night with him or get out of my house now!")

A sharp pain shot through Samantha's ribs. She grabbed her side, a hiss slipping through her teeth. Alison's teasing demeanor evaporated. Her face twisted in concern.

"¿Qué pasó? ¿Qué tienes? ¿Él te golpeó?"
("What happened? What's wrong? Did he hit you?")

"¡No! ¡No! ¿Por qué estaría aquí si lo hubiera hecho?" Samantha snapped back.
("No! No! Why would he be here if he did?")

Alison flustered. "¿Qué pasó?" *("What happened?")*

They both switched back to English, remembering Mike was still there. His eyes widened, he had no idea Samantha spoke Spanish.

Samantha sighed. "Some bitches at *Le Cher* threw me into a table. My side hit the corner so hard, I thought I cracked a rib."

She paused, trying to choke back the words. "I guess I got kicked in the same spot too."

Alison's eyes widened. "Show me, Sami." They both walked toward the bathroom.

Once inside, Samantha hesitated, then pulled back her robe, exposing deep bruising along her ribs.

"¡Dios mío!" Alison gasped. *("Oh my God!")*

Her concern morphed into anger.

"Si yo estuviera ahí, esas perras habrían terminado en el piso."

("If I was there, those bitches would've been on the floor.")

Samantha sighed, shaking her head. "No soy una peleadora, Alison."
("I'm not a fighter, Alison.")

"Pero yo sí." *("But I am.")*

Alison wasn't letting this go.

Samantha hesitated before recounting what had happened.

"They basically sucker-punched me," she said. "I was walking away, and the fat one pulled my hair. I stumbled back, and before I knew it, she yanked me off balance into the corner of the table. I didn't even see it coming."

Alison's jaw clenched, fists curling tight. Samantha knew she'd go to war for her without hesitation.

After a pause, Alison helped her back into her robe, and they walked out of the bathroom together. The tension softened as the conversation drifted into something more casual.

Samantha motioned to Mike for another ice pack. She held it to her ribs through the robe, breathing in the cold relief. Samantha filled Alison in on the plan to pick up their cars from *Le Cher*.

"We'll head over soon. I just need to make some coffee first," she said, making her way to the kitchen.

Mike, who had been observing, followed behind offering to assist. Alison stood against the counter, still visibly fuming.

Samantha moved with quiet purpose, her calm presence helping to lighten the mood as the coffee began to brew. She kept it light. She didn't want the hoopla and worry. Right now she just wanted them to all enjoy a nice cup of joe together.

What's In The Box?

Their conversation shifted to upcoming collaborations, reminding Samantha of the packages piled in the corner of the living room. Six boxes in total, stacked neatly but forgotten. Alison's eyes lit up when she saw them.

"You know I love unboxing," Alison said, already moving toward the packages.

Samantha hesitated, then waved her over. "Fine. Bring them to the table." She just wanted Alison's attention focused elsewhere.

Alison wasted no time dragging all six boxes over, her excitement practically spilling out. Mike followed, curious. As Alison tore into the boxes, Samantha rattled off the brands, most of them high-end and instantly recognizable.

"These all look amazing," Alison said, holding up a pair of gold-accented sunglasses from one of the boxes.

Samantha barely reacted. Collaborations were the last thing on her mind, but Alison was enjoying herself, and that was enough for now.

Then Alison's eyes landed on a sleek pink box. Its glossy exterior stood out from the rest.

"What's in this one?" she asked, holding it up.

Samantha frowned. "I don't remember that one coming in."

"Well, if you don't remember it, let's open it," Alison grinned.

Reluctantly, Samantha nodded. "Fine, but it's weird. I usually keep track of this stuff."

Alison unwrapped the box carefully. The packaging was meticulous, wrapped in soft tissue paper with an unmistakable air of luxury. Placed at the center was a single, elegantly designed bottle of facial product, its pink-and-white label gleaming under the light. The aesthetics were striking.

"It's gorgeous," Alison said, her tone reverent.

Samantha studied the sleek pink box, unease creeping in. "I still can't figure out who sent this," she said. "I don't even remember talking to this brand."

"Here's a note," Alison said, pulling out a sleek card. She read it aloud with deliberate clarity, her tone crisp but casual, as if she might catch herself slipping into her accent.

"Participate in this collaboration with Queen of the Nile Beauty. Try our ageless face serum. Go live and showcase it. Upload your live following the guidelines listed and receive $600."

She lowered the card and nudged Samantha with a grin. "Hey, that's an easy $600."

"There's also another card," Alison said, pulling it from the bottom of the packaging. "It's got deliverable guidelines and payment info. No direct name, just a generic marketing email."

They looked up the company online and it seemed legitimate. Other influencers had worked with them, and there were testimonials across multiple platforms saying the exact same thing: that the brand paid promptly, followed through, and delivered quality products. Everything seemed above board.

"They probably pulled my address from one of the PR lists I'm on. It happens. Some companies just skip the email part and send product.

Mike squinted, skeptical. "That doesn't bother you?"

"It should," she admitted. "But it happens more often than you'd think. I'm signed up with a lot of influencer agencies and networks. My info gets passed around all the time."

Samantha stared at the bottle, her gut screaming that something wasn't right. She flipped it over, scanning the ingredients, then her stomach dropped.

"Oh no." She shook her head. "I can't do this. Nope." She threw a firm thumbs-down.

"Why not?" Alison asked.

"There are three ingredients in here that break me out really bad," Samantha said. "Remember that awful, itchy rash I had last year? That was from a product with these same ingredients."

Alison's brows furrowed as she recalled the incident. "Oh yeah. You looked like a tomato for weeks."

"Exactly. Yeah, I can't risk it. And I don't even know where this came from. Let's just get rid of it," Samantha said, pushing the box aside.

"Hold up, girl," Alison interjected. "I'll do it."

Samantha hesitated, thinking twice. "But it's addressed to me. That could backfire."

"It's fine. I'll do the live and then log into your account to post it. No one's gonna know, and I'll keep the $600. Too easy," Alison said.

Samantha paused, then shrugged. "Fine. Better you than me."

Alison carefully repacked the serum and tissue paper, tucking the sleek pink box under her arm, already thrilled by the thought of easy cash.

Unbeknownst to either of them, the facial serum wasn't a gift, it was a trap. A meticulously crafted weapon disguised in luxury packaging, meant to disfigure. If Samantha had used it, it could've caused irreversible damage. But to Alison, it was just another collab opportunity.

With the packages sorted, Alison bid Samantha and Mike goodbye, promising to catch up soon.

As the door closed behind her, Samantha shook her head. "I love my girl, but she's *too* much sometimes."

Mike chuckled. "She's got energy, that's for sure."

Samantha sighed, shifting gears. "Let's start getting ready for the day. We've got a lot to do."

Mike agreed. Outside, Alison walked off in her wedges, the pink box still tucked confidently under her arm.

CHAPTER 13

WHAT ABOUT THAT SHOWER?

With Alison finally gone, Mike and Samantha could resume their alone time. Watching her disappear through the security cameras on the TV screen, Samantha let out a visible sigh of relief and opened her smart home app.

Last chance if you want to leave," she said smiling.

Mike crossed his arms in playful defiance. "Why? Are you kicking me out?"

She glanced back at him, picked up her home's smart device, and spoke into it. "Seal the outside gate. Arm alarm in 30 seconds, silent countdown."

"Outside gate secured. Motion sensors active. Thirty-second silent countdown initiated," the system responded.

"Geez, it's like Fort Knox in here," Mike said.

Built during Prohibition, Samantha's stunning six-bedroom, nine-bathroom home had been fully restored and modernized without losing its historic charm. Every corner, from the crawl spaces to the attic, had been redone, making it one of the nicest houses on the block.

A true parade-of-homes standout, the house was surrounded by greenery and featured multiple hidden connections, trap doors, passages, and crawl spaces that linked rooms or led outside.

If she were ever in danger, Samantha could easily hide until her private security company, with their incredibly fast response time arrived. She didn't need a panic room; there were plenty of places to take cover. Above her room was a hidden connection to the attic and other parts of the house, making it nearly impossible for anyone to sneak up on her.

A complex security system protected the home, a fog layer that disrupted intruders, heat-signature motion sensors, sound amplification and dampening. It would prove crucial to her survival. She was secure for now, but not safe from deadly intent.

Having grown up here with her grandmother, Samantha knew every inch of the house. Though modernized, she was determined to keep it as a symbol of her family's legacy and the security she had always felt.

But with a killer growing more relentless in his pursuit, she faced a painful choice: abandon the home built from generations of love, or stay and risk becoming its final memory.

"They don't release this kind of alarm system to the public," she said. "It was a gift from my dad since he works in surveillance. My house has a mini defense system, so to speak. I know immediately if someone breaks in. And the front door isn't the only way in or out."

She paused, a small smile forming. "Maybe one day I'll really show you around."

"I'm sure you could get lost in here," Mike joked.

"You actually can," she said with a laugh.

With Alison gone, the mood lightened. Samantha finally relaxed. She took her coffee rituals seriously. A true connoisseur, today's brew came from the mountains of Chiang Mai, Thailand, sourced from Doi Inthanon National Park. It was a rare blend, a souvenir from last year's trip with Alison to complete an unforgettable journey filled with rich flavors and vibrant culture.

"I guess I should rinse off," Samantha said with a sly grin, twirling her hair around her finger, clearly giving Mike the signal.

Mike smirked, catching her drift. "I'm assuming your shower's big enough for two?"

Samantha just smirked back and tapped her phone, switching on one of her afternoon playlists, perfectly mixed to set the mood. A familiar track filled the air— "From the Start (Extended Chill Mix)" by Morgin Madison and Ryan Lucian. The upbeat rhythm pulsed through the room as she extended her hand to Mike.

"Felicia, turn on the master bathroom shower," she said. "Set to lukewarm and transfer my playlist to the bathroom speakers."

From upstairs, the water kicked on. Mike helped Samantha to her feet. She was moving more easily now, her strength gradually returning. Together, they climbed the stairs, her grip on the banister lighter than it had been all morning.

At the bathroom door, she stopped and turned to face him. Her robe slipped off her shoulders, the mellow light catching her curves with natural elegance. Mike's breath caught. Spellbound, he couldn't look away.

She stepped closer, fingers brushing the hem of his shirt before lifting it over his head. He mirrored her, easing the robe the rest of the way down. Their clothes fell to the floor in quiet unison.

Eyes locked. No words needed. Samantha wrapped her arms around his neck, drawing him into a kiss that was breathless, tender, and filled with unspoken want. A faint ache in her side reminded her she wasn't fully healed, but she ignored it, holding on to the closeness she craved.

Stepping into the shower, a large, luxurious space with three shower-heads cascading warm water over them, the steam enveloped them in heat. The built-in bench offered more than just seating. They weren't thinking about anything but each other.

Samantha folded into Mike's touch, his hands strong yet safe, just as her father had once said a man's hands should be. The thought lingered briefly before being swept away in the moment. Their lips met again, the water pouring over them as they explored each other with growing intensity.

Guiding him to the bench, Samantha straddled him, savoring every second. She could feel him inside her, and it felt like something she didn't know she needed, until now.

She pressed her body against his, taking in every inch. Her kisses trailed down his neck until they reached his collarbone, where she playfully sucked, leaving a mark that would linger long after the water dried.

Their movements synced with the rhythm of the music pulsing through the bathroom, as if the song itself guided their pace. Every touch, every kiss, every motion heightened the electricity between them.

Samantha let herself fall back, the stream cascading over her face and spilling between her breasts. Mike held her by the back, steady as he pushed deeper, her spine curving in surrender. Her moans filled the steam-filled space, mingling with the water and the beat. She was taking it from the start, just as the song promised

As the male vocals came in, she stood him up, water dancing over their bodies, steam curling around them like smoke. Mike moved her against the wall, the cool tile sending a sharp, thrilling jolt through her. He slid into her again. Samantha let out a cry, her pleasure echoing through the bathroom, raw and unfiltered.

They moved again, water coursing over them, urgency mounting. Mike sat her on the bench and entered her fully. She gasped, her mouth parting. Her hands gripped his shoulders, nails digging in as her body arched. He began thrusting rocking her back and forth. Her eyes fluttered shut, her breath catching with high-pitched sounds spilling from her lips as she slipped further into ecstasy.

She held onto his back, grounding herself, anchoring him as he pushed harder. Faster.

With one final thrust, Samantha screamed "Oh my God!" as her orgasm crashed through her, unraveling her beneath him. It was, without question, the most intense shower sex she'd ever had.

"I owe you one," she whispered in his ear.

He tasted the words, letting them settle like a promise. A promise of more. And he wanted it.

The thought stayed with him, curling into something deeper, a desire not just for her body, but for time. For presence. For whatever this was becoming.

This was about more than pleasure. This was about Samantha, seeing her let her guard down and revealing pieces of her heart. He wanted to prove he could be the man she needed him to be. And more than that, he wanted the chance.

As the song faded, they stayed in the steam, catching their breath and stealing gentle kisses. A new track began to play, gently pulling them back to reality. They rinsed off together, hands trailing over each other one more time.

Eventually, Samantha reached for the shower controls and turned the water off. They stepped out, hand in hand. She grabbed two towels, passing one to Mike, and they helped each other dry off. Already, her mind was veering toward the day ahead. The errands. The loose ends. The unfinished business.

"Well, that was… unexpected," she said with a sly grin.

"Best shower I've had in a long time," he said, light hearted, but sincere.

They shared one last kiss before facing the day ahead.

CHAPTER 14

LET'S GO GET OUR CARS

After finishing up in the shower, Samantha and Mike dried off. Without his usual supplies, Mike couldn't style his hair the way he liked, and it fell flat in an unassuming way. Samantha liked the change, but Mike admitted this was how he used to wear it back in high school.

Samantha teased, "Oh, you had a glow-up, didn't you?"

"Guess you could say that," Mike replied with a grin.

They exchanged easy banter as they got dressed, completely comfortable around each other now. Samantha slipped into a pair of black leggings that hugged her curves, threw on a loose blouse, and zipped up a cropped leather jacket. She pulled on comfortable boots and adjusted her outfit in the mirror, making sure her bruises were hidden as best she could.

Before finishing up, she had Mike snap photos of her bruises to show the night manager.

Mike, meanwhile, felt self-conscious about wearing the same clothes as the day before. Noticing his discomfort, Samantha offered to help. The only thing she could spare was one of her own T-shirts, which he gratefully accepted. She tossed him a crisp Dodgers T-shirt, one from her limited-edition collection.

"That'll do," Mike said gratefully.

With her makeup finished, Samantha styled her hair, letting it fall naturally over her shoulders. She paused, assessing her movements, still aware of the ache in her ribs.

"Okay," she whispered to herself, barely audible, nodding once. Mentally prepared, she turned to Mike.

"Well, I guess it's time to call the Uber," she said, noting it had taken her slightly longer than usual to get ready.

Mike still insisted she take something for the pain, but she smiled at his concern.

"I appreciate it," she said. "But when it gets insufferable, I'll take something. For now, I'd rather try CBD cream or something holistic."

Once they were both set, Samantha called the night manager directly to arrange the trip. When the car arrived, they were relieved to see it was an XL, which offered plenty of space for a comfortable ride to DTLA.

Before leaving, Samantha armed her alarm, giving it the usual 45-second countdown. Her dog and cat, knowing the house just as well as she did, stayed hidden in their usual spots. She called their names as she left, but neither came out to greet her. She understood why. Her pets were always cautious when she was about to leave.

Sliding her arm through Mike's, she held his hand as they walked to the Uber. He opened the door, and she climbed in, settling in with ease. The ride downtown was quiet, the hum of the city filling the air.

Samantha rested her head on Mike's shoulder, her eyes drifting shut for a little bit..

"Wake me when we get downtown," she murmured.

Mike nodded in response, gently brushing his fingers through her hair. After a quick kiss, Samantha sat back, allowing herself to drift off for the rest of the ride to *Le Cher*.

The Meeting At *Le Cher*

The 30-minute ride downtown came to an end, and Samantha's brief catnap was over. As the Uber pulled up in front of *Le Cher*, Mike opened the door for her. She stepped out, but a sharp grimace crossed her face. Jumping down from the SUV had caught her off guard.

Mike noticed right away. Without hesitation, he slipped his arm around her for support, and together they made their way inside.

The night manager was already waiting at the entrance, offering a friendly welcome, though his concern for liability was obvious. He'd been reviewing footage of the incident on repeat and was already making arrangements to ensure nothing like it ever happened again.

Samantha straightened up, determined to handle the situation. She shook the manager's hand while still holding Mike's, and together, they walked to the office.

"Thank you for meeting with me, Samantha," Jean-Claude said.

She gave a brief nod, wanting to keep things short and to the point. Mike introduced himself, and Jean-Claude gestured toward the chairs.

"Please, have a seat."

Samantha eased herself into the chair. It was lower than she expected, and it took her a moment to settle in.

"How are you feeling?" Jean-Claude asked.

"I'm holding up," she replied.

"Yes, we saw the footage and we're deeply sorry. Those tables have already been removed. But more importantly, are you experiencing any symptoms? Anything unusual right now?"

"That's something I should be discussing with my doctor, not you."

"Oh…of course, absolutely," Jean-Claude said.. "But about the doctor, we'd like to send you to ours as well. We just want to make things right."

"Let's wait until I see my own doctor first," Samantha said. "Then we can talk about everything else you want to offer."

"Don't you want to hear me out?" he asked.

"I can hear you out after I speak with my doctor," she said, firm but controlled. "Right now, I'm just hoping this isn't anything serious."

She rubbed her side instinctively. The back and forth wasn't helping. The ache had started to flare again.

"I'm not looking for anything. So please don't give me a reason to."

Mike sat back in silence, watching the exchange unfold.

"*Le Cher* is not that type of establishment," Jean-Claude said firmly. "We do not allow or tolerate hostilities here. You were assaulted. A police report should be filed."

"What good will that do?"

"It will help us and help you. There needs to be an investigation. Once again, you were physically assaulted, and we have to take this seriously."

Mike shot Samantha a concerned look. She exhaled sharply before responding.

"Okay. For paper trail purposes, I guess."

"Exactly. That way, we have the camera footage to provide to the police in case you decide to press charges."

"Do you really think LAPD is going to waste their time on this?"

"But…what if they don't?"

"I'm not signing anything right now."

Mike glanced at her again, but she waved him off. Jean-Claude sat forward, elbows sliding onto the desk.

"At the very least, we need you to fill out an incident report internally."

"I'm not signing anything," she repeated.

"We're not asking you to sign anything. Just something in your own words about what happened."

"I already told you through DM. Take that as my incident report. Please, I just want to get my car and go."

She rubbed her injured side again, wincing slightly. Just then, the phone rang. Jean-Claude answered, seamlessly slipping into French.

"Oui, j'essaie de raisonner avec elle maintenant. Mais elle est très difficile à convaincre. Êtes-vous sûr qu'elle ne s'est pas cogné la tête contre la table en tombant? Elle n'a pas l'air de réfléchir clairement, et évidemment, c'est elle qui porte la culotte dans leur relation."

("Yes, I'm trying to talk some sense into her now. But she's very tough to reason with. Are you sure she didn't hit her head on the table when she fell? She doesn't seem to be thinking clearly, and obviously, she wears the pants in their relationship.")

Samantha's eyes locked onto him, her expression cold and unrelenting. In flawless French, she spoke.

"Vous ne devriez jamais supposer que personne ne comprend. Cela montre à quel point vous êtes ridicule. Vous essayez de faire la paix avec moi, mais vous parlez de moi comme si je ne comprenais pas le français. C'est impoli, ignorant et non professionnel. Je ne 'porte pas la

culotte' dans une relation imaginaire que vous inventez, mais si je l'étais, ce serait un partenariat égal. "

("You should never assume no one understands. This shows how much of a buffoon you are. You're trying to make peace with me, yet you speak as if I don't understand French. It's rude, ignorant, and unprofessional. I don't 'wear the pants' in whatever imaginary relationship you've made up, but if I were, it would be an equal partnership.")

Mike sat frozen, stunned, unable to take his eyes off her.

Jean-Claude hastily ended the call and began apologizing, but Samantha remained motionless, arms crossed, her expression unreadable. He stepped out of the office and returned later with paperwork and a business card for their doctor's office.

"Please, take this," he said gently. "We want you to have everything you need for your visit. There are no strings attached, we're not trying to buy you off. We're just deeply concerned. What happened was unacceptable, and I take full responsibility. It happened on my watch."

"Je n'ai aucun intérêt à signaler votre comportement pour l'instant, mais ne me donnez pas une raison de le faire. Et laissez cela être une leçon pour vous : ne supposez jamais qu'une personne ne comprend pas ou ne parle pas votre langue, " Samantha said calmly.

("I have no interest in reporting your behavior for now, but don't give me a reason to. And let this be a lesson for you: never assume someone doesn't understand or speak your language.")

"Of course. You are absolutely right. My deepest apologies. Please forgive me."

He handed her the paperwork. Inside, a discreetly tucked apology card held a $1,200 gift card.

"Avec ce que vous avez dit, il sera difficile pour moi de pardonner tout cet incident," Samantha said.

("With what you've said, it will be hard for me to forgive this entire incident.")

"And I truly am sorry again," Jean-Claude said. "I messed up, and I sincerely hope you can forgive me for what I assumed. Please let me know how I can help. Consider this a small gesture. I promise, our entire management team is taking this very seriously."

Samantha nodded, her expression unreadable.

"Faites monter notre voiture, s'il vous plaît," she said coolly.

("Please bring up our cars.")

Jean-Claude called for the valet. Samantha and Mike walked out, leaving him alone in the office, fully aware of the impact of his mistakes.

A Girl Of Many Surprises

As they waited for the valet to bring their cars, Mike couldn't help but break the silence.

"I had no idea you spoke two languages."

Samantha smirked, leaning slightly against the valet stand. "Three, actually."

"Three?" His brows lifted. "How'd you manage that?"

"I'll tell you soon enough… if you manage to stay on my good side," she teased, giving him a playful shove.

Mike chuckled, shaking his head. "And here I thought I was getting to know you. Now you're full of surprises."

"Don't tell anyone," she said in a mock conspiratorial tone. "It would kill my online persona."

Mike laughed, eyes still on her. Her wit, her layers, the way she carried herself were all pulling him in.

"What did you say to him back there? In French, I mean."

Samantha shrugged. "In so many words? I called him a buffoon and told him not to assume nobody understands or judge."

"That's it?" Mike asked with a look of intrigue.

"And that I had to stand up for us since he made some ridiculous, derogatory comment about me 'wearing the pants,'" she added, crossing her arms with a slight roll of her eyes.

Mike let out a low whistle. "Remind me never to get on your bad side."

She grinned. "Trust me, you'd know if you were on my bad side."

Mike laughed, shaking his head. "Fair enough. So, how's the pain level?"

She paused, her hand instinctively going to her side. "I'm at a yellow right now. It's still throbbing, but it comes and goes. Being on my feet is actually helping a little." Her face tensed as she clutched her side.

"I'll need another cold pack soon. If they can't see me today, I'll need to find somewhere to get some ice packs before heading home."

"Okay," he said, nodding. "We'll find a place to stop."

She rested against him, her voice strained, but determined. "I just want to go back home. Let's go shopping first, then head back to my place."

Another invite. Another sign. Another step toward something growing between them.

The valets pulled up and handed them their keys.

"Race you to the store?" she challenged.

"Oh, you're on!" Mike shot back.

They sped off into the night, ready to lose themselves in another wonderful evening together. A calm before the storm of what was soon to come.

CHAPTER 15

THE KILLER'S NEXT VICTIMS

The killer, now disguised as a repairman, moved through the upscale Downtown L.A. gym. Bright neon signage lit the exterior, while marble flooring and the scent of eucalyptus towels inside screamed luxury. His uniform and credentials were flawless, leaving no room for doubt. The security guard at the front desk barely glanced at him, offering only a nod as he passed. He signed in at the front desk with no issues. The girl working didn't second guess him at all.

Inside, the gym buzzed with the energy of late-night workouts. Members meticulously tracked their reps, some filming their exercises for social media. For him, it was the perfect cover.

He moved with purpose, toolbox in hand, clipboard tucked under one arm as he weaved past rows of treadmills, ellipticals, and weight machines. Every detail of the gym was etched in his mind. This wasn't his first time here. He had spent weeks studying the layout, memorizing routines, learning the timing of his targets' sessions.

Jordan And Tabatha: Marked For Death

An influencer couple with millions of followers across multiple platforms, they were nothing short of social media royalty. Their content blended motivational speeches, perfectly lit workout routines, and aspirational wellness tips.

They played the part well on camera, smiling and inspiring, but they were nothing like that in real life. The killer knew their workout routine. He had studied it. And he was going to strike in a way so deliberate, so precise, they'd never see it coming.

He ascended the stairs of the luxury downtown L.A. gym. Entry was easy. A skeleton crew was working, just one girl at the front. The few members inside didn't give him a second glance. His disguise was flawless. After all, who questions the repairman?

At the top floor, he reached the treadmills. Tabatha always used the one in the corner. It had the best lighting for her live streams and a panoramic skyline backdrop. She'd guard it like a hawk, pacing and glaring at anyone who dared claim it. And how hard she pushed herself, his trap would only work on her.

He knelt down. A few flicks of a screwdriver, one clipped wire, and the treadmill was rigged. It would look completely functional… until it wasn't.

He could already picture the instant she'd go flying.

Downstairs, he made his way to the weight machines, eyes fixed on the cable press. Jordan's zone. Always the machine in the back corner, his go-to for filming workouts uninterrupted. He liked to stack the plates, grunt into the camera, and show off for the algorithm.

The killer adjusted the internal pulleys just enough to ensure a catastrophic snap mid-rep.

Satisfied, he wiped his hands and strolled casually toward the lobby, blending seamlessly into the rhythm of gym life.

Now, he just had to wait.

Jordan and Tabatha would be arriving soon.

Unaware that their picture-perfect empire was about to shatter on camera.

Samantha was off his radar for now.

Tonight, it was all about them.

Tonight, the gym would bear witness to their end.

CHAPTER 16

A NIGHT OF TURNING POINTS

Samantha arrived at the grocery store first and waited for Mike to show up. She had underestimated how much sitting for too long would aggravate the pain, her discomfort had climbed to a seven. Parking her car, she took a minute to catch her breath, resting her head on the steering wheel with her eyes closed. Her breaths were measured and controlled, an effort to block out both the persisting pain and the emotional toll of her earlier interaction with Jean-Claude. She wasn't one to cry, but the tears were dangerously close.

A few minutes later, Mike's car pulled up beside hers. He immediately noticed her slumped posture. Concerned, he got out and gently rapped on her window. When she didn't respond the first time, he knocked again, startling her slightly.

"Oh, there you are," she said with a faint smile as she rolled down the window.

"Are you okay, Sam?"

"I'll be fine," she said. "I'm going to the doctor tomorrow morning. Let's just get what we need and head back home."

Back home. Mike caught that. She didn't say my place, she said back home. *Don't overthink it*, he told himself. Still, the words stuck with him.

He nodded, absorbing her words, but stayed close. His eyes lingered on her face, reading between the lines of her resilience.

They were parked in front of one of the city's high-end grocery stores, the kind with polished floors, organic everything, and imported ingredients. Mike was determined to make Samantha a comforting, home-cooked meal.

She opened her door and reached for his hand. "Help me out, please."

They stared walking toward the store together. Samantha keeping stride but she felt the drag in her step.

"Let's hurry," she said, gripping his arm. "I just want to go home."

Alison's Last Glow Up

Alison stood in her spacious, immaculately decorated vanity room, meticulously setting up for what would unknowingly become a stream of life and death.

The collaborations she planned to promote tonight were all on tight deadlines, and she was determined to impress her brands. Her lighting was perfectly angled, her backdrop spotless, and the products she intended to feature were arranged with care.

The countdown timer glowed on her screen, 45 minutes to go. Just enough time to perfect her makeup and rehearse her opening lines.

As she swept a shimmering highlighter across her cheekbones, Alison paused to admire her reflection.

"Perfect," she whispered, tilting her head to catch the light, the beat of Aryn Amante's "Ok, So?" pulsing through the house.

Alison mouthed the lyrics, her voice rising with the chorus, completely lost in her vibe. This song was her anthem, an unapologetic declaration of her lifestyle. Samantha hated it, thought it represented everything wrong with Alison's choices. But to Alison, it was power.

The track's backstory was infamous with it's seemingly controversial lyrics and rumors that had set social media ablaze. But Alison didn't care about the drama. If anything, she related to the song's unapologetic sass.

Scandal was the air she breathed. She lived for the thrill of being desired, pampered, and pursued. There was no shame in her game. She was on the sugaring sites, and she played the role well. Why spend her own money when a line of eager men were ready to bankroll her lifestyle?

Her phone buzzed, a flurry of notifications. DMs from admirers, texts from "business partners," desperate pleas from men she'd left on read. Laughing, she scrolled through them, her perfectly manicured finger dismissing each one. As the song's hook hit, she threw her head back, singing along in mockery of their obsession.

Whatever she could take from a man, she would. Alison never saw herself as the villain. Married, engaged, or taken, if they showed up in her DMs, that was on them, not her.

She was single, detached, and care free. If they got caught, that was their fault. Beneath the glam and confidence, though, Alison was no pushover. Spoiled, sure. But she knew how to handle herself.

She smirked, thinking back to the recent encounter at *The Tummy Shaker,* a swanky rooftop spot in DTLA. One of her "dates" had made the rookie mistake of leaving his location on, and his fiancée had tracked him there. The woman stormed in, screaming, making a scene. Alison had barely glanced up from her drink.

"He should've turned off his location, sweetheart. That's not my problem," she had dismissively said, twirling her straw in her cocktail.

The fiancée wasn't having it. After a string of insults and mockery, she shoved Alison.

Big mistake.

Before anyone could react, Alison struck back, quick as lightning, a sharp two-punch combo. The woman hit the floor. Lights out. Alison could've been a boxer. Seriously.

The restaurant froze. Alison simply smoothed her hair, picked up her purse, and turned to the stunned man.

"Night's over, baby."

Then she walked out, leaving him scrambling to help his unconscious fiancée.

No charges were filed, Alison had technically been assaulted first, but the incident had caused a stir. The restaurant, eager to avoid bad press and litigation, offered her a settlement. The check still sat in her dresser draw uncashed.

Alison didn't care about the money. The satisfaction was payment enough.

At just over five feet, she might look harmless, but don't let the size fool you. Alison's got hands. Push her and she swings back. Hit her and she hits back harder. Just like the woman who found out the hard way: don't lay hands on Alison—because she'll knock you out in high heels and keep it moving.

It was just another story in her ever-growing list of escapades. Another guy discarded, another drama survived. And Alison remained unapologetic. Even

Samantha, who had long accepted Alison's fiery personality, found herself rolling her eyes at the tale.

But Alison? She reveled in it.

Ok, So?

Here Come The Gym Rats

At *Elite24Fit,* you could feel the swagger the moment Jordan and Tabatha walked in. They moved like they owned the place, radiating the kind of arrogance only influencers with millions of followers could muster. They didn't need introductions, everyone in the gym already knew who they were.

They built a brand on sweat and lies. If only their followers knew who they really were when the cameras stopped rolling.

Jordan cracked his knuckles and headed toward one of the machines, already anticipating his workout. This was his stage, his arena, and his ego demanded a flawless performance.

They moved in unison, making their way through the gym like a well-rehearsed act. The first half of their workout, they trained together, feeding off each other's energy. They trained like it was a performance. Their energy loud, dramatic, and made for social media.

Everything was a close-up, a pose, a show. They were impossible to ignore. Even noise-canceling headphones couldn't drown them out. Their desperate need for attention bled through every corner of the gym, like a silent scream: look at me.

No one wanted to be near them, but that didn't matter, and they didn't care. This was their world. Everyone else was just passing through.

They hit every workout: core, cardio, strength and conditioning. Even Cross-Fit. The gym itself was high-end boasting every piece of equipment imaginable. There were even talks of adding in an indoor track. But after tonight, those talks would cease.

The second half of their workout, they split off, each focusing on their own routines. Jordan pushed his limits, loading heavier and heavier weights, determined to test himself. Unaware that his effort was about to come to a grisly end.

The gym's music thumped in the background, a strange, unsettling contrast to the silence creeping into the room. In the shadows, the killer waited patiently, biding his time.

The Final Run

Tabatha paced near her favorite treadmill, the one with a dead-center view of Downtown Los Angeles. The perfect spot for her late-night streams. The lighting was impeccable, casting her against the glowing skyline like a polished ad for the *Elite24Fit* lifestyle.

But someone was already on the machine.

A woman, maybe in her late thirties, walked at a brisk pace. She didn't fit into Tabatha's carefully curated image of the gym. Wearing a slightly baggy sweatshirt and leggings, her face flushed with effort, she wasn't here to impress anyone. No filters, no updates, no clout-chasing, just a quiet determination to make a positive change.

Tabatha watched her like a hawk, tapping her foot impatiently. Minutes dragged by before she finally stepped forward.

"Excuse me." Her voice carried a brittle politeness. "How much longer are you going to be on this treadmill?"

The woman visibly startled, removing her headphones. "Oh, um… just a few more minutes," she said, glancing at the timer.

Tabatha sighed, crossing her arms. "Right. Well, I need this one, so if you don't mind wrapping it up soon."

The woman hesitated, biting her lip. Her heart rate spiked, not from her workout, but from the confrontation she desperately wanted to avoid. With a small, tight smile, she nodded. "Sure, I'll finish up now."

Tabatha smirked, victorious, and immediately stepped onto the treadmill as soon as the woman got off.

The Last Review

As the gym-goer grabbed her water bottle and phone, heading toward the locker room, her hands trembled slightly, not from exhaustion, but from frustration. She had looked forward to this workout all day, hoping for some peace and a chance to clear her mind. Instead, she had been dismissed, pushed aside, made to feel invisible. Like she didn't belong.

Sitting down on a bench, she opened Yelp with a scowl and began typing:

"If you're thinking about joining Elite24Fit, DON'T! This gym is overrun by influencers who think they're better than everyone else. Tonight, one of them rudely forced me off a treadmill because it's her 'favorite.' I'm here to work on myself, not to be harassed by entitled people treating this place like their own personal content studio. Management needs to do something about this, or they'll lose more members. I'm canceling my membership tomorrow."

She hit POST REVIEW with a firm tap and took a deep breath, determined to follow through with what she said.

This wasn't the first complaint about the gym's influencer problem, and it wouldn't be the last. The general manager would see the review in the morning and, with one glance, know exactly who it referred to. Jordan and Tabatha again.

The duo was the bane of his existence. Their antics had sparked a stream of complaints from members. Yet, as much as he wanted to revoke their memberships, his hands were tied.

Jordan and Tabatha were platinum-status members, influential fitness personalities who constantly tagged the gym in their videos, driving in foot traffic. For every member they alienated, they brought in three more, eager to mimic their workouts or simply catch a glimpse of them in person.

They thrived on the attention, feeding off every nod of recognition. Regular members often approached them for advice, and Jordan and Tabatha were always happy to help, so long as they could plug their social channels. Their following grew fast, and with it came new clients. Clients they trained privately, cutting directly into the gym's personal training revenue.

The trainers complained bitterly to the general manager. The message loud and clear.

"They're stealing our business!"

But corporate didn't care. Numbers mattered more than ethics. To them, Jordan and Tabatha were a free marketing goldmine, drawing in new members and boosting referrals through the gym's rewards program.

The manager felt trapped, powerless against the two influencers who treated the gym like their personal playground. His frustration was mirrored by his staff, who had grown equally disillusioned.

But amid the stress and chaos, there was one silver lining: the camaraderie among the staff. They had formed a tight-knit group, united in their disdain for Jordan and Tabatha.

Workplace romance wasn't frowned upon at *Elite24Fit*. If anything, it had become an unspoken glue holding the team together. Friendships had blossomed into something more. Bonds strengthened by late-night venting sessions over drinks.

Still, the general manager couldn't shake his frustration. He urged his team to document every violation and every disruption. If they could find a solid reason to revoke Jordan and Tabatha's memberships, maybe corporate would finally listen. For now, all they could do was endure. It was them versus Jordan and Tabatha.

But, as the manager would begin his shift the next morning, he had no idea what would await him. A negative Yelp review would be the least of his concerns.

By the time the night was over, the gym would face a crisis unlike anything they'd ever seen. And no staff camaraderie, or corporate indifference could prepare him for what was coming.

Setting The Plan In Motion

The killer leered in the shadows of the club, now disguised as just another gym-goer. His lifelike mask ensured the cameras couldn't match his face to anything in the system. He moved freely, working out undetected. But his gaze never left Jordan and Tabatha.

He wasn't going to miss this.

Tabatha's body language said it all as she finally claimed her prized treadmill. Her need to assert dominance radiated from every step. He had studied this pattern: an arrogance so ingrained it became her routine, one that fed directly into his plan.

Downstairs, Jordan was in his element, stacking weights for his live stream. Upstairs, Tabatha basked in the glow of her perfectly staged setup, her audience already watching. The stage was set.

There was a poetic justice to it. Their obsession with appearances. Their casual disregard for others. Tonight, it would all collapse. The traps he had planted earlier were silent, precise, and ready to deliver the reckoning they so richly deserved.

This wasn't just revenge.

It was a message.

By the time the night ended, this gym would never be the same.

Not for its members.

Not for its staff.

And not for anyone who chose to look the other way.

The Night Everything Would Change

Samantha allowed herself to slow down as she and Mike strolled through the store together. For once, she wasn't glued to her phone. Her socials were on autopilot, content scheduled two weeks out, her campaigns already locked in.

All contracts signed. All deliverables met. All payments en route. It wasn't just productivity. It was control. Carefully maintained, deliberately earned. With everything handled, she could finally breathe.

The pain from her injury at *Le Cher* was still a reminder of how fast things could spiral. But Mike's support was helping her heal both physically and emotionally. Somehow, in the blink of an eye, breakfast with him had turned into dinner. And she welcomed the distraction.

She couldn't deny it anymore, Mike had been there for her in ways no one else had. Could she finally allow herself to trust him? Let him in? They'd been on a handful of dates over the last three months, after all. The possibility tugged at the edges of her heart.

But this would be one of the last nights she felt any semblance of normalcy. Tonight was the calm before the storm.

In just 48 hours, everything in Samantha's life would change. While she enjoyed this faint sense of peace, Alison prepped for her next livestream. Jordan and Tabatha powered through their nightly workouts. And somewhere in the city, the killer waited. Silent. Patient. Every step of his next move meticulously plotted.

By the end of the night, what had begun as a quiet murder investigation, intended to be kept low-profile to avoid public panic, would erupt into a full-blown media firestorm. The killer's spree would no longer be seen as isolated.

A serial killer would be on the loose, and Los Angeles would soon be consumed by chaos.

For the LAPD, the wave of gruesome discoveries ahead would leave them scrambling, every resource stretched thin, as they raced to connect the dots of a blood-soaked puzzle.

And for Samantha, Mike, and everyone else caught in the killer's web, life as they knew it was about to be shattered forever.

CHAPTER 17

THE LAST WORKOUT

Samantha and Mike finished shopping, their cart filled with everything they needed for dinner. Mike had planned the perfect meal, salmon pasta Alfredo topped with fresh tomatoes, cilantro, and chives, paired with garlic bread, shrimp cocktail, and a bottle of red wine. Samantha couldn't help but smile as they wandered through the aisles together.

She felt light. The pain dulling, just for now. They laughed, joked and let the night slip away. At the checkout, Mike, ever the gentleman, took care of everything.

As they stepped outside, Samantha turned to him, meeting his gaze. And without a word, she kissed him. A long, lingering kiss, as if time itself had paused. The world around them, the people walking by, it all faded into the background.

When she pulled away, she grinned mischievously.
"What was that for?" Mike asked, a smile creeping across his face.

"Oh, you know. Gotta kiss the cook, after all."

Mike chuckled as he loaded the groceries into her Tesla. When Samantha reached to close the trunk, Mike stopped her, pressing the button himself. They exchanged another long look. And just as she moved closer to kiss him again, she suddenly blurted out:

"Race you to my place!" Her voice was high-pitched with excitement.

Mike laughed, eyes gleaming with the same playful energy. "Oh, you're on."

They both rushed to their cars, flirtatious and giddy, ready for the short drive back to Marina Del Rey, unaware of the deadly countdown taking place elsewhere in the city.

Halfway home, with Mike close behind, Samantha spotted a glowing green cross in the distance. Relief washed over her. Without hesitation, she flipped her blinker on and pulled into the parking lot.

Mike caught the hint following her inside the parking lot and parked beside her. He flashed an approving smile as she rolled down her window.

"I'm gonna run in and grab some CBD cream," she said. "You want anything?"

"No thanks, but take your time," Mike replied.

"Okay, wait for me here."

She disappeared inside and returned a few minutes later, looking visibly relieved. As they backed out of their spots together, she rolled down her window again.

"Oh, the race is still on!" she called out before speeding off.

Mike shook his head, laughing to himself before following suit.

Samantha, always a mix of playfulness and wit. He was starting to see more of her now. Beneath the sassy, high-energy persona of a lifestyle and beauty influencer, something deeper was beginning to emerge. She was slowly peeling back the layers, little by little. And he liked what he saw.

Maybe it was the injury that had sparked the shift. But more than that, he was here, for her. And all the signs pointed to her wanting him here too.

Could this be the start of something real? After three months, he was open to it. He knew she talked to other guys, but he chose to stay optimistic. He had good feelings about her. But only time would tell.

And as the thought slipped from his lips in a quiet whisper, he had no idea how little time they actually had left to exist in that calm, suspended moment before everything would change.

Bye Bye Jordan And Tabatha

The gym was quiet, eerily so. It was late, nearly empty, save for Jordan and Tabatha. They'd been working out for hours, pushing each other harder with every set. Four hours in, they were drenched in sweat and still going. Jordan worked through his strength and conditioning, testing his limits with heavier and heavier weights. He was determined to push himself, unaware that his effort was about to come to a grisly end.

Some lo-fi music drifted through the speakers, the kind of polished, laid-back playlist meant to calm the mind. Tonight, it only added an unsettling layer to the silence. It was a dead Saturday night at the gym. Jordan and Tabatha were alone. Nearby, the killer blended in, posing as just another member. Calm. Patient. Ready to make his move.

Tabatha, upstairs on the treadmill, was focused on her workout, her speed increasing with each passing minute. She was in the zone, pushing herself to the limit while her followers cheered her on through the live stream. She was responding to their messages, laughing and talking about how much harder she could push herself, getting louder as she fed off the fanfare.

Downstairs, Jordan was nearing the end of his workout, the weights heavier than before. He had his tripod set up and was live to his followers. He pushed through each set, determined to complete his reps. But as he lifted the weights, he felt something snap, a strain in his arms.

He pushed harder, but the strain was too much. With one final effort, the cables snapped under the pressure. The killer had thinned the wire just enough that it wouldn't withstand a few more reps under the pressure.

His arms instantly broke and the weights came crashing down onto his neck. It happened too fast for him to react, like his head had been caught in a guillotine.

The force severed it nearly clean from his body, leaving it dangling by a single, sinewy strand of muscle. The gym was silent. No one heard. No one saw. No one knew.

The killer stepped from the shadows, his hands steady as he approached Jordan's lifeless body. With a swift motion, he snipped the last muscle holding Jordan's head to his body and it fell to the floor with a sickening thud.

His eye twitched. Blood pooled around his severed head and streaked across the floor. What a horrible way to go. And it was all captured live. Jordan's followers were stunned in disbelief. The live chat blew up. The comments poured in.

"OMG IS HE DEAD?!!"
"WTF DID I JUST WATCH?!!"
"NO NO NO NO NO!!!"
"Are we being PUNKED right now??"
"Bro his HEAD! Did his eye really just twitch??
"Someone call 911!!"
"I'm out. I can't watch this."

Back upstairs, something went horribly wrong.

Tabatha was on an incline when the treadmill suddenly jerked backward. The springboard launched her into the air, and she crashed through the gym's glass wall with a sickening crack.

Shards exploded into the night as her body sailed through the air. Her scream lost in the wind.

The chat exploded. People were going bananas.

"OMG SHE JUST WENT THROUGH THE WINDOW!"
"WTF! WTF! WTF!"
"Bro, did she just do a Peter Pan out that window?"
"Is someone calling 911?"
"WHAT IS HAPPENING?"
"OMG Tabatha?! I'm going to cry!"
"This has to be AI! It just has to be!"

The killer, having just finished with Jordan, watched from below with cold detachment.

Seconds later she hit the cold concrete, the thud of her body echoing through the quiet streets. The cheap glass, installed as a cost-saving measure by management, had given way instantly, sealing her fate.

The killer stood motionless, the rush of satisfaction sweeping through him. Without a single glance back, he left the gym as calm as he'd entered. He slipped into his car and drove off, disappearing into the night. Behind him, the scene erupted. Screams filled the air as people poured onto the streets, drawn by the chaos.

They gathered at the scene, some still frozen in disbelief. Tabatha's body lay twisted on the pavement, sending a wave of shock through the crowd. Phones then appeared, some trembling. Others capturing the gruesome scene without hesitation. The horror streamed live on the Citizen app. Most watched through their screens, too numbed to feel the humanity slipping away.

"Call the police! Don't just film!" someone shouted, their voice filled with panic and outrage.

Several people waved their hands at those recording, shouting at them to stop, but their words were swallowed by the growing crowd. Tension escalated as arguments broke out among bystanders. Some condemning the gawkers for exploiting the tragedy. Others, brushing off the outrage as a waste of energy.

"It's too late for that! You think the cops can do anything now?" someone snapped back.

The body lay still on the dark asphalt, bathed in the flickering neon glow of downtown. A few brave souls stepped forward, faces pale with disbelief. While the rest lingered at a distance, transfixed by the horror. Some genuinely tried to help. Others stood frozen. A handful, far too late, finally called the police, knowing deep down the killer was already gone.

Then a sharp, high-pitched scream rang out from inside the gym in pure panic. Someone had seen Jordan's severed head and body. Second later, they burst through the doors.

"Yo! Somebody's dead in there! They ended him. Like, for real. Head's on the ground. Blood everywhere!"

More people rushed out from inside the gym. When they saw the body, some gasped. Others recoiled. It was nearly unrecognizable.

Several bystanders tried to push their way inside. Security was minimal, and a few managed to sneak a look before being stopped.

"This is someone's life! How are you trying to sensationalize it, you sick fuck?" the lone security guard shouted, overwhelmed and losing control of the scene outside the gym.

Back over by Tabatha's body, people were clamoring.

"How could you want to take footage of this?" one person asked.

"What should we do? Are we allowed to cover the body?" another citizen asked.

"Where are the fucking cops?!" somebody exclaimed.

And yet, despite the chaos building around her, Tabatha's body remained untouched. Her stillness, so final, so brutal, seemed to paralyze those nearby. Sirens wailed in the distance, growing louder with each passing second. Still, the crowd just stood there.

CHAPTER 18

CHAOS AND SENSATIONALISM

The scene at *Elite24Fit* had erupted into utter chaos. Police cars with blaring sirens cordoned off the area, their flashing red and blue lights reflecting off the glass skyscrapers. A sea of spectators gathered behind police tape, their faces a mix of shock, curiosity, and disbelief. The scene was nothing short of a media frenzy waiting to explode.

Sergeant Blake Ramirez arrived, barking orders to his team. "Secure this area! I don't want a single bystander past this line."

He pointed to the drooping yellow tape, his voice cutting through the noise of murmurs, helicopter blades, and the distant wail of an ambulance.

The area was completely shut down. Pedestrians were rerouted, and LAPD traffic units redirected every vehicle. Overhead, helicopters circled, their spotlights sweeping across the grim scene below. The fire department stood by. The fire department stood by, ceremonial now. The chaos was far beyond their reach.

Sergeant Ramirez spoke into his radio, "Get me Lieutenant Byron Maxwell. We're in some serious shit."

"Copy that," came the response.

As the sergeant surveyed the scene, he muttered under his breath, "Another influencer, another live-streamed death, and another fucking circus."

Ramirez turned to one of his officers. "Keep TMZ out of here. I mean it. I catch one camera crew inside this tape, they'll be leaving in handcuffs."

Too late. The headline was already live on their website:

"High-Profile Fitness Influencers Found Dead At L.A. Gym: Accident or Something More Sinister?"

The article was pure sensationalism, feeding off the mystery surrounding Jordan and Tabatha deaths. It ran wild with speculation, quoting shaken bystanders, hinting at possible motives and relationships, yet offered no real answers. The killer's identity remained unknown, but the public was already drawing their own conclusions.

The crime scene was meticulous in its horror. The shattered gym window loomed high above, casting an eerie frame around the spot where Tabatha had fallen. Broken glass sparkled on the pavement, reflecting the dim streetlights and adding a surreal beauty to the carnage.

A Very Long Night Ahead

Lieutenant Byron Maxwell stepped out of his unmarked car, Detectives Jason Jacobson and Edward Castanon flanking him. He adjusted his tie as the trio pushed through a swarm of reporters and gawkers. Cameras flashed. Questions flew. But Maxwell's stoic expression never wavered.

"Lieutenant Maxwell, is this connected to the other murders?"

"Are social media influencers being targeted?"

"Is the killer sending a message?"

Maxwell raised a hand quieting the crowd. His voice was firm, controlled.

"We're conducting a thorough investigation. Out of respect for the victims and their families, we won't be making any speculative statements at this time."

Turning away from the media frenzy, Maxwell muttered to his colleagues, "They're going to run wild with this."

"They already are," Jacobson replied. "It's all over social media and TMZ. Every armchair detective in L.A. is spinning their theories."

"Let them spin," Maxwell said coldly. "We've got work to do."

The Crime Scene

The gym looked like a war zone. Broken equipment, scattered weights, and shards of glass painted a brutal picture of carnage. Forensics teams moved with purpose, snapping photos and collecting evidence beneath the harsh glare of overhead lights. A white sheet covered the body, but the spreading pool of blood beneath it was impossible to ignore.

"This is the night security guard, Samson," Ramirez said. "He's been cooperative and already shared what he knows."

Maxwell gave the young man a nod. His face was pale and clammy. "We'll speak with you shortly, Samson. Wait by the front desk for now."

As the detectives approached the scene, Castanon let out a low whistle. "What a way to go."

Jacobson crouched by the fallen barbell, inspecting the snapped wire. "Deliberate," he muttered. "No way this happens by accident."

Maxwell nodded, scanning the scene. "Two fitness influencers with massive followings. Dead in one night. Both killed mid-livestream. And both gruesome as hell."

"Don't forget the one from 48 hours ago," Castanon added. "Another influencer. Same age range. Same M.O."

Maxwell's jaw tightened. "This is no coincidence. The killer is sending a message."

As they examined the equipment, the detectives paused at the treadmill Tabatha had been using just minutes before her fall. A torn cord dangled from the machine. Severed clean.

"We need surveillance footage," Maxwell said. "Jacobson, call the judge. Get a subpoena. I want every second of video from tonight."

"On it," Jacobson replied, stepping away to make the call.

A Lead Emerges

Sergeant Ramirez approached the detectives. "The security guard mentioned something. Said a repair guy came in late tonight, supposedly for routine maintenance. But he remembered him because something felt… off."

"How so?" Maxwell asked, interest piqued.

"Tall. About 6'4". Slim, but saggy. Like he lost a lot of weight fast. Long black hair, brown eyes, bronze complexion. Mustache, scruffy beard. Name tag said 'Lester.' Said he was with a company called Griffin Repair Co."

Maxwell exchanged a look with his team. "Call the company. See if they've even got a Lester on the payroll."

Late Night Interruptions

Loud cries echoed through the room, muffled by the sheets.

"Faster… yes, faster…" Megan gasped, her voice breathy and urgent.

She gripped the headboard, her body arching as Greyson moved beneath her. He rose, his face brushing against hers. She moaned again, her head falling back, hair spilling over her shoulders.

Their rhythm quickened.
Her breath caught. Once, then again.
So close. And then, they got swept up in the feeling, losing control.

Their bodies locked, trembling, before collapsing into each other. Greyson settled on her as they caught their breath. Their lips met in a slow kiss. The final chord to their passion.

Greyson and Megan had been together for eight months, their romance blossoming at the gym where they worked. Colleagues had cheered when the "work wife, work husband" banter finally turned real. What began as playful flirtation escalated into something deeper.

Lying tangled in the sheets, Greyson grinned. "Your flexibility, I swear. I don't know how you do it."

Megan laughed, brushing a strand of hair from her face. "And your stamina? I should put you on the roster for my yoga class."

Their laughter was cut short by the buzzing of Greyson's phone. He ignored the first two calls, sending them straight to voicemail. By the third, he groaned and reached for it.

"It's Paul," he said, glancing at Megan.

"What the hell? What does he want at this hour?"

Greyson answered. "Paul, this better be good. Remember our talk about boundaries?"

"Turn on the news. It's the gym. We're all over it."

"Why? Did Tabatha post another workout challenge?"

"No, Greyson. Just turn it on."

Frowning, Greyson grabbed the remote and flipped on the TV. The headline made his stomach drop:

Tragedy at Elite24Fit: Fitness Stars Found Dead in Gym Horror—Police Launch Homicide Investigation

Megan gasped, her hand flying to her mouth. "Oh my God… Jordan and Tabatha…"

Greyson stared at the screen, disbelief washing over him. "This has to be some kind of sick joke."

"It's not," Paul said grimly. "The cops are swarming the gym. They're questioning everyone. We need to get the team together."

"Yeah," Greyson said, rubbing his forehead. "Who was working tonight?"

"Celine and Max," Paul replied.

Greyson nodded, his mind racing. "Right. I'll send a mass text. Megan, can you reach out to the trainers?"

"Already on it," Megan said, grabbing her phone.

A text from Darren, the regional manager, popped up on Greyson's screen:

Emergency meeting tomorrow morning. Be prepared to discuss protocols.

Greyson sighed heavily. "This is going to be a shit show."

"Welcome to bizarro world," Megan muttered, shaking her head as she typed furiously.

Containing The Mess

As the night deepened, detectives inside sifted through fragments of evidence under a heavy perimeter maintained by police. Outside, the media frenzy raged on. Lieutenant Maxwell stood firm, staring into the heart of a city teetering on the edge of panic.

"This isn't just another case," he muttered. "This is a damn storm, and we're right in the middle of it."

The pieces were starting to align, but the full picture remained elusive. And somewhere, the killer was already planning his next move.

CHAPTER 19

A FINAL NIGHT OF PEACE

As Samantha and Mike made their way home, a quiet sense of relief washed over her. The day had been long, the strain still hanging over her, but something about returning into her own space brought comfort.

She pulled up to the house, parked behind the gate, and waited. As soon as Mike arrived, she waved him in, motioning for him to park behind her.

Once inside, she locked the gate, turned on the alarm system, and they began unloading groceries. Mike, ever the gentleman, carried everything in. The routine and its simple grounding tasks felt almost soothing.

She stood up on her tiptoes and kissed him, a breath of calm finally settling between them. "We made it home. I'm really glad you followed me."

Samantha walked to the freezer and pulled out a cold compress for her ribs. The relief was immediate as the coolness pressed against her skin. She sighed in contentment, knowing the tension would ease, even if only for a little while.

She grabbed a muscle relaxer next, deciding her body had earned it. The chaos of the day felt distant now, at least for now.

"Last chance," Samantha called over her shoulder, a playful smile tugging at her lips. "If you need to leave, now's the time."

She walked over to arm the security system, the familiar routine bringing a quiet sense of reassurance.

"It's too late to kick me out," Mike grinned.

"Maybe… maybe not," she teased.

With a nod, Samantha armed the system.

The calm voice chimed through the room: "Home secure. Motion detectors activated."

She turned toward Mike and smiled, relief washing over her.

"Home sweet home," she said in a sing-song tone, high-pitched like a kid getting exactly what they wanted.

Samantha called for her pets, and they came running eager for food and attention. She laughed, petting them as they nuzzled against her legs.

"They only came because they want food," she joked, then turned to Mike with a sly smile. "Be a dear, please feed them for me while I get comfortable?"

Watching the pets warm up to Mike amused her. With them taken care of, she clutched the cold compress to her ribs again and headed upstairs to settle in for the night. She was finally ready to let the day go and rest.

Downstairs, Mike moved through the kitchen, prepping their food and refilling water bowls. His mind stayed focused on the comfort of being there with her. A small slice of normalcy, tucked inside the chaos.

While Samantha was settling in for the evening, Alison was preparing for her live session. Her makeup was flawless. The setup for her beauty stream already in place. It was almost time for *The Alison Hour*.

She smiled as she got into position, eager to showcase the latest products she would be reviewing.

What she didn't know was that the well-meaning gift from Samantha would soon become part of a much darker story than either of them could have imagined. The livestream began, and Alison dove into her routine, oblivious to the storm building around her.

Samantha returned downstairs, her light black silk robe flowing around her as she moved. The robe, one of her favorites, had an delicate gold "S" stitched on the chest.

It fell to mid-thigh, perfect for lounging in comfort while still making a statement.

As she stepped into the living room, she teased over her shoulder, "Maybe one day I'll show you all around this house."

Mike smiled, curiosity piqued. Samantha's home, with its layers of history and hidden spaces, had always intrigued him.

She walked over to a spot he'd barely noticed before, an ordinary-looking wall fixture, he'd assumed. But Samantha unlatched a small, concealed door.

"This one leads to the wine cellar," she said, gesturing toward a darkened stairway.
"Down there, the tunnels split. One exits near the side of the house, the other by the front."

She turned back to him, playful. "Would you believe me if I told you this house was used during Prohibition?"

"The house of secrets," he said, clearly entertained by the thought.

"Just kidding…maybe," Samantha laughed and closed the hidden door, then turned her attention to her phone.

Alison was live, already deep into her beauty tutorial. Samantha stuck around to show support and saw

Alison still in the early stretch of the stream, rambling about her day. Once she got going, there was no stopping her, and she was definitely on a roll.

Samantha lounged on the couch, robe loosely tied, nothing on underneath. As she moved, the robe fell slightly open, and Mike, glancing up from the kitchen, caught a glimpse of her side boob. She didn't seem to notice, still focused on her phone.

While Alison spoke to the camera, Samantha gave a quick shoutout, telling her own followers about their friendship. Comments of support and heart emojis rolled in instantly.

"Wanna join me, Sami?" Alison called out with a teasing grin. "Split screen, come on."

Samantha hesitated, glancing at Mike across the room. He was still at the counter, focused on plating their meal. The soft glow of the kitchen lights caught the angle of his jaw as he worked.

Screw it.

She tossed her hair up into a loose bun, grabbed her laptop and ring light from the living room shelf, and turned toward the mirror, already slipping back into her zone. The polished, performative side of her. The one she hadn't tapped into in days.

"Felicia, switch me to Split Screen Mode."

Within seconds, Samantha's face appeared beside Alison's on the livestream. The comments lit up.

"OMG it's *Simply Samantha*?!"
"Wait! They're friends??"
"I knew I recognized her!"
"Drop the skincare recs!!"

"Hi guys," Samantha said with a warm, easy grin. "Yes, that's my girl. We grew up together."

The two started doing glam side by side, playfully discussing beauty tips and secrets. Samantha read a few usernames out loud, laughing when one fan begged for a hair tutorial.

Across the room, Mike looked up from the counter. He paused, watching her from the kitchen. Her voice, her poise, her radiance on camera. This was a version of her he hadn't fully seen before. Confident. Commanding. Charismatic.

He smiled to himself.

She indulged the stream for a little longer, tossing out a few light comments and reacting along with Alison on some gossip, but careful not to get sucked into another marathon session. That girl could go until the sun rises. Not tonight. Not with company.

Then she glanced toward Mike, still at the counter, prepping their meal.

Alison changed topics seamlessly as she thanked someone for a Superchat and read aloud, "What country have you had the best sex in?"

Time to go. The chat was taking a left turn.

She said her goodbyes as Alison held up the gift with a grin. Samantha blew her a kiss and tapped the screen to end the stream, catching Alison mid-laugh on her way out.

"Felicia, play my night mix number seven," Samantha instructed, eager to set the tone for the evening.

Good music, good food, and good company. She was happy at the thought.

"Didn't know I was dating a livestream queen. You lit up the screen back there."

Samantha rolled her eyes but smiled. "It was just for a second to support Ali. I was on autopilot. Definitely not camera-ready."

She touched her loosely styled hair, the cold compress still pressed to her side.

Mike smirked. "Your autopilot's still better than most people's best."

She let out a soft laugh. "It's like riding a bike. You just don't think about it sometimes."

She eased into the chair a bit more, then added, "But it felt good to do that, just to sort of decompress after all that's happened."

She clutched the cold compress tighter. It was beginning to melt. Her gaze drifted off.

"How are you feeling?"

She didn't answer right away.

"Sam? A pause. "Samantha?"

"Oh. Yes. Sorry." She blinked back to focus. "Was just thinking if I had any unfinished collabs. I don't."

She rested her other hand on her face, voice softening.

"And I'm glad I don't. Come to think of it, I'm not quite ready to put content out there just yet." She gave a small shrug.

"I've got the next two weeks scheduled. And with everything that's been happening… I really need to focus on getting myself right."

She nodded to herself reaffirming the decision.

"I understand," Mike said gently. "It's been a rough couple of days. "You should go upstairs, get in bed. This'll be done soon, and I'll be up."

"Okay. I won't argue," she murmured.

Mike replaced her cold compress before she got up slowly and headed upstairs to settle into bed.

CHAPTER 20

A FACEFUL OF HORROR

Forty-five minutes into her livestream, Alison was getting warmed up. Known for her engaging multi hour live streams, she had perfected the art of connecting with her audience. Her followers adored her, hanging on her every word. Fully monetized with affiliate links, online shops, and a loyal fan base, her viewers often emulated her lifestyle, from skincare routines to restaurant recommendations.

With just under 100,000 subscribers, Alison's channel, *The Unapologetic Life of Alison,* delivers exactly what the name promises. A raw, stylish ride through her everyday world. Part glam, part chaos, all her.

She's not here to be a role model. She's here to be real. No filter. Full transparency. Always.

Between Get Ready With Me videos, beauty hauls, and filter-free vlogs about her dating life, Alison makes one thing clear: she knows her worth, and she expects to be treated accordingly. She's made an art of wrapping men around her finger, and she doesn't shy away from showing her audience just how much they're willing to spend to be in her orbit… and how you can too.

She swears she's not trying to give dating advice, but she does. Constantly. And it's not always pretty. Her takes are blunt, twisted, sometimes toxic… and often exactly what her followers are looking for. Don't subscribe to her channel if you're not ready to hear something you don't want to. That's half the appeal. That's why they keep coming back.

Whether she's flaunting a designer bag from a new fling or breaking down how to ghost a guy without guilt, Alison owns every inch of her lifestyle. Her rotation of men? That's her business, period.

The brunches. The yacht parties. Popping bottles at the club. Getting flown out. The hotel stays. All transactional.

She doesn't chase numbers, or your approval. She posts what she wants, when she wants. She's in her prime. She's unapologetically living her best life, and her audience loves her for it. But if it makes you uncomfortable? That's on you. Unsubscribe anytime.

No, Alison Louise Santiago doesn't apologize for living life on her terms. That's why people subscribed. They knew exactly what they were getting when they tuned in. She had a knack for the livestream. Her signature segment, *The Alison Hour*, became a staple of the channel. Her people were always eager to hear what she had to say or what tea she was about to pour. And tonight's live, was shaping up to be another one of her "all nighters."

"I'm going to share some of my absolute favorites with you tonight. You know me. I only want to steer you in the right direction!"

Alison sat relaxed in her silk baby-blue robe, a delicate white "A" stitched across the chest in cursive.

She reached for a sleek, mysterious package from Samantha's gift box and held it up for the camera to see.

"Oh, I can't forget about this one!" she exclaimed.

She began explaining the product, reading the instructions out loud, preparing to demonstrate it. Dabbing the serum onto her cheekbone, Alison carefully spread it across the right side of her face, marveling at the instant glow.

"Look at that glow!" she said, turning toward the camera to catch the light.

Just as she reached for more product to apply to the left side, her phone buzzed.

"Sorry, guys, I've been waiting for a delivery from one of my favorite restaurants. I can't wait to show you," she explained, her chat still buzzing with comments. "Let me see what's going on."

Her smile faltered as she read the message. The driver was hopefully just lost, idling on the wrong street.

"Ugh. Delivery drivers," she muttered, rolling her eyes. "Okay, BRB, besties. Don't go anywhere!"

She threw on a hoodie and oversized sunglasses even though it was pitch black out. It wasn't about hiding, it was armor. Ego. Persona. She dashed out the door. The driver, clearly confused and unable to follow Alison's directions, was on the next street over, forcing her to walk five houses down to meet him.

She waved him over, scolding him lightly.

"You'd think with a preloaded tip, you'd try harder to find my house. How hard is it to follow GPS directions and read instructions?" she said, snatching the bag of food and shaking her head as she walked away.

"Amateurs," she muttered under her breath.

By the time she returned to her vanity setup, ten minutes had passed. Alison plopped into her chair, flashing an apologetic smile at the camera. Her viewer count had tapered to just under 8,000, but they were still with her.

"I swear, they'll let anyone be a delivery driver these days," she joked, earning a flood of laughing emojis in the chat.

"Now, where were we? Oh, right. The mystery product!"

Unbeknownst to her, the product had already started taking effect. Her right cheek was glowing. A alarming, blotchy red. But Alison, still in performance mode, picked up where she left off, dabbing more of the product onto her face.

Then the chat lit up:

"Wow, glowing goddess vibes!"
"Rosy red cheeks!"
"Girl, is it supposed to be red like that?"
"Did you look at yourself??"
"Alison, your cheeks look… weird!"
"Something's wrong with your face, Alison!"

"What?" she muttered, leaning closer to the camera.
"Nah, it's just the lighting. Chill!"

She shrugged off the concerns, laughing nervously. But as the stinging sensation intensified, her laughter faded. Alison dabbed her face with a tissue, her confidence faltering. When she pulled her hand back, she didn't like what she saw.

A red stain glared back at her.

Shit was getting real.

"Wait a second…" Alison's voice shook, barely above a whisper.

The chat exploded:

"OMG, what's happening?!"

"Your face, how horrible!"
"Is this a prank???"
"Alison, end the stream!"

Alison turned to the mirror, her eyes widening in horror. Her cheek was raw, glistening, and blistering before her eyes.

"Oh my God. OH MY GOD!" she screamed, her voice piercing. Her hand shot up to her face, but she recoiled. Her fingers slick with blood. Her skin was beginning to boil, oozing pus along her cheekbone.

"Felicia, call 911!" she screamed at her home assistant.

"Emergency services are being contacted. Stay on the line," Felicia's voice was calm. Too calm.

"911, what is your emergency?" came the voice on the other end.

"My face! It's burning! Please send help. My address is—"

"Ma'am… is this a joke?"

"IT'S NOT A JOKE!" Alison shrieked. "HELP ME!"

The burning intensified. Blisters bubbled across her skin, peeling in strips before her eyes, like it was being grated away. She froze, staring in horror at her reflection. Her monitor kept rolling, capturing every second as her face unraveled.

"Oh my God! Oh no, oh no… What's happening? Oh my God!" she screamed, bolting up from her chair.

The camera caught only a blur as she bolted to the bathroom. She splashed water on her face in vain, sobbing as her reflection worsened.

"Alison Santiago, your emergency request has been registered. Help is on the way," Felicia's voice returned, neutral and unshaken.

When she stumbled back into frame, her face was raw and glistening. A grotesque blend of blood and blistered flesh. Whatever was in that product was eating through her skin.

"HELP ME!" she screamed directly into the camera.

Her chat exploded panicked.

"Call the cops!"
"Where are the paramedics??"
"Alison, babe, no!"
"End the stream!"

"I'm calling 911!"

Alison's panic shifted into survival mode. The stinging became searing. Unrelenting. Blood mixed with shards of melting skin, dripping down her neck. She bolted to the backyard.

"Location locked. Emergency personnel en route," Felicia announced, barely audible over the open sliding door.

In a final act of desperation, she threw herself into the pool.

The camera, still rolling, captured the eerie glow of the water as her body disappeared beneath the surface.

"Please remain stationary until assistance arrives," Felicia's voice echoed behind her, the final mechanical line before silence.

Seconds later, blood began to rise, swirling in dark clouds through the illuminated water.

Sirens grew louder in the distance. Horrified viewers begged for updates.

"Is she okay?!"
"Alison, where are you?!"
"Someone, DO SOMETHING!"
"ALISON, SAY SOMETHING!"

The livestream stayed on, capturing the rippling pool and the blooming shadow of blood. Siren lights flickered in the water's surface, red, blue, red, as faint voices of first responders echoed in the distance. The chat exploded.

"She's in the pool hurry!"
"WHERE ARE THEY?!"
"Someone help her!"
"Did she come up yet?"

A loud crack sounded, the fence giving way. Heavy footsteps rushed through the backyard. Then came the splash. Two firefighters dove in, dragging Alison's lifeless body toward the edge.

The stream didn't cut. It held steady as CPR began, her pale figure limp on the pavement.

And then, static.

Alison's fate remained a chilling mystery. One the internet would replay endlessly, frame by frame.

CHAPTER 21

MIKE'S BEDSIDE MANNER

As Samantha lay in bed with the cold compress easing her trailing pain, she allowed herself to relax. The smell of dinner drifted through the house, and it smelled good. A smile tugged at her lips as he prepared their meal. She appreciated the quiet he brought with him. A peace she hadn't realized she'd been craving.

From upstairs, she could hear the distant clinking of plates and glasses as he rummaged through the kitchen. She found it cute.

Maybe I should go help him, she thought.

She moved too fast and felt a sharp jolt in her side as she twisted to get out of bed. With a gasp, she collapsed back onto the mattress, sprawled across the middle, taking short, shallow breaths. More cabinets opened below.

He needs my help, she insisted.

She reached for her tablet, pulling it over her chest to access the kitchen intercom. Her voice came through the intercom via a quirky cat-shaped wall clock, the speaker built into its mouth and the control button cleverly hidden in one of its paws. The digital display on its belly glowed as she spoke, guiding Mike step by step as he searched for the special dinnerware she had tucked away for an occasion like this.

She had a deep fondness for these dishes. A pale lavender set with bold gold trim and a polished porcelain finish. They weren't a splurge. Samantha was used to spending money on beautiful things. If something fit the aesthetic of her home, she'd buy it. And tonight felt like the perfect night to use them.

When Mike confirmed he'd found everything, she smiled to herself and closed her eyes, letting the smooth melodies of her playlist wash over her. Tame Impala's "New Person, Same Old Mistakes" played in the background, its hypnotic rhythm allowing her to drift deeper into comfort.

Minutes passed.

The glow from the hallway spilled gently into the bedroom as Mike stepped inside, the lavender and gold dinnerware gleaming in his hands. The scent of creamy Alfredo, garlic, and seared salmon filled the air, blending with the faint trace of Samantha's perfume still clinging to the pillows.

She sat up slowly, her robe slipping slightly along her shoulder as she adjusted the cold compress resting on her side. The room was dim, lit only by the golden hue of her bedside lamp and the flicker from a candle burning on the dresser. Her playlist flowed on, the music a dreamy pulse beneath the stillness.

Mike placed the plate on the bedside tray. The lavender dish was warm beneath the plated silverware, the pasta glistening, steam curling upward in delicate ribbons.

He set down a folded napkin beside her, the cloth matching the trim of the plate almost exactly.

Samantha sighed and laid back against her pillows, her body finally beginning to settle. The music played in the background, the flicker of candlelight on the nightstand casting a tranquil glow across the room.

Dinner in bed. A favorite indulgence.

"You're the best," she murmured, sitting up and reaching for the chilled wine glass he'd brought with him.

"Just doing my part for you, Sam," he replied. His gaze stayed fixated in her.

She smiled, raising her glass. "Well then, cheers to this lovely dinner."

They clinked glasses and took a sip.

"Your dinnerware set looks snazzy," Mike said, glancing down at the lavender and gold plate. "My sister would love them."

"Would she?" Samantha perked up. "I'll send you the link."

She grabbed her phone, found the site, and tapped the link over. A second later, a chime hit Mike's phone. He opened it and paused.

$799.
Regular price: $1,349.

He kept his expression neutral, doing his best to mask the reaction so Samantha wouldn't notice.

"Yeah, she better take advantage of that deal," Samantha casually said, scrolling through the site with a light shrug. "Oh well. I love them. I didn't want to wait."

The price tag was nothing to her. But to Mike, and definitely to his sister, $800 was a luxury that could pay for a dozen more practical things.

"I'll tell her," he said politely, tucking the phone away.

They began to eat. The world outside didn't matter. A calming breeze drifted through her room, and for a second, it felt like everything might be okay. They could finally exhale, unaware of how short-lived that breath of peace would be.

The dinner was perfectly balanced, neither too heavy nor too light. Mike had plated everything with care, serving perfect portions as if they were dining in a high-end restaurant. The salmon Alfredo was rich and creamy, laced with garlic, cilantro, and chives for an aromatic kick. The shrimp cocktail they shared added a delicate, refreshing contrast, and the garlic bread was crisp on the outside, soft and buttery on the inside.

Every bite felt indulgent yet satisfying. The kind of meal that left them full, but not sluggish. A dinner made to be savored.

Mike smiled as Samantha took a bite, her eyes lighting up with pleasure.

"Glad you like it," he said, settling beside her.

"It's perfect."

They both laughed, appreciating the calm. Music filled the room, the atmosphere warm and inviting. For now, it was just the two of them, wrapped in a peaceful bubble, far removed from the rest of the world.

Mike returned with a fresh cold compress and two glasses of wine, his caring nature evident in every movement.

"May I see?"

Samantha looked at him with a mix of trust and amusement.

"Of course, Dr. Mike," she teased, opening her robe slightly to reveal the affected area.

She wasn't wearing a bra. Her breast rested naturally, plush and unguarded, the gentle curve catching the light, highlighting her raw, unfiltered beauty. Even in this vulnerable state, her glow still came through.

Mike saw the swelling and discoloration, and his heart dropped once more. He knew how much she had endured that night at *Le Cher* all because she refused to let it end on someone else's terms.

He gently pressed the cold compress to her ribs. She closed her eyes and placed her hand over his, holding it as he treated her.

"Thank you for taking care of me." She rested her head against his shoulder.

A quiet beat of comfort and connection settled between them. The chaos of the outside world forgotten.

Samantha pointed for the CBD cream and Mike rubbed it onto her injured side. The sensation was soothing as the cream sank into her skin, easing deep into the muscle.

Within minutes, the dull ache that had nagged her all day began to fade. Mike followed it with the cold compress, applying it carefully for a double-action effect.

Feeling good, she couldn't help but smile as she signaled for him to come closer. She kissed his lips. A silent thank you wrapped in affection.

She was slowly developing real feelings for him. Her thoughts clear. She couldn't blame it on the alcohol, the meds, or even the heat of the moment.

It was him being here, showing up in ways that mattered. Helping her manage the aftermath of something traumatic, not with grand gestures, but with patience and care.

She found herself embracing it. The other guys? Slowly she was starting to forget about them.

Samantha had always kept men at arm's length, never allowing anyone close. But whatever happened that night at *Le Cher* had led her to this moment.

To Mike.
To right here, right now.

She reached for his hand as she lay there, rubbing it gently against hers. He had just finished treating her injured side. One of her favorite songs began to play over the speakers— "Footsteps in the Dark" by Cannons, (originally performed by The Isley Brothers.)

As the melody played, something inside her let go. She looked up at Mike, and with her opposite hand, slowly unbuckled his belt. He hesitated for a moment, concern visible across his face.

"Are you sure?" he asked, his hand brushing along her ribs.

"Just don't get on top," she whispered, low and teasing, mischief glinting in her eyes.

She sat up to kiss him, and as she did, her robe fell open, revealing her bare breasts. Mike reached up, cupping her gently. His touch was featherlight, yet the brush of his thumb over her nipple made her breath catch, the sensation washing over her.

She guided him closer, positioning him with care. As their bodies met, he entered her. Her lips parted in silent surrender, her arms instinctively wrapping around his neck.

Their movements matched the rhythm of the music. The sound enveloping around them, pulling them closer and amplifying the heat between them.

Mike pulled off his shirt, the warmth of their bare skin sending a shiver through Samantha. She climbed on top of him, her robe falling away from her body. She let out a sharp gasp, sitting lower on him. Mike started to sit up out of concern, but Samantha pushed him down, shaking her head no.

Slightly breathless, she looked down, their eyes locking with intensity. Then she began to sway, taking him in fully, each motion steeped in pleasure. Every twist of her hips made her moan, her lip caught between her teeth as she moved faster, more deliberately.

Mike laid back, watching her hair whip back and forth, her breasts bouncing in rhythm with each movement. He sat up, taking one into his mouth. He let his tongue dance across it. A breath caught in her throat, trembling out as she collapsed against him. Something in her gave way and she didn't want to stop it. She kissed his neck, then up to his ear.

Mike felt it. The twinge, the heat. She was wet, soaking him. The sensation made his own pleasure build fast. He felt her chest rising and falling with every breath, beads of sweat forming along her brow. He hugged her close, their slick bodies pressed together. And then, with a whip of her hair, she popped back up on top.

Her hips didn't stop, the moans spilling out louder now, nearly tipping into screams, as he kissed her all over.

Their climax neared, each movement more urgent than the last, both nearing the edge. Mike held her tighter, and they moved together, locked in rhythm.

Kissing. Grinding. Deeper. Slower. Then faster again.

Passionate, breathless strokes. Their bodies both completely in sync.

The song neared its end.

They erupted together.

Samantha grabbed him as she climaxed, her hair tumbling across her face. When she looked up, smiling, a dizzy rush swirled through her head. She fell into him, arms folding around his torso as she rested her head on his chest.

Mike, still inside her, kissed her forehead as she relaxed in his arms. Her breath slowed.

For the first time in what felt like forever, Samantha allowed herself to be fully present, safe, cared for, and deeply connected.

They lay together, letting the warmth settle over them.

Their last night of peace.

Tomorrow, everything would change.
Their paths set.
Their fates both already caught in the killer's web.

CHAPTERS 22-26

ORIGINS OF VENGEANCE

In these chapters, we peel back the layers of the killer's past, uncovering the deeply personal reasons behind his gruesome murders. Each victim is intricately tied to his life. Connected through betrayal, humiliation, direct harm, or even death. These influencers are not random targets. They are individuals who have profoundly wronged him and his family, leaving lasting scars.

The murders are acts of vindication and retribution, fueled by the physical and emotional losses he endured. Something inside him snapped. The toll of these injustices became unbearable. He could no longer turn the other cheek while his enemies thrived.

Them gaining followers, clout, wealth, and praise without facing consequences. To him, they embody everything he despises: narcissism, entitlement, egotism, and selfishness.

These influencers ruined his life. They took from him the people and things that mattered most. Now, he's determined to take everything from them. His revenge list is long, and he intends to cross off every name.

Each murder will grow more shocking, more theatrical, creating a wave of panic across the city. The police, stretched thin, scramble to keep up, chasing every lead with growing desperation. They know this killer must be stopped, and by any means necessary.

Yet amid the chaos, one name burns brightest in his mind: Samantha Sinclair.

Little does she know is that she is his ultimate prize. The culmination of his vendetta.

The package that disfigured Alison? It was never meant for Alison. It was meant for Samantha.

The killer would have been satisfied with maiming her. But Alison's mistake forced him to change his plan. Now, he can't afford to take chances. Samantha must die.

For Samantha, life will be a waking nightmare. Shaken by the murders, devastated by what happened to Alison, she struggles to make sense of it all. At first, she's unaware of her connection to the killer. But as he draws closer, the truth begins to surface. It becomes terrifyingly clear: the killer is fixated on her, and she's running out of time.

But Samantha won't be the same woman she once was. As the killer relentlessly pursues her, she will undergo a transformation. Shock, fear, and panic will give way to clarity, strength, and determination. She will realize she cannot rely on the police or anyone else to save her.

If she wants to survive, she'll have to fight for it. She'll have to become her own savior.

CHAPTER 22

THE VIRAL REVIEW OF DEATH

Eating With Jeff had a reputation that could make or break a restaurant. Known for his brutal honesty and refusal to accept sponsorships or collaborations, he prided himself on being untethered and free to deliver opinions without obligation. While his followers adored his unfiltered reviews, restaurant owners feared the power he wielded. His audience followed his praise, or condemnation like sheep.

When Jeff visited the family-owned restaurant, he had no idea the devastation he would leave behind.

The restaurant, run by a single mother and her son, was the family's pride and joy. She had poured their life savings into opening the business, hoping to bring the flavors of their homeland to the community.

"Welcome to our restaurant," the killer's uncle said warmly as Jeff entered. "We're so glad to have you here. Can I recommend a few dishes?"

"Yes, please," Jeff replied with a polite nod.

The killer, still heavyset at the time and working the counter, chimed in.

"These dishes are our specialties," he said with pride. "They're authentic recipes from our country and a representation of our culture. I think you'll really enjoy them."

Jeff smiled, ordered the suggested dishes, and even left a generous tip, as he always did. To the family, he seemed kind and approachable. A valued guest.

They had no idea he was a food reviewer with over two million followers nor that their livelihood would soon hang in the balance.

The Review Of Destruction

Jeff parked his crossover at a nearby park, angling his phone to capture the perfect frame. He adjusted the takeout containers in the passenger seat, set up his camera, and hit record.

"So today, I tried a new place," he began, holding up the neatly packaged food. He butchered the restaurant's name, stumbling through it with zero effort to get it right. "It's, uh… supposed to be authentic… something."

He waved dismissively at the containers, mispronouncing the dishes as he described them. His tone was flippant, but his followers didn't care. His ignorance was part of the charm.

Going through his usual ritual, he smeared black streaks under his eyes like a football player for something he called "Food Warrior Mode," a segment his fans ate up with every review.

"Alright, let's see how it hits on the JeffMeter," he said, grinning as a cheesy thermometer graphic flashed on-screen.

He took a bite of the first dish, paused dramatically, then spat it into a napkin with a loud gag.

"What is this?" he exclaimed, his face contorting in mock disgust. "It's trash. No flavor. No texture. Honestly, it's like they didn't even try. Just gross!"

What Jeff didn't realize, or perhaps refused to understand, was that he was butchering the entire meal. He treated the dishes, a cultural delicacy, like something he grabbed in a fast-food drive-through.

The sauces weren't meant to be dumped together. The food wasn't meant to be eaten cold, alone in a car. But that didn't stop him from tearing into it with misplaced confidence.

"This presentation is a joke," he continued, holding up the carefully plated meal as though it were garbage. The only thing he deemed passable was the drink, and even that praise came laced with backhanded remarks.

"I mean, this is... fine, I guess. But barely."

Leaning dramatically off-camera, he pretended to gag again.

"Nope, never again. Can't do it, won't do it. BLEH!" He slapped his hand on the dashboard for emphasis. "One star, and that's me being generous."

And with that, the JeffMeter plummeted and exploded on screen in a burst of flames, the word TRASH flashing across the graphic in bold red letters.

Satisfied with his performance, Jeff uploaded the video after a quick round of edits. All complete with his over-the-top reactions and snarky commentary. Within hours, the review exploded online, its fallout rippling far beyond his already massive following of over 5 million. His fans, ever loyal, descended on the restaurant's nonexistent digital presence with a wave of negativity.

Except, the restaurant didn't have a social media page, at least, not at first. They were an old-school, family-run business, relying on word of mouth and loyal locals to fill their tables. But Jeff's viral tirade forced their hand. Scrambling to do damage control, the owners hastily created social media profiles in hopes of reaching Jeff and setting the record straight.

The account was a humble start: a single photo of their storefront, accompanied by a caption pleading for understanding.

We are a small family-run restaurant. Jeff's video has hurt us deeply. Please let us explain.

They even tagged Jeff, hoping he would respond. But he never did.

To him, it was just another notch in his content creator belt. Another spectacle that earned him views, praise, and validation. While on the other side of the screen, he had crushed the livelihood of people he never even tried to understand.

The Full Tragedy Of The Killer's Mother

Eating With Jeff was never one for pleasantries when it came to his reviews. His brutal honesty, his refusal to accept compensation, and his unwavering commitment to his "authentic" experiences built his platform. But it also tore lives apart.

Jeff's visit to the family-owned restaurant should have been a crowning achievement for the single mother and her brother who ran it. It was supposed to be their labor of love, an effort to share their country's authentic cuisine with the community. They had poured every last cent into it, hoping to create something long-lasting for future generations. But Jeff's review destroyed that dream.

A Mother's Plea, A Family's Fall

The family's world began unraveling just days after *Eating With Jeff's* brutal review went live. The video spread like wildfire, racking up millions of views and reshares, prompting a flood of negative comments about their restaurant. Because the restaurant was located in a smaller town, the impact was even more devastating. Business plummeted, and the family struggled to understand how everything they had worked so hard to build could collapse in the blink of an eye.

The mother, desperate to save what she had built, turned to social media. After sending multiple DMs to Jeff's Instagram, pleading for a chance to make things right, she eventually decided to call him directly using Instagram's video feature.

When Jeff finally picked up, his face appeared on screen. Casual and disinterested.

"Mr. Jeff," she began, her voice trembling. The stress and tension were visible in her eyes and etched into her voice.

"Please, thank you for answering. I'm begging you… can you take down the review? Or maybe give us another chance? You can come back for a courtesy visit. Everything will be on us."

Jeff shook his head no. "I don't do reviews for compensation," he replied firmly. "That's not how I roll. I pay for my food, I tip, and I give my honest opinion. Accepting anything from you would compromise my authenticity."

"But you didn't understand our food," she said, her voice cracking as tears streamed down her cheeks. "It's meant to be eaten a certain way, and you didn't even pronounce the dishes correctly. You misrepresented everything. If you come back, I'll show you how to eat it and explain everything properly this time."

Jeff sighed. "Look, my review was based on my experience. That's what my followers expect, true honesty. However brutal it may be, that's what I give. I'm not taking it down, and I'm not doing a second review. It wouldn't be authentic."

His tone was smug.

"Authentic?" the mother exclaimed, her voice breaking. "You're destroying us! This was supposed to be our dream! You insulted our culture, our food… everything we worked for! Do you even care what you've done?"

She was both physically and emotionally exhausted, the gravity of the situation breaking her down in real time.

Jeff's expression hardened, now showing visible annoyance. "I'm sorry you're upset, but I'm not responsible for what happens to your business. My review is my opinion reflecting my genuine experience. If you message me again, I'll block you."

With that, he ended the call.

The mother stared at her screen in disbelief, hands slowly covering her face as she began to weep.

She knew, deep down, the days were numbered for their restaurant.

The Fallout

The mother tried to stay strong, but the wave of negative attention was overwhelming. Customers who came after Jeff's review weren't there to enjoy the food, they were there to find something wrong. Their complaints were loud, exaggerated, and cruel.

"Jeff was right about this place," some would mutter as they walked out.

The negativity surrounding the restaurant only grew. Despite a few loyal defenders trying to speak up in the comments, the damage was already done.

The worst was when customers left bad reviews right in front of them.
But what could they do?
They couldn't confront anyone. They couldn't accuse anyone.
And yet, they knew exactly what was happening.

Potential customers would pass by. Some, genuinely curious, would look up the restaurant from the sidewalk. But once they saw the viral post or the flood of one-star reviews, they'd shake their heads and keep walking.

Then came the health inspector, more thorough than usual, possibly influenced by the public outcry. Minor infractions that once might've warranted a warning were now enough to drop them a full grade.

Business dropped to nothing.

Within weeks, the restaurant couldn't turn a profit. Bills piled up. They lost their lease. At the same time, the landlord for their rented three-bedroom, three-bath townhome began pressuring them for overdue rent. Unable to keep up, the family was evicted.

The day they closed their doors was the mother's breaking point.

She stood outside the restaurant, tears streaming down her face as the landlord changed the locks. Then she collapsed to the sidewalk, weeping uncontrollably.

"I'm so sorry, Mom," the killer said, hugging her tightly.

"It's gone," she whispered. "Everything we worked for is gone."

Moving into a cramped two-bedroom, one-bath apartment was a blow that shattered her spirit. The once-vibrant woman who had radiated joy and pride now spent most of her days in silence, staring blankly out the window.

The killer, still heavyset and riddled with self-doubt, watched helplessly as the mother he adored slipped into a dark and devastating depression.

The only peace she found came from sleeping pills. And slowly, they became the only thing she could rely on.

"Mom," the killer said one evening, finding her alone at the kitchen table. "We'll figure something out. I'll find a way to make it better."

She didn't respond. She just shook her head.

"This was supposed to be different," she whispered. "This was supposed to be our future. Now it's gone."

The Breaking Point

One fateful afternoon, the killer and his uncle returned from a trip to the grocery store to find the apartment eerily silent.

"Mom?" the killer called out, his voice echoing through the tiny space.

They reached her bedroom and found her lying on the bed. Her face pale, still, and heartbreakingly serene.

An empty bottle of sleeping pills sat on the nightstand. It told them everything.

"No!" the killer screamed, collapsing to his knees beside her.

His uncle rushed forward, trying to shake her awake. But it was too late.

She was gone.

The killer sat frozen beside her lifeless body, tears streaming down his face.

Grief twisted in his chest. Then something darker crept in.

A resolve. A name.

"She's dead because of him," he whispered, voice trembling with fury.

"Because of Jeff."

The Eulogy

The day of his mother's funeral came with heavy rain, the sky's tears pouring down. It was hard to fathom that he had to bury his mother this way. She didn't deserve this. She had given so much.

She hadn't left much behind. The funeral was small and intimate. Just immediate family, including his aunt, whom he had always been close to. She was from his mother's side, and their bond had always been strong. She'd looked after him often growing up, and now, she was about to take him in, welcoming him into her home. He loved her deeply.

The killer stepped forward to give the eulogy.

"My mom just wanted to share her love for our homeland with people. Where we came from. She wanted to bring that here to the U.S. Her cooking wowed everyone, and she wanted to build something from that.

As an international student, she came here with nothing but a dream. And somehow, she made it work. She stayed. She built a life."

He took a breath, glancing at the casket.

"A few years later, she had me. I remember growing up, I was her little helper at pop-up events. I remember the lines of people waiting for her food. She would sell out fast."

His voice cracked slightly.

"And I remember the joy it brought her. To see how much people genuinely loved her food. She'd take future orders right there at the market. You could see how happy it made her, sharing herself and her heart through her cooking."

He blinked hard, his mind drifting to *Eating With Jeff.* Sadness and rage swelled inside him. For what had been taken. For his sweet, beloved mother. Still, he pushed through the eulogy.

"She believed food was a great unifier. That's why she put so much passion into her recipes. She never wanted to lose the joy of cooking."

He paused, then continued.

"She wanted me to take over, but I don't think I'm ready. Her recipes are like none other. She even tried to teach me. Her restaurant provided for us. She put me through school with it."

He stopped again.

"But I keep coming back to her joy. How she found happiness and purpose. How she provided for me after my father died so early in my life. Cooking gave her fulfillment. And through it, she made sure I never went without."

He swallowed.

"I will miss her.
I love you, Mom."

As the casket was lowered into the ground, the priest prayed over her body.
It was goodbye. One final, devastating goodbye.

Tears streamed down his face.
She was gone.
Taken far too soon, with so much more to give.

Planting The Seeds Of Vengeance

In the months that followed, the killer's sorrow hardened into rage. Jeff's indifferent dismissal of their family's pleas echoed in his mind. His mother's death wasn't just a tragedy. It was an injustice.

The killer would begin to transform himself, slowly and deliberately, shedding the weight and weakness he had carried for years. Every pound lost would be one step closer to the man he needed to become.

Eating With Jeff had taken everything from him.

Now, he would take something back.

He skimmed the pages of his mother's Bible for peace, flipping through pages that once brought his mother comfort. But only one verse spoke to him:
"An eye for an eye, and a tooth for a tooth."

Exodus 21:24

He stared at the words.

Then, slowly, he closed the Bible.

His decision was made.

He would figure out what mattered most to Jeff—and take it from him.

He would do it for his mother.

CHAPTER 23

PUBLICLY SHAMED, PRIVATELY BETRAYED

Months had passed since his mother's death. Her burial had left the killer in a haze of grief and anger. Now renting a studio apartment from his aunt, he tried to rebuild his life. In his culture, family looked after one another in times of crisis. Though cramped, the space offered a glimmer of support as he navigated his despair.

The killer worked a simple job as a forklift operator that allowed him to remain anonymous. He spent his days in isolation, his thoughts cycling through the tragic loss of his mother and the botched SWAT raid that had killed his father years ago when he was just a child. Losing his father, an innocent man, at the hands of an overzealous officer had scarred him deeply. Now, his mother's death, triggered by *Eating With Jeff's* scathing review, felt like a final blow.

But it wasn't going to be the final blow.

Grief fueled his emotional eating, and his obesity only deepened his isolation. One day, while scrolling through social media, he came across an ad for a weight loss program run by fitness influencers Jordan and Tabatha. Their promises of fast results and supportive coaching struck a chord. So he signed up.

Little did he know, the very people he trusted to guide his transformation would betray him. They would expose his vulnerabilities. And in time, both Jordan and Tabatha would become the next names on his list.

The Clout Couple

Jordan and Tabatha weren't just a fitness couple. They were a brand. With over 6 million subscribers, their fans were glued to their all-access YouTube channel: *Get Fit With Taby & Jay.*

Their joint page was a machine curated with slick edits, couples workouts, motivational content, "day in the life" videos, and viral challenges. But that was just the surface. They both had their own solo pages as well, each with hundreds of thousands of followers and fully monetized.

Together, they built a small fitness empire: sponsorships, cross-promos, paid brand deals, influencer cameos, and collabs with everyday people just hoping for a shot. Their DMs were packed with training requests, program sign-ups, and event invites.

Wake up. Work out. Post. Repeat.

But off-camera?

They were cold. Self-absorbed. Egotistical. Narcissistic.

They didn't truly care about their clients' success
They only pretended to.
Fake. No real support. Nothing genuine.

Everything was transactional.
If you didn't boost their clout, line their pockets, or fit their image, you didn't matter to them.

Jordan thrived on the admiration. Tabatha thrived on control. They fed off the attention. Every like, every view, and every comment was just another high.

On camera? They were the couple you wanted to be. Polished. Positive. Perfect.

In real life? They were the kind of influencers people rolled their eyes at, with their constant theatrics.

And as the killer came to learn… there was nothing inspiring about them at all.

The Start Of The Program

At first, the killer found solace in the program. Jordan and Tabatha were charismatic, their enthusiasm infectious. They seemed genuinely invested in his progress by offering personalized support through group chats and one-on-one calls. They guided him through meal plans and workouts, always peppering their messages with motivational platitudes.

"You've got this," Tabatha wrote one evening. "Small steps lead to big changes."

"Thank you for your support!" he replied, feeling a flicker of hope.

"We'll make sure you're unstoppable," Jordan chimed in.

The exercises were grueling and often left him sore, but he appreciated their patience. Their consistent encouragement kept him going.

Until the cracks began to show. It started when they suggested he begin filming his journey. For content. For their growing channel. At first, he hesitated. The request felt invasive.

"I'm camera shy, guys," he said during one of their accountability sessions. "I'm more comfortable behind the scenes. I'll take a before-and-after photo, but that's as far as I'll go."

Jordan and Tabatha exchanged a subtle glance, their smiles tightening.

"It's just not the same," Tabatha said, leaning closer. "We want people to connect with your journey. You'd be a real-life inspiration for others like you. For people afraid to take that first step."

"I don't know..." the killer began, uneasy. "I just don't think I can do it."

Jordan cut him off, striding over and clapping a hand on his shoulder.

"Listen, man. We've been here for you since day one. This journey? It's not just yours, it's ours too. Me, Taby, and you... all teamwork, bro. Together, we can inspire so many people."

"I get that," the killer replied hesitantly, "but I'm just not comfortable being on camera."

"You sought us out because you wanted to change," Jordan pressed, his tone firm but friendly. "And by showing your story, we're helping others who don't even know where to start. It's bigger than just you."

"Seek and ye shall find," Tabatha added smoothly, her tone almost reverent.

"Exactly!" Jordan nodded, feeding off her energy. "And what they'll find is us. Our program. Transforming you means showing everyone else we can transform them too. It's really inspiring."

"And impactful!" Tabatha beamed.
"Yes!" Jordan chimed in again.
"Your weight loss journey will be impactful for others. So many people are in your shoes," he added pointedly.

Their words overlapped, each feeding into the other, like a well-practiced pitch perfected over time. But beneath their smiles and encouragement, there was an unmistakable undertone of exploitation. This wasn't about helping him. It was about branding.

They wanted him to be the proof of their method. A walking, talking advertisement. He would be their prop.

Jordan and Tabatha saw him as the perfect before-and-after case. If they could make it work on him, they could sell the dream to everyone else who was obese. All they saw was a cash grab.

"You let us document the journey," Jordan continued, his voice dripping with faux camaraderie, "and we'll hook you up with even more support. All access! Personalized sessions, advanced plans, all the meal prep, the works. And it'll cost you next to nothing. Think about it, bro."

He slapped the killer hard on the upper back, the sting remaining longer than expected. Tabatha smiled wide, nodding along.

"We're only after your best interest and your health," she added with mock sincerity.

"Just think about it," Jordan said again. His tone now more of a command than a suggestion.

Their Escalade was pulled up outside the DTLA gym, gleaming and pristine. They walked off without waiting for a response. Their departure was as abrupt as their pitch.

The killer stood there, silent. For the first time, he began to question their motives. What had started as a glimmer of hope now felt like a trap. A trap lined with smiles, hidden agendas, and manipulation.

Their encouragement had strings.
And he wasn't sure he wanted to pull any of them.

A Shift In Attitudes

Several weeks passed, and while the killer had lost about 20 pounds, his progress was slow. Emotional eating continued to hold him back, a fact that didn't sit well with Jordan and Tabatha. During an accountability session after a grueling workout, their patience finally snapped.

"Look, bro," Jordan said bluntly, crossing his arms. "We're giving you the tools, but you're still fat. I don't get it. Do you, Taby?"

Tabatha tilted her head, her tone dripping with false sweetness. "No, honey, I don't. Especially since I've been cooking all your meal preps personally and you're still not following through."

"This is a three-part program," Jordan continued, his voice rising with frustration. "The shit works. It's proven, man. You gotta stick to the script for total success." He shook his head in disgust, looking the killer up and down.

The killer bristled, feeling the sting of their words. "I'm dealing with some personal issues," he said, trying to keep his composure.

Tabatha scoffed, mirroring Jordan's disdain. "And your weight's gonna cause more issues if you don't get it together. Do you want to stay some fat ass no woman would ever touch?" She laughed, her tone mocking. "You're like a real-life Eric Cartman!"

Jordan smirked, leaning into the insult. "She's right, man. Women look at us the same way we look at them. No one wants to roll over on a blimp in bed."

"I really don't think this is what I signed up for," the killer said, his voice trembling as he protested their harsh treatment.

Jordan got up from his seat, walking over to loom over him. "Hey, bud, look. If we're being harsh, it's because it's time for some tough love."

"Tough love because we care!" Tabatha chimed in, positioning herself next to the killer.

"Because we care," Jordan reaffirmed, pointing at her. "All we're hearing are excuses. And you know what? It's time for the excuses and limiting beliefs to stop."

"That's right! Once the excuses stop, the results can start," Tabatha said, her tone softening just enough to seem reassuring. "But you have to stick to the program. We're giving you the tools because we care about your progress."

The killer nodded, trying to absorb this new, harsher form of motivation. "I'll try harder, I promise."

Jordan's demeanor darkened. "Yeah, you said that the last two accountability sessions, and your fat ass is still struggling to keep up with the class. That's why we've been giving you these extra one-on-one sessions for free the past two weeks. We're investing in you, man. You've gotta invest in yourself."

Tabatha threw her hands in the air, exasperated. "You can lead a horse to water…"

"…but you can't make him drink," Jordan finished, the two of them exchanging smug grins.

"If you're not gonna follow through, this program isn't gonna work for you," Jordan said sharply.

"And then where will you be? Some stinky fat guy no woman will touch unless you pay for it like some John," Tabatha said, her tone condescending.

Jordan added with a cruel grin, "That's if you can even find your junk under all that fat to make it happen."

They both burst out laughing at their own crass joke, their mockery echoing in the killer's ears.

Humiliated and on the verge of tears, the killer excused himself, mumbling something about needing air. He stepped outside the gym, fists clenched.

For the first time, the killer felt a simmering anger bubbling beneath his shame.

It was no longer just about losing weight. Now, it was about something more.

The Clip That Broke Him

During a group workout session, Jordan and Tabatha recorded their class for their fitness channel, *Get Fit with Taby & Jay*. The killer already knew since everyone had signed waivers. What he didn't realize was that they were specifically targeting him, filming his worst lows to turn them into viral content.

One particularly grueling session pushed him past his limit. Exhausted, overheated, and humiliated, he lost control and soiled himself mid-squat.

They caught it all on camera.

Later that night, the footage became the centerpiece of their newest upload:
POV: Your Worst Gym Nightmare.

Right as it happened, they added a cartoon fart sound. The screen zoomed in on his horrified face, froze in place, and cut to a slow-motion replay with meme text and dramatic music.

Then came the final stamp:
WORKOUT FAIL, splashed across the screen in bold red letters.

Jordan's voice came in, smug and casual:
"Don't be this guy."

The internet laughed.
Jordan and Tabatha gained thousands of new followers across their platforms.
And the killer became a joke.

He wasn't a client.
He wasn't a person.
He was content.

The Confrontation

The killer couldn't hold back his fury any longer. The humiliation, the betrayal, the violation, it had all built to a breaking point. After the grueling session, he waited for the class to thin out, eyes locked on Jordan and Tabatha. Then he stormed toward them, his face flushed with rage.

"I told you not to film me!" he shouted, his voice echoing off the gym walls. "You've ruined my life!"

Tabatha turned, calm and almost amused. "You agreed to the program. Filming is part of the deal. You signed the waiver, remember?"

"Not like this," he snapped, voice breaking. "I didn't agree to be mocked and paraded like some fucking joke!"

Jordan, grinning, leaned lazily against one of the spin bikes.
"You're a viral hit, bro. You should be thanking us. You're Insta-famous! And best of all, you inspired others to join the program." His smugness only poured fuel on the fire.

"Fuck you, Jordan!" the killer roared, lunging forward and shoving him hard. Jordan stumbled back against a machine, his shirt pulled in the scuffle.

"You asshole," the killer spat, chest heaving.

Jordan's smile disappeared.

He lashed out fast and hard. A brutal two-punch combo landed squarely on the killer's nose and jaw, sending him sprawling to the floor. Blood dripped down his face.

But Jordan wasn't finished. With fury in his eyes, he delivered a sharp kick to the killer's ribs, knocking the wind from his lungs.

"Jordan, stop!" Tabatha shouted, grabbing his arm to pull him back. "Stop!"

He let her, but the damage was done.

The killer lay there, bloodied, humiliated, wheezing. Jordan straightened his shirt, his grin returning.

"It's funny when fat people fall," he said coldly, towering over him. "I think the ground actually shook."

He laughed. Tabatha rolled her eyes, but a faint smile tugged at her lips.

"You're such an ass," she said, brushing her hand along his arm condoning everything.

Across the gym, a staff member gasped as she witnessed the scuffle unfolding.

"Oh my gosh! No, no, no," she called out, rushing forward a few steps. "You can't do that. Stay here. I'm getting the manager."

She turned and bolted. "Greyson! Greyson, there's an altercation happening. It's Jordan and Tabatha again!"

But it wouldn't matter.
Security footage would show the killer as the one who threw the first shove.

Jordan would claim self-defense, and it would stick. Jordan and Tabatha gathered their things, completely unfazed. They ignored the staff's concerned glances and the GM's attempts to stop them as they headed for the valet.

To them, it was nothing, just a hiccup. A chance to flex on someone beneath them. They were protected by clout, money, and the security footage backing up their version of events.

The killer remained on the ground, blood pooling beneath his nose. His dignity shattered. A few staff members rushed to help bringing tissues and towels. Their concern evident. But their sympathy only deepened the sting.

Outside, Jordan and Tabatha climbed into their sleek black Escalade, laughing as if nothing had happened.

To them, he wasn't a person. Just a prop.

They drove off, leaving chaos behind.

And inside the man they had humiliated, something dangerous began to take root.

Bruised And Bloodied

With the help of concerned staff, the killer was brought to his feet. He winced, dabbing at his swelling jaw as pain radiated through his ribs with every breath. A few minutes later, Greyson, the general manager, appeared. He was led by the young woman who had witnessed the entire confrontation and rushed to get him.

Greyson's expression was calm, but his eyes darted between the injured man and the now-empty doorway where Jordan and Tabatha had walked out.

"I'm so sorry this happened," Greyson said, polite but measured. "Are you okay? Do you need medical assistance?"

The killer shook his head, voice hoarse. "No. I'll be fine."

"Let's at least get you off your feet." He gestured to a nearby chair. "Sit. I'll grab you some water."

As Greyson turned, he looked to the woman at his side. "Celine, please grab more towels and an ice pack."

"Of course," she said, already moving.

Moments later, she returned, standing nearby with everything in hand holding them out carefully. Greyson nodded his thanks. She hovered close, but kept her eyes on the floor.

"Can you walk me through what happened?" Greyson asked gently, crouching slightly to meet the killer's eye level.

The killer rubbed the back of his neck with the ice pack, still avoiding direct eye contact. "They've been humiliating me online. I just… I snapped. But I pushed him first. I shouldn't have done that."

Celine cleared her throat. "I saw it happen, Greyson. He's telling the truth. Jordan was provoking him the whole time."

Greyson nodded, his voice even. "I see. All physical altercations are serious, no matter who starts them. We'll need to investigate this."

The killer looked down. "I just lost my temper. It won't happen again."

"I appreciate your honesty," Greyson said, his voice still neutral. "I'll need to review the security footage to understand the full situation. For now, let's focus on making sure you're okay. That's the priority."

The killer nodded reluctantly, sipping his water.

Greyson excused himself, promising to follow up. But once he turned away, his expression hardened. He walked briskly toward his office, pulling out his phone to call corporate. His tone stayed professional, but frustration simmered beneath the surface.

Jordan and Tabatha had pushed boundaries before. This? This crossed a line.

Still, he said nothing. The gym's reputation, and his own, depended on discretion.

Meanwhile, the killer sat silently, surrounded by well-meaning staff unsure how to comfort him. Their concern felt hollow. It couldn't undo what had just happened.

No apology, no corporate policy, not even a desperate call to headquarters could erase this.

This wasn't over.

Not for him.

Jordan And Tabatha Get Away With It Again

Greyson stormed into his office, slamming the door behind him. His jaw clenched as he picked up the phone and dialed Darren, the regional manager at corporate.

"Hey Darren, it's Greyson. We've got another issue with Jordan and Tabatha. Specifically Jordan. I think this is it for him. He physically assaulted a guest."

Darren's voice came through, calm but firm. "That's a serious accusation. Were there any witnesses?"

"Some staff heard the aftermath. I was notified immediately. Darren, this is just one more problem in a long list. It's time we revoke their membership."

"Hold on," Darren said. "Let's take this step by step. Have you looked at the cameras?"

"I'm pulling them up now." Greyson's fingers clacked aggressively on the keyboard, irritation spilling into every movement.

"Good. Let's see what the footage shows. We can't act rashly," Darren said, measured as ever.

Greyson gritted his teeth, eyes locked on the screen. After a brief pause, he spoke again.

"There. Jordan punches the guy. Twice. Then kicks him while he's down. This was brutal, Darren. We need to act."

"Were the police called?" Darren asked.

"He's hesitant, but I'm going to ask him again."

"Alright. Let's look at the footage together once again," Darren said. "Share your screen."

Greyson clicked into the gym's camera system and hit PLAY hard. "Watch how Jordan reacts. This wasn't self-defense. This was excessive."

They watched in silence.

Then Darren spoke. "Back it up. Do you see it?"

"See what?" Greyson snapped.

"Wait, pause it here," Darren said. "The guest shoved Jordan first. That's an act of aggression."

Greyson pleaded his case. "So? Look at how Jordan escalates it! That kick alone. He could've broken a rib!"

Darren's voice didn't budge. "It's self-defense. The shove initiated the physical contact. Jordan had every right to defend himself."

Greyson threw up his hands. "He responded by punching the guy twice and kicking him in the ribs!"

"Greyson, we have to be consistent. Jordan was physically assaulted first. That's the story. In fact, the footage supports revoking his membership. Not Jordan's."

Greyson sat back in disbelief. "You've got to be kidding me."

"Jordan and Tabatha bring in positive press and traffic. This isn't grounds for banning them," Darren said, finality creeping into his tone. "Tell the guy his membership will be terminated. His behavior leaves us no choice."

Greyson swallowed his frustration. "At least give me time to break it to him."

"Wrap it up by the end of the week. Don't waste too much energy on this. It's a clear-cut case." Darren ended the call.

Greyson sat back, his eyes fixed on the ceiling in defeat. His attempt to hold Jordan and Tabatha accountable had backfired spectacularly.

Now he had to tell the injured guest, the man who had been mocked, punched, and kicked, that he was no longer welcome at the gym.

Once again, Jordan and Tabatha walked away unscathed. And Greyson was left to clean up the mess.

The Turning Point

Greyson let out a heavy sigh as he hung up the phone. The frustration from his conversation with Darren lingered, but he knew he had to stay composed. Pushing back his chair, he stood and made his way out of the office.

The killer sat silently in the lounge area, head down, a bloodied towel pressed against his face. Greyson approached with a professional demeanor, careful not to betray the storm raging inside him.

"Thank you for your patience," he began. "I want you to know we're taking this seriously. There's going to be an internal investigation, and I'll be in touch once it's completed."

The killer looked up, his eyes clouded with a mixture of hurt and simmering anger.

"I understand," he said,. "I'm not going to call the police. I don't want anything. This isn't your fault. I don't need to go to the hospital. But what happened today…"

He paused, swallowing hard.

"It's deeply upsetting. Still, I appreciate your concern, and how quickly you addressed this."

Greyson nodded, keeping his expression neutral. "I'm sorry this happened. We'll do our best to get to the bottom of it. I'll be in touch, but please don't hesitate to reach out if you need anything in the meantime."

"Thank you," the killer replied, standing slowly.

As Greyson walked away, the killer stayed motionless, his mind racing. The ache in his ribs and the sting of humiliation were nothing compared to the fire building inside him.

This would be the last time he was a victim.

The bullying. The mockery. The sheer disregard for his dignity.

It ended here.

Something inside him had shifted.

A part of himself he hadn't known existed was now fully awake.

He wasn't seeking justice anymore.

Justice was too kind.

He wanted Jordan and Tabatha to suffer for every moment they do to humiliate him.
This day marked the beginning of something new.

He was no longer the man who had entered the gym that same morning.

The King And Queen Of Cringe

Jordan and Tabatha parked their blacked-out Escalade in a secluded spot, far from prying eyes. Their adrenaline from the gym incident hadn't faded. It had twisted into something primal.

Tabatha, aroused by Jordan's display of dominance, rushed him. Their kisses grew frantic, hands roaming, breath hitching as they tugged clumsily at each other's clothes.

Tabatha straddled Jordan, her movements rushed and uncoordinated as she yanked off her top. Her flat, muscular frame stayed rigid as she pushed in for another kiss.

Their passion, though intense, was far from elegant. It was awkward, loud, over the top, a chaotic clash of egos masquerading as intimacy.

Tabatha moaned dramatically. "Rock me! Oh yes! Rock me!" She threw her head back theatrically, her movements stiff and robotic.

She was wearing a tennis skirt, making it easy for Jordan.

"Oh, I'm gonna. You want this?!" he grinned smugly, flexing his muscles.

The SUV started rocking, but not smoothly. Tabatha bounced up and down in a jerky rhythm, her head banging against the ceiling a couple of times. She didn't seem to care.

"Yes, yes! Oh God, yes!" Her tone was more aggressive than sensual.

Jordan grabbed her waist, his grip overly firm as if he were performing for an invisible audience, chest puffed out.
"You like that? You like all this power?" he grunted, his movements just as offbeat and graceless as hers.

"Oh yeah! Oh yeah!" she screamed, her volume comically excessive.

"I'm gonna take you to the moon and back!" Jordan shouted, his hands awkwardly patting his chest like he was hyping himself up.

"Take me there, baby!" she squealed, her voice hitting a pitch more shrill than seductive. She tried tossing her hair back, but it snagged on the headrest. Yanking it free without missing a beat, she let out a little scream.

The two moved faster, their efforts looking more like a workout gone wrong than a romantic encounter. Jordan's grunts grew louder, blending with Tabatha's nonsensical cries.

"Fuck me! Fuck me harder!" she screamed, her tone swinging wildly between demanding and absurd.

"I'm the king, baby!" Jordan roared, smacking the Escalade's roof like he was about to bench press the entire SUV. Pure theatrics.

"Yes, King Jordan! Yes! Yes! Oh my God, yes!" Tabatha howled, her arms flailing as she tried to exaggerate her movements even more. One wild swing sent her elbow banging into the window with a dull thud. She let out a little "oof" but didn't miss a beat.

Finally, they let out synchronized screams, though it sounded more like pain than ecstasy. Tabatha collapsed against Jordan, panting like she'd just run a marathon. Jordan, smirking smugly, clearly pleased with himself.

The SUV fell silent except for their ragged breathing. The windows fogged over, but the atmosphere wasn't steamy. It was cringe-worthy awkward, like an overacted scene from a bad reality show.

"That was incredible," Tabatha said, her tone breathless but unconvincing as she reached for her tank top.

"Yeah," Jordan replied, flexing again. "You're welcome."

Their love wasn't tender or intimate. It was built on ego, spectacle, and narcissism, culminating in an unromantic romp that said more about their need to perform than to connect.

And once again, they got away with everything.

A Dark Resolve

The backlash from the viral incident hit hard. The killer quit the program and left his job soon after, retreating into isolation as he spiraled into a deep, consuming depression. Even his gym membership was revoked for instigating the altercation.

Twice now, influencers had shattered his life. First Jeff. Now Jordan and Tabatha. They all had one thing in common: a relentless pursuit of fame and profit at the expense of others.

Narcissistic. Self-absorbed. Main character syndrome, embodied.

Sitting alone in his room, he stared into the mirror. The pain and humiliation etched on his face were hardening into something else, a dark resolve. His transformation wouldn't just be physical. It would be psychological.

It started now.
He would no longer be the victim.
He would take control.
One by one, they would pay.

CHAPTER 24

THE BALLAD OF AUNTIE GLORIA

onths after the killer set out to reclaim his life and plan his revenge, his aunt, the family matriarch who took him in, was finally close to achieving her lifelong dream of buying her first home. She had immigrated to the United States in pursuit of the American Dream, and now, after years of sacrifice, that dream was within reach. The house was modest. Three bedrooms, two bathrooms, but it was everything to her.

Now, she'd entrusted the home-buying process to Carly Rivers, who had quickly built her own brokerage, *Rivers Luxury Properties,* gaining a reputation for her flashy personality and an Instagram feed packed with luxury homes and glowing testimonials.

From the start, the killer had been skeptical. Carly's wide, toothy smile felt performative. Her constant need to "create content" during showings came off as self-serving, and her wardrobe didn't exactly scream professionalism. With a full menu of cosmetic enhancements, including lip fillers, Botox, breast implants, and a conspicuously sculpted BBL, Carly seemed less like a professional and more like someone cast to "play realtor" in a TikTok skit.

Hair extensions, long lashes, and claw-like nails completed the look. She wore smart glasses, not to see better, but to be seen. Always filming. Always branding. Stylish in her mind. Clueless in his. But his aunt was charmed. She liked the "Miss Busy Cute Real Estate Girl" routine.

"She's got connections," she said one evening, scrolling through Carly's carefully curated feed. "She's young, energetic, and knows what she's doing. She found this place quick!"

He tried to push back, but his aunt waved him off. "This is my dream, not yours," she said firmly.

All Glitter, No Glitz

The house Carly had found seemed perfect at first glance: freshly painted walls, a cozy backyard, and a location close to the family's community. It was in the Franklin Hills area of Los Angeles. But the killer noticed cracks, both literal and metaphorical.

"I'm telling you, Auntie, this place doesn't look right," he said one afternoon as they toured the property. He pointed to water stains faintly visible behind the newly painted drywall, uneven floors that creaked ominously, and a musty smell hovering in the air. "It's like they're covering something up."

Carly, ever attentive, swooped in before his aunt could respond. "Oh, don't worry about that. All older homes have their quirks," she said, her voice honeyed with reassurance. Flashing her signature dazzling smile, she added, "This one's a steal at this price. Trust me, I wouldn't let you sign on a bad deal."

His aunt looked unsure, but Carly brushed it off, lowering her voice like she was sharing a secret.

"This neighborhood? It's well-to-do. In a year or two, this house will double in value," she said.. "And you're getting it for thirty-five thousand below asking. That's practically unheard of in this market!"

His aunt's skepticism wavered, but she didn't fold just yet.
"Since this is a fixer-upper, forty-two thousand below asking would be better," she said thoughtfully. "That'd leave more room for the things I actually want to do with it."

Carly didn't even pause. "Yes! Absolutely. Forty-two thousand below asking gives you a ton of flexibility. I'm going to be real with you, this is pre-pandemic pricing for this neighborhood. You're getting a fixer-upper, sure. But one with bones and location. You will not find turnkey in Franklin Hills for this price. Not even close."

"You really think it'll go up that fast?" her aunt asked.

"I *know* it will," Carly answered without hesitation.. "And don't worry, I know people who will make this house fab."

The killer stayed silent, watching his aunt's defenses crumble. She was putty in Carly's hands.

Then, Carly's phone buzzed. Her face lit up. "Forty-two thousand below asking is confirmed!"

His aunt beamed, excitement flooding her face.

"There's a small but," Carly added smoothly, as if it were barely a wrinkle. "You'll just need to sign a couple of disclosures and a hold harmless agreement. Since you're getting such a deal, the sellers don't want to be on the hook for repairs."

"What kind of repairs?" the killer asked.

Carly turned to him, her voice clipped but composed. "It's a fixer-upper, *like* we said. Nothing scary. Just modern updates. Totally normal in this kind of situation."

His aunt hesitated. "I'm okay with that… as long as it's not major."

"It won't be. You're going to love making this your own," Carly assured her, gently guiding her toward the next room to begin preparing the paperwork for escrow.

The killer stood back, frustration simmering as his aunt, swept up in Carly's confident pitch, agreed to everything and signed her life away. Outside, Carly practically glowed as she recorded a manifestation-style Instagram video with the caption:

Another family finds their dream home! So blessed to make this happen for them! #DreamHome #Manifest #RealtorLife #Sold

She tagged the aunt, smiled wide, and posted.

The killer remained in the background, silent. The cracks he had spotted in the house now mirrored a bigger realization. No one was really listening to him. Not about the house. Not about his instincts. And soon, not even about what would come next.

Creaks, Leaks, And Band-Aid Fixes

The first several weeks felt good. His aunt celebrated with everyone, hosting dinner parties that filled the house with laughter, joy, and music. Family visited often. She turned the patio into a cozy haven, stringing up lights and surrounding it with potted plants. The house itself was quaint, tucked away on a shady low-traffic street, had a tree out front that cast just enough shade to make it feel like home.

But just after Thanksgiving, the shine began to wear off. The creaks grew louder. The leaks came more often. And those quick band-aid fixes? They were peeling away, revealing everything she'd tried not to see.

It didn't take long for the "dream home" to turn into a nightmare.

Within months, the roof began leaking during a heavy rainstorm. Not long after, the plumbing gave out.Severely outdated, with frequent backups she hadn't been warned about. Mold crept through the basement, and the issues kept piling up, each one more costly than the last.

She tried to stay hopeful, but the house was falling apart faster than she could hold it together. The aunt video-called Carly in desperation, but her tone had shifted.

"You bought the house as-is," Carly said curtly during a phone call. "These are issues you're going to have to fix. Just call a contractor; they'll fix it up in no time."

"But I don't have the money for all this!" the aunt cried. "You said the repairs weren't excessive. You said,"

"Look, I understand you're frustrated," Carly interrupted, her patience thinning. "But you signed the papers. You signed the disclosures and the hold harmless agreement. You knew what you were getting. My job was to find you a home, and I did. You're a homeowner now. Congratulations. Bye-bye now."

The killer listened to the conversation from the next room, his fists clenched. He wanted to grab the phone and confront Carly himself, but his aunt shook her head, tears streaming down her face.

"We'll figure it out," she whispered.

This wasn't the time for "I told you so's." His aunt was hurting, scared, and vulnerable. This was a time to support her, to stay by her side, and to help financially however he could.His entire focus was on that. But his anger brewed at the mess Carly had caused for his aunt.

The Writing's On The Wall

Figuring it out wasn't an option. The mounting repairs drained his aunt's savings, and when she couldn't keep up with the mortgage, the foreclosure notices started arriving. She was on the brink of losing everything.

Carly, meanwhile, had already moved on. She was posting new listings, flaunting her wins at influencer events, and celebrating her latest sales. To her, the aunt was just another closed deal.

One evening, the killer confronted his aunt after dinner.

"Why didn't you listen to me?" he asked, his voice shaking with anger and frustration.

She looked up, her eyes hollow. "I wanted to believe her," she confessed. "She made me feel like I could finally have something of my own."

"But now we're worse off. Everything's in limbo. She wins, and you lose."

His aunt didn't argue. "I just wanted to believe she was a good person. I took her at face value. I was wrong."

She stood up, taking a bottle of wine with her as she left the table. Drinking had become her only escape. Her words gutted him. First his mother, now his aunt. Both left broken by influencers who came into their lives and delivered ruin.

Rock Bottom In Pink Satin

The day the foreclosure notice arrived, something inside the killer shifted.

His aunt's sobs echoed through the house, heartbreak woven into every box she packed. Though they managed to short-sell the house before the foreclosure was finalized, the damage was done. Her financial stability was obliterated. She still owed the bank a significant balance, and they were preparing to sue her for it. Her credit was destroyed. Her dream of a better life, gone. The family would have to return to a cramped apartment, a bitter reminder of everything they'd lost.

"Drinking isn't the way to handle this," the killer said calmly, watching her stagger into the living room. It was the middle of the afternoon, but she was still in her pink and white satin nightgown, stained with wine and days of neglect. Her hair was matted, her breath sour with stale alcohol.

"Just leave me alone and let me cope. Or get out!" she snapped, her voice slurred. Her trembling hands rummaged through the kitchen drawers for another bottle of wine. When she found one, she fumbled with the corkscrew, struggling to open it.

The killer stood silently, his disapproval heavy in the air. She finally pulled the cork free but stumbled backward in the process, splashing wine across her chest.

"Just let me enjoy my last few nights here!" she shouted, pain cracking through her voice. "Just allow me that peace damn it!"

"I'm trying to help you," he said, his voice tight with frustration.

"Leave now, damn you!" she screamed, clutching the bottle like a lifeline. She staggered toward her bedroom, using the wall for support.

He didn't follow. He simply grabbed his coat and walked out.

"I'll come back when you're sober. However few hours that lasts," he muttered, slamming the door behind him.

Left alone, she finally had the silence she'd been chasing. Sitting on the edge of her bed, she poured another glass of wine. After a long pause, she reached for the muscle relaxers on her nightstand and popped one into her mouth. Relief swept through her almost instantly, a welcome numbness.

She didn't care anymore. Not about the house. Not about the lawsuit. Not even about herself.

Laying against the headboard, she clutched the wine glass in her hand. The stains on her gown, the boxes in the hallway, the foreclosure notice crumpled on the floor, all of it faded into the background as she slipped into unconsciousness.

For now, the pain gave way. Numbed by alcohol, dulled by pills, buried beneath the wreckage of a dream that wouldn't be coming back.

The Meltdown

The day had come. It was time to leave the house for good. Gloria had locked herself in the bathroom, dragging out every second she could in the place she once called her dream home. Inside, she hummed a familiar tune, off-key and unsteady, as she took swigs straight from a wine bottle she'd snuck in. Her eyes landed on the pill bottles on the counter. With a resigned sigh, she popped two into her mouth and chased them with wine, letting the mix blur her emotions into something dull and distant.

When she finally emerged, she wore jeans and an oversized T-shirt. Her hair was tangled, her movements sluggish. Outside, the family was already loading boxes into the moving truck. She made a lazy attempt to help but mostly loitered, swaying, shouting the occasional unhelpful direction.

"She's no use like this," a family member muttered, but no one intervened. They knew she was too far gone.

Gloria drifted through the house like a ghost, grazing the walls, murmuring slurred goodbyes to the rooms. Her tone bounced erratically between wistful and weirdly cheerful, as if she were trying to pretend the collapse wasn't happening in real time.

The killer couldn't take it anymore. He pulled her aside, voice tight with frustration.
"Auntie Gloria, what kind of example are you setting for everyone?"

"What do you want from me?" she snapped, her speech thick. "I'm at peace. It's over. I've accepted it."

"You're not at peace. You're drunk, taking pills. And you're embarrassing yourself. You're not helping anyone."

Their exchange drew glances. A younger cousin approached cautiously.
"Is she okay?"

"She needs to lie down," the killer muttered, trying to protect her dignity.

"I'm not lying down!" Gloria screamed, suddenly lunging and shoving him in the chest. He caught her wrists, restraining her gently but firmly, guiding her into a chair.

One of the uncles shook his head. "This is out of control. Get her out of here before this turns into a scene."

Gloria lashed out again, venom in her voice. "I don't need any of you! Piss off!"

An elder stepped forward without a word and slapped her. The crack echoed through the nearly empty house.

"Get it together!"

Gloria blinked, stunned. She tried to fight back, but her limbs were heavy, uncoordinated. She sagged into the chair, muttering curses through gritted teeth.

The killer stepped in again, calmer now.
"If we don't get her out of here, we'll never finish this move. Just… take her somewhere. Anywhere."

The family exchanged looks. Two cousins stepped in and gently lifted Gloria. She flailed half-heartedly, but offered no real resistance. As they carried her toward the car, she mumbled incoherently. The door shut behind her with a dull thud.

The rest of the family returned to the task in tense silence, the weight of her breakdown hanging in the air.

At The Bottom Of The Bottle

The day that would forever change the killer's family was drawing near. Weeks after the short sale, his aunt Gloria had fallen even deeper into darkness. Refusing help from anyone, she spent her nights drinking in bars and often woke with no memory of how she got home... or who she was with.

One night, she brought a man from a bar back to the house she'd already sold. It was still in escrow, technically hers for now, but she knew the end was near. Still, she clung to the keys like they meant something.

They slept together on a makeshift pallet on the floor. When she woke the next morning, she stared at the stranger beside her, feeling numb, hollow, and ashamed, then slipped out without a word and started drinking again.

Her family, desperate to stabilize her, gave her a private room in their already-cramped two-bedroom apartment. But no amount of kindness seemed to help. Gloria rarely came home, often disappearing for days at a time. And when she did, she was either too drunk or too hungover to speak. She refused any intervention, and the drinking only got worse.

In the days before the accident, from October 11th to 14th, Gloria drank heavily every day. Her days and nights blurred into a haze of alcohol and pills. On October 15th, her life and the lives of several others changed forever.

When The Demons Took The Wheel

On October 15th, in the mid-afternoon, Gloria decided to drive to the store. She was intoxicated, heavily impaired by both alcohol and prescription drugs. As she merged onto the 405 freeway, her eyelids grew heavy, and she fell asleep at the wheel. Her car veered into oncoming traffic, triggering a devastating multi-car pileup.

The aftermath was horrifying. A husband and wife in one of the vehicles were killed instantly. Rescue teams managed to free their toddler from the wreckage, but the child would now face life as an orphan. The freeway was shut down for hours. Debris scattered everywhere. Multiple injuries. Twisted metal. Sirens. The scene was chaos. Flashing lights, emergency personnel, and the anguished cries of shaken witnesses.

Gloria was pulled from her vehicle with a deep gash above her brow, bruising along her ribs, and a sprained wrist. Miraculously, she was otherwise intact. A toxicology report was taken, and authorities awaited confirmation. Once the results were in, her fate would be sealed. She'd be facing a slew of charges.

Trial By The Comments Section

The news spread like wildfire. The crash dominated headlines, with photos of the mangled vehicles plastered across every media outlet. By evening, every local news station was covering the tragedy.

A suspected DUI driver caused a fatal crash on the 405 Freeway earlier today, one report read. *Two people are dead, a child is hospitalized, and several others are injured. The driver, a woman in her 50s, remains hospitalized. Authorities have not yet released her name, pending the results of a toxicology report.*

But Gloria didn't have to wait for the police to name her. She saw it happen in real time from her hospital bed.

Her name was plastered all over the internet thanks to a rage-bait content creator who ran a site and YouTube channel called *You Ain't Safe*. The host, Barry, who called himself "B Tone", specialized in exploiting public tragedies for clicks, spinning half-truths and public data into viral outrage.

That night, Gloria saw the video go live.

"Her name is Gloria. Gloria M.," B Tone said, pacing in front of a green screen. "Thanks to one of our Eyes, we've confirmed she's the driver in yesterday's deadly freeway crash. Witnesses say her luxury SUV veered across lanes in broad daylight and BOOM—two lives were gone, just like that. A husband and wife… gone.

Their child? Orphaned. There are more injuries too, another driver in critical condition."

He leaned closer to the camera. "Toxicology's pending, but the talk is she'd been drinking. A lot. You connect the dots. This woman didn't just crash, she tore a family apart. And if that report comes back the way I think it will, then congratulations, Gloria M… you blew the candle out on two lives."

The footage cut to clips of the crash site with ambulance lights flashing, still shots from the freeway, and even a filtered image of Gloria pulled from an old Facebook post. It was smeared with red tones and glitch effects.

Meet the woman who killed a family. More on YouAintSafe.net. #DUI #405Killer #RotInJail

The video exploded within hours. Her social media pages that were previously low-key and unassuming were now bombarded with hate. Death threats and doxxing campaigns flooded her inbox, with people calling her a monster, a murderer, and a drunk slut who should've died in the crash.

It was a full-blown trial by the comments section.

Post-Crash Day 1–2: The Realization

Gloria woke up in a sterile hospital room, her body aching, her mind foggy. An officer stood at the foot of her bed and informed her of what had happened. She already knew, but she played along, pretending it was the first time she was hearing it.

It got harder when he mentioned they were waiting on the toxicology report, though he hinted they already had their answer.

A crash.
Two lives lost.
Multiple injuries.
A toddler left orphaned.

Her world had shattered in an instant. The crash itself was a blur. She couldn't remember getting behind the wheel, let alone the impact. When the nurse returned with her chart, she caught a look of passive judgement in her eyes.

The reality hit like a freight train. Her drinking had caused this. The guilt was suffocating. For two days, she stared at the ceiling, refusing all visitors. Her family tried to reach out, but she turned them all away.

I don't deserve to see them she thought, tears rolling down her face.

She replayed the nights she spent drinking alone. The ignored warnings. The pleas from her nephew. They had all been right. Now, two innocent people were gone because of her.

The officer excused himself but made it clear that the police would be back. His parting words to her:

"You may talk to me again… or to a detective. Either way, we'll be back. Have a good night, Miss."

The door closed and she just laid in sterile sobering silence.

Day 3–5: The Prison Of Her Mind

The physical recovery was slow, but the emotional toll was worse. Gloria withdrew into herself, barely eating or speaking to the nurses. Her hospital room felt like a prison cell and she knew real prison was likely next.

The story was everywhere. Any time she turned on the TV or overheard voices in the hallway, it was about her. The victims were beloved figures in Los Angeles, deeply connected to their community. Their family stood alongside Mothers Against Drunk Driving (M.A.A.D.), demanding justice.

The press conference was devastating.

"These were two incredible souls taken too soon," the victim's sister said, holding back tears.

Gloria winced when they mentioned the toddler, an orphan now because of her. She saw the pain on their faces, heard the calls for accountability.

The empty liquor bottles in her car became the public's rallying cry. The toxicology report hadn't even come back, but the narrative was set: she was the villain.

Each report chipped away at her spirit. The guilt and shame consumed her, and the thought of enduring a trial was unbearable.

On Day 4, the story exploded even further. The other driver in critical condition succumbed to his injuries.

Barry's rage-bait channel, *You Ain't Safe,* dropped a new video titled *"Drunk Woman Destroys Lives: The Face of Recklessness,"* with **"EXCLUSIVE INFO"** flashing across the screen. In it, Barry alleged that *"sources close to the investigation"* had confirmed **empty liquor bottles** were found inside Gloria's car.

Though the police hadn't publicly released that information, the claim spread like wildfire. Gloria saw it playing on a nurse's phone and knew instantly there was no coming back. The narrative was already set. She was the villain.

The nurses couldn't say anything directly, but she saw the shift in their eyes. The unspoken verdict. The whispered updates behind the curtain.

Day 6–10: A Final Goodbye

Gloria finally allowed one visitor, her nephew. He entered the room cautiously, unsure of what to expect.

She greeted him with a tired smile, though her eyes were heavy with sorrow. "I needed to see you, Richie."

The killer hadn't heard that nickname in years. It brought back memories of a simpler time when his aunt was a source of love and joy.

She handed him a letter, her hands shaking slightly.

"Please give this to the family. They need to know how sorry I am."

Richie hesitated, looking at her with pleading eyes. "Auntie, wait. You were sick. This wasn't you."

"They don't care about that," she replied, shaking her head. "The world doesn't care. I don't blame them. I did this."

"No, Auntie Gloria. They need to hear the whole story. I'll make sure Carly is exposed. They'll know what pushed you to this."

She turned her head away, a tear slipping down her cheek. "It's still on me, Richie. No one else."

He reached out and held her hand. "We'll find a way through this. Please, stay strong."

Gloria squeezed his hand, her lips forming a faint smile. "You've always been like a son to me. I love you, Richie."

"I love you too, Auntie Gloria."

As the nurses entered to run more tests, Richie left, clutching the letter. He had no idea it would be the last time he would see her alive.

A Quiet Resolve

The hospital room was dimly lit, the hum of distant monitors filling the silence. Gloria stared blankly at the ceiling, her mind replaying every mistake that led her here. She had overheard the nurses talking about shift changes earlier in the evening. A spark of clarity pierced through the haze of her grief, this was her window, her chance to escape the endless torment.

The room's heavy curtains caught her eye. Their cords were thick and sturdy, tied neatly to hooks along the wall. She sat up, testing their strength in her hands. She spent the rest of the night planning, careful not to arouse suspicion.

The Morning She Let Go

At 6:47 a.m., the shuffle of feet outside her door signaled the end of one nursing shift and the start of another. It was now or never. Gloria moved quickly, untying the curtain and fastening a noose.

She climbed onto the windowsill, taking one last look at the city she had called home. "I'm so sorry," she whispered. Her hands trembled as she secured the other end to the window, testing its strength one last time. With tears streaming down her face, she whispered a final prayer to the empty room.

The sun was rising, painting the skyline in shades of orange and pink, a cruel contrast to her inner darkness. A song played over the speakers in the room as she stepped outside onto the ledge: Belau & Beth Hirsch, "Ethereal." The melody and lyrics felt like an acceptance, a true resolution to her decision.

Without hesitation, she stepped forward, closed her eyes, and jumped.

The Tragic Discovery Of Gloria

At 7:02 a.m., a nurse entered the room to check vitals. The first thing she noticed was the open window, curtains billowing gently in the morning breeze. Her eyes followed the cord leading outside.

Then she screamed.

Hospital staff rushed to the room. A collective gasp filled the air as they looked outside the window to see Gloria's lifeless body swaying against the side of the building. The scene was gruesome and surreal, her shadow cast long and haunting by the morning light.

The Last Thread Snapped

The phone call came hours later. The killer was at a storage facility, carefully organizing his aunt's belongings. His phone buzzed, it was one of his cousins.

"Hello?" Richie said.

"Hey, man. It's about Gloria," the cousin stammered. "She's… she's…"

"What happened?" Richie asked frantically.

"She's gone," the cousin said, voice trembling. "She hung herself at the hospital."

The words didn't register at first. He stood frozen, the box in his hands slipping to the ground. Its contents spilled out, framed family photos, old recipes, a bundle of letters.

"No," he whispered, his voice barely audible.
"Not her."

Richie drove to the hospital in a daze, barely aware of his surroundings. When he arrived, the sight of the covered body bag being wheeled out confirmed what he didn't want to believe.

Inside, the family gathered together grieving. He walked to the window where it happened, staring out at the ground below. Rage and grief bubbled inside him.

This is what they've done. This is all their fault, he thought bitterly.

This was no longer just about his mother. They had taken Auntie Gloria too.

The Catalyst For Revenge

Later that night, alone in his room, Richie scrolled mindlessly through Instagram until he landed on Carly's profile.

One post stood out.
Carly lounged poolside, her caption read:
Another day, another blessing. Don't let the haters bring you down! #StayBlessed #PositiveVibes

His jaw tightened.

Then came the final blow.

A notification popped up from *You Ain't Safe,* B Tone's rage-bait channel. The headline read:
"Drunk woman who caused multi-car pileup on the 405 takes the coward's way out."

Below was a blurred screenshot, grainy hospital surveillance showing Gloria's body hanging outside her window.

Richie's stomach turned. His hand trembled as he hurled the phone against the wall. It hit hard, screen shattering on impact.

He doubled over, his breath coming in short, raw gasps.

These people… these influencers…
They destroy lives.
They walk away without consequence.
They take and take and take.

His thoughts twisted and fragmented as he sank to his knees, fingers clawing the carpet. Grief swallowed him, then rage shoved it aside.

He crawled toward the window and looked out into the pale moonlight, the glow catching in his eyes.

"They don't get to walk away from this," he muttered.

For the first time in weeks, Richie felt something sharper than pain.

Purpose.

Retribution would be his.

Two Graves Down

A gray sky loomed overhead, threatening rain as the small group gathered around the grave. The killer stood slightly apart from the rest, his hands stuffed into the pockets of his black slacks, shoulders hunched against the cold. The priest's voice droned on, offering comfort and prayers for the departed, but the words barely registered.

First, his mother. Her life snuffed out by an influencer's cruel and tasteless viral video. Now his aunt. Her spiral into alcoholism and reckless decisions, a direct result of another influencer's greed. Two women he loved, gone because of people who treated others like props and stepping stones, then walked away without a glance back.

He tried to stay present, but it was impossible. The sting of loss was too raw, and the rage too close beneath the surface. Carly. Tabatha. Jordan. Barry. Their faces flashed in his mind like a reel of nightmares. He thought of the viral video mocking him at his lowest. The cruel nicknames. The laughter. The way the world joined in, oblivious to the real pain they caused.

And Barry? Barry had taken it further. He didn't just profit off Richie's humiliation, he turned his aunt's tragedy into clickbait. His YouTube channel, *You Ain't Safe,* had made her the face of drunken destruction, using her image to entice rage, mockery, and threats. Gloria had been spiraling, but that video? That video helped push her over the edge.

As the casket lowered, Richie's jaw tightened. He couldn't cry. Not anymore. Not here.

"This is the last time," he whispered. "The last time they get away with it."

The priest's voice faded. Mourners began to leave, offering final condolences as they trickled away. Richie stayed behind. He watched the dirt cover the casket, the sound of shovelfuls dull against the wood.

The world had let them trample over his life, over the women who had helped raise him, without even noticing.

But they would.

Soon.

He turned from the grave with a darker, sharper purpose behind his eyes. Grief had shaped him. But it was vengeance that would now define him.

It was time to bury a few more.

Gloria's Goodbye

After the funeral, the killer sat alone in his dimly lit apartment. The weight of the past few days bore down on him like an anchor. He reached into his jacket pocket and pulled out the folded letter his aunt had entrusted to him.

With trembling hands, he opened it, bracing himself for her final words.

My dearest family,

My loving and enduring family, you have always been my greatest joy. All these years, I've tried to be the rock for all of you, the one who led by example. I've watched you grow, each of you, into the remarkable people you are. I've seen the kids blossom into their own, and it's brought me so much pride and happiness. You've been my joy, my purpose, and my light in every dark time.

My life was always about control, about working hard and providing for my nieces and nephews after my son died. Everything I did, I did for you. When I finally got the house, I thought I'd achieved my dream. It wasn't just a home; it was my sanctuary, my safe space. I wanted you all to share in my happiness, to see the fruits of my labor. I opened it to each of you because it was a part of me, a reflection of my love for this family.

But I didn't see what was coming. I didn't know that what I loved so deeply would become my downfall. Richie tried to warn me, bless him for his persistence, but I was blinded by my own happiness, my own pride. I was so focused on holding onto the house that I didn't notice I was losing myself. Slowly, without even realizing it, I became sick. I started to unravel, and I turned to something that I thought could soothe the pain. But it only made it worse. I became an alcoholic and an addict.

I'm so sorry I couldn't see the signs. I'm sorry for what my actions have caused all of you. I let my sickness take hold, and it led me to this terrible place. It led to a tragedy that I can never undo. I took three lives because of my actions. Three innocent people. And in doing so, I orphaned a little girl, a little girl who will never know the warmth of her parents because of me. That guilt, it's unimaginable, unbearable. I've replayed the moment in my mind every night, and I haven't slept since. I've become the person I never thought I could be, someone I hated.

And now, I can't face it anymore. I can't bring more shame to this family, the family I love more than anything. I hope you can forgive me someday, but I understand if you can't. Just know this: I love you all. More than words could ever say.

Find peace for yourselves, even if I couldn't.

Forever in your hearts,

Gloria

Richie read the letter twice, his hands gripping the edges of the paper so tightly it began to crumple. His vision blurred as hot tears filled his eyes.

"She was already gone," he muttered to himself. "Long before the crash. And none of us could save her."

But even through the grief, anger bubbled to the surface. It wasn't just her sickness. It wasn't just her choices. There was another piece to this puzzle, the influencers, the exploitation, the toxic culture that had pushed his family to the brink.

Two family members, gone because of their actions.

This letter wasn't just a goodbye.

It was a reminder.

He folded the letter carefully and placed it back into his pocket.

"They must pay," he whispered. "For all of it."

CHAPTER 25

THE INSURANCE COMPANY DEVIL

Two weeks had passed since Aunt Gloria's death, and Richie had quit his job. The viral gym video had made it impossible to show his face there again. The mocking laughter followed him everywhere, both online and in real life. There was no way he could return to that version of his life.

But the humiliation became fuel. It burned within him, stoking a fire that had long been dormant. Richie was changing. He followed a strict workout and meal plan, dedicating himself to becoming leaner, meaner, and stronger.

He joined an all-inclusive gym where the rule was simple: no filming allowed. For the first time in years, Richie felt free from judgment. Here, he trained with purpose, pushing himself to the limit, physically and mentally. His hair was now cropped short, just long enough to tie into a ponytail, and a thick beard framed his face. He looked hard, focused, resolved. He would shed his old self, one rep at a time.

Richie kept to himself. He didn't want new friends or small talk. The gym was his sanctuary. His place to focus, train, and plan. Every drop of sweat reminded him: the man he used to be was dead. He was building someone who could take control. Someone who could finish what had been started.

The shadow of Gloria's death lingered, not just emotionally, but mentally. As her closest relative and the primary beneficiary of her will, Richie took charge of the final arrangements, determined to give her the dignity the world had denied her in the end.

Then came the life insurance policy.

Years earlier, Gloria had signed up with Hathaway Insurance. At the time, the company was known for compassion and simplicity. No invasive questions. No fine print.

Their slogan stuck with her: *We make the hardest days easier*. That's what sold her. But everything changed after the founder, Albert Hathaway, passed away. His son, Danny, took over and buried everything his father had built.

Under Danny's leadership, Hathaway Insurance became cold and ruthless, drowning grieving families in red tape and driven by one thing: profit.

Richie didn't realize how much that change would matter, until he filed the claim. He believed the policy would honor his aunt's wishes.

But Danny Hathaway had other plans.

And when that denial would arrive, it would set off a chain of events that changed everything — the final push over the edge.

Because once Richie snapped, there was no stopping what followed.

No warning.
No mercy.
Just consequences. Long overdue.

The Man Behind The Denial Letters

Danny Hathaway thrived on attention. Flamboyant and eccentric, he craved the spotlight and soaked up the camera.

Unlike his father, who built Hathaway Insurance on integrity and a no-nonsense mission to protect grieving families, Danny treated the company as a vehicle for self-promotion.

Now he was the face of the company. His grinning mug appeared on billboards, commercials, and every digital ad campaign: always paired with his annoyingly catchy tagline:
Life's better with a Dandy-Tastic deal!

It was cheesy. It was everywhere. And it worked. Danny had turned Hathaway Insurance into a brand and himself into an influencer, leveraging social media to boost both visibility and ego.

They called him a visionary, but his "vision" was nothing like what Albert Hathaway had intended. Under Danny's leadership, the company abandoned its compassion. It no longer prided itself on simplicity or service. Now it was all about the bottom line.

Denials skyrocketed. Claims were rejected faster and more aggressively than ever, with Danny personally reviewing each one. Not because he cared, but because control made him feel powerful.

His rise to power had been seamless. Groomed from childhood to inherit the empire, Danny took the reins with ease. His three sisters held little sway over the company's operations. He was the heir, and with that title came unchecked authority.

But now his sisters were growing uneasy. Negative press was mounting. Allegations of unjust denials and claims that Hathaway Insurance had abandoned the principles that once made it a trusted name. They wanted to distance themselves from the backlash, fearful of the damage to the family's legacy.

His wife, Justine, stood firmly behind him, silently drinking in the power as much as he did. Their bond had been forged in childhood love and hardened by ambition. Even when Danny was wrong, she clung to the belief that there was still good in him and that he would come around and do the right thing. At least, she hoped so. She always backed him up. Together, they were untouchable. For now.

But like most families with generational wealth, there were secrets buried beneath the surface. Secrets no one wanted unearthed.

Albert Hathaway, the man behind the brand, had a long-term mistress who bore him a biracial son the public never knew about, a boy with hazel-green eyes, just like Danny's.

The child was born to a Black woman outside the family, and while Albert never publicly acknowledged him, a DNA test confirmed the truth. The family was mortified. Their prejudice ran deep. They wanted the scandal buried.

But Albert secretly cared for the boy and his mother.

Albert's wife had always known. In her world, infidelity wasn't a dealbreaker. It was the cost of luxury. She had long since built her own empire, a successful makeup line now sold at high-end retailers, including the very store where Samantha worked—*Glam Haven*.

Albert had bought her silence with the best of everything. In return, she smiled, waved, and played the role of the elegant wife.

Rumors persisted even as Albert grew old and sick. Whispers of more women. More children. He traveled often, and not always for business. But nothing ever stuck, only whispers.

His PR team was elite. Hush money. NDAs. Crisis managers on speed dial. The media never got a whiff. Albert's legacy stayed clean because he made sure it would.

Upon his death, His longtime attorney, Spencer, ensured all of Albert's illegitimate children were discreetly taken care of. But it was the biracial son who caused the biggest stir.

Albert had arranged a moderate trust for the boy, along with a small but symbolic stake in Hathaway Insurance with a few shares. Not enough to influence anything, but enough to disrupt their perfect narrative. And it rocked the family.

The Hathaway name, once a tightly polished brand of wealth and tradition, now carried a scandal the boardroom couldn't scrub clean.

The boy's mother received $10,000 a month in child support, locked in until he turned twenty-one. No loopholes. No early terminations. Albert had made sure of it.

The money flowed. The boy thrived. And Danny and his sisters could do nothing but grit their teeth and pretend it wasn't happening.

The Family Table Of Privilege And Prejudice

The Hathaway Building stood tall in Century City, offering sweeping views of the skyline. A fitting headquarters for a family empire. It was here, at the heart of their wealth and influence, that Danny and Justine sat across from his sisters: Lyndsay, Hayley, and Whitney.

The triplets, all in designer suits that flattered their slender frames, shared more than just their appearance. They shared a way of life steeped in privilege and power.

Matching designer purses and accessories, nails perfectly manicured, glamour defined them. Their clothes were similar yet distinct, each sister flaunting her own style but united by a common entitlement.

"Just how long do you think you're going to continue with this thinking?" Lyndsay's voice cut through the air, sharp and challenging.

"Danny, if Papa were here, there's no way he'd allow this," Hayley added, her tone equally loaded with disdain.

"I don't think you and your wife over there fully understand what it means to carry the legacy Papa built," Whitney said, her words laced with rising frustration.

Together, the sisters spoke in unison. "We won't claim this!"

Hayley, her voice dripping with accusation. "All these angry letters? Addressed to you."

"All of these pleas for coverage? Addressed to you," Whitney added, her gaze ice cold.

"All of the denials? From you… and her," Lyndsay finished, pointing directly at Justine, who sat beside Danny, her face a mask of cool detachment.

"That's enough!" Danny barked, his voice rising in a rare burst of fury. "You have no idea what's going on!"

"Because you shut us out!" Whitney snapped, her frustration spilling over.

"Yes, and you fail to realize we have insiders reporting to us. That's how we know what you're doing, and what you're planning to do," Hayley added with a knowing glare.

"And when I find out who they are, they'll be fired," Danny growled, gripping the edge of the table.

"You won't!" Hayley shot back, defiant.

"You don't have total power, Danny," Whitney said, her voice rising. "I know that's what you want, but Daddy made sure there were checks and balances."

"You three only hold 36% combined," he reminded them with a smirk. "I don't need your vote at the board meetings. The decision rests with me, and me alone."

"Changes can be made," Lyndsay said, her words resigned, though she knew it was an empty threat. She slumped back into her seat, and the sisters followed suit.

Hayley sank into her seat with a sigh, fanning herself as she muttered about vertigo. Whitney, ever the caretaker, hugged Hayley asking if she was alright. Their unity in protest remained strong, but the exhaustion from the argument was starting to show on them all.

Danny noticed it too. He wasn't the oldest, but he could see his sisters were trying to save face. Despite the tension, he made an effort to ease the tension.

"Girls, my sisters, I'm doing this because we need to save money. We're spending too much. We have to cut back on the claims we pay and how we pay them. All existing and new policies have been modified," he explained, his tone almost pleading.

"I have the numbers here," Justine offered, trying to add her voice to the discussion. But her words barely registered. The sisters shot her a look of icy contempt, and she quickly fell silent.

"Cutting back while buying up more billboards and TV time? You're full of shit, you know that?" Whitney's voice was sharp.

"Advertising and marketing are number one," Danny countered, but his words held little weight in the face of his sisters' disdain.

"You're so deluded," Hayley said, her voice tinged with condescension. "This isn't Daddy's vision. You're too young, Danny. You don't have the maturity to lead this company."

The triplets were all in their late twenties, while Danny, at just twenty-one, was still struggling to prove himself.

"I don't think you realize how much money Papa had to spend silencing all his women," Danny said, his tone firming. "There are more children out there too. Children younger than us."

"You've got to be kidding me," Lyndsay rasped.

"I'm not," Danny replied flatly. "And one of them… well, we already know about the hood baby."

Hayley scoffed, shaking her head. "God, don't remind me. That whole thing was so embarrassing."

"He's also got another one with some Asian lady," Danny added casually.

"You're kidding? *Another* side baby? With *an* Asian woman?! Lyndsay blurted out, scandalized.

"Oh god! We're not about to add *their* New Year to our family calendar." Whitney fumed.

"Imagine the holiday cards. 'Love, Peace, Pan-African day, Asian holy day, I *just* can't! And I'm *sure* she's looking for some handout," Hayley said crossing her arms in protest.

"Actually, she has her own money," Danny continued. "They only agreed that the daughter would get private school and college covered. So dear old dad set up an account just for that."

"Such a model minority," Lyndsay said sarcastically, rolling her eyes. "They're all over the road in their Teslas. Watch out everyone!"

"Right? It's like they're personal starter pack," Hayley chimed in, laughing. "Teslas, golf clubs, tennis rackets…"

"Don't forget about the matcha drinks," Lyndsay said with a smirk, doubling down.

"And they all pose like this too," Whitney said throwing up a peace sign and scrunching her face into a fake smile.

They all broke into laughter that was catty, condescending, and cruel.

Across the table, Justine shifted in her seat, visibly unsettled by the insidious, ignorant banter. The blanket stereotyping struck a nerve. "Maybe we shouldn't use language like that," she said. "It reflects *badly* on all of us.

Lyndsay snapped around to face her. "*Then* don't sit at this table, sweetie."

"I have the numbers here," Justine offered gently, sliding a folder toward them. "The cuts you've made are already getting heat in the press, Danny. And if people catch wind of any racially charged language coming out of this building on top of all the denied claims—"

"*Oh, here we go*," Lyndsay groaned, rolling her eyes.

"—it could be catastrophic," Justine continued, her voice firm. "We're not just playing with policy terms. We're playing with reputation. Legally and publicly, the optics matter."

"Oh, how noble," Hayley sneered. "The voice of morality joins us."

"She said optics. What is that, the *buzzword* of the day?" Lyndsey huffed, rolling her eyes.

"I'm not comfortable with—" Justine began, but Whitney cut her off sharply.

"You're not even a Hathaway," Whitney snapped. "So maybe sit this part out."

Justine froze, her jaw tightening as she shot Danny a vulnerable look, a silent plea for backup.

"Enough," Danny said, his tone sharp. "She's right. We don't need a PR disaster on top of everything else. Let's be mindful."

"And demure," Whitney added. The sisters exchanged a glance and then laughed, cold and cutting.

Justine gave Danny a grateful look, but he only shrugged, a sly grin creeping across his face. "Listen, I don't care whose money we take. It's all one color in the end."

Laughter rippled through the room, leaving Justine on the outside looking in. Her words had fallen on deaf ears. She didn't smile. This wasn't support. It was survival. A business decision.

"And Mom?" Hayley asked after the laughter faded.

"She forgave him a long time ago," Lyndsay shrugged.

"Yeah, she gets mad if we bring it up," Danny added. "She just wants it all to go away."

The family sat in the uncomfortable silence that followed. United not by love, but by a shared disdain for their father and the women he'd betrayed them with. They sneered at the mention of illegitimate children, each revelation another stain on the Hathaway name. The room, once filled with insults and mockery, now simmered with hushed contempt.

Danny was the first to speak. "So… our father paid off these women, and it's cost us a lot. Naturally, to keep our money where it belongs, I'll have to make some cuts."

"But don't forget what Daddy built," Hayley said, her voice sharp. "What he and Granddaddy built. You didn't build this empire. You inherited it."

"Yes. Do better," Whitney added flatly, her eyes locked on him.

"Don't fuck this up," Lyndsay said, her words edged with sisterly venom.

Danny smirked. "*Hey*, if I do, and I won't, but if I do, it's *my* ass they'll come for. *Not* yours. I'll shield you all from the fallout."

One by one, the sisters stood, each casting a final look toward Justine. Hayley, the last to leave, paused at the door, turning just long enough to twist the knife.
"We love you, dear brother. But keep your bitch in line!"

The door clicked shut.

Justine sat frozen, her eyes wide and jaw tight, humiliated but silent. Danny sighed and turned toward her.

"They'll never accept me, will they?" she asked.

"You don't need their approval," Danny replied. "You never will. They can't accept anything that doesn't fit their perfect little image."

His words were meant to comfort, but they rang hollow.

Justine opened her mouth, paused, then closed it again. She wanted to tell him something, something that could change everything. But not now. Not like this.

She had taken a pregnancy test that morning.

It was positive.

Danny didn't know it yet, but by denying a claim he shouldn't have, he was setting off a chain reaction that would cost him far more than just the company.

One Denial Too Many

The clock ticked on, each second sharpening the eerie silence of the office. Danny sat hunched over his desk, the cold glow of his monitor casting hard shadows across his face. File after file flashed before him.

Each click of the mouse was another claim reviewed, another denial marked. The gravity of it no longer fazed him. This was business. Every rejection was a line item. A calculated move.

"I'm going home," Justine's voice broke through the silence. She stood in the doorway, coat draped over her arm. "Sebastian's bringing the car around."

Danny looked up, his eyes tired but composed. "I just have a few more files. I'll be right behind you."

She lingered, her hand still on the doorknob.

"You can send him back after he drops you off."

A sigh slipped from her lips as she stepped toward him. The room felt heavier with each footfall, a shared silence stretching between them. When she reached his desk, they didn't speak. Instead, they embraced.

Her body met his and Danny felt something stir. Not just physically, but emotionally. The office, the decisions, the claims, everything began to fade.

He kissed her like he didn't trust words to carry the feeling. His hands moved against her body, his fingers trailing along familiar paths. Justine embraced his touch with no hesitation and no pulling back. Only the echo of something unresolved.

Maybe this was her chance to tell him that she was three weeks late. That she had taken two tests. That she was pregnant.

But she didn't.

Danny had no idea. His mind was on numbers, denials, deadlines. On cutting costs and dodging scandals. On a future he was convinced he was shaping alone.

So she said nothing.

Not yet.

They pulled back. She smiled, grabbed her coat, and looked at him. Her hand cupped his face.

"I'll see you at home."

"Yes. I'll see you soon."

"I hope so. Esperanza's preparing a special dinner for us," she added.

"Alright. I'll leave as soon as Sebastian gets back," he said, placing both hands on her face before kissing her again.

She kissed him. Her eyes fell shut as she embraced him. Then, lips brushing his ear, she whispered,
"Hurry."

He held her gaze, their foreheads nearly touching. "I promise."

They broke the embrace. She smiled once more and turned toward the door. Her heels echoed across the polished floor as she stepped out into the hallway. At the far end, Sebastian stood waiting by the elevators.

One thing about Danny was clear: he wasn't a cheater like his father. Justine loved him for that, for his commitment and his steadiness. But Danny wasn't perfect. His cold-blooded decisions on denied claims revealed a darker truth about who he had become. To him, it wasn't personal. It was just business. Efficient, streamlined, profitable.

But tonight, he would make a decision that set something irreversible in motion.

With over two hundred files left to review, it was just another name in the queue. Another form. Another policy.

Then he saw it. Gloria M.

He opened the file, his eyes scanning the details. Cause of death: suicide.

He cross-referenced the claim against internal policies, toggling between folders of updated disclosures, addendums, and signatures. And there it was. A loophole.

Though Gloria had never signed a new contract, she had acknowledged a yearly update letter. Routine. Standard-looking. Most wouldn't think twice. But the language had shifted subtly, burying new exclusions in layers of legal gray. One of those exclusions now applied to her.

Technically, her death should have been covered under her grandfathered plan. There was room for argument, even grounds for a court case. But Danny didn't care. He wasn't here to honor legacy contracts or gamble with legal semantics. If her family wanted a fight, his lawyers were ready to drag it out until they couldn't afford to breathe.

He had what he needed. That was enough.

With one swift stroke of his pen, the decision was made.

Denied.

Quick. Clean. Final.

What Danny didn't know was that this denial would seal his fate.

His status as a pseudo-celebrity, a grinning face on every billboard, had made him a public figure. And that made him a target for someone who had nothing left to lose.

As he clicked to the next file, his phone buzzed. A notification flashed: another influencer had tagged him in a rooftop cocktail shot, promoting Dandy-Tastic Deals. His brand was alive and thriving.

But out there, in the dark, someone is watching.

Grief is tightening around them, feeding a rage that's dangerously close to erupting.

And when it does, no one will be ready.

Lighting The Match To Madness

Three weeks after Gloria's death, the denial letter arrived from Hathaway Insurance. Cold. Mechanical. Signed by none other than Danny Hathaway himself. It was a generic form letter, with no empathy and no remorse. Just a copy-pasted apology from a faceless empire.

The killer stared at the page, his grip tightening until the paper crumpled in his fist. It was the final insult, proof that the systems meant to protect had only caused more suffering.

He tried calling Hathaway Insurance, desperate for answers. It was useless. Danny's decision was final. No appeal. No exception. No justice.

Richie collapsed to the floor, grief and rage consuming him. The pain wasn't just emotional anymore. It tore through his chest, raw and physical. Sobs wracked his body in waves, each one breaking something deeper inside.

That was it. The last thread of his sanity snapped. Furious. Unhinged. The final thing that could have brought Gloria peace, one simple gesture, denied by an insurance mogul turned social media celebrity. Danny Hathaway couldn't even honor her death claim.

When he discovered who Danny really was, with his flair for the camera and smug face plastered across every cheesy commercial, something dark settled in Richie's chest. Danny's name went on the list. Another influencer building a platform on selfishness and spectacle.

If that hadn't already pushed him madness, Barry's rage-bait channel delivered the final blow. Richie knew that in the days after the crash, Barry had incited his followers to flood Gloria's Instagram with threats, mockery, and hate.

His twisted commentary and viral spin turned a woman's lowest moment into public spectacle. Gloria had seen it. She had felt it. And it helped push her over the edge. Now Richie was going to make him pay for it in blood.

The TV hummed in the background, one of Danny's ads looping again:
"Get yourself a Dandy-Tastic deal!"

Richie didn't blink. He sat there, staring through the screen, already thinking of how to get to Danny Hathaway. How we was going to kill him. And How to get to Barry Mintone.

"A.K.A. B Tone."
The rage-bait king of *You Ain't Safe.*
The man who turned grief into content and tragedy into currency. His mind twisted at the ways he could kill him for maximum shock value.

Once, Richie believed in fairness. In the system. In second chances.

That man was gone.

Down the rabbit hole he went.

Now, he was hellbent on vengeance.

Jeff. Jordan. Tabatha. Carly. Barry. Danny.

They were all on the list.

And Samantha Sinclair?

She wasn't off the hook.

Not if Richie had anything to say about it.

CHAPTER 26

SO, WHY SAMANTHA SINCLAIR?

Leonard Sinclair: The Weight of Mistakes and Family Sacrifices

Leonard Sinclair never stopped missing his mother. Even now, years after her passing, he still caught himself reaching for the phone to call her, especially on long nights when the quiet felt too loud. She had been his anchor. Her strength and poise had been his compass, guiding him through a life that often felt too complex to navigate alone.

Born in Lyon, France, to a French-American diplomat mother and a father of Arab descent who had immigrated to Latin America and become an academic, Leonard's childhood unfolded across continents. His mother, later stationed at the U.S. embassy in Geneva, stayed deeply connected to French culture, especially its café life and cuisine, traditions she had lovingly passed down to him.

Leonard grew up speaking French and Spanish at home. His mother enrolled him in an international school, where he was also taught English from an early age to prepare him for a global career. His father spent weekends and summers teaching Leonard conversational Arabic, determined to pass on their cultural roots.

After his parents divorced, Leonard's mother brought him to the United States for a brief period while working an interim assignment in Washington, D.C. Soon after, she was reassigned to Europe, where Leonard completed much of his adolescence in Geneva.

Years later, Leonard returned to the U.S. permanently for college, earning degrees in international relations and criminology. His linguistic fluency, global perspective, and academic record caught the attention of the FBI, where he was recruited straight out of graduate school.

Deadly Rookie Mistakes

Leonard joined the FBI at 24, initially assigned to the Los Angeles field office, specializing in counterterrorism. By 27, his reputation as a rising star was solidified by his ability to manage high-pressure situations and conduct negotiations in multiple languages. However, Leonard lacked field experience and he yearned for it, eager to prove he was capable of catching the big fish. That ambition would lead to a fatal mistake that changed his career trajectory forever.

He was tapped to lead an intelligence-based raid on a family suspected of harboring terrorists. The operation, relying on faulty intel, targeted the wrong household: a quiet immigrant family of five. Leonard, overseeing the SWAT team, unknowingly ordered the raid that resulted in the death of a hard-working father. Their young son (the future killer) and two sisters survived the traumatic event. Leonard had been the trigger man.

Though the FBI conducted an internal investigation and cleared him of wrongdoing, Leonard was removed from field service. The tragedy became a scarlet letter on his conscience. His peers saw him as someone who could compartmentalize guilt, but inside, Leonard carried the weight of that decision every day. He buried himself in his work, striving for perfection as if it could erase the past.

Leonard never returned to field service, but he made a lasting impact behind the scenes. He led operations that broke up multiple terrorist cells. His strategies were sharp and his instincts unshakable. He stayed three steps ahead of the criminals, eventually becoming one of the bureau's most brilliant criminal minds.

Placing Career Over Love

Leonard met Laura, a criminal behavioral psychologist originally from Puerto Rico, during an international security conference in Los Angeles. Laura, an Afro-Latina woman with a striking balance of beauty and intellect, was drawn to Leonard's calm demeanor and strong moral code. They fell in love and married quickly. Their daughter, Samantha, was born soon after in L.A.

But Leonard's career demands took a toll. His constant travel and emotional distance left Laura feeling isolated. Despite her efforts to bridge the gap, Leonard's inability to connect outside of work created a void in their marriage. After years of feeling unloved and unsupported, Laura left Leonard when Samantha was only seven, running off with another man to start a new family. She never looked back. It would be another ten years before Samantha saw her mother again.

Samantha remembered that final day clearly. Her mother picked her up from school, dropped her off at her grandmother's, and spoke to her in Spanish, always making it a point to keep their culture alive. That last kiss? Unknowingly, a goodbye. There would be many nights Samantha cried herself to sleep, knowing her mother was gone.

Samantha's Upbringing

With Laura gone, Leonard juggled career and single parenthood. Recognizing Samantha needed a stable maternal figure, he turned to his mother, recently retired from diplomatic service.

The Los Angeles estate she returned to had been willed to her by her American grandfather, a family home passed down through generations. There, she raised Samantha with warmth, love, and structure.

Samantha grew up in a multilingual household: her grandmother often spoke to her in French, while the Spanish her mother once used to keep their culture alive remained with her and reinforced by the comforting presence of the family's longtime Latina housekeeper Magdalena.

English was her primary language, but French and Spanish served as emotional touchstones. Languages of memory, comfort, and identity. Arabic, though her most challenging, was still part of her world.

Introduced early by her strict grandfather and later nurtured by her father with more patience, she could hold a conversation when needed. However, it never came as naturally.

During a two-week trip to the Middle East with her father, visiting extended family for the first time, the pressure to speak fluently in daily life had nearly overwhelmed her. So she improvised and claimed partial hearing loss in one ear. It bought her grace and sympathy, giving her the space to listen more carefully and absorb tone and context.

She'd repeat the phrases later in private, letting them settle. By the second week, she could respond with enough ease that no one questioned her. What began as a defense mechanism became a private triumph. Fluency born not from mastery, but from resilience.

Leonard's mother became Samantha's rock. She encouraged independence and curiosity, nurturing the resilience that would define her. Leonard remained present, but their relationship was more functional than emotional. Career came first. Because without a career, there would be no provision for family. That was how he saw it.

Leonard's Career Shift

By his late 40s, Leonard transitioned out of the FBI into private security and surveillance, serving high-profile clients. His multilingual abilities and deep connections made him one of the best in the field. The shift allowed him to stay closer to Samantha, but the emotional distance between them had already settled in.

Samantha admired her father's career, but often felt like an afterthought. Her strongest bond was with her grandmother, who remained her true source of comfort and emotional grounding. Even when Samantha went through her bratty influencer phase as a teen, her grandmother's love never faltered.

A Child's Grudge Turned To Hate

For the boy who survived the botched raid, Leonard's actions had destroyed his family and stolen his childhood. As he grew older, he tracked Leonard obsessively, watching the man who killed his father build a life of success and respect. Then he discovered Samantha.

She became the perfect final target.

In the killer's eyes, Samantha represented everything Leonard still had—love, legacy, and family. Taking her would balance the scales. Make Leonard suffer the same unimaginable loss. This wasn't just revenge.

It was justice.

The sins of the father would fall on the her, his first born and only child.

CHAPTER 27

ALL EYES ON SAMANTHA

Back at the crime scene, the gym was an eerie shell of what it once was. Officers combed the area for evidence under the sterile glow of flickering fluorescent lights. The coroner had already removed the bodies, but the air still carried a heavy sense of unease. Lieutenant Byron Maxwell stood near the entrance, pressure mounting. With the murders stacking up and no concrete leads, the case was quickly turning into a race against time.

Captain Cunningham entrusted Maxwell with full authority over the investigation. Now, Maxwell faced the unenviable task of solving what felt like an unsolvable puzzle. Detective Castanon approached just as Maxwell ended a call with Captain Cunningham.

"The captain said we've got a briefing in the morning," Maxwell reported. "All divisions are to be present. Orders from the Chief."

Castanon nodded, his tone firm. "Understood."

"But before that, I need something concrete out of here tonight. Keep the press backed off, lock down the perimeter, and make sure no one gets in who doesn't belong."

"Right away," Castanon said, moving to carry out the orders.

Maxwell watched him go, brow furrowed. Castanon had potential, but his overzealous nature made Maxwell wary. This case required precision and restraint. Not bravado. And Castanon hadn't mastered that yet.

Before Maxwell could dwell on it, Sergeant Ramirez approached.

"Lieutenant, we've got a 911 call out of Mar Vista. A young woman. Her face was… melting off on a livestream. It's going viral. She's been rushed to the hospital. Police and fire are already on scene."

Maxwell's eyes narrowed. "Another influencer, tonight," he muttered. "This isn't isolated. It's all connected."

He turned to leave, issuing orders as he went.

"Castanon, Jacobson, wrap up here. I want a full report by sunrise."

"But shouldn't I go—" Castanon started.

"You have your assignment Detective," Maxwell said, already heading to his car.

The streets were empty as Maxwell sped down the 10 Freeway, sirens slicing through the silence of early morning. The clock on his dash read 3:00 a.m., but sleep wasn't even a consideration. His mind spun with questions. The pressure was mounting.

His phone buzzed again. Captain Cunningham.

"Maxwell here."

"I'm hearing about Mar Vista," the captain said, voice tense. "There's no containing this anymore. The Chief's agreed to a press conference Monday morning at City Hall."

Maxwell sighed. "Guess I'll wear my best suit," he muttered.

"Byron, we need leads. Fast," Cunningham pressed. "Pacific Division is backing you up. Detective Lawrence Miller is already on site. Consider him your extension out there."

"Got it," Maxwell said. "We're working every angle. But Castanon's… over zealous. Might not be the time for it."

"This is your case," Cunningham reminded him. "Handle it however you need to. Just deliver results."

"I will," Maxwell replied, resolute.

"Good. We're counting on you, Byron."
The line went dead.

Maxwell tightened his grip on the steering wheel. The weight of responsibility bore down, but it wasn't unfamiliar. A transplant from Detroit, he'd made his name cracking cases others couldn't.

Drug rings. Human trafficking. Killers with no patterns. His drive came from loss. His brother, gunned down in gang violence when Maxwell was still a teen. That tragedy had shaped his life's mission.

Now in his late 40s, he was a seasoned detective with a reputation that preceded him. Federal offers still came his way, but the thought of starting over never appealed. This case, though… it felt different. Like a turning point.

One that might redefine everything.

Alison's House On LockDown

Maxwell pulled up to the scene. Alison's house was a chaotic swarm of activity. Patrol cars lined the street, and neighbors stood on their lawns, whispering to one another. The story was already blowing up on the Citizen app, drawing even more onlookers.

Flashing his badge, Maxwell made his way past the patrol officers guarding the perimeter and stepped inside. The house was crawling with investigators, and he quickly spotted Detective Lawrence Miller.

"Lieutenant Maxwell," Miller said, extending a hand. "I've heard a lot about you. Your reputation precedes you. It's a pleasure to work with you."

"Likewise," Maxwell replied, shaking his hand. "I've heard you're one of Pacific Division's rising stars. Glad to have you on this."

"Thanks. Here's where we stand," Miller said, diving into the details. He outlined the timeline of events and explained that Alison's condition had been linked to a facial serum she'd applied during a livestream. Forensics was already analyzing the package the serum came in, but no one had touched it directly. It was still being dusted for prints. They planned to send the contents to the lab for further analysis.

"We traced the package to a Samantha Sinclair," Miller continued. "She's in Marina del Rey. On paper, she and Alison are friends. But we don't know what that really means."

"We'll pay her a visit," Maxwell said. "She's a person of interest for now. Hopefully, she has some answers."

Back at the gym, Castanon and Jacobson were winding down their investigation. There wasn't much to go on. No usable prints, just a bloody footprint left behind and scattered witness statements. The scene remained active, but progress was slow.

Meanwhile, across town, Samantha and Mike lay peacefully asleep, unaware of the storm about to descend on them. Samantha's night playlist drifted in the background, a soothing melody that would soon be shattered by the news of Alison's fate.

Tomorrow, the first crack in her world would appear. A sharp jolt that would set everything in motion.

CHAPTER 28

SAVING ALISON

The ambulance screeched to a halt at the hospital, paramedics rushing Alison through the emergency room doors on a stretcher. Her body trembled from the pain and the cold wetness of her clothes. Despite their efforts to stabilize her, she was barely conscious. Her surroundings a blur of harsh fluorescent lights and urgent voices.

"She's got severe burns, likely third degree on the right side of her face," one paramedic briefed the ER team as they wheeled her in. "Burns spared the eye and hairline, but there's extensive tissue damage to her cheek and jaw. No airway compromise so far, but she's been in and out."

Alison's mind clung to fragments of the ordeal. The burning sensation. The plunge into the pool. The suffocating darkness as she sank. She had acted on pure survival instinct, but the chlorine had only magnified the pain. She vaguely remembered someone pulling her out.

"Get her inside," the attending doctor barked. "Clean the wounds. Poor girl's going through hell. We need to prep her for emergency surgery. There's too much necrotic tissue to leave untreated."

The word surgery cut through the haze like a blade. Alison's body jerked instinctively, her survival reflex kicking in again. Hands, too many hands, gripped her. For a split second, she couldn't tell who was touching her.

"Don't," she gasped, voice raw and broken.

"You're safe, young lady. Let us help you," one of the nurses said, her tone calm and firm, like a lighthouse in fog.

Still, her limbs twitched. Her breathing quickened. The shock of her being in a hospital. The realization that she was the victim of an attack. Someone is out there who did this. And that someone could still find her.

A softer voice came next, closer to her ear. "You're safe now, mija." A woman's voice. Spanish. Warm. She didn't know it, but it anchored her long enough to stop fighting.

The trauma team moved with practiced urgency. IV lines were inserted to manage her pain and hydration. Monitors beeped steadily above her. She blinked against the fluorescent light, her senses in overdrive. The beeps, the voices, the cold air on her damp skin.

Female nurses carefully peeled off her wet clothes, dried her, and modestly covered her before tending to the burns. Despite their best efforts, Alison flinched as they began cleaning the ravaged skin. Her body recoiled, trembling as nerves screamed beneath every touch.

The doctors winced. The burns were severe. Angry, raw tissue and cartilage exposed, with some flesh charred beyond recognition. Half her face had melted away, dead skin hanging in grotesque patches around her cheek.

Dr. Duncan Pearce entered the room, his presence instantly commanding the room's attention. He was one of the best reconstructive surgeons in the state, and known for his precision, calm, and unshakable demeanor.

"Alright," he said, authoritative but gentle. "We'll clear the necrotic tissue and stabilize her tonight. There's a long road ahead, but we'll give her the best chance possible."

His team nodded, already prepping Alison for surgery. The ER staff carefully dressed her wounds, trying not to cause further trauma. Alison's breath hitched as antiseptic touched her skin, her body trembling with pain, fear, and exhaustion.

"Hang in there, Miss," a nurse whispered, brushing a hand gently over her arm. "You're in good hands now."

As the stretcher rolled into the operating room, Alison's eyes fluttered shut. Her body finally surrendering to sedation and fatigue. Dr. Pearce and his team followed closely, their expressions set with focus and resolve.

For Alison, the nightmare was far from over. The physical scars would take months, maybe years to heal. But the emotional ones?

Those would run even deeper.

Outside Alison's Home

The first rays of daylight stretched across the horizon as Lieutenant Maxwell and Detective Miller stepped out of Alison's house. The chaos had mostly died down. Patrol officers maintained the perimeter, and though a few neighbors lingered, the scene was quieting.

Maxwell rubbed a hand over his face, fatigue settling deep in his bones. "There's nothing else we can do tonight," he said.

"I agree," Miller replied, just as worn. "We've documented everything we can. We'll need fresh eyes in the morning."

Maxwell pulled out his phone and dialed Detective Castanon. The upstart answered quickly, his voice alert despite the hour.

"Castanon, that's it for the night," Maxwell said. "You and Jacobson get some rest. We regroup at 11:00 a.m. to go over everything. The gym stays locked down. Alison's house stays under surveillance. Both are active crime scenes. I don't want anything slipping through the cracks."

"Understood, Lieutenant."

Maxwell ended the call and turned to Miller. "Tomorrow, we find Samantha Sinclair. There's a connection here and we need to figure out what she knows."

"For now, we call it a night?"

Maxwell nodded. "We're racing the clock. And with the press conference on Monday, that's only going to add more pressure."

"Anything coming out of Hollywood Division yet?" Miller asked.

"Nothing solid. We're hitting resistance from residents up there who don't want us searching near their property lines. Arson team's still combing the area, but we can't get to where we need to. It's been a drag."

Miller nodded. "Pressure's building."

Maxwell's jaw tensed. "Pressure's part of the job. Let's just hope tomorrow gives us the break we need."

As the last patrol car pulled away, the sun rose over the houses, casting a golden hue across the calm street. The yellow police tape fluttered in the morning breeze, bright and impossible to ignore.

Inside The Operating Room

Two hours had passed since Alison was wheeled into surgery, and Dr. Pearce's focus hadn't wavered. The room was hushed, the machines carrying its steady beat. His team moved in unison, following each command without hesitation.

"Carefully now," Dr. Pearce instructed. "We need to excise the damaged tissue without compromising the healthy areas."

He peered closer, gloved hands unwavering as he meticulously removed the charred skin from Alison's cheek. Each motion was deliberate, the tension in his brow betraying the weight of the task.

The burns were staggering, spanning much of her right cheek and creeping toward her jawline. The tissue damage was severe, but not hopeless. Her eye and hairline had been spared. Still, the scarring would be life-altering.

"This is step one," Dr. Pearce said. "Stabilize her. We'll need multiple reconstructive surgeries down the line, but this initial cleanup is critical."

His team responded in sync, passing instruments, assisting as he worked. Alison's vitals remained steady, but the emotional and psychological toll loomed like a shadow over the room.

Dr. Pearce had treated dozens of burn victims, but this case felt different. Alison wasn't just another patient.

She was part of something bigger now. A story gripping the city. A chilling pattern of violence aimed at influencers.

"She's stable," a nurse finally said, completing the first phase of surgery.

Dr. Pearce exhaled and stepped back. "Good work. Monitor her closely over the next 24 hours. Keep her comfortable. Prep for the next stage."

As Alison was wheeled into recovery, Dr. Pearce removed his gloves and looked to the clock. The hospital was still, the hour late. This was only the beginning of a long, grueling journey for Alison… and for the team trying to bring her back.

CHAPTER 29

SUNDAY NOT SO FUN DAY

Morning sunlight crept into the room, waking Samantha slowly. Samantha shifted toward Mike, who was still beside her. He felt her move, turned his head, and kissed her forehead.

"I thought you were still here," she said, a soft smile touching her lips. "At least now I know I didn't dream it."

"Good morning, Sam," Mike said gently. "How are you feeling?"

She sat up carefully, grimacing as her hand brushed her bruised ribs. "Oh yeah, the *Le Cher* thing. I almost forgot for a second." A small chuckle escaped. "It's getting a little better… I think. At least I hope."

"What time is your appointment?"

"They're seeing me at 1:00 p.m. at urgent care," she replied.

Mike nodded, slipping out of bed to freshen up. "That gives me time to make breakfast."

Samantha watched as he slid on his boxers and walked toward the bathroom. She admired his physique, a playful smile tugging at her lips.

As she lay back, she took her phone off Do Not Disturb. A flood of notifications hit the screen. Free Meal Jason had been texting non-stop.

Free Meal Jason: *Hey, you okay? Haven't heard back. You still want to meet?*

Samantha sighed, annoyed, typed her reply.

Samantha: *I'm not going to be available anytime soon.*

He replied immediately.

Free Meal Jason: *When will we meet then?*

Rolling her eyes, she shut the door on that chapter.

Samantha: *We won't be. I'm sorry, but I'm talking to someone else now.*

A pause. Then:

Free Meal Jason: *Can we at least stay friends?*

Without replying, she deleted the conversation and his number.

Just then, another message came in. This time from Free Meal Keith.

Free Meal Keith: *Samantha, where are you? Did you forget about us?*

He'd always been good company, but it was time to cut this tie too.

Samantha: *Keith, we had some good dates, but I'm talking to someone else now.*

Free Meal Keith: *Wow. Wish you'd told me sooner.*

Samantha: *It just sort of happened. I'm sorry.*

Free Meal Keith: *So that's it, then?*

Samantha: *For now, yes.*

Free Meal Keith: *Can we stay friends?*

She stared at the screen, hesitating.

Samantha: *Maybe… I don't know. I don't want to think about that right now. Goodbye, Keith. Take care.*

She deleted his number and the chat log, setting her phone down with a sense of finality. It felt freeing, like she was finally clearing space for something, or someone real.

She reached for her tablet and moved too suddenly, gasping as the pain in her ribs flared. Grabbing the controller for the house speakers, she spoke into it.

"Should I come down so we can eat at the table?"

Mike's voice echoed through the system. "Don't come down. I'm coming up to you."

"Okay, Mister! It smells amazing." The delight was evident in her voice. "Oh, and do you see the digital cat clock on the wall? Press the button on its paw. It connects to the speakers, so no yelling needed."

Mike chuckled pressing the button. "Got it. I'll be up in about fifteen minutes."

"I'm looking forward to another one of your delicious breakfasts."

Samantha laid back, a smile tugging at her lips. Peace was something she hadn't known in a long time, but it was creeping in. Mike was thoughtful, kind, and real. And that was worth making space for.

The savory aroma of breakfast drifted through the house, wrapping her in warmth. She closed her eyes, finally ready to start letting go of the past and embrace what was next.

More Than Meets The Eye

Mike focused on breakfast, determined to make it special. He was preparing breakfast tacos, a perfect mix of hearty and fresh. Eggs, sausage, bacon, shredded cheese, cilantro, diced onions, and limes sat ready. He had both red and green salsa, sour cream, and a bowl of freshly cut fruit to balance it out. He arranged everything with care, thinking not just about the meal, but about Samantha.

She had been through so much, yet somehow held it together, pushing through the pain without complaint. It wasn't lost on him how strong she was. But he also noticed the times when her vulnerability slipped through. Those glimpses weren't weaknesses, they were something deeper, something real.

There was a part of Samantha that craved companionship. He could tell it wasn't easy for her to admit. Not even to herself. She had kept her walls up for so long, even with him. But after what happened at *Le Cher,* something had shifted. In those instances when she let him in, he felt her need. Not just for someone to lean on, but for someone she could trust completely.

Last night had been different. The way she moved, savoring everything. It wasn't just physical, it was emotional. There was passion in her touch, but also apprehension. She looked at him with eyes that almost pulled back, as if reminding herself not to hope too much and not to believe this could be real. But she didn't back away. She had thrown her arms around him and held on tight, not wanting to let go.

Mike felt it. This wasn't just about sex, even though that part of their connection was undeniable. It was something deeper. The way she was starting to trust him.

The way she was letting him see her real self, it felt different.

As he stood over the stove flipping bacon, he thought about the decision he'd made the night before while she slept beside him.

He wanted this. He wanted her.

Samantha wasn't just someone he was seeing; she was starting to matter to him in a way he hadn't expected.

He knew being with her wouldn't be easy. Chaos came with the territory. But that didn't faze him. If anything, it only solidified his decision to stick around.

Mike finished plating the tacos, adding a small bowl of lime wedges and a colorful plate of fresh fruit. He took a step back, gave a small nod of approval, and grabbed the tray.

Balancing it carefully, he started up the stairs. He wasn't expecting a big reaction, but he hoped it would make her morning a little easier. That was the point. Showing up and keeping her steady, one small thing at a time.

Piecing The Puzzle Together

The air inside Alison's house was heavy with tension as the team scoured for clues. Maxwell paced the living room, scanning for anything that might tie the killer to the scene, when Miller called out.

"We found something with this gift box!" Miller said, holding up a small, intricately designed container. "It looks like it was made by a small business in Venice."

Maxwell walked over to examine it. "What's the name of the business?"

Miller turned the box to reveal a faint logo. *Diana's Custom Gifts*.

Maxwell quickly pulled out his phone and typed in the name. "The shop's closed today, but we'll pay her a visit first thing tomorrow."

Miller nodded, carefully placing the box into an evidence bag.

The customized gift box was an unexpected lead. The woman who owned *Diana's Custom Gifts* also bartended at *Le Cher*, the same bartender who had served Mike and Samantha that night. The discovery raised more questions than answers. Could the killer have a connection to her? Did she unknowingly provide a clue?

Meanwhile, a separate lab was still running tests on the chemical compound found in the bottle that burned Alison's face. Preliminary analysis suggested it had been tampered with, traces of a face serum from a high-end brand called *Queen of the Nile Beauty* were identified in the residue.

The killer hadn't just weaponized a beauty product. He'd carefully selected one designed to destroy.

The police planned to visit the shop for security footage and a few questions. The owner's cooperation might be the breakthrough they needed.

Maxwell stepped away and called Castanon for an update.

"Sir," Castanon began, "we've got another witness from the gym willing to describe the killer, but the accounts are conflicting."

Maxwell's brow furrowed. "How so?"

"One witness described the killer as a repairman. The other saw a gym-goer hovering near Jordan before… before the attack. And the descriptions don't match."

"Shit," Maxwell muttered. "He's using disguises."

"That's what I thought," Castanon replied. "The gym's corporate team has agreed to cooperate. They're sending over all the security footage."

"Good. What about the staff?"

"That might be tricky," Castanon admitted. "Corporate has already briefed them on what to say. We'll have to tread carefully. They're being coached."

Maxwell exhaled sharply. "Fine. We'll meet the gym manager after the press conference tomorrow. Any update on the footprint analysis?"

"Nothing yet, but we're still working on it."

"Keep at it," Maxwell said, ending the call.

Without hesitation, he punched in Jacobson's number.

"Detective," Maxwell began, "I want round-the-clock police presence at the hospital. Two officers stationed at all times, and one assigned to her floor. Make it happen."

"Absolutely," Jacobson replied. "We've got one officer there now. I'll double it."

"I also need you to coordinate with hospital security. No one gets onto her floor unless cleared. And make sure the press doesn't report where she's being treated. We can't risk the killer finding her. If he's really using disguises, he could slip in dressed as staff."

"Understood. "I'm heading there now."

"Good," Maxwell said ending the call.

He turned to the team. "We need to dig deeper into Samantha. If she's another target, she might be the key to figuring out who this bastard is."

The pressure was mounting. The killer was resourceful, intelligent, and relentless.

Every second counted.

I Think He's A Keeper

Back at Samantha's, they had just finished breakfast. Her morning playlist filled the room with an upbeat, infectious energy that matched her mood. Whether it was the music, the food, or simply Mike's presence, Samantha was all smiles. Her playful spirit resurfaced, making her feel lighter than she had in weeks.

"Wow, Mikey, these were wonderful," she said, setting her fork down with a grin. "You're over here spoiling me. I can't remember the last time someone cooked for me like this."

Mike leaned back. "Just wanted to make sure you had a good start to your day, especially with that doctor's appointment coming up."

"And I am," she replied, moving closer to press a soft kiss to his lips.

"I'm glad." He smiled reaching for the plates. "I'll take these down. I know you need to start getting ready."

Before he could finish, Samantha reached out and touched his hand.

"Mike?"

He looked at her, their eyes locking. There was a look there that made him pause. Her lips parted slightly, but it was her eyes doing all the talking.

"If you don't have anything to do today… will you come with me to the doctor? "I don't want to be there alone," she confessed.

Her voice trembled slightly as she glanced down at their hands. Her fingers brushed his, and when she looked back up, her hair slipped into her face, half-concealing her expression. But Mike saw it, unguarded vulnerability that hit him straight in the chest.

"Of course I'll come," he said without hesitation.

Her face lit up with relief. "Great," she said, sliding out of bed. "I'll start the shower."

Mike stepped out of the room with the dishes, and Samantha sank back against the pillows. A deep exhale escaped her lips as her thoughts drifted. Grateful, nervous, and maybe… a little bit hopeful.

It's too late, she thought. *I can't hide how I'm feeling about him anymore.*

A wry smile tugged at her lips. *What can I say? I think he's a keeper.*

Her mind drifted back to the last time she'd felt this safe with someone. Years ago, with her college sweetheart. They'd been inseparable until graduation, when life pulled them in different directions. After that, the walls went up.

A lot of that traced back to her father. His absence made emotional commitment hard. *Will they leave like he did?* She often wondered. Her parents' divorce had left a scar that never fully healed. One that made her skeptical of love and wary of getting hurt.

But with Mike, it felt different. It wasn't just the way he treated her, it was how he made her feel. Safe. Seen. Like she didn't have to keep her guard up.

It felt like a schoolgirl crush happening all over again… only deeper.

Don't make me regret falling for you, Mike, she thought, closing her eyes.

A soft smile crept across her face as the sound of running water drifted in from the bathroom. *I could get used to this, if he plays his cards right.*

The Blur Between Dreams And Pain

Alison's surgery had lasted six grueling hours. As the anesthetic began to wear off, she slipped in and out of consciousness. Her mind foggy and disoriented. She had no idea where she was, only vague impressions of light and sterile surroundings.

The sharp, clinical smell of the hospital mixed with the low hum of nearby machines. It felt like a dream, but not quite. Her thoughts were too scattered to form any sense of reality. Each time she drifted into a sleep-like state, she couldn't tell if it was real or just part of the blur of sedation.

The pain was distant, barely perceptible through the drug-induced haze. She could feel the weight of her body, the pressure of the bandages, but it didn't fully register. She didn't know how much time had passed since the surgery, or even what exactly had been done. Her mind was a cloud, shifting between fragmented memories and half-formed thoughts. Was she in a dream? Was the blood, the chaos, the terror all just a nightmare?

When she finally stirred, it felt like waking from a foggy slumber. Her eyes fluttered open, blinking against the sterile white ceiling above. Her body felt foreign, heavy, unresponsive. The faint beeping of machines and the soft shuffle of footsteps told her she wasn't alone, but she couldn't make sense of the figures around her. They were shadows at the edge of her perception, blurred and faceless.

Her phone lay silent beside her, its battery long dead from the barrage of missed calls and messages. She was too disoriented to remember it, let alone check it. The hospital staff had confiscated it during triage, and in her unconscious state, she was unaware of the outside world moving on without her. The messages she couldn't read, the notifications she couldn't see. It had all slipped away in the depths of sedation.

Alison was alone in the sterile room, unable to speak, disconnected from the world. Her body felt locked in place, confined to the bed, the weight of her situation pressing down like a lead blanket. Vitals were monitored constantly, but all she could do was slip deeper into unconsciousness as the next shift of nurses arrived. Her mind drifted, untethered, lost in a sea of confusion and silence.

Her recovery had only just begun. Alison, adrift in her fractured world, had no idea how long or painful the road ahead would be.

Steam and Surrender

Samantha had the shower running, her hair pinned up and her robe loosely tied. The air was thick with steam when Mike came upstairs. Hearing the water, he stepped into the bathroom, slipped his arms around her waist, and gently tugged at the sash of her robe. It fell open, revealing her bare body. A rush surged through him, not just from the heat.

His erection pressed against her from behind as Samantha turned, letting the robe slip to the floor. Her breasts were soft and full, her skin flushed from the steam. She took his hand and led him into the shower. Water cascaded over them, drenching their bodies in warmth as their hands found each other, washing and exploring with slow, searching strokes.

Mike's hand slid between her legs, drawing a soft moan from her lips. Their breathing deepened, the intimacy thickening between them even before the music filled the air.

"Don't U Wanna (Medsound Remix)" by DJ Aristocrat and T. Say began playing over the house speakers. The beat pulsed through the tiles, slow and electric, a rhythm that seemed to sync perfectly with their bodies.

Samantha turned, her wet hair clinging to her back as she came closer, lips brushing his ear. "You got the feeling…" she whispered, the lyrics melting into her voice as she kissed him with full intent letting herself go slip into his firm grasp, her passion overflowing, unrestrained.

Water danced across their skin as Mike pulled her closer, drawn in by her rhythm, her scent, the way her mouth met his so perfectly. She climbed into his lap, sinking down onto him with a soft gasp. He groaned, gripping her waist as she adjusted, water streaming down their shoulders and arms. The lyrics continued. She added a playful twist.

"It keeps breaking me, breaking me, all the time," she whispered, her breath hot against his ear as her hips rocked slowly. The words melted into the song's echo, weaving through the fog of desire filling the shower. Her hands looped around his neck, her body pressing into his as he matched her rhythm, gripping her tighter.

The lyrics throbbed in their ears as the beat built. Samantha arching back, her movements intensifying, Mike steadying her with firm hands. Her eye locking with his. Heavy with raw intensity.

"You found the meaning of wondering, wondering how I…" she breathed, her voice barely above the sound of water hitting tile.

And then it hit. A surge of pleasure overtook them both, bodies trembling, gasps and moans lost in the hiss of water and the beat of the song. Their mouths met in one last kiss as the track faded. Their skin from their afterglow as they stepped out, the air warm against their bodies.

CHAPTER 30

THE STRONGEST NEED HELP TOO

The fluorescent lights of the urgent care waiting room buzzed faintly, blending with the soft hum of an '80s playlist on the speakers. A football game flickered on the mounted TV, momentarily catching Mike's eye. Beside him, Samantha clutched her intake papers with a white-knuckled grip. Her tension was unmistakable. Gently, Mike reached over and took her free hand.

"Hey," he murmured. "Relax. You're going to be okay."

Samantha sighed, resting against him. Her oversized purple cashmere sweater slipped slightly off one shoulder, casually chic against crisp white leggings and metallic sandals. Her designer purse rested beside her, its gold chain catching the light.

"Samantha Sinclair?" a nurse called from the doorway.

She exhaled, adjusted her sweater, and stood slowly. Mike helped her up, his hand resting gently on her back as they followed the nurse to the exam room. Samantha eased onto the table, her legs swinging slightly while Mike settled into the chair beside her.

A few minutes later, the door opened and a polished, older doctor entered. His white coat was polished, and his demeanor was professional but warm.

"Good afternoon, I'm Dr. Wallace," he said, extending a hand. Samantha shook it firmly, defiance evident even in the small gesture.

"How did this happen?" he asked, glancing over her paperwork.

Samantha recounted the fight at *Le Cher*, her tone brisk and almost clinical. But she softened when she mentioned how Mike had helped her afterward.

Dr. Wallace nodded thoughtfully. "Tell me about your pain."

"It's manageable," Samantha replied quickly fixing her hair. "Sharp sometimes, mostly throbbing. I've been icing it and doing what I can. Found a lot of information online."

Mike shot her a knowing look. The kind that gently called her out without a word. His gaze softened, but the message was clear to be honest. Samantha caught it, but still lifted her chin, clinging to her independence.

"And on a scale of one to ten?" the doctor asked.

"It was a six the morning after, but now it's a three. I'm fine. Really."

Dr. Wallace chuckled. "You sound like someone who doesn't like to sit still."

"I can't afford to sit still," Samantha shot back. "I need to get back to my routine."

"Well, let's assess the damage first," he replied evenly. "We'll start with some X-rays."

Samantha followed him to the imaging room. Her movements deliberate, almost performative, as if to prove she didn't need help. Mike stayed in his seat, quiet but attentive, letting her be.

In the imagine room, Dr. Wallace gently palpated her ribs. As his fingers brushed the bruised skin, Samantha gasped despite herself.

"Still tender," he said, stepping back.

"I'm *fine*," she insisted, irritation creeping in.

Dr. Wallace calmly instructed Samantha toward the imaging machine. She rolled her eyes, let out a dramatic sigh, and complied, every step radiating exaggerated irritation. He didn't react, clearly used to difficult patients.

"I hate being here," Samantha said, flipping her hair.

Join the club, Dr. Wallace thought.

Instead, he offered a smooth smile. "I won't have you here much longer. Wait for me in the next room, and I'll share the results."

"Fine," Samantha replied strutting out.

A few minutes later, he returned with the X-ray results.

"Good news. Nothing's broken. But, two ribs are badly bruised, and there's soft tissue damage. You're lucky. Your core strength probably prevented something worse."

Samantha straightened. "So, I'm good to go back to my normal routine?"

"Not so fast," Dr. Wallace said. "Recovery will take two to six weeks. I'm prescribing pain meds and muscle relaxers, and I want you to rest. No strenuous activity."

"I don't have two to six weeks," she protested. "I can handle it. I've *been* handling it."

The doctor turned to Mike. "You'll need to make sure she follows the instructions."

Samantha's eyes flared. "He's not my keeper!"

Mike raised his hands in mock surrender. "Just here to help, Sam."

Her shoulders tensed, then dropped. "I can take care of myself," she said, crossing her arms.

"I don't doubt that," Dr. Wallace said kindly. "But even the strongest people need help sometimes. Let yourself heal."

Mike stood and placed a hand on her shoulder. "I know this is hard right now," he began. "But he's speaking from a place of care. Take a break, Sam. You're allowed to."

Samantha didn't look at him, but she didn't move away either. "Okay, Doctor."

The doctor extended his well wishes and concluded the visit. Later, the nurse returned with her prescriptions, and as they prepared to leave, Samantha snatched her paperwork with practiced flair. She marched out ahead of Mike, her exaggerated confidence a final act of defiance. The nurse rolled her eyes. Mike just shrugged and followed.

Outside, he opened the car door for her. Samantha slid in, her body finally relaxing.

"I'm fine," she said, more to herself than to him.

"I know," Mike replied, leaning in to buckle her seatbelt. "But let me help anyway."

As he stepped back, Samantha looked over at him, her fingers toying with the edge of her purse.

"Are you sure?" she asked. "You have your new role at work. I don't want to be a distraction."

Without a word, he reached over and gently pressed a finger to her lips.

"I told the doctor I'd look after you," he said, nudging her shoulder. "And I meant it. Sorry Sam. You're stuck with me now."

Samantha stared at him for a second. Then, instead of replying, she leaned over and hugged him tight, wrapping her arms around his shoulders.

That was her thank you.

Brace Yourself, Samantha

Mike drove Samantha home, planning to stay the night, cook, and keep her company. She didn't mind; she welcomed it. The thought of another dinner made her smile. Her mood had lifted. Some of it painkillers, but mostly Mike. They chatted and laughed all the way home.

Mike's car, a sleek fully loaded black Honda Accord with tinted windows, cruised through the streets as dusk settled in. It wasn't flashy, but it reflected him. Understated, but always sharp. And Samantha noticed. She always did.

"Oh no, no!" Samantha groaned. "*Change* that shit. *Immediately.*"

Mike glanced at her, amused. "What? Isn't it a hit? Why the hate?"

"Ok, So?" by Aryn Amante played faintly through the car speakers.

"That's Alison's song," she said, her tone dripping with disdain. "I can't stand it."

"Why not? You're blonde like her," Mike asked. "I thought she'd be all over your *many* playlists."

Samantha rolled her eyes. "Do you even know what this song is about?"

"Not really," Mike said with a grin. "But I'm sure you're about to tell me."

"Cheating." Samantha began. "The rumors were that Aryn Amante and the guy she hooked up with were both still in relationships. His girlfriend was also Aryn's friend, which made the whole thing even messier. She even lost a ton of followers on social media over it. And Alison? She treats 'Ok, So?' like it's her anthem. Makes me sick."

Mike shook his head. "Get outta here. I had no idea."

"Please. You think I don't know my pop culture? I've done my homework. Now, do me a favor and *turn it off.*"

Mike chuckled as he changed the station. "Fine, you win. No homewrecker anthems tonight."

The car slowed as they pulled into Samantha's driveway. She sighed contentedly, ready to enjoy a peaceful evening at home.

But that wasn't going to happen tonight.

An unmarked police SUV was parked nearby. The detectives were clearly waiting for her. Inside Detective Castanon watched Samantha and Mike exit the car.

"You think she knows?" Detective Castanon asked, his tone casual.

Detective Maxwell, seated behind the wheel, adjusted his tie. "Let's find out. Keep it professional. Stay calm, *not* aggressive. We need her cooperation, not a reason to shut us out."

"Didn't know she was a baddie," Castanon said, unable to resist commenting.

Maxwell shot him a sharp glance. "Let's not get sidetracked."

"Hey, just an observation," Castanon replied, raising his hands in mock defense. "Strictly professional, of course."

Detective Miller sat in the passenger seat, his eyes fixed on the house. After watching Samantha and Mike walk in, the three officers stepped out and approached the gate.

Inside, Samantha hadn't noticed the detectives on her cameras. She was too caught up in the lightness of her evening with Mike, grateful for his presence as she navigated her recovery. But the peace wouldn't last. This visit was about to shatter it.

CHAPTER 31

THE QUEEN OF HER CASTLE

As Samantha and Mike were deciding on what to cook for dinner, the peaceful atmosphere was interrupted by the sharp chime of the security system.

"Motion detected, front gate," the system announced.

"What the fuck is this?" Samantha muttered, her irritation matching the sudden halt in Mike's movements.

She grabbed her tablet, flipping through the cameras until the front gate appeared on-screen. The figures at the gate were ringing the bell again.

Her voice, tinged with annoyance, crackled through the call box. "Umm… who are you?"

The men paused, looking up for a camera.

Samantha's voice rang out again. "I see you. Don't worry about where the camera is, but I see you."

Detective Maxwell looked up and, after a beat, introduced himself and the others. "Samantha Sinclair?

We'd like to come in and talk to you. You know an Alison Santiago, right?"

Samantha's eyes narrowed. "What is this? She's my best friend."

"May we come in? It's urgent," Maxwell pressed.

Samantha's voice remained cold, her tone hardening. "I don't let strange men into my house. How do I know you're really cops?"

She glanced back at Mike, who stood behind her, nearly forgotten in the tension.

"I don't take chances," she continued. "And I'm not just letting anyone in."

Mike stepped forward too quickly. Samantha flinched before she could stop herself, her body on edge, her nerves pulled tight like piano wire.

"Okay," she said, "if you are who you say you are, put your badges next to the call box. I need to verify you."

Detective Castanon looked baffled. "Ma'am, what are you talking about?"

"This is my house. My rules," she snapped. "Put your badges up to the call box, and I'll scan them for verification."

A new side of her had emerged. Commanding. Composed. Tactical. Mike had not seen this before. She navigated the system like she was trained for this, flipping between monitors, messaging her security contact, activating multiple layers of defense.

Mike could see the strain in her eyes. She was holding it together, but just barely. Her breaths were short and quick, her posture rigid.

He stepped in, wrapping an arm around her. "Don't worry. Whatever this is, I'm here."

She leaned into his touch briefly, then kissed his hand and pulled away. Still strong. Still standing.

"Do it now, or leave my gate," her tone sharp despite the shake behind it.

The officers exchanged glances. Maxwell gave in. "Alright, Miss Sinclair, if this is what it takes."

One by one, they raised their badges to the call box. Samantha scanned and uploaded the data, eyes fixed on the screen until the security company confirmed:

Verified.

"Alright, detectives," she said, some tension loosening. "I'll stand down my security system."

"Felicia, disengage the system and open the front gate," she said.

"Acknowledged. Disengaging now."

The gate clicked open.

Samantha grabbed her side with a sharp wince. One hand braced against the counter as she breathed through the pain. Then she stood tall. This wasn't the time for weakness.

Mike moved to her side again, staying just behind her. Ready, but letting her lead. She gave him a quick glance. He nodded.

Drawing strength from his presence, she exhaled, stood tall, and opened the door.

Good Evening, Officers

Samantha opened the door, letting the detectives file in. She moved to the far side of the kitchen counter , the power dynamic clear. Mike stood off to the side, like a line judge. The detectives held authority, but she remained composed, in control of her space despite the tension.

"Detectives, may I help you? What is this about Alison? What's happened?" she asked, her voice calm but tinged with concern.

"First, my name is Lieutenant Byron Maxwell. These are my colleagues, Detective Lawrence Miller and Detective Edward Castanon. We hate to meet you under these circumstances," Maxwell said, his expression grave.

Mike introduced himself as Samantha's friend. Samantha, clearly annoyed, wanted the encounter to be brief and without unnecessary banter.

"Detectives, please state your business with me," she said, urging them along.

"Of course," Maxwell replied. He cleared his throat clearing choosing his next words carefully. "We're investigating a series of murders that have taken place over the past 72 hours."

Samantha stared at him, blankly unaware.

Maxwell exchanged a glance with his colleagues before continuing. "You haven't seen the news yet, have you? Three high-profile influencers have been killed. Miss Santiago was also a victim."

"Alison?" Samantha's voice rose. "What's going on? I've been at the doctor all day."

Maxwell took a breath. "Miss Sinclair, your friend was the target of a horrific attack. A package linked to you was delivered to her. Inside was a facial product. And… it disfigured her. Third-degree burns. She was rushed into emergency surgery."

Samantha's face went pale. She collapsed to her knees, sobbing uncontrollably.

"No… no… no… Alison!" Her body trembling as Maxwell's words crashed down on her.

Mike rushed to her side, kneeling with her, his hand on her back. He helped her up, feeling the shock and pain radiating through her.

Maxwell stepped back to give her space. "Miss Sinclair, I know this is a huge shock, and I'm so sorry. But we do need to ask a few questions. This is part of a much larger investigation. Anything you can share might help us find the person responsible."

Samantha agreed still shaken. Her body leaning into Mike's as she fought to stay composed.

"Whatever this package was, it had your name on it," Detective Miller added.

Her eyes widened in disbelief. Tears streamed down her face like a running faucet. Mike held her close, guiding her head to his chest as she wept. Her tears soaked into his shirt.

Mike spoke up. "Detectives, she may need a moment."

"Of course," Miller replied, following Maxwell's lead. "We understand. Please… take your time."

"I told her not to take it," Samantha whispered, wiping her tears with a tissue. "I didn't recognize the sender, but I figured it was just another PR agency. I get packages all the time. I had no idea. I even looked up the company and it seemed legit."

Maxwell nodded, taking notes. "So did we. But we're still looking into them. Anything you can recall is helpful. This is a race against time."

Mike stood behind Samantha with his hands on her shoulders. His silent presence grounded her.

"I had a weird feeling about the package," she continued, voice shaky. "But she insisted on opening it."

"We opened it together. The instructions said to go live with a product demo and get $600. I really thought it was just another collab. Just like the others," she added, concern laced through her words.

Maxwell nodded. "That's consistent."

"I was here for the whole thing," Mike added. "I can give a statement."

"That would help," Maxwell replied.

Samantha looked directly at him. "Do you know where she is?"

"She's at L.A. Medical," Maxwell answered, his eyes lowering briefly.

"I need to see her," Samantha said, her voice cracking. "She's not answering her phone. I even have been texting her. Nothing."

Maxwell's tone grew firmer. "We're doing everything we can. But right now, you'll need to be patient, Miss Sinclair."

"Patient?" Samantha snapped, her hands gripping the counter. "She's alone in a hospital room and you're telling me to be patient?"

She broke free of Mike's touch, stepping forward with determination to confront Maxwell, but the pain caught up and she faltered. Her next words caught in a gasp, the sharp pang stealing her breath. She stumbled, catching herself against the counter.

Mike moved instinctively to help, but she lifted a hand—not to push him away, but to hold the moment still. Their eyes locked. His concern was written all over his face. She gave the smallest shake of her head, a quiet *I'm okay,* then mouthed, *thank you.*

"How did you come into contact with the package?" Maxwell asked, cutting back in.

She didn't answer right away.

Her eyes stayed on Mike as the rest of the room seemed to fade. A pull, like a shared breath. He glanced at Maxwell, then back at her, his jaw set. A slow, deliberate nod that said, *I'm with you.*

A fleeting smile touched her lips. It didn't last long, but it was enough. He steadied her just by being there.

She turned toward the detectives, not flustered but poised. Her shoulders squared as if bracing against a storm. The motion was subtle, yet defiant.

"It was dropped at my gate, mixed with the others," she said, her voice clear. She pointed toward the packages still stacked in the corner. "Alison came by the next day and wanted to use it. I couldn't. I'm allergic to some of the ingredients. I begged her not to take it. She insisted."

"She did," Mike confirmed. "I was here."

Just then, Samantha's phone buzzed on the counter. It was her father, calling after seeing the security alert from the officer verification.

"Honey, is everything alright?" Leonard asked.

In Spanish:

"Sí, la policía está aquí. Es sobre Alison… ha resultado gravemente herida," Samantha said, trying to hold back tears.

(Yes, the police are here. It's about Alison… she's been seriously injured.)

"¿Qué pasó?" her father asked urgently.
(What happened?)

"Llegó una crema facial en un paquete. Pensé que era una colaboración de marca. Había ingredientes que no podía usar por mis alergias. No lo reconocí, pero le dije que no lo tomara. Ella lo usó de todos modos. Tenía un mal presentimiento… y ahora Alison está herida," she said, crying.

(A facial cream came in a package. I thought it was a brand collab. There were ingredients I couldn't use because of allergies. I didn't recognize it, but I told her not to take it. She used it anyway. I had a bad feeling… and now Alison is hurt.)

"Está bien. Ya veo que la policía está allí y que todos están presentes… ¿Quién es ese chico?" her father asked, referring to Mike.

(It's okay. I see the police are there and everyone's present… who's that guy?)

"Un amigo. Estaba aquí cuando…" she paused. Noticing Castanon eavesdropping, she shot him a look and spoke sharply in Spanish.

(A friend. He was here when—)

"¿Hablas español?" she asked, raising an eyebrow.
(You speak Spanish?)

"Sí," Castanon replied curtly.
(Yes.)

Samantha held his gaze, then calmly switched back to her father, now speaking in fluent French.

In French:

"Papa, je veux qu'ils partent. Il faut que j'aille voir Alison," Samantha said, her voice firm.
(Daddy, I want them gone. I need to see Alison.)

Detective Castanon's irritation was obvious. He shot a look at Maxwell and gestured, but Maxwell waved him off with a shake of his head. Miller, still following Maxwell's lead, stepped closer and rested a hand on Castanon's shoulder, to try and calm him. This was a sensitive situation. Tact was key.

"Je vais voir ce que je peux faire, ma chérie. Tu devrais rester sur tes gardes," her father replied, his voice calm but urgent. "Je vais renforcer la sécurité de la maison."

(I'll see what I can do, honey. You should stay on your guard. I'll reinforce the house security.)

"Surveillance 24 heures sur 24 ?" Samantha asked, her voice trembling.
(Round-the-clock monitoring?)

"Bien sûr," he assured her. "Je vais mettre l'équipe d'intervention en alerte. Ce colis portait bien ton nom, n'est-ce pas ?"
(Of course. I'll put the response team on standby. That package had your name on it, didn't it?)

"Oui," Samantha replied. Though her mind raced.
(Yes.)

"D'accord. Je vais m'en occuper. J'ai scanné leurs dossiers. Tu peux collaborer avec les autorités. Dis-leur tout ce qu'ils doivent savoir, et je te rappellerai plus tard."
(Okay. I'll take care of it. I've scanned their records. You can cooperate with the authorities. Tell them everything they need, and I'll call you back later.)

"Oui, papa. Je t'aime," Samantha said.
(Yes, Daddy. I love you.)

"Moi aussi, je t'aime," her father replied before hanging up.
(I love you too.)

She's Not Your Suspect

Samantha hung up, set her phone down, and let out a heavy sigh. The tension in the room loomed like a shadow. She needed time to process.

She didn't realize how long she had been lost in thought   until Mike's voice broke the silence. "Is everything okay, Sam?"

Regaining her focus, she looked up. "So what do you need, detectives?"

"If you have the surveillance from the night you received the package, we'd like to compare it with footage from another crime scene," Detective Maxwell said.

"Of course. I can download it and either email it to you or put it on a flash drive," Samantha offered.

"A flash drive would be best, if you have one," Maxwell replied.

"Yes, I do." She wiped at her eyes and walked over to retrieve a flash drive.
"I'll just need a few minutes to access the date and download it," she said. Her voice supportive, but edged with exhaustion.

She retrieved her laptop and began typing, pulling up the security footage from that day. The timestamp appeared. The killer came into view on camera, disguised as a delivery driver.

Her stomach twisted. He had arrived the same night she'd met Mike at *Le Cher*.

She gasped at how close the timing was. The cameras had caught her pulling out of the driveway just minutes before the figure appeared, walking up to place the package at the gate. Unaware of the surveillance, the killer hadn't even tried to hide his face. Every feature was clear.

Every angle of him was captured in pristine, high-resolution detail. More than enough to run facial recognition. It could be the break they needed.

The police and Mike saw it all. Samantha, sensing the weight of the moment, wiped away a few stray tears.

"I'll start downloading this," she said, regaining her composure. She tapped away as the download progress bar appeared, preparing to hand the flash drive to the detectives.

But Castanon couldn't help himself.

"This helps, but it isn't going to release you from any more questions we have," he said.

Samantha, shaken, turned sharply. "Excuse me?"

Things were about to unravel for the detectives.

Maxwell jumped in.. "We just still need to…"

"No, no, no, no." Samantha cut him off. "Am I a suspect in this? Because that's *exactly* the vibe I'm getting from you now. I'm giving you this to leave me alone, not to come back. I told you everything I knew," she insisted, her voice rising.

"Ma'am, this is an ongoing investigation, and we need to assess your involvement. If we have more questions, we will be back to ask them," Castanon unequivocally said.

As Castanon's questions became more aggressive, Samantha's hand tightened on the counter. She shifted her weight, careful not to jar her injury. But her breath caught with every word Castanon spoke, as if the tension of the moment only made the pain worse.

"You've been at the center of this from the start. How do we know you're not withholding something?" Castanon pressed. .

Was this about the footage... or was she already a suspect in their eyes?

Mike saw her flinch. That was enough.

He immediately stepped forward, his body tense. "What the hell is wrong with you?" he snapped, placing himself between Samantha and Castanon. "She's the victim here. She's been stalked, attacked, terrorized, and you're treating her like she's the criminal?"

"Miss Sinclair, we really need your help with the footage," Detective Maxwell said gently. "Please."

But it was too late. Samantha's blood boiled. The injustice of being treated like a suspect had finally pushed her over the edge. Mike turned to her, reading the tension in her posture, the way she braced against the counter.

"Don't let him get in your head," he urged.

She said nothing and just stared, her eyes like ice-cold daggers aimed straight through Castanon.

"I'm not doing the good cop, bad cop routine. Felicia, terminate the download," she snapped, her voice hard and unwavering.

"Termination confirmed. Download canceled," Felicia's calm voice replied.

Detective Maxwell moved to step closer, but Mike was already between them. "Don't," he said sharply, his voice low but filled with an authority that made Maxwell pause. "Samantha doesn't need this right now."

Mike turned to Castanon. "I think it's time for you to leave," he said, his tone commanding. The threat of what would happen if they didn't leave hanging in the air.

"Samantha?" Mike interjected, looking at her, his voice calm but firm. He then turned to Maxwell, his expression serious. "This isn't the way to handle this. If you want her help, you need to back off and show some respect."

Maxwell glanced from Mike to Samantha, then gave a reluctant nod and waved Castanon off. The download was at 87%. A crucial piece of evidence. And now, they weren't getting it. All because of Castanon's arrogance.

"I'm just doing my job," Castanon grumbled, but he didn't argue further. With one last glare at Samantha, he retreated outside.

"No," Mike shot back, his voice rising. "You're pushing her too far. She's grieving, and now you're throwing out baseless accusations? You seriously need to dial it back."

"You're right," Maxwell admitted, throwing another glare at Castanon. "This got out of hand. We're here to help, not make this harder for you. But… we really do need that footage to help us." Still pressing.

Making sure Castanon heard as he left, Samantha said,
"If I'm being investigated, I'll be directing you to my lawyers at Weinstein, Strasburg, and Gambino. Julian Weinstein represents me."

Her voice trembled slightly. She tried to hold her composure, but the way her hand gripped the counter betrayed her unease.

The detectives shifted uncomfortably. They knew he was one of the top attorneys in town. Things had just gone from bad to worse. A major delay in the investigation, triggered by Castanon's mishandling.

"I'm really sorry for my partner's behavior," Maxwell said earnestly. "But we still need that footage. Please, Miss Sinclair, don't let his attitude jeopardize this case. We're trying to help you, and we need your help as well."

Samantha crossed her arms, standing her ground. "*Help me*?" she repeated, incredulous. "Your partner just accused me of being involved. You think I'm going to hand over anything to people who can't even decide if I'm a victim or a suspect?"

"Accusing her is not going to gain cooperation," Mike said, backing up Samantha.

"Again, I apologize, Miss Sinclair, but we believe the killer will try to target you again. We would like you to consider leaving," Maxwell said.

Maxwell's words registered with Mike as he realized the looming threat posed to Samantha.

"Sam, maybe you should consider their request," Mike said with concern.

Samantha pulled away from Mike's grip, the isolation setting in. If she was going to fight for her home, she'd do it on her own. She stepped forward, bracing herself to face the officers, and even Mike if she had to.

"I'm *not* leaving. I'm *not* going to be pushed out of my home. I'm safe here," she insisted.

She was breathing heavier, fighting to stay strong, but the strain showed. Stress pulsed through her body, sharpening every ache. The tension in the room pressed in from all sides. It was too much at once. The edges of the room began to spin, but this wasn't the time to waver. She forced herself to hold on.

I need them all to leave, she kept thinking. *Mike can go too if he doesn't understand me.*

The detective's gruff voice snapped her back to attention.

"But we can put you under surveillance and take you somewhere safe," Detective Maxwell said, trying to convey his willingness to protect her.

"My house is already under 24-hour surveillance. I don't need you," she said sternly.

"What are you talking about?" Detective Maxwell asked.

Samantha, still boldly making her stand against the officers, didn't mince words. She moved between them and Mike, fighting to stay upright, refusing to stumble. This was her home. Her ground. And no matter how much it hurt, she wasn't giving it up. No one was going to force her out.

I'll face them all if I have to, she thought, jaw clenched as she fought to steady her breath.

Breathing heavily, she said, "If someone broke in, I'd know exactly what to do. I know this house like the back of my hand. I know where to hide. I have high-level defenses here. Do you really think I'd call 911? Fuck no. You're too slow. My system alerts a private armed security team, and they'll be here faster than any cop. So, once again, I'm not leaving my home. Everything is on camera. We've been on camera this entire time. I'm fine, and I will stay fine. I don't need you."

It was becoming increasingly clear to Mike just how close she was to unraveling. The look on her face said it all. She felt cornered. Her defiance was starting to crack. Her eyes flicked from person to person, silently pleading:

Back off.

"Miss Sinclair, you should really consider—" Maxwell began.

"I'm not leaving my home!" she shrieked, cutting him off.

The strain finally boiled over. A sharp stab of pain shot through her ribs. She winced, gasping, one hand flying to her side as the other clutched the counter for support.

The throbbing surged back, stronger now with every passing second, pulsing with every breath.

"Are you okay?" Maxwell asked, visibly concerned.

Mike stepped closer, his eyes scanning Samantha's pained expression before turning to face them.

"Listen, guys, you're really upsetting her. You're making this a lot worse," he said.

"Get out now!" she screamed again, tears welling in her eyes. Samantha was breaking down. Seeing the distress on her face, Mike gently wrapped his arm around her.

Maxwell made one final attempt to reconcile everything. "Look, I'm really sorry for my colleague's attitude. I never wanted you to feel like you couldn't trust us."

He cleared his throat and pulled a card from his pocket, placing it on the counter. "If you think of anything else or want to talk, you can reach me directly. I'll make sure this stays professional from now on, and you'll only deal with me."

Samantha barely registered his voice through the tears.

Mike turned to Maxwell. "Thank you. I think it's best if we wrap this up for tonight. Samantha needs time to fully process everything."

A tear fell down her face. Mike respected the gravity of the situation.

"Felicia, initiate security protocol in ninety seconds," Samantha said, her voice a little hoarse.

"Of course, Samantha. Security protocol will initiate in ninety seconds," Felicia replied, her voice soft but precise.

The detectives hesitated, exchanging a look before glancing back at Samantha. One last silent urge for her to reconsider, to do the right thing.

"Security protocol will activate in sixty seconds."

But there was no more talking. The line had been drawn. Samantha's gaze made it clear. This was her final word.

"Forty-five seconds to full protocol engagement."

Detectives Miller and Maxwell began making their way out, tension in their shoulders.

"Protocol engaging in thirty seconds. Please exit or override."

With tears still in her eyes, Samantha followed them to the door. As they stepped out, she slammed it with her free hand, the other still gripping her injured side.

"Final warning. Ten seconds to full security lockdown."

She walked back to her screens and watched them head toward their car, taking short breaths, trying to calm herself.

"Final confirmation. Security protocol engaging now."

A pause.

"Samantha, your home is secure. Protocol is active."

With them gone, she stumbled toward the stairs in a haze. Her body weak. Every step a struggle. The stress of everything, the news about Alison, how it all happened rocked her. It felt like icepicks stabbing into her. She reached out to balance herself, but it wasn't enough. Her body betrayed her, and she collapsed at the foot of the stairs.

Her composure shattered. She sank to the floor, burying her face in her hands, sobbing.

Mike was at her side in an instant, kneeling beside her. Without a word, he wrapped his arms around her. She folded into him, sobbing uncontrollably. He held her tightly.

"I've got you," he murmured. "I'm here. I've got you."

Mike gently pulled her into his chest, his arms a barricade around her. His heartbeat thudded in her ear, grounding her to the moment. Every ragged breath she took, he matched, his grip tightening as if he could absorb the pain for her.

"I'm so tired," she whispered, her voice barely audible between sobs. "I don't know how much more I can take. And Alison…"

"You don't have to do this alone," he said. "I'm here. Whatever happens, I'm here."

For a long moment, they stayed there, Samantha leaning into him as the weight of the world bore down on her.

Finally, she pulled back, her eyes watery and red. "I really need to lie down," she said weakly.

Mike helped Samantha to her feet holding her upright as she made her way up the stairs.

"I'll stay here with you tonight," he said.

She nodded, too drained to argue. She pulled him into the room with her, not letting go of his hand, not wanting him to leave. They both took off their shoes, and Mike helped her into bed, propping her up in a semi-upright position against the headboard to ease her injured ribs.

She immediately rested her head against him and fell asleep shortly after. A slight snore escaped her. She shifted lower, her arm draping across his chest.

Poor Samantha. Mike couldn't shake the image of her breaking down, the fear in her eyes, the way her body trembled. He made a solemn vow right then: whatever came next, she wouldn't face it alone.

CHAPTER 32

BREAKING RANKS

The detectives left Samantha's house, Still sensing her glare long after they turned away as they walked to their car. Detective Miller radioed for a squad car to pick him up. Minutes passed. An awkward silence stretched between them all. Now wasn't the time to rehash what had happened inside Samantha's home.

"I'll meet you tomorrow," Miller said as he climbed into the vehicle.

Maxwell nodded, his tone clipped. "Yeah. I'll call you when I'm ready."

As Miller's car pulled away, Maxwell turned to Castanon without a word and motioned toward their vehicle. They climbed in. Tension settled thick between them. The low hum of talk radio filled the silence as Maxwell gripped the steering wheel, the leather creaking beneath his hands. Several minutes passed before he finally spoke.

"Detective Castanon, when did you make detective?"

Caught off guard, Castanon hesitated. "Uh… about two years ago.."

Maxwell glanced at him briefly, then focused back on the road. "What kinds of cases have you worked?"

"Mostly robberies. A lot of those in my precinct. But I closed *all* of my cases."

"So this is your first homicide case," Maxwell said. Not as a question, but a statement.

Castanon nodded. "Yes sir. And I'm grateful to have the opportunity to—"

Maxwell cut him off. His voice was calm, but cutting. "If you were really grateful for this opportunity, you wouldn't have made the mistakes you did back there,"

Castanon frowned. "Mistakes? Like what?"

"Like not following my lead." Maxwell's tone was calm, but the edge cut deep. "You walked in there puffing your chest, acting like you had something to prove."

"I was just trying to—"

"No," Maxwell said, cutting him off. "Stop right there. I had everything under control. She was about to give us a key piece of evidence, and you blew it. You pushed too hard, and now we're set back."

Castanon bristled. "Sir, I was doing my job. She's at the center of this. We need answers."

"Doing your job?" Maxwell's grip on the wheel tightened. "Your job is to listen, observe, and communicate with your team. Not alienate the one person who can help us possibly crack this case."

Castanon crossed his arms. "I don't think it's fair to blame me for—"

"You're off the case," Maxwell said flatly.

"What?" Castanon's voice jumped. "You can't just pull me off the case!"

"I can. And I just did." Maxwell's voice was flat, final. "This case is too important for ego trips. I need a team that follows direction. You clearly can't."

"Ego trips? You're kidding me right now?"

Maxwell said nothing. Just stared ahead.

That silence burned more than any words could.

"I see what this is about, Lieutenant," Castanon snapped. "This is personal. Clearly personal."

"Detective Castanon," Maxwell said evenly. "I'm going to give it to you straight. I can't have hotheads on my team. Simple. You'll be reassigned where the department needs you."

Castanon let out a dry, mocking laugh. "I'll be reassigned where the department needs me," he echoed, voice dripping sarcasm. "So procedural. So matter-of-fact. So…"

Maxwell shot him a cold look. "Careful with your next words, Detective. That's your final warning."

Castanon's jaw clenched. "I'm taking this up with the captain," Castanon snapped.

Maxwell replied emotionless. "Go for it. Maybe he'll give you five minutes. If you can catch him."

They pulled up to Downtown L.A. LAPD headquarters. Castanon flung the door open and disappeared into the bustling crowd, the slam echoing behind him. Maxwell watched him disappear, then shook his head before driving off.

Sleepless Nights In The Fashion District

Maxwell took the scenic route home, weaving through downtown as city lights washed over the streets. He'd lived here since moving to Los Angeles, drawn to its constant energy, the skyscrapers, the late-night buzz, the hum of life that never stopped.

A historic building turned loft in the Fashion District. Top floor. Two bedrooms. Plenty of space. Maxwell liked the view, a constant proof he hadn't wasted his shot.

Tossing his keys onto the counter, Maxwell collapsed onto the couch. The day had left a bitter taste in his mouth. Castanon's mishandling of the situation with Samantha had set them back, and the heaviness of the investigation hung over him like a storm cloud refusing to break.

Maxwell rose, a stack of documents in hand, and started building a flowchart on the wall. Photos of the victims: Tabatha, Jordan, and Jeff, lined up in a grim row and connected by red lines. It was the beginnings of a pattern he was desperate to crack.

"Why these influencers?" he muttered, studying the arrangement. "What's the connection? And how does Samantha Sinclair fit into this?"

He paused, thinking about her. She was… different. Her wit and grit had caught him off guard. And that security setup? Possibly military-grade. There was a story there, one she hadn't told. She clung to that house like leaving it meant leaving pieces of herself behind. The desperation in her voice hadn't escaped him.

There were layers to her. Layers she wasn't ready to peel back.

With a sigh, he picked up his phone and texted the captain:

Castanon's off the case. He broke rank. I can't have that from someone on my team. Kids not ready for something like this. I'll fill you in more tomorrow.

The reply came back almost immediately:

Your case. Your call. See you tomorrow at the press conference.

Maxwell set the phone aside and sat down, eyes drifting to the flowchart again. The killer was still out there and time was running out. They needed a break.

He jotted down a rough to-do list for the morning, then fixed himself a drink and stepped out onto the balcony.

The cool night air brushed against his face as he looked out over the city. For a moment, he let his mind wander. Not to the case, but to the choices that had led him here. The failed marriage. The distance from his son. The relationships he'd let die so he could serve justice.

He was a slave to the job.

And nights like this reminded him of the cost.

"This is it," he said, swirling the drink in his glass. "The last night of rest I'll have for a while."

Tomorrow, the manhunt would begin again.

CHAPTER 33

FALLOUT AND FLASHBULBS

City Hall — Monday, 9:00 AM

The press conference was underway, broadcast across Southern California. Every major local outlet was present, joined by a handful of national reporters. The press pit buzzed with reporters jockeying for position, cameras flashing, and microphones crowding the podium.

Among the crowd stood Jessica Ryder, a striking figure in a form-fitting black suit that hugged her curves while maintaining an air of professionalism. Beneath her blouse, a black and gold necklace with a center opal caught the light, accentuating her complexion. Her diamond-cut earrings caught the sunlight with every sharp turn of her head.

A sleek smartwatch and a delicate bracelet completed her ensemble, adding a touch of elegance to the powerful image she projected. Her long legs carried her with confidence in high heels. She stood tall, her posture commanding attention.

Jessica was no stranger to the chaos of a press pit; in fact, she thrived in it. As the host of *The Ryder Report,* she'd earned a reputation for dismantling anyone who tried to hide the truth.

Mayor Victor Lang stepped up to the podium, his expression somber, and the crowd drew silent.

"Ladies and gentlemen," he began. "The brutal and grotesque murders we've seen have left our city shaken. I want to assure you that every resource is being utilized to bring the person responsible to justice. We are working tirelessly to find the connection between these crimes and to protect our city."

Nearby, interpreters translated his words into sign language. The telecast was being simultaneously translated as well.

"Mr. Mayor, what more can you tell us?" a reporter called out.

"We're not going to rest until we find out who's behind this," the mayor replied. "This is a race against time."

"Any leads, any details, anything?" another voice chimed in.

The mayor raised a hand to calm the growing frenzy. "I'll hand this over to LAPD Chief Christopher Parks, who will address your questions."

Chief Parks, a tall man with a commanding presence, stepped up to the microphone. His tone was measured but firm.

"What the mayor said is true. We at LAPD are utilizing every resource to investigate these crimes and ensure the safety of our city. We urge the public to remain calm as we work to uncover the truth."

"What information do you have?" Jessica Ryder's voice broke through the crowd, clear and direct.

Chief Parks glanced at her, his expression tightening. "We have evidence suggesting there is a connection between the victims. However, this is an ongoing investigation, and we are calling on anyone with information to come forward. Your city needs you."

Jessica wasn't satisfied. "These murders were live-streamed. Even with takedowns, underground sites still show the videos. Is this how the killer's trying to send their message?"

The chief's jaw tightened. "We are not going to speculate on the killer's motives."

"But isn't it your job to speculate? The city is comparing this to the 'Night Stalker' spree, and you're saying you won't address that? How do you expect us to have confidence in this investigation?"

The crowd murmured, all eyes turning to the chief. He cleared his throat, visibly irritated by Jessica's question.

"Miss Ryder, wild speculation without evidence is dangerous. We work with facts, not hypotheticals."

Jessica smirked. "Sounds like you've got nothing. Typical."

Chief Parks ignored her and continued. "I'll now turn things over to Captain Eugene Cunningham and our lead investigator, Lieutenant Byron Maxwell."

Maxwell stepped forward, his tailored blue suit framing his broad shoulders perfectly. The crisp white shirt and matching tie added to his air of command. His sliver hair caught the morning sun, his sharp features were softened by a calm and composed demeanor. Jessica couldn't help but notice how well put-together he was. He was a man who clearly took care of himself. She felt a flicker of intrigue.

Maxwell scanned the crowd before speaking.

"Good morning. We are horrified by these killings, as I'm sure all of you are. While it's true that the victims so far have been influencers, our investigation is still developing. We are exploring every lead, and we need your help."

"Lieutenant Maxwell," Jessica interjected again. What's your message to the killer? And to the people of Los Angeles?"

Maxwell's gaze locked onto hers. He noticed her confidence, the sharp gleam in her eyes, and how her suit emphasized her poise. For a split second, he allowed himself to acknowledge her beauty before answering.

"My message to the killer is this: We're coming for you. You can run, you can hide, you can change your face a thousand times, but we will find you. And to the people of Los Angeles: stay vigilant, but don't let fear control you. This city is stronger than one man's reign of terror. And we will prove it."

Jessica smirked, impressed by his poise. As the press pit erupted with more questions, Maxwell handled them with an almost stoic professionalism. His ability to command the room only intrigued her further.

As the conference ended and reporters began to disperse, Jessica made her move, weaving through the crowd to catch Maxwell.

"Lieutenant Maxwell, over here! Lieutenant Maxwell!" Her voice rang out with a confidence that cut through the clamor of the crowd. It was so recognizable, you could pick it out from any sea of reporters.

Maxwell paused, his body stiffening for just a moment before he turned, facing the unmistakable voice.

He locked eyes with Jessica as she approached, the press pit around them seemingly fading for a brief moment.

"Lieutenant, I have more questions. There's more to this story, and it would be beneficial if we could arrange to talk more," she said, her tone professional, but there was urgency in it.

Maxwell studied her for a moment, his features unreadable. "I'm familiar with you, Miss Ryder. I know how aggressive you are when it comes to getting a story. I respect it, but I want to be careful with how I speak with you."

Jessica's expression softened. "I understand this is a sensitive time, and I know how to conduct my reports. I'm offering you my platform to help quell some of the fears surrounding this case. I think we should talk more."

Maxwell hesitated. "I don't think I can assist beyond this."

But Jessica wasn't backing down. "I have sources. I have information that can help. I can be a friend to your investigation." She met his eyes, her expression unwavering. She had nothing concrete yet, but she hoped he wouldn't call her bluff.

"Miss Ryder."

"Jessica," she interrupted, her gaze never leaving his.

"Jessica," he repeated, his voice softening. He took a deep breath before continuing. "I'll take whatever information you can share. I do mean that for investigative purposes."

He reached into his jacket pocket and pulled out his business card, offering it to her.

She accepted it without hesitation, her fingers brushing his lightly. "Likewise. I only want to present you in the best light," she said, offering him her own card in return.

Maxwell took it, his gaze flickering briefly to the card before looking back at her. "I hope so. But if you burn me, I'll never speak to you again," he warned.

Jessica's lips curved into wide smile. "Hey," she said with a flirtatious tone, "I did set you up right with my last question. And great message, by the way."

Maxwell chuckled, his lips pulling into a slight grin. "And I appreciate that too," he returned, his eyes holding hers for a moment longer than necessary.

"We're on the same side," she said. Thank you, Lieutenant Maxwell."

"Byron," he corrected her, the corner of his mouth twitching as he fought back a smile.

"Thank you, Byron," she replied, her voice sending a ripple of unspoken curiosity between them.

With that, Maxwell turned and rejoined his colleagues, but not before sneaking one last glance at Jessica. She watched him go, her thoughts racing. As she made her way out of the press area, her steps were poised, heels striking against the pavement. A smile played at the corners of her lips. She knew she had made an impression. Both of them, in their own way, were already considering when they might meet again.

CHAPTER 34

HE'S OUT THERE WATCHING

Richie's Hideaway — Monday, 10:00 AM

The remote clicked, turning off the TV. The TV cut to black, but the aftermath of the press conference still hovered in the air. Richie let out a soft, amused chuckle. The police and their so-called "manhunt" were laughable. All the heightened security, all the promises of justice, it wouldn't stop him. They were chasing shadows, and he was a ghost.

Breathing heavily, Richie rose from his creaking chair, the worn leather sticking slightly to his back. His movements were slow and deliberate, as if savoring the weight of his next steps. He crossed the small, dimly lit space to his makeshift workstation: a beat-up wooden table cluttered with a laptop, professional camera, and a tangle of cords.

His hashtag mask hung ominously above, watching like a specter. In the corner, latex face molds lined the wall, tools of his deception. Each one was eerily lifelike, designed to transform him into someone new. A small walk-in closet held the clothes and wigs to match, completing every persona he built from scratch.

His flat, tucked deep in the grittiest corner of the Toy District in Skid Row, was where the city's glow barely reached. Below him sat an old warehouse and a stretch of run-down storefronts, their graffiti-covered walls offering anonymity. The building housed a revolving cast of struggling artists and ghosts of the system. People too consumed by their own survival to ask questions. Richie's disheveled, grungy appearance let him disappear into the backdrop.

He didn't need much. Just a single-room studio. No AC. Creaky floors. Peeling paint. A sagging mattress in the corner. It was all he required.

The space was dominated by a rolling whiteboard, a chaotic shrine to revenge. Photos, maps, timelines. Richie's lips curled into a smirk as he scanned the board.

Names, scrawled in thick black marker:

- **Jeff** – Crossed off.
- **Tabatha** – Crossed off.
- **Jordan** – Crossed off.
- **Samantha** – Circled, with the word "DONE?" scrawled next to it.
- **Carly** – Her photo was centered on the board, a bright red bulls-eye drawn over it.
- **Barry**
- **Danny**

Richie still believed Samantha had been taken out by the corrosive product. The media hadn't revealed Alison's survival, or the truth about what really happened. As far as he knew, Samantha was maimed, broken, and finished. Just another notch on his justice board.

He pulled down Jeff's photo. Then Tabatha's. Then Jordan's. Each takedown came with a swell of satisfaction. Then he pinned Carly's photo in the center, the bullseye framing her face.

"Your turn," he muttered.

The room was silent, save for the soft hum of his computer and a TV faintly replaying the press conference. Maxwell's face flashed on screen. His words echoed again.

"We're coming for you."

Richie scoffed. "Yeah, sure you are."

He stepped into the bathroom and flipped on the light. The bulb flickered, then buzzed to life. His reflection stared back. His greasy hair lay in strands, hollow, bloodshot eyes, a trimmed but unkempt beard. He gripped the sink hard enough to crack porcelain, his face inches from the mirror. His breath fogged the glass.

"This is their fault," he murmured. "They drove me to this."

A flash of doubt passed over him but he crushed it. There was no room for second thoughts. Vengeance was the only fuel he had left.

Back at his workstation, he began planning Carly's death. Her name, underlined and circled. Around it, notes, sketches, details of her routine. His camera sat nearby, loaded with candid shots he'd taken of her. Every movement. Every angle. The prep had begun.

This one, he would savor.

Carly wouldn't just die.

She would suffer.

Richie reclined back in his chair, lit a cigarette, and watched the smoke swirl toward the ceiling. Sirens wailed in the distance, but he didn't flinch.

The city was reeling

And he was just getting started.

Samantha's House — Monday, 10:30 AM

Samantha woke up still in the clothes from yesterday, her body heavy with exhaustion and her mind clouded by the events of the past few days. She blinked against the dim light of her room, disoriented and groggy. It hadn't been her intention to sleep through the night, especially with Mike there, but everything had become too overwhelming. It all collapsed on her, dragging her into a restless slumber she hadn't even realized she needed.

The cooling sensation on her injured side was the first thing she noticed. It dulled the pain, offering a rare flicker of relief. Slowly, she sat up, wincing as she shifted her weight, but she was managing better than the day before. She made her way to the bathroom, brushed her teeth quickly, and avoided the mirror. The dim lighting was intentional; she wasn't ready to face herself just yet.

From downstairs, the faint sound of the TV pulled her back to the present. Her heart eased slightly as she thought of Mike.

"Mike?" she called out, her voice cracking as she made her way down the stairs.

She found him on the couch, a plate of breakfast in his lap, his attention split between the food and the TV.

"Oh my God, Mike! I'm so sorry." Her voice cracked with guilt. "I can't believe I slept that long."

Mike looked up, his expression soft. He set the plate on the coffee table. "It's okay. I wanted you to rest."

"But I kept you stuck here." She ran a hand through her hair, flustered. "I didn't even ask if you needed to leave. I should've set an alarm or something. God... I'm such a mess."

"Sam," he said gently, rising to his feet. As he walked over, he took her hand and guided her to the couch.

"You don't have to explain or feel bad. I wanted to be here. I needed to be here with you. You're going through a lot. You need support."

His reassuring words sank in. Samantha's chest tightened.

"Mike," she said, a small smile breaking through her overwhelmed expression. "I don't think I could've gotten through yesterday with the police without you. Thank you again."

Her arms folded around him, and with a long breath out, she let go of a tension she hadn't even noticed building.

"How's your side feeling?" he asked.

"Better today," she murmured, her words slightly muffled against his chest. "Not as much pain. I can move easier."

"I kept treating you while you slept," Mike said. "I refreshed the ice packs and reapplied the numbing cream."

His words struck her heart. She pulled back to meet his eyes, a tear slipping down her cheek.

"Thank you," she whispered, her voice breaking. She gave him an endearing kiss. One that spoke all the words she couldn't.

"I really feel good with you, Mike," she confessed. "I'm so glad you're here."

Mike smiled. "I feel good with you too, Sam." His hand rested on her back.

"You should eat," he said, nodding toward the kitchen. "There's a plate in the microwave."

"I'll try," she murmured, though she didn't move. "I just want to stay here with you a little longer."

She let herself be close to him, her cheek resting against his chest. His heartbeat thumped beneath her ear, a strength that calmed her. She was beginning to see and feel the good in Mike. It was unexpectedly comforting.

Alison's Awakening — 11:00 AM

Alison's eyes fluttered open, the harsh fluorescent lights of the hospital room blinding her. She blinked, trying to focus, but everything felt distant. Like she was trapped underwater. The constant beeping of the heart monitor filled the room, a monotonous reminder that she was alive... though she wasn't sure she wanted to be.

Her body felt like it was weighed down by bricks, her limbs unwilling to obey.

Get up. Get up now. She told herself. But as she tried, her face throbbed, a searing pain flooding her senses. Her breathing quickened, shallow gasps slipping past her lips as the monitors beeped in protest.

The cold, sterile air stung her nostrils. That's when she noticed the breathing tube.

Her face… it felt wrong. Half of it was numb. The other half burned like it was missing.

Panic crept in.

Her hands trembled as they moved instinctively to her face. First, she touched the side that felt untouched, fingers grazing familiar, whole skin. It's still there, she thought, a flicker of relief sparking in her chest. But as her hand drifted to the other side, it stopped. Bandages—thick, tight, suffocating—wrapped around what she already knew were deep, disfiguring wounds.

Her fingertips hovered. The rawness beneath the surface burned with every inch.

Then the memory hit, like a tidal wave.

The package. The product. The searing pain.

Alison's mind replayed everything in excruciating clarity. The horror clawed its way back, and a guttural scream ripped from her throat.

She thrashed in the bed, breathing ragged as panic surged through her. Screams tore from her throat, sharp and unrelenting, echoing through the sterile room. Machines erupted with piercing alarms as her body went into full revolt.

Within seconds, medical staff rushed in. Nurses surrounded the bed, trying to subdue her.

"Miss Alison, you're safe," one of them said, but the words barely registered.

"Hold her down!" another shouted as she continued to scream, her voice raw and wild.

Finally, Dr. Pearce entered the room, his face drawn with concern. He surveyed the chaos.

"Sedate her," he ordered.

A nurse readied the injection. Within seconds, the sedative took hold. Alison's body stilled. Her screams faded to whimpers, then silence. She sank into the bed, her chest rising and falling in a shallow rhythm as the medication drew her into a deep, merciful sleep.

Dr. Pearce stood at the foot of the bed, eyes on the monitors. The nurses exchanged worried, shaken looks. What they had just witnessed hung heavy in the air.

"I want a nurse checking on her every thirty minutes," Dr. Pearce ordered. "The shock is too much for her to handle alone. I need to be here when she wakes up again."

He paused, glancing at her motionless body.

"And someone please charge her phone," he said. "Her friends or family might be trying to reach her. She's all alone right now."

The staff acknowledged. One nurse stayed behind, adjusting the IV line, as the rest slowly filed out.

The only sound left in the room was the constant beep of the machines. The sole witnesses to Alison's pain.

LAPD DTLA Headquarters — 11:30AM

Detective Maxwell stood at the front of the conference room, a whiteboard behind him filled with names, notes, and victim photos. The air was tense but focused. Detectives Jason Jacobson and Lawrence Miller sat at the table, while Sergeant Blake Ramirez stood near the door, arms crossed. His role in securing the gym had been critical, and his readiness to assist was clear.

Maxwell cleared his throat. "First off, Detective Castanon is officially off the case. Sergeant Ramirez, I'll be leaning on you more from here."

"Understood," Ramirez said with a firm nod. "We've got a tight perimeter around the gym. It'll stay sealed for the next 48 hours. Management's been cooperative so far."

"Good. Anything else from the scene?" Maxwell asked.

"We're combing through the camera footage now," Ramirez replied. "There's a footprint still being analyzed, and we found some residue. If we can ID it, we'll run comparisons. But with the disguises he's been using, it's tough. He's slippery."

Maxwell nodded. "Stay on it!

He then turned his attention to the next task at hand. "Jacobson, what's the status on Alison? How's the hospital detail?"

"All secure," Jacobson replied. "Her room's under constant watch. Police detail posted. So far, her name hasn't leaked. No press involvement."

"Good," Maxwell said. "The killer may think he succeeded with Alison, but once he realizes she's alive, he might circle back. I want that floor locked down. No mistakes."

"Want me to assign one of my guys to the hospital rotation?" Ramirez offered. "I can reinforce the team."

"Do it," Maxwell said. "Keep our comms tight. Any shift, I want to know immediately."

Ramirez nodded, already pulling out his phone to reassign two officers.

Maxwell turned to Miller. "What's the latest from Alison's house?"

"Wrapping up today," Miller reported. "We've collected everything. No signs of forced entry. Nothing beyond the package drop."

Maxwell's gaze shifted to Jacobson. Reach out to the gym manager. I want a full list of members, guests, and staff. Anyone with access in the past few weeks. And Jeff? Any leads?"

Jacobson flipped open his notes. We've been combing through Jeff's socials along with Tabatha's, Jordan's, Samantha's, and Alison's. Cyber Crimes is flagging anything out of the ordinary. Any comments, posts or patterns. They'll let us know if something connects."

You're in the loop now," Maxwell said, nodding at him. "With Castanon gone, we'll be relying on you more often to coordinate support from your end."

Ramirez straightened. "Understood, sir. I won't let you down."

"Boss," Jacobson added, "I'm heading to meet the gym manager again. We're requesting extended footage from the last few months. Maybe we'll catch something."

"Good," Maxwell said, tapping the whiteboard with his pen. "Let's hope today gives us something. Miller, you're with me. We'll try contacting Miss Sinclair again."

He turned back to Jacobson. "The minute Alison wakes up, I want to be alerted. Her statement could give us a real break."

The room fell quiet as that sank in. Finally, Maxwell spoke again.

"Let's get to it. Dismissed."

The group stood and dispersed to their assignments. Maxwell stayed at the whiteboard, eyes locked on the names.

They weren't close. Not yet. Too many gaps remained. Too many questions unanswered. And out there, in the shadows, the killer was still moving... still watching... still plotting.

CHAPTER 35

RUNNING ON FUMES

Elite24Fit — Monday 3:00PM

Greyson sat in his office, fingers drumming the desk in barely concealed irritation. Across from him, Detective Jacobson stood silent, calm, waiting for the gym owner to comply. Greyson had only just been allowed back into his office, escorted by Jacobson, to retrieve the requested security footage. *Elite24Fit's* higher-ups had reluctantly authorized limited cooperation, but Greyson wasn't happy about it.

The whole ordeal was a nightmare for business. His trainers weren't making money. Memberships were on hold. The gym's reputation was hanging by a thread. Sure, the deaths were tragic, but if he was honest, it was the financial hit that kept him up at night.

Jordan and Tabatha? Horrific as their ends were, they hadn't exactly been saints. Years of boasting, bullying, clout-chasing, and stirring drama. They'd made plenty of enemies. Deep down, Greyson couldn't shake the thought: *They finally crossed the wrong person.*

He shook the thought away, ashamed it had even crossed his mind. Still, he was going to do what the police asked so they could be done with his gym.

"So," Greyson said, breaking the silence, "I can only access footage from the past month. Anything older gets automatically wiped."

"I'll take what I can get," Jacobson replied evenly. "You mentioned Jordan and Tabatha had a lot of confrontations here. I need anything that gives insight into their interactions with other members."

Greyson sighed. "They weren't exactly beloved, Detective. This place sees traffic all day. I don't know what you're looking for, but it sounds like a reach."

Jacobson didn't flinch. "That's exactly what I'm doing. And I appreciate your help."

Greyson pursed his lips. "Well, I can't spend all day scrubbing footage."

"No one's asking you to," Jacobson said evenly.

"However," Greyson added, "I can pull their check-in times and match those with the security feed. Your team can take it from there."

"That's helpful. Thank you," Jacobson replied, his tone genuine.

Greyson accessed the gym's system, pulling the logs for Jordan and Tabatha and queuing up the footage. As the download started, he printed a backup list and handed it to Jacobson.

"So… when do I get my gym back?" Greyson asked, his tone edged with impatience.

"Tomorrow afternoon, most likely," Jacobson replied without looking up.

"What a mess," Greyson muttered.

Jacobson ignored the comment. "Can you think of any specific incidents involving them and other members?"

Greyson let out a heavy sigh. "Detective, we've been over this. I told you everything I could. Feels like we're beating a dead horse at this point."

"I'll decide that," Jacobson said, his voice edging sharper.

Greyson's jaw tightened. "I just want my gym back. My staff's losing money. This isn't sustainable."

"Any major altercations? Anything worth noting on record?" Jacobson pressed.

Greyson shrugged. "Plenty. None that stand out. Complaints, bad reviews, a few heated emails."

"I'll take those too."

Greyson's eyes narrowed. "Maybe we should end this conversation here."

Jacobson didn't flinch. His tone calm but unyielding. "I can subpoena the records if I have to."

Greyson's expression hardened. "Some of that's private. Your case is about two people, not my entire client list."

"*My duty*," Jacobson said, "is to stop a killer. If any of your records help with that, they're relevant. I appreciate your cooperation…but I don't need your permission."

His eyes darted to the still-downloading flash drive. He rubbed at his jaw, tension creeping in. "I need to clear this with my higher-ups," he said reaching for his phone.

Jacobson didn't move. He sat back in his chair, expression unreadable and watched as Greyson stepped out to call Darren, the regional manager.

He Can't See Me Like This — 3:30PM

Samantha's eyes fluttered open slowly. She was still on the couch, lying on her side. The cold compress on her injury provided a revitalizing sensation, dulling much of the pain that had consumed her the day before. The sound of the downstairs shower brought her back to reality.

Oh no… she thought. *Not again.*

She had fallen asleep again, leaving Mike to fend for himself. Her chest tightened with guilt. She did not want this for herself, and she certainly did not want it for Mike. As much as he reassured her it was fine, she could not shake the heaviness in her heart.

I must be holding him hostage, she thought.

Her mind spiraled. Alison's face was burned into her thoughts. The image of her, alone and unreachable in that hospital room, haunted her. She had not heard back from her texts or calls, and the uncertainty was eating her alive. She pressed the cold compress tighter against her side, eyes shut, trying to quiet the storm of thoughts crashing in her head.

I have to see her. I must see her.

But then there was Mike. Lately, he had become a comforting presence, reliable in the middle of a storm she couldn't seem to escape. She had always admired his mild-mannered, cool-headed nature, but she wasn't used to depending on anyone like this. Being taken care of made her feel exposed. Off-balance. She glanced down at herself, her hair messy, her clothes rumpled. She felt like a stranger in her own body. Unrecognizable.

I can't let him keep seeing me like this, she thought. *I'm unraveling... and he's still here.*

The shower turned off. The sound of running water gave way to silence. Samantha sat up slowly wincing as her injury reminded her to move carefully.

I'm no good like this. I need to be alone.

She stood and walked to the bathroom door. Pausing, she pressed her hand against it, the cool surface grounding her. Her fingers lingered, gently rubbing the wood as if it were Mike's chest, letting the imagined warmth settle through her. But this wasn't right. Not like this. She straightened, lifting her chin as if summoning courage.

"Mike… Mike… honey?" she called to him her voice cracking. The word slipped out like a whisper, and startled her nonetheless.

Did I really just say that?

"Yes, babe?" came the reply from the bathroom.

Her breath caught. *Shit! He heard that.*

"Um, um…" she stammered, her mind fogged. She gripped the doorframe, unable to think of what to say. Finally, the words stumbled out. "I'm no good like this. It might be best for you to go home."

"You don't mean that, Sam. I know you don't," Mike replied.

Her chest clenched. He was right. She didn't mean it. But the storm in her head was tearing her apart.

"Mike… I just…" she bit her lip. "It's for the best. I'm not myself right now. I've been sleeping too much. I can't expect you to stay here with me like this. I'm a wreck."

"Sam, can we talk when I get out of here?" he insisted.

"But… but my mind's made up. I… I just need to be alone. Yes… I do," she protested. Her voice barely carried. The words felt like shards of glass.

"Don't let the door be a barricade. "Let's talk face to face. I'm almost done."

"Mike, please…" Her voice broke.

The door opened and there he was. Wrapped in a towel, his hair damp, droplets of water still clinging to his chest. She froze. Her eyes locked on his body before darting away.

"Wait!" she blurted, rushing to a nearby closet. She retrieved a towel and walked back to him, beginning to dry him off. "Let me do this… at least."

Mike stood still, eyes closing as the towel moved across his chest, her touch light against his skin. She tossed it onto the couch, and their eyes met. Unspoken thoughts stirred between them.

"So… do you really want me to go?" Mike asked again.

She couldn't look at him. Her hair fell across her face like a curtain. "I think… I think it might be best."

Mike reached out, brushing the hair from her eyes. She flinched slightly at the tenderness.

"You really mean that?"

She opened her mouth, but no words came. Her breath caught. Before she could speak, he closed the distance and kissed her.

She let herself go, feeling the kiss, her arms winding around his neck, pulling him closer. A sigh escaped her lips. Perhaps resolve, perhaps something more. Her kisses quickened. Their foreheads touched as she backed him against the wall, still kissing him. Her breathing deepened, driven by emotions she couldn't quite name. His hands rested at her waist.

A tear slipped down her cheek as they pulled apart. She quickly wiped it away, hoping he hadn't noticed. Their foreheads rested against each other.

"You're worried about Alison?"

Samantha looked away, fighting back tears.

"I know," his hands finding hers. "So am I."

Samantha's eyes watered. She reached for a tissue.

"I can't expect you to stay with me like this,"she said giving his hands a squeeze. A silent acknowledgment that she wanted him to stay, even if she couldn't bring herself to say it outright.

"If you really want me to leave, I will," Mike said. "But not before we have dinner together tonight. You need to get out. If you don't, you'll burrow down the rabbit hole of worry and grief. I don't want you getting depressed on me ok?

Samantha nodded. Her voice was too shaky to argue.

"Okay," she whispered. "I'll get ready."

She could not say no to him. Not after everything. Not after the kiss. Not after his unwavering care.

As she turned toward the stairs, she felt something changing. Mike wasn't pushing, just showing up, being real. And somehow, it was getting to her. At the top of the stairs, she glanced back to him.

"Thank you, I do feel much better."

Mike smiled, then blew her a kiss.

She laughed. Her feelings were growing. She still struggled to fully let go with him, but slowly, he was getting past walls she never thought anyone could.

The One Name No One Wants To Hear At *Elite24Fit* — 4:00 PM

Greyson finally made the video call to Darren.

Darren answered. "Hey, what's up, Greyson?"

"Hey, Darren. I'll just get into it. The cops want emails and other data access. How much are we willing to give them?"

Darren responded, "Give them what they need to assist with their investigation. This is a top-down decision," he said, emotionless.

"But all my emails about Jordan and Tabatha? All the complaints from my team? All the emails I've sent to corporate over the years, including you? The incident reports that guests filled out about them? What about anonymity? Don't we have to respect that, especially for our guests?" Greyson rebutted.

"These are company emails. They were sent and responded to from our company email address. Ergo, the emails are company property. And as a company, we have decided to give the police whatever information they need on Jordan and Tabatha to assist in their investigation." Darren's tone remained unwavering.

"I'm having a hard time with this decision. We've talked so many times, with guests notifying us of complaints and concerns. Now the detectives expect me to recall every interaction I or my staff had, even with gym patrons. I understand what's happening, but this is getting to be too much. I'm not sure I want to keep engaging with them like this."

"You don't have to keep talking to them. But privacy is irrelevant, and your comprehension isn't a prerequisite for your cooperation in this," Darren said.

"I'll need tomorrow to get the emails to them," Greyson said. "So… when are we reopening? My team and I want to get back to work."

"About that…" Darren hesitated.

"What do you mean?" Greyson sounded alarmed.

"I was going to call you tomorrow, but we're still 50/50 on reopening with everything that's happened."

"But this gym is the second most visited in L.A., just behind New York. Our members will miss us, including our celebrity clients. What do you mean, 50/50? We bring in so much money?"

"Greyson, it's the way the murders happened," Darren said.

"So what? We just reopen and move on? People will get over it. They'll forget. Attention spans are short, and half our clients don't even pay attention to the news with how self-consumed they are," Greyson argued.

"No, Greyson. It's not that simple. We're facing tough questions. We're being accused of using cheap glass that gave way, causing her to fly off the side of the building. We're staring down legal battles from the victims' families."

"Darren, if I may be frank, no matter how thick or thin the glass was, with the speed she was running and how fast the treadmill was going… once it lurched and launched her into the glass, she would've died on impact anyway. She went through back first."

"We don't know that. And now we're fighting with building management. It's turning into a blame game. For now, we're closed for the rest of the week. And there's real talk about shutting down indefinitely because of this."

"Wait, what? No, no, no. What about my team? My team has to work. We *have* to move on from this. We *have* to move on from Jordan and Tabatha. This isn't fair to my team."

"We are prepared to pay your team until a final decision is made after Rebecca arrives."

"Thank you, but… what happens after?"

"I would advise you to prepare your team for the possibility of closure, or relocation. Corporate's trying to do as much damage control as possible. There's too much bad energy surrounding this," Darren said, hoping Greyson would read between the lines.

A beat of silence passed between them. The heaviness of it hung in the air. Greyson sat with it, trying to process. Once again, even in death, Jordan and Tabatha were making life hell for him and his team.

God, what am I thinking?

Two people were dead. Horrifically. Tragically. And all Greyson could think about was getting his gym back. Jordan and Tabatha had been awful. He'd seen through them from the start, and so had his team. Corporate had overlooked years of toxic behavior, from bullying to arrogance to entitlement. The resentment had built, and that's where his disdain came from.

Could their deaths be liberating for me? Greyson thought. *Am I a horrible person for thinking this?*

He just wanted his gym back. He felt a creeping sense of separation anxiety and zoned out, forgetting for a moment that Darren was still on the call.

But was this now a sense of poetic justice? After finally being rid of those two, his world would be on the brink of collapse.

How were Jordan and Tabatha bigger than the gym? Bigger than everyone else there? Our lives didn't revolve around them, but could it be that they did? He was losing himself in his thoughts.

"Greyson. Greyson, you okay?" Darren asked, noticing his silence.

"Yeah, yeah. I just… this detective's pressing too much," he said, trying to deflect his real thoughts.

Don't crash out now, he told himself.

"Greyson… there's more," Darren said, pausing. "Rebecca from Philadelphia is coming next week. I'll be driving down to be there."

"Shit. You've got to be kidding me," Greyson said. A chill ran down his spine. He knew what that meant.

Rebecca Falcone from Philadelphia was a feared name in *Elite24Fit*. A lioness in the company. When she showed up, it meant something serious was going down and usually, changes followed. She didn't come to make friends. She came to assess liability. And she cut that liability, whoever or whatever it was. Philly suited her icy nature. Cold as Ice, like the song goes.

She was tall—athletic tall—the kind you spotted in a crowd. Broad shoulders, strong legs, and curves that hadn't gone anywhere since her college basketball days. Cute, if you could see past the resting bitch face.

Rebecca didn't care for office romance. She knew it was going on, but said nothing. Her rules were simple: keep it professional, keep it clean. As long as she didn't have to get involved, you were safe. In college, she played basketball, and played it well. Led her team to five straight NCAA tournaments. A certified sports girl. Diehard Eagles fan. Season ticket holder. Face-painter. Intense.

She was already in a bad mood about this trip. It was pulling her away from an Eagles game, and they were having another winning season. Her list of people she liked was short. Luckily, Greyson made the cut.

But that could change depending on her mood.

She was the type who, if she sneezed, the whole company heard it. Get on her bad side, and you wouldn't last long. She could fire you mid-conversation, sandwiched between small talk and a smile. You wouldn't even see it coming.

"Yes, she's coming to look at everything with you," Darren said. "That's why I'm saying, we may not reopen this location. We've got to be ready for whatever decision she makes. You know her word carries weight."

Greyson knew that firsthand. Rebecca had vouched for him to run DTLA after seeing his standout numbers as an assistant manager in San Diego.

And once she vouched for you, that was it. The job was yours. The internal interview had been a formality. He was handpicked by Rebecca, and that was all that mattered. Their interactions had been minimal, but when Rebecca gave Greyson a directive, it was always carried out to the letter.

"I understand. I'll be here, and I'll be present," Greyson said.

"Good. Because I need your help taming the beast that is her," Darren said, alluding to Rebecca's personality.

Greyson bristled at the comment, wondering if it was a veiled tall joke. He didn't let it slide.

"If you need my help, then follow my lead when we talk to her," he said firmly. "I manage this place every day. I talk to everyone here, including building management. I know my staff. I know what this gym needs. And I know Rebecca's going to ask some very tough questions."

Greyson wasn't finished. "With her, less is more. Keep your answers short. Better to let me do the talking."

"Of course," Darren said, realizing his own head might be on the chopping block too.

The power dynamic would shift the instant Rebecca set foot in Los Angeles. Darren was willing to cede control to Greyson, but not without issuing one last directive.

"Greyson, give the detectives what they need. You don't have to answer their questions, but hand over the emails."

"Understood," Greyson replied.. "I'll see you this week."
And with that, the call ended.

Greyson let out a deep breath, trying not to let the anxiety overtake him.

A new battle was about to begin. He had to fight for his team. He had to fight for his gym. But deep down, he knew this could be a losing battle.

Still, he would try.

It all came down to what Rebecca was going to say next week.

He quickly texted the group chat:

Whoever is available, let's meet at Page in downtown tonight. I have very important updates.

The messages flooded in immediately. Everyone was available. After days of silence, any form of contact felt like a breakthrough. And now, they had it.

Putting his phone back in his pocket, he returned to his office to let Detective Jacobson know he'd have everything by tomorrow.

He was eager to be rid of him, ready to join his team for dinner. But the uncertainty of what was coming weighed heavily. Greyson and the team would have to brace for impact. Rebecca's impact.

Alison's Meltdown — 8:00 PM

Outside the room, night nurses traded updates in hushed voices as the shift change began. Alison stirred. Her eyes opened slowly, blinking against the sting of the fluorescent lights. Everything felt distant, like she was underwater. But her mind was racing, adrenaline already kicking in.

Get up. Get out, she told herself.

The rhythmic beeping of her monitors grated on her nerves. Every sound was too loud, too sharp.

I'm alone, she thought. The realization slammed into her chest. Panic took hold.

With clarity born of desperation, she gritted her teeth and moved her hands. Trembling, she grabbed the IV line and yanked. Pain exploded through her arm as the needle tore free, a sharp scream escaped her lips. Alarms blared. She reached for the nasal cannula.

"No, no, no," she rasped, her voice hoarse. Her movements were frantic, the pain radiating through her fragile body no match for her raw will to escape.

The noise caught the attention of one of the Filipina nurses passing by. She froze, eyes widening as she saw Alison yanking the breathing tubes from her nose.

"Room 812! Room 812! We've got to hurry!" she shouted.

"Oh no!" another nurse gasped as they rushed in. Two more nurses appeared within seconds, led by a tall male nurse. Alison sat upright in bed, bandaged face trembling with effort, her breathing ragged.

"Leave! Leave!" she cried, voice garbled but forceful.

"Miss, calm down," one of the nurses said, trying to soothe her.

But Alison wasn't hearing them. She thrashed as they approached, her legs kicking with surprising strength. One of her feet connected with a nurse's thigh, sending her stumbling back into a rolling tray table.

"Miss Alison, stop! Please!" another nurse pleaded, but Alison only fought harder, her arms swinging wildly as they tried to restrain her.

Dr. Pearce burst into the room, his face a mixture of concern and determination. "What's going on?"

"She's pulling everything out, Doctor. We're trying to restrain her!" the male nurse replied, struggling to hold Alison's arm.

"Sedate her!" Dr. Pearce ordered. "Quickly!"

Alison's eyes widened at the word, her panic escalating.

"No, get away from me!" she screamed. She spotted the tray with the syringe and kicked it with her right foot, sending it clattering to the floor.

"Miss Santiago, listen to me!" Dr. Pearce pleaded. "I want to help you. Please, you're safe here!"

But there was no reasoning with her. Her fight was instinctual. Primal. The team struggled to contain her, nurses wrangling her flailing body, dodging her kicks.

"No, no, no! Let me go!" Alison screamed.

Suddenly, the head Filipina nurse slipped in with precision, moving like a shadow. She retrieved the syringe from the floor. Thankfully, it was still capped and sealed. She prepared it quickly and darted forward. In a smooth, practiced motion, she injected Alison with the sedative.

Alison flinched, her eyes wild.

"No… I want out! I want… to go…" she gasped, her voice breaking as the drug took hold.

Her limbs went heavy. The fight drained from her body in slow, twitching waves.

"Rest," the nurse gently said.. "Rest easy. Rest, honey. We will help you. But please, rest."

The words cut through Alison's haze. The nurse placed her hand gently on Alison's head, stroking her hair as her body began to relax. The combination of the sedative and the nurse's calming presence lured her back into sleep.

"You're not alone, dear," the nurse whispered again, her accent warm and soothing.

Alison, barely conscious, reached out with one trembling hand. The nurse took it, firm and comforting, and didn't let go as Alison drifted back into sleep.

Dr. Pearce exhaled.. "Everyone okay?"

The staff nodded, shaken but intact.

"We should probably restrain her," Dr. Pearce said reluctantly. "Just in case…"

"No." The head nurse's voice was calm, but resolute.

Dr. Pearce looked at her, surprised.

"She doesn't need restraints," the nurse said. "She needs someone waiting for her. I'll be the first voice she hears next time she wakes up."

After a pause, Dr. Pearce nodded. "Alright. Monitor her closely. Call me at any change."

As the others cleared out, the head nurse stayed by Alison's side, still holding her hand. The assurance that Alison wasn't alone.

Dinner Plans — 8:30 PM

Samantha stood in front of the mirror, brushing her hair in slow, deliberate strokes. The cool, soft breeze from the open window swirled around her, a subtle contrast to the unease in her chest. She stared at her reflection, zoning out as her thoughts wandered to Alison.

No answer... no confirmation... no word, she repeated silently, her mind looping.

She had been calling Alison's phone to no avail. The hospital remained tight-lipped leaving her in limbo and unable to get any updates. The stress of it bore down on her.

"Sam, how are you doing up there?" Mike's voice called from downstairs, breaking her trance.

Samantha blinked, realizing how much time had slipped away. *I'm doing it again... losing track of everything,* she thought, guilt creeping in.

"I'm fine, Mike," she called back. "I'll be down soon. I'm sorry!"

She snapped out of the haze and moved to the closet, fingers gliding over hangers until she landed on a go-to look: a sleek black cutout one-piece swimsuit that doubled as a bodysuit, paired with a flowing blue-and-white floral skirt that hit mid-thigh.

The light fabric skimmed her legs, flattering her calves. Simple, yet chic. Stylish without trying too hard. She added glittery earrings, a matching necklace that caught the light just right, and a white bracelet to complement her smartwatch.

At the bottom of the closet, her eyes landed on a pair of heels. They were sleek, black, open-toe stilettos from Aquazzura, with a delicate ankle strap and glimmering heart-shaped embellishments across the front. Alison had given them to her. Samantha picked them up gingerly, a tear slipping down her cheek before she quickly wiped it away.

As she slipped them on, the shimmer of her toenail polish mirrored the sparkle of the crystal hearts. The light seemed to catch both at once, highlighting a look that was intentional, elegant, and entirely her.

Focus, Sam, she told herself, forcing a smile as she grabbed a sleek silver purse and a fitted leather jacket. Her hair wasn't perfectly styled. Some pesky strands of frizz had won this round, but she tossed a brush into her bag and let it go. As she descended the stairs, she spotted Mike standing by the door, and her eyes widened slightly.

Is he saving this outfit somehow? she thought, unable to hide her surprise.

Mike had cleaned up sharply. His diamond earrings caught the light, and his hair was freshly styled. He wore a black-and-gold patchwork button-down, the sleeves rolled just enough to reveal his designer watch. Stone-washed jeans fit him perfectly, paired with a sleek belt and crisp sneakers.

"You really clean up nice, Mikey," Samantha teased. She gave him a once-over, appreciating the effort.

"And you look great yourself," Mike said, his eyes focused on her. "You truly look like a hot date."

Samantha let out a small laugh. "Oh, please. This was a quick outfit, and I totally gave up on my hair," she confessed, brushing a hand through the stubborn strands refusing to cooperate.

"Still," Mike said with a grin, stepping closer, "you make it look second nature."

Their gazes locked. He moved in for a kiss, and she met him halfway. She wrapped her arms around his neck as he took the lead.

This boy can kiss, she thought, surprised by how much she didn't want it to end.

"I'm okay right now," she said, sensing the question behind his eyes. She gave his arm a gentle squeeze.

The phone chimed, breaking the moment. Their Uber had arrived.

"Shall we?" Mike asked, holding the door open.

Samantha nodded and moved toward the console disarming the alarm before rearming it with proximity sweeps every twenty minutes. Alerts would ping her phone and the security company. Hyper-sensitive motion detection activated, and the exterior lights flared to life, illuminating the property like a fortress.

As they stepped outside, Samantha called out to her pets, knowing they were likely hiding as usual. "Be good, you two," she said, more to herself than to them.

With everything set, they climbed into the car and headed downtown to *Page*. Samantha glanced out the window, letting the city lights blur into streaks of color.

She needed this night. Even if she wasn't sure how much she could enjoy it. They were getting close now, approaching the 110 freeway, about to make the final turn into the downtown. Mike had been right to suggest this. She needed to get out. The stress was already eating her alive from the inside out, and Mike could see it.

She glanced back at him, her eyes lingering for a moment before turning away, watching as the city lights came into view.

Ali, baby, please hang on. You've always been the fighter between us, Samantha thought.

She exhaled bracing herself. *A normal night out? Okay. I can do this.*

Little did she know, this "normal" night out would set the stage for something far more meaningful.

CHAPTER 36

STRONGER TOGETHER

Greyson walked up to *Page*, nestled on 6th and Hope in Downtown Los Angeles. The bar's cozy, bookish aesthetic was a welcome reprieve from the chaos of the past few days. Tucked among towering skyscrapers, *Page* offered a rare charm, a mix of modernity and nostalgia.

The décor stood out. Bookshelves climbed the walls, packed with worn classics and fresh covers, while low amber lighting and leather armchairs gave the space a literary-lounge feel. Near the bar, a DJ booth sat idle, ambient music playing from the speakers. From the entrance, you could look up and catch a perfect view of the city library and the *National Bank Tower*, their lights gleaming against the dusk.

Greyson wasn't alone. Megan walked beside him.

The entire team had agreed to meet tonight. A much-needed gathering after the emotional turbulence of the past week. Outside the bar, they greeted each other with hugs and familiar smiles, like a family falling back into step.

Paul, Celine, Max, Raul, Rasheed, Constance, Lupe, Darlene, Taylor, and Brandon all arrived. Each flaunting their personal flair. After living in gym attire day in and day out, everyone welcomed the excuse to dress up. From sharp jackets to bold colors, each outfit was a reflection of their unique energy.

Darlene, naturally, was the first to arrive. She'd already secured a section for the group.

"Guys, I'm three drinks in. Don't make me drink alone anymore!" she called out, raising her glass as the others trickled in. She had that magnetic, larger-than-life energy. Darlene was like the team's self-appointed auntie, always making sure their nights out were ones to remember.

"You're the one who lives for this stuff, Dar," Raul teased as they headed over.

"Damn right I do," she fired back, motioning for everyone to sit.

Laughter and hugs followed as they settled in. It had only been a few days, but the aftermath of the murders and the uncertainty surrounding the gym made it feel like much longer. Still, for now, they soaked in the familiarity and one another's company, even as the shadow of recent events loomed.

A few minutes later, a sleek black Uber pulled up outside the bar. Mike stepped out first, buttoning his shirt as he rounded the car to open Samantha's door.

"You don't have to do that you know," Samantha said, looking up at him.

"Call it good manners," Mike replied, offering his hand.

She took it, but smirked. "Hey, I'm not a senior citizen yet."

Mike chuckled. "You sure about that? All those naps you've been taking say otherwise."

Before she could fire back, her expression softened. "Thank you, Mikey. For suggesting we go out," she said, pressing a quick kiss to his cheek. Then she hooked her arm through his, letting him lead her inside.

Find Us A Table

Inside, the hum of conversation and clinking glasses enveloped them. Samantha scanned the room, taking in the vibe of *Page*. The books lining the walls gave it the feel of an old library, but the modern furniture and curated music kept it lively. It felt familiar yet distinct—like stepping into a storybook that hadn't been written yet.

"Nice pick," Samantha said, squeezing his arm as they found a small table near the bar. Mike pulled out a chair for her, and she eased into it, careful not to strain her side.

"You good?" he asked, concern flickering across his face.

"I'm good," she reassured him. "But I might need one of those drinks soon."

Mike grinned. "I'll handle it. You just sit tight."

She scanned the crowd, unfocused, until a face gave her pause. She wasn't sure… but it looked like Greyson, the manager of the *Elite24Fit* she used to workout at.

Their laughter was contagious, but as she caught snippets of their conversation, her chest tightened.

"…Poor Jordan, poor Tabatha. But man, it's crazy to think of their last moments," Max said, shaking his head.

"It's still insane how fast it all happened," added Celine, who had worked the night of the murders. "I can't stop replaying it in my head."

Max had also worked that night but had stepped out for a quick food run for himself and Celine. The murders happened in that brief window.

"I'm so sorry, Celine. How are you holding up?" Megan asked, her voice gentle.

"I'm okay. I'm just trying to gather myself. I know the police are going to want to talk to me," Celine said with dread.

"We have protocols in place," Greyson reassured her.

"I don't mind talking to them… I just don't know what I can say that will help. It was a normal Saturday night. Whoever did this blended in like anyone else, including to me." She rested her face in her hands and muttered, "Did I fuck up somehow?"

The group immediately rushed to comfort her, each one offering words of reassurance. They all agreed that it wasn't her fault. Their unity wrapped around Celine like a blanket, and she felt the warmth in their support.

"You think we'll ever go back to the gym? Or is this it for us?" Raul asked, leaning back in his seat.

Samantha's ears perked up, curiosity tugging at her. She tried to sneak another glance, but before she could catch more, Mike returned with drinks and a menu.He set down two cocktails and two shots, sliding into his seat with a casual grin.

Samantha blinked back into focus, brushing a few stray strands of hair from her face. It was warm inside, and the humidity wasn't helping. She sighed, breaking the silence.

"I guess it's going to be one of those nights again for me," she said, gesturing to her frizz-prone curls. She rolled her eyes letting out a defeated sigh.

"Relax, Sam," Mike said, his tone warm and reassuring. "You look great, as always."

She laughed shaking her head. Deciding to get more comfortable, she reached for her cropped jacket. As she slipped it off, she tilted her head back, shaking her hair free. The motion was fluid and sexy. Her necklace caught the light just right, and the way her top hugged her figure made Mike momentarily forget what he was doing.

"That's better," Samantha said, draping the jacket over her chair. She caught him looking and offered a small, knowing smile that said, It's okay.

Mike snapped back into focus lowering the drinks. "Cheers?" he said, sliding a shot glass toward her.

She smiled and picked it up, her fingers brushing his. Their eyes met just for a second, but the spark between them was undeniable.

"Cheers," she echoed, clinking her glass against his.

Slowly Peeling Back The Layers

Samantha set the empty shot glass on the table, letting the warmth of the alcohol settle in her chest. She sat back, crossing one leg over the other, her fingers absently tracing the rim of her cocktail glass. When she glanced at Mike, his easy smile was still there, encouraging her to let her guard down.

"Mike," she began with a hint of hesitation in her voice. "You've been… really amazing through all of this.

I'm going through so much, I can't even begin to explain it." Her throat tightened. "I don't think I've said it enough, and I'm sorry I haven't, but thank you."

Mike rested his forearms on the table. "You don't have to thank me, Sam. I'm here because I want to be. I care about you."

Her lips curved into a faint smile. "I know you do. That's why I feel like I owe you more. I've been closed off, and you've been nothing but patient. You deserve more than half of me."

"Take your time. It's okay. I understand."

Samantha exhaled, coming forward as if to meet him halfway emotionally.

"It's just… growing up, I never really had anyone I could lean on. My dad was always busy. FBI cases took him away for weeks. Sometimes months. And my mom?" She paused. "She left when I was seven. I was in elementary school. He was never home. She was raising me alone, and one day, she just… got fed up. Picked me up from school, dropped me off at Grandma's, and never came back."

Samantha swallowed. "She told me she was going shopping. I didn't see her again for ten years… just before I turned eighteen. She ran off with another man, started a new life. A new family. She's a retired lawyer now and teaches at a community college where she heads up the paralegal program."

"How's your relationship now?" Mike asked.

"It's better. I understand her now. I understand why she left. But I had to learn early that if I wanted something done, I had to do it myself. That's how Grandma raised me."

"She raised you to be a survivor," Mike said backing her up.

"My grandmother was both nurturing… and strict," Samantha continued. "Her love was there for me, yes, very deeply. She filled the void after my mom left. Ten years."

She paused, her expression shifting. Something deeper flickered in her eyes as if recalling a memory or a lesson.

"But yeah," she said, nodding, as if reciting something she'd heard a hundred times. "It was always about survival instincts. That's how she raised me."

"She never said it directly, but I always knew that it was up to me to hold it all together."

Mike listened "That explains a lot. Your house, your security system… even your attitude. It's all about control."

She shook off the look that had settled on her face, re-centering herself as his words sank in. "It is," she admitted, fidgeting with her necklace. "But it's exhausting, Mike. And now with everything that's happened… Alison, the killer… it's like my whole world is unraveling. I feel helpless." Her voice cracked. She took a sip of her cocktail to calm her nerves.

Mike reached across the table, his hand covering hers. "You're not helpless, Sam. You have an inner strength. Even if you don't see it yet, I do. Let me help you find it. Let me be that for you."

She looked down at his hand, her fingers curling around his. "I want to let you in. I do. But it's hard. I've spent my whole life building walls, and now I don't know how to take them all down."

"You don't have to," Mike reassured. "Not all at once. Little by little. Brick by brick. I'm not going anywhere. I'm here."

Her eyes met his. A flicker of vulnerability breaking through.

Something in her was softening, and she didn't know what to do with that. She could feel it beginning to happen, but the idea of losing control still terrified her.

"I know you are," she said. Bouncing back with energy, she added, "You're really good at this, you know?"

"At what?"

"At being… safe. It's unnerving," she said with a small laugh, shaking her head.

Mike smirked. "What can I say? It's a talent."

Before she could respond, a burst of laughter from a nearby table caught her attention. Her eyes drifted toward the group seated a few tables over.

Their animated conversation was lively, but certain words hit her like a jolt: *Tabatha. Jordan. Murder. Burn victim. Livestream.*

Her focus sharpened. She leaned slightly toward Mike. "Did you hear that?" she asked, pointing subtly toward the group.

Mike turned his head, catching bits of their conversation. "Yeah… sounds like they're talking about the gym murders."

"I wonder if they know about Alison."

"Some probably do. Anyone who saw the livestream would. But no one knows what hospital she's at from the reports I've seen so far."

Samantha's heart pounded. Her mind was racing.

Did they know more than they were saying? Did anyone know where Alison was?

The feeling in her gut wouldn't let up. tight, insistent, undeniable.

She had to find out. She had to know for herself.

No Love Lost

"Ssshhh, am I being horrible right now?" Raul asked, lowering his voice with mock concern. "They were both horrible people. Jordan and Tabatha. No, no, no." He waved his hand dramatically, nearly spilling his drink.

"Beyond horrible," Celine chimed in, taking a quick sip of her cocktail.

"Remember that whole incident with you, Lupe?" Raul added, his tone shifting. "They both ganged up on you."

"Oh, I remember," Lupe replied, her jaw tightening at the memory. She let out a rapid stream of Spanish, her words biting and raw. "Son dos pedazos estúpidos de maldita basura arrastrados por el viento."

Her voice cut like a knife, furious and unfiltered.

"What did she say?" Max asked.

"She said they're both pieces of trash blowing in the wind," Darlene translated with a grin.

That sent Raul, Darlene, and Lupe into a fit of laughter, their camaraderie cutting through the tension. Max held his head shaking it.

"They should've had their memberships revoked that same day," Rasheed said, his tone more serious now.

"But Darren and corporate, you know how they were. Always taking their side," Constance added with an eye-roll. Her head fell against Brandon's shoulder as she rested a hand on his knee. Their closeness didn't go unnoticed.

"Wait... when did this happen?" Raul asked, eyes widening in mock scandal as he fluttered his lashes dramatically.

"The night we closed together last week," Constance said, smirking as she glanced at Brandon.

"Bitch, no way!" Raul gasped, feigning offense.

"It did. And here we are now," Constance said with a shrug, her smile warm.

The group erupted into laughter, their energy infectious.

"A toast then, shall we?" Paul called out, lifting his glass and cutting through the noise.

Paul flagged down a server, and the table fell silent.

"Don't worry, it's on me," he said. "Got a nice stock payout today. I want to celebrate."

"You're damn right you're buying the shots!" Raul teased, nudging him with an elbow.

As they waited, the group's chatter grew louder, their corner of the bar buzzing with life. Their outside world didn't exist.

Across the bar, Samantha kept sneaking subtle glances in their direction. She couldn't help herself. Ear hustling, nosy, and fully aware of it. Mike noticed her distraction and followed her gaze. The gym crew was too caught up in their own banter to notice, but something about their conversation tugged at Samantha.

There was a familiarity in the way they spoke of names, details, and tones that wouldn't let her go.

Racing Thoughts

"Sam, what else did you want to tell me?" Mike asked, guiding the conversation back.

Samantha looked at him, but her attention drifted toward the gym team's table across the room. Her thoughts swirled.

"Sorry… it's that table," she said, her voice trailing off as she tried to pin down the feeling gnawing at her. "I think they worked at the gym I used to go to."

Mike glanced over, curiosity flickering in his eyes. He didn't recognize anyone. "Oh yeah?"

"Did they release the other names?" she asked.

"Yeah, they did. Jordan and Tabatha."

"Oh my God," Samantha whispered. The names hit her like a wave. She hadn't connected the dots until now, but she knew who they were. Fitness influencers. Loud. Flashy. Impossible to ignore. "Wow… that was them?"

Mike nodded, his expression dimming. "Tragic."

"I wonder how," Samantha asked, her voice low.

Mike hesitated. "We probably shouldn't talk about it over dinner… but the murders were grisly. They're saying that Tabatha was thrown from the building."

A loud gasp escaped her lips. She darted her eyes in disbelief.

"I know," Mike said.

Before the thought could settle, their server arrived with the food. He placed her plate on the table. A fresh hummus platter with veggies, pita, and olives. She smiled faintly. It was light. Simple. She wasn't very hungry, but she needed to eat.

Mike's meal was a different story. Nashville hot chicken sandwich with a mountain of fries. He dove in, giving the moment a break from the heaviness.

Samantha poked at her hummus like a rabbit. Her thoughts still spinning. She couldn't let go of the other table's conversation, or the lingering dread over Alison. Her fingers hovered over her phone, tempted to call again, but she stopped. The hospital had already shut her out. It left her feeling stuck and helpless.

The silence between her and Mike wasn't uncomfortable, but it wasn't their usual lightness either. She felt like there was so much she wanted to say... but the words wouldn't come.

Taking another small bite, she glanced up. Mike's focus was on his food, but his expression was soft and attentive. It made her feel safe enough to try again.

She pressed her thumb against the edge of her glass, grounding herself. Her voice came out softer than she expected.
"Mike... I'm scared."

He paused mid-bite, set his sandwich down, and looked up. "Talk to me, Sam."

Tears welled in her eyes, but she blinked them back. Now wasn't the time. Or maybe it was. She didn't know anymore.

She took a breath and shook her head. "I don't know. I just… I feel like I'm losing control. Like I'm being pulled in too many directions. Now the police. And I can't stop thinking about Alison. What if something happens? What if she doesn't make it? It's this weight I can't shake."

Mike reached across the table, his hands covering hers.

"You don't have to carry it all, Sam. Not alone. I'm here."

She squeezed his hand, grateful. But the pressure in her chest didn't ease. She was in too deep. The chaos was already inside her.

"I keep calling. There's no answer. I need to know she's okay," she said, her voice trembling.

Mike pushed his plate aside, now fully locked in. "I know. But it'll take time. We'll get answers."

"Maybe Daddy can find something," she said. "But I'm trying to be patient with the police." Her fingers tightened around her drink. "He's been keeping an eye on the house. He set up the alarm system himself with top-of-the-line everything.”

Mike looked impressed. “Like what? Or is it classified?”

Samantha laughed at his joke, genuinely amused.
“Well… aside from the cameras and infrared sensors,” she said, a small smile forming, “if someone breaks in, the house floods with fog. Blinds anyone inside. But I know every inch so I’d be able to get out.”

She went back to picking at her plate.

“Damn. No kidding,” Mike replied. “Your dad doesn’t play.”

She nodded, then added, “I can throw my voice through the system, control certain doors. And if all else fails… I’ll just activate Sindel’s scream.”

Mike tilted his head. “What’s that?”

Before she could answer, the gym team’s tables conversation changed. She caught mention of Alison. They didn’t say her name, but Samantha’s body tensed. Her ears tuned in. It was the tone. The fragments. The way their voices dropped.
It was about that night. About the attack.

The hairs on the back of her neck stood up. She leaned in, trying to catch more.

Mike noticed. "What's going on?" he whispered.

Samantha blinked and shook her head, grounding herself as she returned to the conversation.

"He installed the alarm because he wanted to protect Grandma and me. "My grandmother worked for the State Department. Daddy just… always wanted us protected. Beyond the usual."

Mike heard every word. He flashed her an understanding smile. Samantha sensed he wanted to ask more about her past, so she steered the conversation toward him instead.

"What about you? Do you have a security system at your place?"

"I've got what I need right here," he said, tapping his side.

Samantha blinked. "Wait… you have your gun now?" Her voice pitched up, surprised.

"Shhh," Mike cut in, his eyes scanning the room. "They didn't pat me down when we walked in. Probably wouldn't have let me stay if they had, even with my CCW."

Samantha, intrigued. "How long have you had a CCW?"

"Four years," he said, taking a sip of his drink like it was nothing. "I never leave home without it. Honestly, I hate the rare times I'm not carrying."

She watched him, a strange flutter rising in her chest. "What kind of gun is it?"

"This one? Glock 42. Compact. Six shots. Easy to conceal, quick to draw. No bulge, no suspicion. I've got others at home too."

Samantha shifted. "I've… never even held a gun," she admitted.

"Your dad never taught you?" Mike asked, his brow lifting.

She shook her head. "No. Even though he was FBI, he never did. I think he wanted to shield me from that part of the world. Maybe he knew I just wasn't ready."

Mike's tone changed, lower now, more serious. "You've got your house, your defenses, sure. But what about when you're not home?"

Samantha let out a soft laugh. "Isn't that what pepper spray's for?" I never really thought about it."

"You're a woman, Sam," Mike pushed back. "And with everything going on, it's not just smart, it's empowering. You need more than just your house to feel safe.”

She slowly nodded, her fingers tracing the rim of her glass. His words landed hard. They felt true.

“I know,” she whispered. After a pause, she looked up at him. Her voice small but clear. “Help me, Mike.”

Mike smiled. “I’d love to. Whenever you’re ready. No pressure.”

A rush of relief filled her chest. Gratitude, fear, and something harder to name. He was offering her control. A way forward. But deep down, she wasn’t sure it would ever be enough.

Her eyes dropped back to her drink. Thoughts of Alison crept in. The package. The gnawing sense that all of this… was meant for her.

A tear slipped down her cheek.

“Protect me,” she whispered. The words too faint for him to hear.

Mike, unaware of the plea, gave her hand a gentle squeeze. “We’ll take it one step at a time,” he said. “You’ve already got the instincts, Sam. We’ll sharpen them together.”

She shook her head, brushing away the tear before he could see it. Her hair slipped forward over her face. She let it stay there a moment, trying to collect herself. She hated how much she needed that, how much she needed him. But God, she did.

"Thank you," she said, her voice stronger now. "I mean it."

"I know you do, Sam," he replied with a soft smile.

They returned to their meal. She managed a few more bites. No more words were needed, just the gentle support of someone who stayed. For now, that was enough.

The Bombshell Announcement

"So, I called you here today because I wanted to wait until we were all together to tell you this," Greyson began, his voice heavy. "There's no easy way to say it, so I'm just going to say it."

"Say what?" Max asked. "What is it, boss?"

"We're not going back to work tomorrow," Greyson said. "The gym is closed for the rest of the week."

"You've got to be kidding me!" Brandon blurted, nearly knocking over his drink.

"But, I've got five clients booked this week!" Rasheed added, shaking his head. "That's going to fuck up my cashflow."

"I know," Greyson said, hands raised in a calming gesture. "Trust me, I've been fighting with Darren. But corporate isn't budging."

The group groaned, frustration simmering. Greyson took a breath and ripped off the rest of the Band-Aid.

"And… it's not just that," he said, pausing. "Rebecca from Philadelphia is coming."

The air vanished from the table. Raul froze, then let out a dramatic scream, clutching his forehead like he'd just been told his dog died.

"Yeah. That's exactly how I felt," Greyson muttered.

The table erupted in shocked murmurs. Everyone knew what it meant when Rebecca Falcone showed up. She wasn't just corporate's enforcer, she was the executioner.

"Didn't she fire the entire team in Seattle?" Taylor asked, eyes wide.

"Not just fire them," Megan said. "She had a 'You're Fired' cake delivered to the gym. Everyone thought it was a celebration, until they opened the box and saw the message. On a video call. She even made them cut the cake.”

“And then flew out the next day to oversee the replacements,” Paul added. “Didn’t even miss her Eagles game that Sunday.”

“I heard she had the new team prepped the second she landed,” Lupe said. “She’s ruthless.”

“Well, my buzz is officially gone,” Darlene muttered, downing her drink.

A mix of anxiety and disbelief settled over the group as the conversation shifted back to the murders.

“Whoever did this… they’re insane,” Celine said. “Jordan and Tabatha were awful, but no one deserves that.”

“So because they died in our gym, we’re the ones on the chopping block?” Rasheed asked, incredulous. “That’s why Rebecca’s coming?”

“Yeah,” Greyson said. “But let me be clear, Rebecca doesn’t show up to ask questions. She shows up to make decisions. I’ll do my best to advocate for each and every one of you.”

“You’re the only one who can, boss,” Brandon said. “Everyone else just walks on eggshells when she’s around.”

Murmurs of agreement passed around the table.

"I'm so sick of corporate," Raul muttered. "They never cared until it was too late."

"And now, it's cleanup time. And we're the ones paying for it," Lupe added.

Greyson exhaled, the weight of their frustration pressing on him. "Look, let's not let this ruin tonight. We'll figure it out. Together. One way, or another."

The conversation drifted again back to the murders.

"You think they'll catch this guy?" Constance asked, leaning into Brandon.

"They have to," Max said. "The city's on edge. This can't drag on."

"And the poor woman who got horribly burned," Celine added, . "Does anyone know what happened to her?"

"No clue. But it sounds awful," Darlene said, shaking her head. "That poor girl."

"She didn't deserve that," Constance murmured.

At her table, Samantha's ears perked up. Her stomach tightened. She knew exactly who they were talking about—Alison.

Without missing a beat, she signaled to the waitress. Minutes later, a tray of shots was delivered to the gym team's table.

The group looked up in confusion, until they saw Samantha and Mike standing nearby.

"Compliments of the lady," the waitress said, setting down the tray.

Samantha took a deep breath and stepped forward, Mike beside her.

"Hi," she said, her tone warm and friendly. "Sorry to interrupt… I couldn't help overhearing. I think we might have something in common."

The gym team looked at her. Surprised, curious. Greyson was the first to speak.

"Wait… do I remember you? Were you a member at our gym?"

Samantha nodded. "I was. And… I knew the victims." She chose her words carefully, not wanting to reveal too much too soon. "I figured it might be worth talking. Maybe share what we know."

The group exchanged glances before Greyson gave a slight nod.

"Well, small world," he said. "Have a seat."

Samantha and Mike joined the table. The ice was broken.

A Unity Against A Looming Threat

Samantha's voice softened as she glanced around the table. "The girl who was burned… she's my best friend."

The group froze. Her words cut through the murmurs like a blade. She didn't say Alison's name out of respect, but the concern behind her tone gave it away.

Greyson studied her a moment longer. "You're not just a former member. There's something more, isn't there?"

Lupe's expression shifted, curiosity turning to surprise. "Wait a second. I follow you. I subscribe to you."

Samantha blinked, caught off guard. "You do?"

Lupe nodded, a tentative smile forming. "Yeah. *Simply Samantha,* right? I've seen your videos. You're really inspiring."

A faint flush rose to Samantha's cheeks. She wasn't used to being recognized like this. At least not outside curated events or brand launches.

"Thank you," her voice tinged with surprise. The compliment felt sincere.

Greyson nodded, his tone easing. "Yeah. I've seen your content too. It's solid. You're definitely putting in the work."

Samantha smiled, the warmth catching her off guard. "Thanks. That means a lot. I didn't mean to interrupt your evening, but I overheard you talking… and I thought maybe we could help each other."

Greyson gestured to the open seats. "Please. Sit. Let's talk."

Mike pulled out a chair for Samantha, then took the one beside her. Their arms brushed. Under the table, he reached for her hand. Their fingers laced in silence, firm and grounding.

The group settled in again, conversation weaving back together with the soft hum of the bar.

"I mean, we don't even know what this guy wants," Paul said. "It's not like he's leaving a manifesto."

"It feels random," Constance added. "But why influencers?"

Rasheed shrugged. "Maybe he hates the whole lifestyle. I've seen people rant online. How fake it is, how influencers don't deserve their platforms. Maybe he's one of those."

Samantha's fingers tightened around her cocktail glass. "I don't think it's random. That package, it was meant for me."

Silence again. Heavy. Real.

"You're saying he's targeting you?" Darlene asked, concern sharpening her voice.

Samantha shifted in her seat, flustered but trying to stay composed. "It came to my house disguised as a paid brand collaboration. A whole media kit, even a thank-you card. Everything about it looked real. Everything we googled came back legit… on brand, even."

She paused, swallowing hard. "I didn't open it… my friend did. And now…" Her voice cracked, eyes glistening.

"That's terrifying," Lupe whispered. "But… why you? Have you had stalkers? Weird messages?"

"Nothing I took seriously," Samantha admitted. "In this line of work, you get trolls and creeps, but nothing that ever made me feel unsafe."

Greyson leaned forward. "We don't know his motive yet. But he's escalating. Live-streaming murders, targeting influencers… he's trying to send a message. And the police?" He shook his head. "They're moving too slow."

"That's why I think we need to stick together," Samantha said firmly. "If he's going after people like us, then any of us could be next. We might need each other to figure this out, to stay safe."

Mike chimed in, calm and resolute. "Samantha's right. The police are doing what they can, but that doesn't mean we can't be proactive. Share info. Watch each other's backs. It might make all the difference. And something tells me this isn't over."

Samantha turned to him, her eyes soft with gratitude. Her fingers curled around his hand, holding it tight. A silent plea. He squeezed back, wordless but present.

"Is this your boyfriend?" Raul asked, a teasing grin breaking through the tension.

"We're dating," she said with a soft smile. "But yeah… he's definitely boyfriend material."

Mike smirked, squeezing her hand again. "I'll take that."

The table smiled, the energy easing. Then Greyson cleared his throat.

"Alright. Let's do it. Let's stay in touch. If anything weird happens like messages, packages, or anything else, we share it. No secrets. Agreed?"

"Agreed," the group echoed, raising their glasses.

"Here's to not letting this bastard win," Darlene said, her voice low and fierce.

They clinked glasses, a pact forged in shadows, against a threat still out there. She looked around the table, then at Mike. She wasn't alone in this anymore, and neither were they.

It's About Us, Not Him

Samantha, Mike, and the gym team connected instantly, bonding over laughter, shared stories, and a new sense of unity. Samantha quickly emerged as the bridge between everyone, weaving herself into conversations with a natural charm that left Mike amazed.

He saw a side of her tonight he hadn't fully seen before. This social butterfly who drew people in with a mix of warmth, charisma, and substance. It wasn't just her energy, it was her authenticity.

Lupe, Darlene, and Raul lit up when they learned Samantha spoke three languages. When Lupe, originally from Mexico, learned Samantha's late grandmother had once taken a brief diplomatic assignment in Mexico City, the connection hit deeper.

Darlene, nurturing and bold, reminded Samantha of her own aunt. They clicked instantly. Raul, ever dramatic and fashion-forward, was floored by Samantha's style, and they quickly launched into a spirited back-and-forth about favorite designers and shopping haunts.

Constance and Celine, always polished and composed, were quick to admire Samantha's makeup skills. Before the drinks were halfway gone, they'd both booked appointments at *Glam Haven* when she returned to work.

Every interaction Samantha had left an impression so much that everyone at the table seemed eager to stay connected with her beyond tonight.

Meanwhile, Mike couldn't take his eyes off her. He watched how she brought people together and how she made everyone feel seen. There was something so naturally magnetic about her. It didn't just impress him, it drew him in deeper. To him, she didn't just have presence… she had leadership, even if she didn't realize it.

Mike found his own rhythm with the group. He, Brandon, and Rasheed hit it off swapping college sports stories. Rasheed repping his basketball days at UC Berkeley, Brandon chiming in with track and football memories from Fresno State, and Mike adding his own from the UCLA basketball team. The three of them laughed like old friends.

Even Paul joined in, chatting stocks with Mike and swapping tips. Greyson floated the idea of a group paintball outing. Mike was all in. The vibe was relaxed with drinks, laughter, and easy side conversations. The kind of chemistry you don't have to force.

Mike took the liberty and ordered another round of shots. "To meeting new friends in new places," he toasted.

The group echoed the toast. Glasses clinked. Laughter carried through the bar. By the time numbers were exchanged, it was clear tonight had sparked something real.

The rest of the bar faded into background noise. Buzzed and glowing, Samantha pulled Mike up when one of her favorite songs came on—"Electric Company" by Hector Gachan.

She couldn't resist the melody. Wrapped in Mike's arms, she pressed her head briefly against his chest before tilting back to meet his gaze. He held her close, the two of them swaying to the rhythm like nothing else existed.

Nearby, Brandon and Constance danced, lost in their spark. Greyson and Megan sat under each others arms as the rest of the team moved freely. The turmoil of the past few days finally giving way.

For the first time in what felt like forever, Samantha let go. She sank into the music, into Mike's arms, and let herself feel something other than fear. The stress. The grief. The dread. It all fell away, if only for this one song.

She tilted her face up, lips mouthing the words:

"I need electric company

Said I need electronic company
Said I need, said I need
Your electric company."

Then she kissed him. The song carried on as she rested her head on his chest, mouthing the lyrics while he stroked her hair.

"You got to light the way in the night all day
You got to dance the night away."

The moment wrapped around them like a blanket. They were all reclaiming something tonight.

As the night wound down, Samantha and Mike stayed near the bar, saying goodbyes as the gym team trickled out in clusters. Samantha felt lighter than she had in days. Sure, the drinks helped. But it was more than that. It was them, the dynamic, the people. The closeness.

As they were about to leave, a striking flash of white hair caught Samantha's eye. She knew that look from anywhere.

"Aya! Bobby!" she called, her face lighting up.

Aya turned, surprised, then beamed. "Samantha? Oh my gosh, hey!"

Without hesitation, Samantha walked over, unbalanced on her feet, but glowing with joy. She pulled Aya in a tight hug, her arms holding on longer than usual.

"It's so good to see you again," she said, slightly slurring, but warm. Mike chuckled beside her, drink in hand.

"Well, this is a surprise. What are you two doing out here? Another collab night?"

"We live out here," Aya said. "This is one of our spots. And tonight, no collaborations. Just vibes."

"That's right! You told us that," Samantha said, leaning into Mike as he placed a calming hand on her back.

Mike gave them a polite nod. "Small world, huh?"

"Yes, indeed. L.A. is big and small at the same time," Bobby said, extending his hand to Mike with a relaxed smile.

Samantha, still buzzing from the high of the night, waved over the bartender. "Hey! Drinks for them. And us too!" she called.

"Oh wow, you don't have to do that," Aya laughed.

"No, no," Samantha insisted, beaming. "It's on me. I'm just so happy to see you. Familiar faces, random places, and new friends." She placed her hand on Aya's shoulder.

The bartender brought over the drinks.
"Cheers," she said, raising her glass. "To seeing you again. And Aya, seriously, I need your hair tips girl."

They all laughed as Aya playfully struck a pose, running her fingers through her white hair.
"Anytime, love! But you're looking amazing too!"

"We're on our way out, take our table!" Samantha offered. She signaled for another one round of drinks.

After another round of drinks, Samantha hugged Aya again. "Let's stay in touch, okay?"

Aya smiled. "Of course hun."

"Thanks for the table. Pretty clutch!" Bobby added with a wink.

Samantha paid the bill, her words tangled with excitement. Aya and Bobby took their seats, still smiling. But before Samantha left, she added something extra to their night, a bottle from the top shelf discreetly sent over.

"Wait, we didn't order this." Aya blinked in surprise.

The server smiled. "Maybe it was ordered before she closed her tab. Compliments of your friend."

As Samantha walked out with Mike, she glanced back and saw Aya scanning the room, bewildered until her eyes landed on the bottle.

Bobby was already pouring two glasses.

"Cheers to Samantha," he said. "You better give her those hair tips now."

"What do I know?" Aya replied, clinking his glass.

"You better figure something out. This is an expensive-ass bottle," Bobby added, already googling the label.

Aya's smile faded, concern setting in. "Something's on her mind," she murmured. "I can feel it. Like she's fighting something heavy."

"She's sweet. And she clearly likes you," Bobby said. "Reach out to her."

"Oh, I will. Definitely. Just to say thank you," Aya replied, her eyes still scanning the room for one last glimpse of Samantha.

Outside, Mike and Samantha reunited with rest of the gym team for final hugs and farewells. The cool night air swirled around them, crisp and full of promise.

Tomorrow would bring challenges. But tonight? Tonight, they had found connection, hope, and something worth fighting for.

Facing What's Next Together

Mike and Samantha walked down the street hand in hand, city lights casting soft shadows along their path. The cool night air swirled around them, but the warmth of his touch kept it at bay. A silent promise seemed to pass between them to weather the days ahead side by side.

For her, it meant peeling back the layers she had long kept hidden, learning to trust and rely on him.

For him, it meant showing her through word and action that he was here for the long haul.

Step by step, they moved forward together, stronger for the bond that had begun to form. Ready to face whatever, or whoever, came next.

END OF BOOK ONE

Coming Soon

The Hashtag Killer: Reckoning

She survived the first attack. But the nightmare is far from over.

Bruised, fractured, and emotionally wrecked, Samantha Sinclair is doing everything she can to hold it together. Both for herself, and for Alison. But when relentless journalist Jessica Ryder invades their privacy, Samantha lashes out in defense of her best friend, even as her own injuries threaten to break her.

The killer known only by his hashtag is still watching and still planning. He knows Samantha is alive. And while he has other names to cross off first, she's never far from his mind.

As a deeper connection with Mike begins to form, Samantha wrestles with where those feelings are coming from. Are they real, or rooted in trauma? And if they are real, is she strong enough to let love in while danger closes in around her?

In the fight between love and survival, Samantha must face the truth: she's going to have to prepare herself to fight back. Healing isn't the end, it's the beginning of the next battle. Continue Samantha's story in Book Two: Reckoning.

The Unofficial Soundtrack For The Hashtag Killer: Awakening

Just some music and inspo that helped create the mood behind the story…

1. "Summer Feelings" – Lennon Stella ft. Charlie Puth
2. "Summer Madness" — Kool & The Gang
3. "A Night Off" – Drake ft. Lloyd
4. "Don't Love Away" – Adrian Marcel
5. "Come Together" – Chris Brown ft. H.E.R.
6. "Come Back Around" — Moon Boots ft. Cherry Glazerr
7. "From the Start" (Extended Chill Mix)" – Morgin Madison & Ryan Lucian
8. "New Person, Same Old Mistakes" – Tame Impala
9. "Footsteps In The Dark" – Cannons (The Isley Brothers Cover)
10. "Ethereal" – Belau & Beth Hirsch
11. "Don't U Wanna (Medsound Remix)" – DJ Aristocrat & T. Say
12. "Electric Company" – Hector Gachan